000003058164

Billionaire Boss

Billionaire Boss:
Hot. Single.
Billionaire.

MAUREEN CHILD

MICHELLE CELMER

LUCY GORDON

MIX
Paper from
responsible sources
FSC
FSC C007454

This book is produced from independently certified FSC™ paper
to ensure responsible forest management.

For more information visit: www.harpercollins.co.uk/green

Printed and bound in Spain
by CPI, Barcelona

MILLS & BOON

First Published in Great Britain 2020
By Mills & Boon, an imprint of HarperCollins*Publishers*
1 London Bridge Street, London, SE1 9GF

BILLIONAIRE BOSS: HOT. SINGLE. BILLIONAIRE. © 2020
Harlequin Books S.A.

Fiancé in Name Only © 2017 Maureen Child
One Month with the Magnate © 2011 Michelle Celmer
Miss Prim and the Billionaire © 2012 Lucy Gordon

ISBN: 978-0-263-28209-2

FIANCÉ IN NAME ONLY

MAUREEN CHILD

To my mom, Sallye Carberry, and my aunt, Margie Fontenot, for too many reasons to list. They are the original Matriarchs. Love you.

One

"Sorry about this," Micah Hunter said. "I really liked you a lot, but you had to die."

Leaning back in his desk chair, Micah's gaze scanned the last few lines of the scene he'd just finished writing. He gave a small sigh of satisfaction at the death of one of his more memorable characters, then closed the lid of the laptop.

He'd already been working for four hours and it was past time for a break. "Problem is," he muttered, standing up and walking to the window overlooking the front of the house, "there's nowhere to go."

Idly he pulled out his cell phone, hit speed dial, then listened to the phone ring for a second or two. Finally a man came on the other line.

"How did I let you talk me into coming here for six months?"

Sam Hellman laughed. "Good to talk to you, too, man."

"Yeah." Of course his best friend was amused. Hell, if Micah wasn't the one stranded here in small-town America, he might be amused, too. As it was, though, he didn't see a damn thing funny about it. Micah pushed one hand through his hair and stared out at the so-called view. The house he was currently renting was an actual Victorian mansion set back from a wide street that was lined by gigantic, probably ancient, trees, now gold and red as their leaves changed and died. The sky was a brilliant blue, the autumn sun peeking out from behind thick white clouds. It was quiet, he thought. So quiet it was damn near creepy.

And since the suspense/horror novels Micah was known for routinely hit number one on the *New York Times* bestseller list, he knew a thing or two about *creepy.*

"Seriously, Sam, I'm stuck here for another four months because you talked me into signing the lease."

Sam laughed. "You're stuck there because you never could turn down a challenge."

Harsh but true. Nobody knew that about Micah better than Sam. They'd met when they were both kids, serving on the same US Navy ship. Sam had run away from his wealthy family's expectations, and Micah had been running from a past filled with foster homes, lies and broken promises. The two of them had connected and then stayed in touch when their enlistments were up.

Sam had returned to New York and the literary agency his grandfather had founded—discovering, after being away for a while, that he actually *wanted* to be a part of the family business. Micah had taken any construction job he could find while he spent every other waking moment working on a novel.

Even as a kid, Micah had known he wanted to write books. And when he finally started writing, it seemed the words couldn't pour out of his mind fast enough. He typed long into the night, losing himself in the story developing on the screen. Finishing that first book, he'd felt like a champion runner—exhausted, satisfied and triumphant.

He'd sent that first novel to Sam, who'd had a few million suggestions to make it even better. Nobody liked being told to change something they thought was already great, but Micah had been so determined to reach his goal, he'd made most of the changes. And the book sold almost immediately for a modest advance that Micah was more proud of than anything he'd ever earned before.

That book was the precursor of things to come. With his second book, word-of-mouth advertising made it a viral sensation and had it rocketing up the bestseller lists. Before he knew it, Micah's dreams were a reality. Sam and Micah had worked together ever since and they'd made a hell of a team. But because they were such good friends, Sam had known exactly how to set Micah up.

"This is payback because I beat you at downhill snowboarding last winter, isn't it?"

"Would I do something that petty?" Sam asked, laughter in his voice.

"Yeah, you would." Micah shook his head.

"Okay…yeah, probably," Sam agreed. "*But*, you're the one who took the bet. Live in a small town for six months."

"True." *How bad could it be?* He remembered asking himself that before signing the lease with his landlady,

Kelly Flynn. Now, two months into his stay, Micah had the answer to that question.

"And, hey, research," Sam pointed out. "The book you're working on now is *set* in a small town. Good to know these things firsthand."

"Ever heard of Google?" Micah laughed. "And the book I set in Atlantis, how'd I research that one?"

"Not the point," Sam said. "The point is, Jenny and I loved that house you're in when we were there a couple years ago. And, okay, Banner's a small town, but they've got good pizza."

Micah would admit to that. He had Pizza Bowl on speed dial.

"Like I said, in another month or so, you'll feel differently," Sam said. "You'll be out enjoying all that fresh powder on the mountains and you won't mind it so much."

Micah wasn't so sure about that. But he had to admit it was a great house. He glanced around the second-floor room he'd claimed as a temporary office. The ceilings were high, the rooms were big and the view of the mountains was beautiful. The whole house had a lot of character, which he appreciated, but damned if he didn't feel like a phantom or something, wandering through the big place. He'd never had so much space all to himself and Micah could admit, at least to himself, that sometimes it creeped him out.

Hell, in the city—any city—there were lights. People. Noise. Here, the nights were darker than anything he'd ever known. Even in the navy, on board a ship, there were enough lights that the stars were muted in the night sky. But Banner, Utah, was listed on the International Dark-Sky roster because it lay just beyond a ridge that wiped out the haze of light reflection from Salt Lake City.

Here, at night, you could look up and see the Milky Way and an explosion of stars that was as beautiful as it was humbling. He'd never seen skies like these before, and he was willing to acknowledge that the beauty of it took some of the sting out of being marooned at the back end of beyond.

"How's the book coming?" Sam asked suddenly.

The change in subject threw him for a second, but Micah was grateful for the shift. "Good. Actually just killed the bakery guy."

"That's a shame. Love a good bakery guy." Sam laughed. "How'd he buy it?"

"Pretty grisly," Micah said, and began pacing the confines of his office. "The killer drowned him in the doughnut fryer vat of hot oil."

"Damn, man…that is gross." Sam took a breath and sighed it out. "You may have put me off doughnuts."

Good to know the murder he'd just written was going to hit home for people.

"Not for long, I'll bet," Micah mused.

"The copy editor will probably get sick, but your fans will love it," Sam assured him. "And speaking of fans, any of them show up in town yet?"

"Not yet, but it's only a matter of time." Frowning, he looked out the window and checked up and down the street, half expecting to see someone with a camera casing the house, hoping for a shot of him.

One of the reasons Micah never remained in one place too long was because his more devoted fans had a way of tracking him down. They would just show up at whatever hotel he was staying in, assuming he'd be happy to see them. Most were harmless, sure, but Micah knew "fan" could turn into "fanatic" in a flash.

He'd had a few talk their way into his hotel rooms, join him uninvited at dinner, acting as though they were either old friends or long-lost lovers. Thanks to social media, there was always someone reporting on where he had been seen last or where he was currently holed up. So he changed hotels after every book, always staying in big cities where he could get lost in the crowds and living in five-star hotels that promised security.

Until now, that is.

"No one's going to look for you in a tiny mountain town," Sam said.

"Yeah, that's what I thought when I was at the hotel in Switzerland," Micah reminded his friend. "Until that guy showed up determined to pummel me because his girlfriend was in love with me."

Sam laughed again and Micah just shook his head. Okay, it was funny now, but having some guy you didn't know ambush you in a hotel lobby wasn't something he wanted to repeat.

"This is probably the best thing you could have done," Sam said. "Staying in Banner and living in a house, not a hotel, will throw off the fans hunting for you."

"Yeah, well, it should. It's throwing me off, that's for sure." His scowl tightened. "It's too damn quiet here."

"Want me to send you a recording of Manhattan traffic? You could play it while you write."

"Funny," Micah said, and didn't even admit to himself that the idea wasn't half bad. "Why haven't I fired you?"

"Because I make us both a boatload of money, my friend."

Well, Sam had him there. "Right. Knew there was a reason."

"And because I'm charming, funny and about the only

person in the world who's willing to put up with the crappy attitude."

Micah laughed now. He had a point. Right from the beginning, when they'd met on the aircraft carrier they'd served on, Sam had offered friendship—something Micah had rarely known. Growing up in the foster care system, moving from home to home, Micah had never stayed anywhere long enough to make friends. Which was probably a good thing since he wouldn't have been able to *keep* a friend, what with relocating all the damn time.

So he appreciated having Sam in his life—even when the man bugged the hell out of him. "That's great, thanks."

"No problem. So what do you think of your landlady?"

Frowning, Micah silently acknowledged that he was trying to *not* think about Kelly Flynn. It wasn't working, but he kept trying.

For the last two months, he'd done everything he could to keep his distance because damned if he didn't want to get closer. But he didn't need an affair. He had to live here for another four months. If he started something with Kelly, it would make things…complicated.

If it was a one-night stand, she'd get pissy and he'd have to put up with it for four more months. If it was a long-running affair, then she'd be intruding on his writing time and spinning fantasies about a future that was never going to happen. He didn't need the drama. All he wanted was the time and space to write his book so he could get out of this tiny town and back to civilization.

"Hmm," Sam mused. "Silence. That tells me plenty."

"Tells you nothing," Micah argued, attempting to convince both himself *and* Sam. "Just like there's nothing going on."

"Are you sick?"

"What?"

"I mean, come on," Sam said, and Micah could imagine him leaning back in his desk chair, propping his feet up on the corner of his desk. He probably had his chair turned toward the windows so he could look out over Manhattan.

"Hell," Sam continued, "I'm married and I noticed her. She's gorgeous, and if you tell Jenny I said that I'll deny it."

Shaking his head, Micah looked down and watched Kelly work in the yard. The woman never relaxed. She was always moving, doing something. She had ten different jobs and today, apparently, still had the time to rake up fallen leaves and bag them. As he watched, she loaded up a wheelbarrow with several bags of leaves and headed for the curb.

Her long, reddish-gold hair was pulled into a ponytail at the back of her neck. She wore a dark green sweatshirt and worn blue jeans that cupped her behind and clung to her long legs. Black gloves covered her hands, and her black boots were scarred and scuffed from years of wear.

And though she had her back to the house, he knew her face. Soft, creamy skin, sprinkled with freckles across her nose and cheeks. Grass-green eyes that crinkled at the edges when she laughed and a wide, generous mouth that made Micah wonder what she would taste like.

Micah watched her unload the bags at the curb, then wave to a neighbor across the street. He knew she'd be smiling and his brain filled with her image. Deliberately, he turned his back on the window, shut the image of Kelly out of his mind and walked back to his chair. "Yeah, she's pretty."

Sam laughed. "Feel the enthusiasm."

Oh, there was plenty of enthusiasm, Micah thought. Too much. Which was the problem. "I'm not here looking for a woman, Sam. I'm here to work."

"That's just sad."

He had to agree. "Thanks. So why'd you call me again?"

"Damn, you need to take a break. You're the one who called me, remember?"

"Right." He pushed one hand through his hair. Maybe he did need a damn break. He'd been working pretty much nonstop for the last two months. No wonder this place was starting to feel claustrophobic in spite of its size. "That's a good idea. I'll take a drive. Clear my head."

"Invite the landlady along," Sam urged. "She could show you around since I'm guessing you've hardly left that big old house since you got there."

"Good guess. But not looking for a guide, either."

"What are you looking for?"

"I'll let you know when I find it," Micah said, and hung up.

"So how's our famous writer doing?"

Kelly grinned at her neighbor. Sally Hartsfield was the nosiest human being on the face of the planet. She and her sister, Margie, were both spinsters in their nineties, and spent most of their days looking out the windows to keep an eye on what was happening in the neighborhood.

"Busy, I guess," Kelly said, with a quick glance over her shoulder at the second-story window where she'd caught a glimpse of Micah earlier. He wasn't there anymore and she felt a small twist of disappointment as she turned back to Sally. "He told me when he moved in that he would be buried in work and didn't want to be disturbed."

"Hmm." Sally's gaze flicked briefly to that window, too. "You know, that last book of his gave me nightmares. Makes you wonder how he can stand being all alone like that when he's writing such dark, scary things…"

Kelly agreed. She'd only read one of Micah's seven books because it had scared her so badly she'd slept with a light on for two weeks. When she read a book, she wanted cheerful escape, not terror-inducing suspense. "I guess he likes it that way," she said.

"Well, everybody's different," Sally pointed out. "And I say thank goodness. Can you imagine how boring life would be if we were all the same?" She shook her head and her densely-sprayed curls never moved. "Why, there'd be nothing to talk about."

And that would be the real shame as far as Sally was concerned, Kelly knew. The woman could pry a nugget of information out of a rock.

"He is a good-looking man though, isn't he?" Sally asked, a speculative gleam in her eyes.

Good-looking? Oh, Micah Hunter was well beyond that. The picture on the back of his books showed him as dark and brooding, and that was probably done purposefully, considering what he wrote. But the man in person was so much more. His thick brown hair was perpetually rumpled, as if he'd just rolled out of bed. His eyes were the color of rich, dark coffee, and when he forgot to shave for a day or two, the stubble on his face gave him the air of a pirate.

His shoulders were broad, his hips were narrow and

he was tall enough that even Kelly's own five feet, eight inches felt diminutive alongside him. He was the kind of man who walked into a room and simply took it over whether he was trying to or not. Kelly imagined every woman who ever met him had done a little daydreaming about Micah. Even, it seemed, Sally Hartsfield, who had a grandson as old as Micah.

"He is nice looking," Kelly finally said when she noticed Sally staring at her.

The older woman sighed and fisted both hands on her hips. "Kelly Flynn, what is wrong with you? Your Sean's been gone four years. Why, if I was your age..."

Kelly stiffened at the mention of her late husband, automatically raising her defenses. Sally must have noticed her reaction because the woman stopped short, offered a smile and, thank heaven, a change of subject.

"Anyway, I hear you're showing the Polk place this afternoon to a couple coming in from California of all places."

Impressed as well as a little irked, Kelly stared at the older woman. Honestly, Kelly had only gotten this appointment to show a house the day before. "How did you know that?"

Sally waved a hand. "Oh, I have my ways."

Kelly had long suspected that her elderly neighbors had an army of spies stationed all over Banner, Utah, and this just cemented that idea. "Well, you're right, Sally, so I'd better get going. I still have to shower and change."

"Of course, dear, you go right ahead." She checked the window again and Kelly saw frustration on the woman's face when Micah didn't show up to be watched. "I've got things to do myself."

Kelly watched the woman hustle back across the street,

her bright pink sneakers practically glowing against all of the fallen leaves littering the ground. The ancient oaks that lined the street stretched out gnarly branches to almost make an arbor of gold-and-red leaves hanging over the wide road.

The houses were all different, everything from small stone cottages to the dignified Victorian where Kelly had grown up. They were all at least a hundred years old, but they were well cared for and the lawns were tidy. People in Banner stayed. They were born here, grew up here and eventually married, lived and died here.

That kind of continuity always comforted Kelly. She'd lived here since she was eight and her parents were killed in a car accident. She'd moved in with her grandparents and had become the center of their world. Now, her grandfather was dead and Gran had moved to Florida, leaving the big Victorian mansion and the caretaker's cottage at the back of the property to Kelly. Since living alone in that giant house would just be silly, Kelly rented it out and lived in the smaller cottage.

In the last three years, the Victorian had rarely been empty and when it wasn't rented out by vacationers, the house and grounds had become a favorite place for weddings, big parties and even, last year, a Girl Scout cookout in the huge backyard.

And, she thought, every Halloween, she turned the front of the Victorian into a haunted house.

"Have to get busy on that," she told herself. It was already the first of October and if she didn't get started, the whole month would slip past before she knew it.

Halfway up to the house, the front door opened and Micah stepped out. Kelly's heart gave a hard thump, and down low inside her she felt heat coil and tighten. Oh, boy. It had been four long years since her husband, Sean, had died, and since then she hadn't exactly done a lot of dating. That probably explained why she continued to have this over-the-top reaction to Micah.

Probably.

He wore a black leather jacket over a black T-shirt tucked into the black jeans he seemed to favor. Black boots finished off the look of Dangerous Male and as she admired the whole package, her heartbeat thundered loud enough to echo in her ears.

"Need some help?" he asked, jerking his head toward the wheelbarrow she was still holding on to.

"What? Oh. No." *Great, Kelly. Three. Separate. Words. Care to try for a sentence?* "I mean, it's empty, so not heavy. I'm just taking it around to the back."

"Okay." He came down the wide front steps to the brick walkway lined with chrysanthemums in bright, cheerful fall colors. "I'm taking a break. Thought I'd drive around. Get my bearings."

"After two months of being in Banner?" she asked, smiling. "Yeah, maybe it's time."

His mouth worked into a partial smile. "Any suggestions on the route I should take?"

She set the wheelbarrow down, flipped her ponytail over her shoulder and thought about it. "Just about any route you take is a pretty one. But if you're looking for a destination, you could drive through the canyon down to 89. There are a lot of produce stands there. You could pick me up a few pumpkins."

He tipped his head to one side and studied her, a flicker of what might have been amusement on his face. "Did I say I was going shopping?"

"No," she said, smiling. "But you could."

He blew out a breath, looked up and down the street, then shifted his gaze back to hers. "Or, you could ride with me and pick out your own pumpkins."

"Okay."

He nodded.

"No," she said. "Wait. Maybe not."

He frowned at her.

Having an audience while she argued with herself was a little embarrassing. She could tell from his expression that Micah didn't really want her along so, naturally, she really wanted to go. Even though she shouldn't. She already had plenty to do and maybe spending time with Micah Hunter wasn't the wisest choice, since he had the unerring ability to stir her up inside. But could she really resist the chance to make him as uncomfortable as he made her?

"I mean, sure," she said abruptly. "I'll go, but I'd have to be back in a couple of hours. I have a house to show this afternoon."

His eyebrows arched high on his forehead. "I can guarantee you I won't be spending two hours at a pumpkin stand." He tucked his hands into the pockets of his jacket. "So? Are you coming or not?"

Her eyes met his and in those dark brown depths, Kelly read the hope she would say *no*. So, of course, she said the only thing she could.

"I guess I am."

Two

"**W**hy are you buying pumpkins when you're growing your own?"

They were already halfway down the twisting canyon road. The mountains rose up on either side of the narrow pass. Wide stands of pine trees stood as tall and straight as soldiers, while oaks, maples and birch trees that grew within those stands splashed the dark green with wild bursts of fall color.

"And," Micah continued, "isn't there somewhere closer you could buy the damn things?"

She turned her head to look at his profile. "Sure there is, but the produce stands have the big ones."

Kelly could have sworn she actually *heard* his eyes roll. But she didn't care. It was a gorgeous fall day, she was taking a ride in a really gorgeous car—even though it was going too fast for the pass—and she was sitting beside a gorgeous man who made her nervous.

And wasn't that a surprise? Four years since her husband Sean had died and Micah was the first man to make her stomach flutter with the kind of nerves that she had suspected were dead or atrophied. The problem was, she didn't know if she was glad of the appearance of those nerves or not.

Kelly rolled down the window and let the cold fall air slap at her in lieu of a cold shower. When she got a grip, she shifted in her seat to look at Micah. "Because I grow those to give away to the kids in the neighborhood."

"And you can't keep some for yourself?"

"I could, but where's the fun in that?"

"Fun?" he repeated. "I've seen you out there weeding, clipping and whatever else it is you do to those plants. That's fun?"

"For me it is." The wind whipped her ponytail across her face and she pushed it aside to look at him. "Besides, if I was going to take lessons on fun from somebody, it wouldn't be you."

He snorted. "If you did, I'd show you more than pumpkins."

Her stomach swirled a little at the implied promise in those words, but she swallowed hard and stilled it. He was probably used to making coded statements designed to turn women into slavering puddles. So she wouldn't accommodate him. Yet.

"I'm not convinced," she said with a shrug. "You've been in town two months and you've hardly left the house."

"That's work. No time for fun."

"Just a chatterbox," she mumbled. Every word pried out of him felt like a victory.

"What?"

"Nothing," she said. "So, what's your idea of fun then?"

He took a moment to think it through, and said, "I'd start with chartering a private jet—"

"Your own personal jet," she said, stunned.

He glanced at her and shrugged. "I don't like sharing."

She laughed shortly as she thought about the last time she'd taken a flight out of Salt Lake City airport. Crowded onto a full flight, she'd sat between a talkative woman complaining about her grandchildren and a businessman whose briefcase poked her in the thigh every time he shifted in his seat. Okay, she could see where a private jet would be nice. "Well sure. Okay, your jet. Then what?"

He steered the Range Rover down the mountain road, taking the tight curves like a race-car driver. If Kelly let herself worry about it, she'd be clinging to the edges of her seat. So she didn't think about it.

"Well, it's October, so I'd go to Germany for Oktoberfest."

"Oh." That was so far out of her normal orbit she hardly knew what to say. Apparently, though, once you got Micah talking about something that interested him, he would keep going.

"It's a good place to study people."

"I bet," she murmured.

He ignored that, and said, "Writers tend to observe. Tourists. Locals. How people are interacting. Gives me ideas for the work."

"Like who to murder?"

"Among other things. I once killed a hotel manager in one of my books." He shrugged. "The guy was a jackass so, on paper at least, I got rid of him."

She stared at him. "Any plans to kill off your current landlady?"

"Not yet."

"Comforting."

"Anyway," he continued, "after a long weekend there, I'd go to England," he mused, seriously considering her question. "There's a hotel in Oxford I like."

"Not London?"

"Fewer people to recognize me in Oxford."

"That's a problem for you?" she asked.

"It can be." He took another curve that had Kelly swerving into him. He didn't seem to notice. "Thanks to social media, my fans tend to track me down. It gets annoying."

She could understand that. The photo of Micah on the back of his books was mesmerizing. She'd spent a bit of time herself studying his eyes, the way his hair tumbled over his forehead, the strong set of his jaw.

"Maybe you should take your photo off your books."

"Believe me, I've suggested it," Micah said. "The publisher won't do it."

Kelly really didn't have anything to add to the conversation. She'd never been followed by strangers desperate to be close to her and the farthest she'd ever traveled was on her last flight—to Florida to visit her grandmother. England? Germany? Not really in her lifestyle. She'd love to go to Europe. Someday. But it wouldn't be on a private jet.

She glanced out the window at the familiar landscape as it whizzed past and felt herself settle. Micah's life was so far removed from her own it made Kelly's head spin just thinking about it.

"One of these days," she said suddenly, shifting her gaze back to his profile, "I'd like to go to Scotland. See Edinburgh Castle."

"It's worth seeing," he assured her.

Of course he'd been there. Heck, he'd probably been *everywhere*. No wonder he stuck close to the house. Why would he be interested in looking around Banner, Utah? After the places he'd been, her small hometown probably appeared too boring to bother with. Well, maybe it wasn't up to the standards of Edinburgh, or Oktoberfest in Germany, but she loved it.

"Good to know," she said. "But until then, I'll plant pumpkins for the kids." She smiled to herself and let go of a twinge of envy still squeezing her insides. "I like everything about gardening. Watching the seeds sprout, then the vines spread and the pumpkins get bigger and brighter orange." Smiling, she continued. "I like how the kids on the street come by all the time, picking out the pumpkins they want, helping water, pulling weeds. They get really possessive about *their* pumpkins."

"Yeah," he said wryly. "I hear them."

He never took his eyes off the road, she noted. Was it because he was a careful driver, or was he just trying to avoid looking at her? Probably the latter. In the two months he'd been living in her Victorian, Micah Hunter had made eluding her an art form.

Sure, he was a writer, and he'd told her when he first arrived in town that he needed time alone to work. He wasn't interested in making friends, having visitors or a guided tour of her tiny town. Friendly? Not so much. Intriguing? Oh, yeah.

Could she help it if tall, dark and crabby appealed to her? Odd though, since her late husband, Scan, had been blond and blue-eyed, with an easy smile. And *nothing* about Micah was easy.

"You don't like kids?"

Briefly he slanted a look at her. "Didn't say that. Said I heard them. They're loud."

"Uh-huh," she said with a half smile. "And didn't you say last week that it was too quiet in Banner?"

His mouth tightened but, grudgingly, he nodded. "Point to you."

"Good. I like winning."

"One point doesn't mean you've won anything."

"How many points do I need then?"

A reluctant smile curved his mouth, then flashed away again. "At least eleven."

Wow. That half smile had come and gone so quickly it was like it had never been. Yet, her stomach was swirling and her mouth had gone dry. Kelly took a breath and slowly let it out again. She had to focus on what they were talking about, *not* what he was doing to her.

"Like ping-pong," she said, forcing a smile she didn't feel.

"Okay." He sounded amused.

"All right, good," Kelly said, leaning over to pat his arm mostly because she needed to convince herself she could touch him without going up in flames. But her fingers tingled, so she pulled them back fast. "Then it's one to nothing, my favor."

He shook his head. "You're actually going to keep score?"

"You started it. You gave me a point."

"Right. I'll make a note."

"No need, I'll keep track." She looked ahead because it was safer than looking at him. Then she smiled to herself. She'd gotten him to talk and had completely held her own in the conversation—until her imagination and hormones had thrown her off.

As long as she could keep those tingles and nerves in check, she could handle Mr. Magnetic.

For the next few days, Kelly was too busy to spend much time thinking about Micah. And that was just as well, she told herself. Mainly because the minute they returned from their pumpkin-shopping expedition, Micah had disappeared and she'd gotten the message.

Clearly he wanted her to know that their brief outing had been an aberration. He'd slipped back into his cave and she hadn't caught a glimpse of him since. Probably for the best, she assured herself. Easier to keep her mind on her own life, her own responsibilities if the only time she saw Micah was in her dreams.

Of course, that didn't make for restful sleeping, but she'd been tired before. One thing she hadn't experienced before were the completely over-the-top, sexy-enough-to-melt-your-brain dreams. She hated waking up hot and needy. Hated having to admit that all she really wanted to do was go back to sleep and dream again.

"And don't start thinking about those dreams or you won't get any work done at all," Kelly told herself firmly.

It wasn't hard to push Micah into the back of her mind, since she juggled so many jobs that sometimes she just ran from one to the next. Thankfully, that gave her little opportunity to sit and wonder if sex with Micah in real life would be as good as it was in her dreams.

Although if it was, she might not survive the experience.

"Still," she mused, "not a bad way to go."

She shook her head, dipped a brush into the orange tempera paint, wiped off the excess, then painted the first of an orchard of pumpkins onto the Coffee Cave's front window. Of all her different jobs, this was her favorite. Kelly loved painting holiday decorations on storefronts.

But she was also a virtual assistant, she ran websites for several local businesses, and was a Realtor who had just sold a house to that family from California. She was a gardener and landscape designer, and now she was thinking seriously about running for mayor in Banner's next election, since she was just horrified by some of the current mayor's plans for downtown. As she laid the paint out on the glass, her mind wandered.

Kelly had a business degree from Utah State, but once she'd graduated, she hadn't wanted to tie herself down to one particular job. She liked variety, liked being her own boss. When she'd decided to go into several different businesses, a couple of her friends had called her crazy. But she remembered Sean encouraging her, telling her to do whatever made her happy.

That had her pausing as thoughts of Sean drifted through her mind like a warm breeze on a cool day. A small ache settled around her heart. She still missed him even though his features were blurred in her mind now— like a watercolor painting left out in the rain.

She hated that. It felt like a betrayal of sorts, letting Sean fade. But it would have been impossible to keep living while holding on to the pain, too. Time passed whether you wanted it to or not. And you either kept up or got run over.

On that happy notion, Kelly paused long enough to look up and down Main Street. Instantly, she felt better. Banner was a beautiful little town and had been a great place to grow up. Coming here as a heartbroken eight-year-old, she'd fallen in love with the town, the woods, the rivers, the waterfalls and the people here.

Okay, Banner wasn't Edinburgh or Oxford or wherever, but it was…cozy. The buildings were mostly more than a hundred years old with creaky floors and brick walls. The sidewalks were narrow but neatly swept, and every one of the old lampposts boasted a basket of fall flowers at its base. In another month or so, there would be Christmas signs up and lights strung across the streets, and when the snow came, it would all look like a holiday painting. So, yes, she'd like to travel, see the world, but she would always come home to Banner.

Nodding to herself, she turned back to the window and quickly laid out the rest of the pumpkin patch along the bottom edge of the window.

"Well, that looks terrific already."

Kelly turned to grin at her friend. Terry Baker owned the coffee shop and made the best cinnamon rolls in the state. With short black hair, bright blue eyes and standing at about five foot two, Terry looked like an elf. Which she didn't find the least bit amusing.

The two of them had been friends since the third grade and nothing had changed over the years. Terry had been there for Kelly when Sean died. Now that Terry's military husband had deployed for the third time in four years, it was Kelly's turn to support her friend.

"Thanks, but I've got a long way to go yet," Kelly said, taking a quick look at the window and seeing a spot she'd have to fill in with a few baby pumpkins.

"Hence the latte I have brewed just for you." She held out the go-cup she carried.

"Hence?" Kelly took the coffee, savored a sip, then sighed in appreciation. "Have you been reading British mysteries again?"

"Nope." Terry stuffed her hands into her jeans pockets. "With my sad love life, I'm home every night watching the British mysteries on TV."

"Love lives can be overrated," Kelly said.

"Right." Terry nodded. "Who're you trying to convince? Me? Or you?"

"Me, obviously, since you're the only one of us with a man at the moment."

Terry leaned one shoulder against the pale rose-colored brick of her building. "I don't have one, either, trust me. It's impossible to have phone sex on an iPad when half of Jimmy's squad could walk in at any moment."

Kelly laughed, grabbed another brush and laid down a twining green vine connecting all of the pumpkins. "Okay, that would be awkward."

"Tell me about it. Remember when he called me as a surprise on my birthday and I jumped out of the shower to answer the call?" Terry shuddered dramatically. "I can still hear all the whistles from his friends who were there in the room."

Still laughing, Kelly said, "Well, that'll teach Jimmy to surprise you."

"No kidding. Now we make phone appointments." Terry grinned. "But enough about me. I hear you and the writer went for a long ride the other day."

"How did you—" Kelly stopped, blew out a breath and nodded. "Right. Sally."

"She and her sister came in for coffee yesterday and told me all about it," Terry admitted, tipping her head to one side to study her friend. "The question is, if there was something to know, why didn't I already know it?"

"Because it's nothing," Kelly said, focusing on her painting again. She added shadows and depth to the curling vines. "He took me to buy some pumpkins."

"Uh-huh. Sally says you were gone almost two hours. Either you're really picky about your pumpkins or something else was going on."

Kelly sighed. "We went for a ride."

"Uh-huh."

"I showed him around a little."

"Uh-huh."

"Nothing happened."

"Why not?"

Kelly just blinked. A couple of kids on skateboards shot down the sidewalk with a roar that startled her. "What?"

"Honey," Terry said, stepping close enough to drop one arm around Kelly's shoulders. "Sean's been gone four years. You haven't been on a single date in all that time. Now you've got this amazing-looking guy living in the Victorian for six months and you're not going to do anything about it?"

Laughing a little, Kelly shook her head again. "What should I do? Tie him up and have my way with him?"

Terry's eyes went a little dreamy. "Hmm…"

"Oh, stop it." But even as she said it, a rush of heat filled Kelly. She only enjoyed it for a second or two before tamping it right down and mentally putting out the fire.

Honestly, she didn't want or need the attraction she felt for Micah. He clearly wasn't interested and Kelly had already loved and lost. She really had zero interest in a romance. Of any kind.

"Okay, fine," Terry said, laughing. "If you're determined to shut yourself up in a closet, wrapped in wool or something, there's nothing I can do about it. But I swear, if the CIA ever needs more spies, I'm going to recommend Sally and Margie. Those two have their fingers on the pulse of everything that happens in town."

And lucky Kelly lived right across the street from them. Sean used to laugh when he saw the older ladies, noses pressed to the windows. He would sweep Kelly into an elaborate dip and kiss her senseless, saying, *"The reason they're so nosy is no one's ever kissed them senseless. So let's give them something to talk about."*

That memory brought a sad smile that she just as quickly let slide away. Remembering Sean meant not only the good times, but the pain of losing him. She'd lost enough in her life, Kelly told herself firmly.

First her parents when she was just a kid, then her grandfather, then Sean. Enough already. And the only way to ensure she never went through that kind of pain again was to never let herself get that close with anyone again.

She had Terry. Her grandmother. A couple of good friends.

Who needed a man?

Micah's image rose up in her mind and she heard a tiny voice inside her whisper, *You do. He's only here temporarily, why not take advantage? There's no future there, so no risk.*

True, Micah would only be in Banner for four more months, so it wasn't as if—no.

Don't think about it.

Sure. That would work.

"You know," Terry said, interrupting Kelly's stream of consciousness, "there's a guy in Jimmy's squad I think you'd really like…"

"Oh, no." Kelly shook her head firmly. "Don't go there, Terry. No setups. You know those never go well."

"He's a nice guy," her friend argued.

"I'm sure he's a prince," Kelly said. "But he's not *my* prince. I'm not looking for another man."

"Well, you should be." Terry folded her arms over her chest.

"Didn't you just say there was nothing you could do about it if I wanted to lock myself in a closet?"

"I hate seeing you alone all the time."

"*You're* alone," Kelly reminded her.

"For now, but Jimmy will be home in another couple of months."

"And I'm happy for you." Deliberately, Kelly turned back to her paints. She picked up the yellow and a small brush, then laid in the eyes on the first pumpkin. With the bright yellow, it would look like the pumpkin was lit by a candle. "I had a husband, Terry. Don't want another one."

From the corner of her eye, Kelly saw her friend's shoulders slump in defeat. "I didn't say I wanted you married."

"But you do."

"Not the point," Terry said stubbornly. "Sweetie, I know losing Sean was terrible. But you're too young to live the rest of your life like a vestal virgin."

Kelly laughed. "The virgin ship sailed a long time ago."

"You know what I mean."

Of course she did. Terry had been saying pretty much the same thing for the last two years. She just didn't understand that Kelly was too determined to avoid pain to ever take the kind of risk she was talking about. Loving was great. Losing was devastating, and she'd already lost enough, thanks.

"Yeah, I do, and I appreciate the thought—"

"No, you don't," Terry said.

"You're right, I don't." Kelly glanced at her friend and smiled to take the sting out of her words. "Honestly, you're as bad as Gran."

"Oh, low blow," Terry muttered. "She's still worried?"

"Ever since Sean died and it's gotten worse in the last year or so." She focused on the paints even while she kept talking. "Gran's even started making noises about moving back here so I won't be lonely."

"Oh, man." Terry sighed. "I thought she loved living in Florida with her sister."

"She *does*." Kelly crouched down to paint in the faces of three other pumpkins. "The two of them go to bingo and take trips with their seniors club. She's having a great time, but then she starts worrying about me and—"

Her cell phone rang and Kelly stood up to drag it from her jeans pocket. Glancing at the caller ID, she sighed and looked at Terry. "Speak of the devil…"

"Gran? Really?" Terry's eyes went dramatically wide. "Boy, her hearing's better than ever if she could catch us talking about her all the way from Florida!"

Kelly laughed. With a wince of guilt, she sent the call to voice mail.

"Seriously?" Terry sounded surprised. "You're not going to talk to her?"

"Having *one* conversation about my lack of a love life is enough for today."

"Fine." Terry held up both hands in surrender. "I'll back off. For now."

"Thanks." She tucked her phone away and tried not to feel badly about ditching her grandmother's call.

"*But*," Terry added before she went back into the coffee shop, "just because you're not interested in a permanent man…"

Kelly looked at her.

"…doesn't mean you can't enjoy a temporary one. I'm just saying."

After she left, Kelly's brain was racing. *A temporary man.* When she went back to her painting, she was still thinking, and as an ephemeral plan began to build in her mind, a speculative smile curved her mouth.

Three

Micah hated cooking, but he'd learned a long time ago that man cannot live on takeout alone. Especially when you're in the back end of beyond and can't get anything but pizza delivered.

He took a swig of his beer and flipped cooked pasta into a skillet with some olive oil and garlic. Adding chopped tomatoes and sliced steak to the mix, he used a spatula to mix it all together. The scent was making him hungry. Most people would think it was way too early for dinner, but Micah didn't eat on a schedule.

He'd been wrapped up in his book for the last several hours, hardly noticing the time passing. As always happened, once the flow of words finally stopped, he came out of his cave like a grizzly after six months of hibernation.

"Hi."

Micah turned to look at the open back door. It was late afternoon and the cool air felt good. Of course, if he'd known he'd be invaded, Micah would have kept the door shut. Too late now, though, since there was a little boy standing there, staring at him. The kid couldn't have been more than three or four. He had light brown hair that stuck up in wild tufts all over his head. His brown eyes were wide and curious and there was mud on the knees of his jeans and the toes of his sneakers. "Who are you?"

"I'm Jacob. I live there." He waved one hand in the general direction of the house next door. "Can I go see my pumpkin?"

The sizzling skillet was the only sound in the room. Micah looked at the kid and realized that he was one of the crew who made so much noise in Kelly's garden. That still didn't explain why the kid was here, talking to Micah. "Why are you asking me?"

"Cuz Kelly's not here so I have to ask another grown-up and you're one."

Can't argue with that kind of logic. "Yeah. Sure. Go ahead."

"Okay. What're you doin'?" Jacob came closer.

"I'm cooking." Micah glanced at the boy, then, dismissing him, went back to his skillet. "Go look at your pumpkin."

"Are you hungry, too?" The boy gave him a hopeful look.

"Yeah, so you should go home," Micah told him. "Have lunch." What time was it? He looked out the window. The sky was darkening toward twilight. "Or dinner."

"I hafta see my pumpkin first and say good-night."

That was a new one for Micah. Telling a vegetable

good-night. But the boy looked so…earnest. And a little pitiful in his dirty jeans with his wide brown eyes. Micah didn't do kids. Never had. Not even when he *was* a kid.

He'd kept to himself back then, too. He'd never made friends because he wouldn't have been able to keep them. Moving from home to home to home kept a foster kid wary of relationships. So he'd buried his nose in whatever books he could find and waited to turn eighteen so he could get out of the system.

But now, staring into a pair of big brown eyes, Micah felt guilt tugging at him for trying to ignore the kid. The feeling was so unusual for him he almost didn't recognize it. He also couldn't ignore it. "Fine then. Go ahead. Say good-night to your pumpkin."

"You hafta open the gate for me cuz I'm too little."

Rolling his eyes, Micah remembered the gated white-picket fence Kelly kept around her garden patch. She'd told him once it was to discourage rabbits and deer. Even though the deer could jump the fence with no problem, she wanted to make vegetable stealing as hard as possible on them.

With a sigh, Micah turned the fire off under his skillet, and said goodbye to the meal he'd just made. "All right." Micah looked at the boy. "Let's go then."

A bright smile lit the kid's face. "Thanks!"

He hustled out of the kitchen, down the back steps and around to the side of the house.

Micah followed more slowly, and as he walked, he took a second to appreciate the view. All around him fall colors exploded in shades of gold and red. The dark green of the pines in the woods beyond the house made them look as if they were made of shadows, and he idly plotted another murder, deep in the forest.

"I could have some kid find the body," he mumbled, seeing the possible scene in his mind. "Freak him out, but would he be too scared to tell anyone? Would he run for help or run home and hide?"

"Who?"

Coming back to the moment at hand, Micah looked at the child staring up at him. "What?"

"Who's gonna run home? Are they scared? Is it a boy? Cuz my brothers say boys don't get scared, only girls do."

Micah snorted. "Your brothers are wrong."

"I think so, too." Jacob nodded so hard his hair flopped across his forehead. He pushed it back with a dirty hand. "Jonah gets scared sometimes and Joshua needs a light on when he sleeps."

"Uh-huh." Way too much information, Micah thought and wondered idly if the kid had an off switch.

"I like the dark and only get scared sometimes." Jacob shifted impatiently from foot to foot.

"That's good."

"Do you get scared?"

Frowning now, Micah watched the boy. For a second he was tempted to say no and let it drop. Then he thought better of it. "Everybody gets scared sometimes."

"Even dads?"

Micah had zero experience with fathers, but he suspected that the one thing that would terrify a man was worrying about his children. "Yeah," he said. "Even dads."

"Wow." Jacob nodded thoughtfully. "I have a rabbit I hold when I get scared. I don't think my dad has one."

"A rabbit?" Micah shook his head.

"Not a real one," Jacob assured him. "Real ones would be hard to hold."

"Sure, sure." Micah nodded sagely.

"And they poop a lot."

Micah hid the smile he felt building inside. The boy was so serious he probably wouldn't appreciate being laughed at. Did all kids talk like this? And whatever happened to not talking to strangers? Didn't people tell their kids that anymore?

"There it is," Jacob said suddenly, and pointed to the garden as he hurried to the gate and waited for Micah to open it. Once he had, Jacob raced across the uneven ground to one of the dozen or more pumpkins.

Micah followed, hands in his jeans pockets, watching the kid because he couldn't very well leave him out here alone, could he? "Which one?"

"This one." Jacob bent down to pat the saddest pumpkin Micah had ever seen.

It was smaller than the others, but that wasn't its only issue. It was also shaped like a lumpy football. It was more a pale yellow than orange, and it had what looked like a tumor growing out of one side at the top. If it had been at a store, it would have been overlooked, but here a little boy was patting it tenderly.

"Why that one?" Micah asked, actually curious about what would have made the kid pick the damn thing.

Jacob pulled a weed, then looked up at Micah. "Cuz it's the littlest one, like me." He looked at the vines and all of the other round, perfect orange blobs. "And it's all by itself over here, so it's probably lonely."

"A lonely pumpkin." He wasn't sure why that statement touched him, but he couldn't deny the kid was getting to him.

"Uh-huh." Smiling again, Jacob said, "None of the other kids liked him, but I do. I'm gonna help my mom draw a happy face on him for Halloween and then he'll feel good."

The kid was worried about a pumpkin's self-esteem. Micah didn't even know what to say to that. When *he* was a kid, he'd never done Halloween. There'd been no costumes, no trick-or-treating, no carving pumpkins with his mom.

Micah had one fuzzy memory of his mother and it drifted through his mind like fog on a winter night. She was pretty—at least, he told himself that because the mental picture of her was too blurred to really tell. She had brown hair and brown eyes like his and she was kneeling on the sidewalk in front of him, smiling, though tears glittered in her eyes. Micah was about six, he guessed, a little older than Jacob. They were in New York and the street was busy with cars and people. He was hungry and cold and his mother smoothed his hair back from his forehead and whispered to him.

"You have to stay here without me, Micah."

Fear spurted inside him as he looked up at the dirty gray building behind him. The dark windows looked like blank eyes staring down at him. Worried and chewing his bottom lip, he looked back at his mother. "But I don't want to. I want to go with you."

"It's just for a little while, baby. You'll stay here where you'll be safe and I'll be back for you as soon as I can."

"I don't want to be safe, Mommy," he whispered, his voice catching, breaking as panic nearly choked him and he felt tears streaking down his face. "I want to go with you."

"You can't come with me, Micah." She kissed his forehead, then stood up, looking down at him. She took a step

back from him. "This is how it has to be and I expect you to be a good boy."

"I will be good if I can go with you," he promised. He reached for her hand, his small fingers curling around hers and holding tight, as if he could keep her there. With him.

But she only walked him up the steps, knocked on the door and gave Micah's fingers one last squeeze before pulling free. Fear nibbled at him, his tears coming faster, and he wiped them away with his jacket sleeve. "Don't leave..."

"You wait right here until they open the door, understand?"

He nodded, but he didn't understand. Not any of it. Why were they here? Why was she leaving? Why didn't she want him to be with her?

"I'll be back, Micah," she said. "Soon. I promise." Then she turned and left him.

He watched her go, hurrying down the steps, then along the sidewalk, until she was lost in the crowd. Behind him, the door opened and a lady he didn't know took Micah's hand and led him inside.

His mother never came back.

Micah shook off the memory of his first encounter with child services. It had been a long, confusing, terrifying day for him. He was sure he wouldn't be there long. His mother had said so. For the first year, he'd actually looked for her every day. After that, hope was more fragile and, finally, the hope faded completely. His mother's lies stuck with him, of course.

Hell, they still lived in a tiny, dark corner of his mind and constantly served as a reminder not to trust anyone.

But here, in Banner, those warnings were more silent

than they'd ever been for him. Watching as Jacob carefully brushed dirt off his pumpkin, Micah realized that this place was like stepping into a Norman Rockwell painting. A place where kids worried about pumpkins and talked to strangers like they were best friends. It had nothing at all to do with the world that Micah knew.

And maybe that's why he felt so out of step here.

That's how Kelly found them. The boy, kneeling in the dirt, and the man standing beside him, a trapped look on his face—as if he were trying to figure out how he'd gotten there. Smiling to herself, Kelly climbed out of her truck and walked toward the garden at the side of the house. Micah spotted her first and his brown eyes locked with hers.

She felt a jolt of something hot that made her knees feel like rubber, but she kept moving. She had to admit it surprised her, seeing Micah here with Jacob. She hadn't pictured him as the kind of guy to take the time for a child. He was so closed off, so private, that seeing him now, walking through a fenced garden while a little boy talked his ears off gave her a warm feeling she couldn't quite describe.

"What're you guys up to?" she asked as she walked closer.

"I showed Micah my pumpkin," Jacob announced. "He likes mine best, he said so."

"Well, of course he did," she agreed. "Yours is terrific."

The little boy flashed Micah a wide grin. Micah, on the other hand, looked embarrassed to have been caught being nice. Interesting reaction.

"It's okay I came over, right?" Jacob asked, looking

a little worried. "Micah was cooking, but he opened the gate for me and stuff."

"Sure it's okay," Kelly told him.

"Okay, I gotta go now," Jacob said suddenly, giving his pumpkin one last pat. "Bye!"

He bolted through the gate and tore across the backyard toward the house next door.

Micah watched him go. "That was fast."

Kelly laughed a little, then looked over at Micah. "You were cooking?"

He shrugged. "I was hungry."

She glanced at the lavender sky. "Early for dinner."

"Or late for lunch," he said with a shrug. "It's all about perspective."

What did it say about her that she enjoyed the sharp, nearly bitten off words he called a conversation? Kelly wondered if he'd been any easier with Jacob, but somehow she doubted it. The man might be a whiz when typing words and dialogue, but actually speaking in real life appeared to be one of his least favorite things.

"So, why keep the fence when you told me it doesn't stop the deer?

She looked around at the tall, white pickets, then walked toward the still-open gate. Micah followed her. Once through, she latched the gate after them and said, "Makes me feel better to try. Sometimes, I could swear I hear the deer laughing at my pitiful attempts to foil them."

He looked toward the woods that ran along the back of the neighborhood and stretched out for at least five miles to the base of the mountains. "I haven't seen a single deer since I've been here."

"You have to actually be outside," she pointed out.

"Right." He nodded and tucked his hands into his jeans pockets.

"There's a lot of them and they're sneaky," Kelly said, shooting a dark look at the forest. "Of course, some of them aren't. They just walk right into the garden and sneer at you."

He laughed and she looked at him, surprised. "Deer can sneer?"

"They can and do." She tipped her head to one side to stare at him. "You should laugh more often."

He frowned at that and the moment was gone, so Kelly let it go and went back to his first question. "The fence doesn't even slow them down, really. They just jump right over it." Shaking her head, she added, "They look like ballet dancers, really. Graceful, you know?"

"So why bother with the fence?"

"Because otherwise it's like I'm saying, *It's okay with me guys. Come on in and eat the vegetables.*"

"So, you're at war with deer."

"Basically, yeah." She frowned and looked to the woods. "And, so far, they're winning."

"You've got orange paint on your cheek."

"What? Oh." She reached up and scrubbed at her face.

"And white paint on your fingers."

Kelly held her hands out to see for herself, then laughed. "Yeah, I just came from a painting job and—"

"You paint, too?"

"Oh, just a little. Window decorations and stuff. I'm not an artist or anything, but—"

"Realtor, painter, website manager…" He just looked at her. "What else?"

"Oh, a few other things," she said. "I design gardens, and in the winter I plow driveways. I like variety."

His eyes flared at her admission and her stomach jumped in response. Not the kind of variety she'd meant, but now that the thought was in her brain, thank you very much, there were lots of other very interesting thoughts, too. Her skin felt heated and she was grateful for the cold breeze that swept past them.

Kelly took a deep breath, swallowed hard and said, "I should probably get home and clean up."

"How about a glass of wine first?"

Curious, she looked up at him. "Is that an invitation?"

"If it is?"

"Then I accept."

"Good." He nodded. "Come on then. We can eat, too."

"A man who cooks *and* serves wine?" She started for the back door, walking alongside Micah. "You're a rare man, Micah Hunter."

"Yeah," he murmured. "Rare."

Naturally, she was perfectly at home in the Victorian. She'd grown up there, after all. She'd done her homework at the round pedestal table while eating Gran's cookies fresh out of the oven. She'd learned to cook on the old stove and had helped Gran pick out the shiny, stainless steel French door refrigerator when the last one had finally coughed and died.

She'd painted the walls a soft gold so that even in winter it would feel warm and cozy in here, and she'd chosen the amber-streaked granite counters to complement the walls. This house was comfort. Love.

At the farmhouse sink, Kelly looked out the window at the yard, the woods and the deepening sky as she washed her hands, scrubbing every bit of the paint from her skin. Then she splashed water on her face and wiped that away, too. "Did I get it all?"

He glanced at her and nodded. "Yeah."

"Good. I like painting, but I prefer the paint on the windows rather than on me."

Kelly got the wine out of the fridge while Micah heated the pasta in the skillet. She took two glasses from a cabinet and poured wine for each of them before sitting at the round oak table watching him.

What was it, she wondered, about a man cooking that was just so sexy? Sean hadn't known how to turn the stove on, but Micah seemed confident and comfortable with a spatula in his hand. Which only made her think about what other talents he might have. Oh, boy, it had been a long time since she'd felt this heat swamping her. If Terry knew what Kelly was thinking right this minute, she would send up balloons and throw a small but tasteful party. That thought made her smile. "Smells good."

He glanced over his shoulder at her. "Pasta's easy. A few herbs, some garlic, olive oil and cheese and you're done. Plus, some sliced steak because you've gotta have meat."

"Agreed," Kelly said, taking a sip of her wine.

"Glad to hear you're not one of those *I'll just have a salad, dressing on the side* types."

"Hey, nothing wrong with a nice salad."

"As long as there's meat in it," he said, concentrating on the task at hand.

"So what made you take up cooking?"

"Self-preservation. Live alone, you learn how to cook."

Whether he knew it or not, that was an opening for questions. She didn't waste it. "Live alone, huh?"

One eyebrow lifted as he turned to look at her. "Did you notice anyone else here with me the last couple of months?"

"No," she admitted with a smile, "but you do write mysteries. You could have killed your girlfriend."

"Could have," he agreed easily. "Didn't. The only place I commit crimes is on a computer screen."

"Glad to hear it," she said, smiling. Also glad to hear he could take some teasing and give it back. But on to the real question. "So, no girlfriend or wife?"

He used the spatula to stir the pasta, then gave her a quick look. "That's a purely female question."

"Well, then, since I am definitely female, that makes sense." She propped her chin in her hand. "And it was very male of you to answer the question by not answering. Want to give it another try?"

"No."

"No you won't answer or no *is* the answer?"

Reluctantly, it seemed, his mouth curved briefly into a half smile. "I should know better than to get into a battle of words with a woman. Even being a writer, I don't stand a chance."

"Isn't that the nicest thing to say?" But she stared at him, clearly waiting for his answer. Finally he gave her the one she was looking for.

He snorted. "No is the answer. No wife. No girlfriend. No interest."

"So you're gay," she said sagely. Oh, she knew he wasn't because the two of them had that whole hot-buzz thing going between them. But it was fun to watch his expression.

"I'm not gay."

"Are you sure?"

"Reasonably," he said wryly.

"Good to know," she said, and took a sip of wine, hiding her smile behind the rim of her glass. "I'm not, either, just so we're clear."

His gaze bored into hers and flames licked at her insides. "Also good to know."

Her throat dried up so she had another sip of wine to ease it. "How long have you been a writer?"

"A writer or a published writer?" he asked.

"There's a difference?"

He shrugged as he plated the pasta and carried them to the table. Sitting down opposite her, he took a long drink of his wine before speaking again. "I wrote stories for years that no one will ever see."

"Intriguing," she said, and wondered what those old stories would say about Micah Hunter. Would she learn more about the closed-off, secretive man by discovering who he had been years ago?

"Not very." He took a bite of pasta, "Anyway, I've been published about ten years."

"I don't read your books."

One eyebrow lifted and he smirked. "Thanks."

She grinned. "That came out wrong. Sorry. I mean, I read one of your books a few years ago and it scared me to death. So I haven't read another one."

"Then, thank you." He lifted his glass in a kind of salute to her. "Best compliment you could give me. Which book was it?"

"I don't remember the title," she said, tasting the pasta. "But it was about a woman looking for her missing sister and she finds the sister's killer, instead."

He nodded. "*Relative Danger*. That was my third book."

"First and last for me," she assured him. "I slept with the light on for two weeks."

"Thanks." He studied her. "Did you read the whole book? Or did you stop because it scared you?"

"Who stops in the middle of a book?" she demanded,

outraged at the idea. "No, I read the whole thing and, terror aside, it ended well."

"Thanks again."

"You're welcome. You know, this is really good," she said, taking another bite. "Your mom teach you how to cook?"

His face went hard and tight. He lowered his gaze to his plate and muttered, "No. Learned by trial and error."

Sore spot, she told herself and changed the subject. She had secret, painful corners in her own soul, so she wouldn't poke at his. "How's your book coming? The one you're working on now, I mean."

He frowned before answering. "Slower than I'd like."

"Why?"

"You ask a lot of questions."

"The only way to get answers."

"True." He took a sip of wine. "Because the book's set in a small town and I don't know small towns."

"Hello?" Laughing, she said, "You're *in* one."

"Yeah. That's why I came here in the first place. My agent suggested it. He stayed here a couple of years ago for the skiing and thought the town would work for my research."

"*Here*, here?" she asked. "I mean, did he stay at the Victorian?"

"Yeah."

"What's his name?"

"Sam Hellman. He and his wife, Jenny, were here for a week."

"I remember them. She's very pretty and sweet and he's funny."

"That's them," Micah agreed.

Kelly took a drink of her wine. "Well, first, I'm glad

your agent had a good time here. Word of mouth? Best advertising."

"For books, too," he agreed.

"But if you want to use the town for its setting and ambience, it might help if you left the house and explored a little. Get to know the place."

He ate for a couple of minutes, then finally said, "Getting out doesn't get the typing done."

Kelly shrugged and set down her glass. "But you can't get to know the town by looking through a window, either. And, if you don't know what it's like here, you've got nothing to type anyway, right?"

"I don't much like that you've got a point."

Kelly grinned. "Well, that makes two points for me, doesn't it? I'm still winning."

Unexpectedly, he laughed and the rich, warm sound seemed to ripple along her spine.

"Competitive, aren't you?"

"You have no idea," Kelly admitted. "I used to drive my grandparents crazy. I was always trying to be first in my class, or the fastest runner or—"

"Your grandparents still live here?"

"No." She picked up her wineglass and watched the light play on the golden wine. "My grandfather died six years ago and my grandmother moved to Florida to live with her sister a year later." Kelly took a sip, let the cold liquid ease her suddenly tight throat. "When my husband died four years ago, Gran came home for a few weeks to stay with me."

"You were married?" He spoke quietly, as if unsure exactly what to say.

No surprise there, Kelly thought. Most people just immediately said, *I'm sorry.* She didn't know why. Social convention? Or was it just the panic of not being able to think of anything else?

She lifted her gaze to his. "Sean died in a skiing accident."

"Must've been hard."

"Yeah," she said, nodding. "It was. And thanks for not saying you're sorry. People do, even though they have nothing to be sorry about, you know? Then I feel like I have to make them feel better, and it's just a weird situation all the way around."

"Yeah. I get that."

The expression on his face was sympathetic and that was okay. Telling someone your husband was dead was a conversation killer. "It's okay. I mean, no one ever really knows what to say, so don't worry about it." Another sip of wine to wash down the knot in her throat. "Anyway, it wasn't easy to get Gran to go back to her new life—she thought she was abandoning me. And I love that she loves me, you know? But I don't want to be a worry or a burden or a duty—not really a duty, but that little nudge of worry. I don't want to be that, either." She took a breath and smiled. "Whoa. Rambling. Anyway, Gran's still worried, and unless I can convince her I'm just fine, she's going to move back here to keep me company."

"And that's a bad thing?"

She looked at him. "Yes. It's bad. She's having a blast in Florida. She deserves to enjoy herself, not to feel like she has to move back to take care of an adult granddaughter."

Nodding, Micah leaned back in the chair, never taking his gaze from hers. "All right. I can see that. So you know what you want. How're you going to manage it?"

Good question. There was a ridiculous idea worming its way through her mind, but it was so far out there she felt weird even entertaining the idea while Micah was here.

"I don't know yet." She smiled, had another sip of wine and said, "But, hey, as fascinating as my whirlwind life can be, enough already. I've given you my story. What's yours?"

He stiffened. "What do you mean?"

"Well, for starters," Kelly said, "have you ever been married?"

Micah shook his head. "No."

Kelly just stared at him, waiting. There had to be more than just a no.

Finally, he scowled and added, "Fine. I was engaged once."

"Engaged but not married. So what happened?"

"It didn't take." His features were tight, like the doors of a house locked against intruders.

Okay, that was obviously a dead-end subject. "You know, for a writer—someone supposedly good with words—you're not particularly chatty."

He snorted and the tension left him. "Writers *write*. Besides, men aren't 'chatty.'"

"But they do talk."

"I'm talking."

"Not saying much," she pointed out.

"Maybe there's not much to say."

"Oh, I don't believe that," Kelly told him. "There's more, you're just stingy about sharing."

He started to speak—no doubt protest, Kelly told herself, but she stopped him with another question.

"Let's try this. You're a writer and you travel all over the world, I know. But where's home?"

"Here." He studiously avoided her gaze and concentrated on the pasta.

"Yeah," she said. "For now. But before this. Where are you from?"

"Originally," he answered, "New York."

Honestly, it would probably be easier if she asked him to *write* the information and let her read it. "Okay, that's originally. How about now—and not this house."

"Everywhere," he said. "I move around."

She hadn't expected that. Everyone was from *somewhere*. "What about your family?"

"Don't have any." He stood up, took his plate to the sink, then came back for his wineglass. Lifting it for a drink, he looked at her. "And I don't talk about it, either."

Message was clear, Kelly thought. He'd put up his mental No Trespassing signs. His eyes were shuttered and his jaw was tight.

Whatever bit of closeness had opened up between them was over now. Funny that while they were talking about *her*, he was all chatty, but the minute the conversation shifted to him, he clammed up so tightly it would take a crowbar to pry words from his mouth.

It surprised her how disappointed she was about that. Since Sean died, she hadn't been as interested in a man as she was in Micah. And for a while, as they sat together sharing a meal, she'd felt that buzz humming between them like an arc of electricity. And now it was fizzling out. The expression on his face told her he was waiting for her to pry. To ask more questions. And since she hated being predictable, Kelly said simply, "Okay."

Suspicion gleamed in his eyes. "Just like that."

"Everybody's got secrets, Micah," she told him with

a shrug. "You're entitled to yours." Tipping her head to one side, she asked, "Why so surprised?"

"Because most women would be hammering me with questions right now."

"Well, then, it's your lucky day, because I'm not like most women." Besides, hammering him wouldn't work.

"Got that right," he muttered.

She heard that and smiled to herself as she carried her dishes to the sink, then turned for the back door. Kelly didn't want to leave, but she knew she should. Otherwise, she might be tempted to be like every other woman in the world and try to get him to open up some more—which would be pointless and exactly what he expected.

"So, thanks for lunch or dinner or whatever. And the wine."

Micah was right behind her. "You're welcome."

His voice came from right behind her. At the open doorway, she turned and almost bumped into his chest.

"Oh, sorry." Wow, was his chest really that broad, or was she just so close it *looked* like he was taking up the whole world? Heat poured from his body, reaching for her, tingling her nerve endings. And he smelled so good, too.

Kelly shook her head, and ignored the flutter of expectation awakening in the pit of her stomach. Deliberately, she fought for lighthearted, then tipped her head back and smiled up at him. "You know, I think I should get another point."

"For what?"

"For surprising you by not asking questions." She held up three fingers and gave him a teasing smile. "So that makes it three to nothing my favor and don't you forget it."

"Not a chance in hell you would *let* me forget, is there?"

"Nope." Kelly grinned. "And how nice that you know me so well already."

"That's what I thought." He studied her as if he were trying to figure out a puzzle. But after a second or two, he nodded. "You want to keep score? Then add this into the mix."

He pulled her in close and kissed her.

Four

Everything inside Kelly lit up like a sparkler, showering her head to toe in red-hot flickers of heat and light. Instinctively, her eyes closed and her body swayed closer to him. His mouth covered hers and his arms came around her, molding her to him, and she lifted both arms to hook them around his neck.

It had been so long since she'd been kissed she was dizzy with the sensations pouring through her. God, she'd forgotten how sensations poured through her system in a kiss, the tangle of feelings that erupted. She couldn't think. Couldn't have spoken even if she had wanted to pry her mouth from his. His tongue stroked hers and the groans lifting from her throat twisted with Micah's, the soft sounds whispering into the twilight.

Breathing was becoming an issue, but she didn't care. She wanted to revel in the feeling of her body awakening as if from a coma. Fires quickened down low inside her and a tingling ache settled at her core. Need clawed at her and she moved in even closer to him. She might have stood there all night, taking what he offered, feeling her own desires tearing at her. But, as suddenly as he'd kissed her, he ended it.

Tearing his mouth from hers, he lifted his head to look down at her. From Kelly's perspective, his features were blurry. She swayed unsteadily until she slapped one hand to the door frame just for balance. As her mind defogged, her vision cleared and her heart rate dropped from racing to just really fast.

He still held her waist in a tight grip, and when he looked down into her eyes, Kelly saw that *his* eyes were a molten brown now, shot through with the fires that were burning her from the inside out.

"I think that makes it three to one now, doesn't it?" His voice was low, a deep rumble that was almost like thunder.

Points? Oh, yeah. Kelly's brain was just not working well enough at the moment to count points. But since her body was still smoldering, she had to say, "Oh, yeah. Point to you."

He gave her a slow, satisfied smile.

Reluctantly, her mouth curved, too. "You're enjoying this, aren't you?"

"I'd be a fool not to," he admitted.

"Yeah. Well." She lifted one hand to touch her fingers to her lips. "Let's not forget, I've still got three points to your one."

His smile faded and his eyes flashed as he let her go. "But the game's not over yet, is it?"

"Not even close to finished," she said, then turned

and started the short walk home. She felt him watching her as she walked away and that gave her a warm rush, too. Kelly had the feeling that this game was just getting started.

She couldn't wait for round two.

Micah watched her go for ten agonizing seconds, then he shut the door firmly to keep himself from chasing after her. God, he felt like some girl-crazed teenager and that just wasn't acceptable. He was a man who demanded control. He didn't do spontaneous. Didn't veer from the plan he had for his life. And that plan did *not* include a small-town widow who tasted like a glimpse of heaven.

He wanted another taste. Wanted to feel her body pressed to his, the race of her heart, the warmth of her arms around his neck.

"Damn it." He took a deep breath to steady himself, but her scent was still clinging to him and it invaded his lungs, making itself a part of him.

His own heartbeat was a little crazed and his jeans felt like an iron cage around his hard body. Micah didn't know what had made him grab her like that. But the urge to taste her, hold her, had been too big to ignore. If he'd been thinking clearly, he never would have done it. The problem was, every time he was around Kelly, thinking was an impossible task.

"Maybe Sam's right," he told himself. "Maybe an affair is the answer." Something had to give, he thought. Because if he spent the next four months as tied up in knots as he was at the moment, he'd never get any writing done.

Something to think about.

* * *

Kelly walked home across the wide front lawn, mind racing, nerves sizzling from that unexpected but amazing kiss. She stopped halfway to the carriage house, turned around and looked at the big Victorian.

In the deepening twilight, the house looked as it had to her when she was a child—like a fairy tale. The house was painted a deep brick red with snow-white trim that seemed to define every little detail. Three chimneys jutted up from the shake roof, indicating the tiled fireplaces—in the living room, the master bedroom and the kitchen. The wide, wraparound porch was dotted with swings, chairs and tables, inviting anyone to sit, enjoy the view and visit for a while. Double front doors were hand-carved mahogany with inset panes of etched glass. The last of the sunset glanced off the second-story windows, making them glow gold, and downstairs a lamp in the living room flashed on, telling Kelly exactly where Micah was in the house.

She lifted one hand to her mouth as she looked at that light, imagining him striding through that front door, marching across the yard to her and kissing her again. God, one kiss and all she could think was she wanted more.

"Oh, man, this could be bad..." Deliberately then, as if to prove to herself she *could*, she turned away and continued to the cottage.

It was a smaller version of the big house. Same colors, same intricate trim, made by a long-dead craftsman more than a hundred years ago. Just one bedroom, bathroom, living room and kitchen, the cottage was perfect for one person and normally, when Kelly stepped inside, it felt like a refuge.

She'd moved out of the Victorian not long after Sean's death because she simply couldn't bear the empty rooms and the echo of her own footsteps. Here, in this cottage, it was cozy and safe and, right now, almost suffocating. But that was probably because she still felt like there was a tight band around her chest.

Kelly dropped into the nearest chair and snuggled into the deep cushions. The comfort and familiarity of the cottage didn't relax her as it usually did. Shaking her head, she sighed a little and told herself to get a grip. But it wasn't easy since Micah Hunter had a real gift when it came to kissing. So, naturally, she had to wonder how gifted he was in...related areas. Oh, boy. She was in deep trouble.

The worst part was that she wanted to be in even deeper.

When her cell phone rang, she dug it out of her pocket, grateful for the distraction. Until she saw the caller ID. Guilt rose up and took another healthy bite out of Kelly's heart. She'd forgotten all about returning her grandmother's call. Seeing Micah, sharing a meal with him, had thrown her off, and then that kiss had completely sealed the deal on her mind, shutting down any thought beyond *oh, boy*!

Taking a breath, she forced a smile into her voice and answered. "Hi, Gran! I'm sorry, I just didn't have a chance to call you back before."

"That's okay, honey," her grandmother said. "I hope you were out having fun..."

Kelly sighed a little and leaned her head back against the cushioned chair. She could hear the worry in her grandmother's voice and wished she couldn't. Ever since Sean died, Gran had been worried and it didn't seem to be easing. If anything, it was getting worse. As if the older Gran got, the more she was concerned about eventually leaving Kelly on her own.

Kelly had been trying for months to convince Gran that she was fine. Happy. But nothing worked because the only thing Gran would accept was Kelly in love and married again. She wanted her settled with a family and no matter how many times Kelly told her that she didn't need a husband, Gran remained ever hopeful.

Even knowing that Kelly had just been kissed until her brain melted wouldn't be enough to satisfy Gran. Not unless she and Micah were married or—

Suddenly, the idea she'd played with earlier came back to her. Maybe it was the kiss. Maybe it was sitting across that table from Micah, talking, laughing, sharing dinner. Whatever the reason, Kelly made a decision that she really hoped she didn't come to regret. "Actually, Gran," she said, before the still-rational corner of her brain could stop her, "I was with my fiancé."

"*What?* Oh, my goodness, that's wonderful!"

The joy in her grandmother's voice made Kelly smile and wince at the same time. Okay, yes, technically she was lying to her grandmother. But, really, she was just trying to give the older woman some peace. The chance to enjoy her life without constant worries about Kelly. That wasn't a bad thing, was it? It's not like she was pretending to be engaged for her own sake. This was completely altruistic.

"Tell me everything," Gran insisted. "Who is he? What does he do? Is he handsome?"

"It's Micah Hunter, Gran," she said, hoping a lightning bolt didn't streak out of the sky and turn her into a cinder. "The writer who's renting the Victorian for six months."

"Oh, my, a writer!"

Kelly's eyes closed tightly on another wince, but that didn't help because Micah's image rose up in her mind and gave her a hard look. She ignored it.

"He's very handsome and very sweet." Oh, it was a wonder her tongue didn't simply rot and fall out of her mouth. *Sweet?* Micah Hunter? Sexy, yes. Prickly, oh, yeah. But she'd seen no evidence of sweet. Still, it was something her grandmother would want to hear. And as long as Kelly was lying through her teeth to the woman who had raised her, she was determined to make it a *good* lie.

"When did this happen?" Gran asked. "When did he propose? What does your ring look like?"

Before Kelly could answer, Gran covered the receiver and shouted, "Linda, you won't believe it! Our girl is engaged to a writer!"

Gran's sister squealed in the background and Kelly sighed.

"I'm putting you on speaker, sweetie. Linda wants to hear the story, too."

Great. A command performance. Boy, it was a good thing they didn't do video chatting.

"It just happened tonight," Kelly blurted. Her grandmother's friends in Banner no doubt gave her updates on Kelly, so she would know that nothing had happened between her and Micah any sooner.

"How exciting!" Linda exclaimed, and Gran shushed her.

"Tell us everything, honey," Gran urged. "I want details."

"He cooked dinner tonight," Kelly continued, and consoled herself that at least that part of the story wasn't a lie. "He proposed while we were sitting out on the porch."

"Oh, that's lovely." Gran gave a heavy sigh and Kelly felt terrible.

She was already regretting this, but she was in so deep now there was no way to back out without admitting she had lied. Nope. Couldn't do it.

"Yeah, it was lovely." Kelly nodded and kept going, making it as romantic as she could for her grandmother's sake. The woman loved watching Hallmark movies and had been known to cry at particularly touching commercials, so Kelly knew Gran would expect romance in this story.

Thinking fast, she said, "He had flowers on the porch and those little white twinkle lights hung from the ceiling. Music was playing, too," she added, telling herself to remember all of these details. "He brought out a bottle of champagne and went down on one knee and when I said yes, he kissed me."

Kissed her brainless, apparently, because otherwise why would she be inventing all of this? Oh, God, just remembering that kiss had her blood humming and heat spiraling through her body. One kiss and she was making up an engagement.

What was she doing?

"Well, good, I'm so glad to hear he gave you romance, sweetheart. I'm so happy for you." Her grandmother sniffled a little and her sister said, "Oh, Bella, stop now. The girl's happy. You should be too."

"These are happy tears, Linda, can't you tell?"

"They're still tears, so stop it."

Kelly grimaced. Could you actually be *devoured* by guilt?

"Pay no attention to my sister," Gran said softly. "You know, honey, since you lost Sean, I've been so worried."

"I know." Kelly told herself she was doing the right thing. She was easing an old woman's heart. Making her happy. It wasn't hurting anyone. Not even Micah, really. He was only here temporarily. Heck, he didn't even have to meet her grandmother. And, when he left in four months, Kelly would simply tell Gran that they'd broken up. Maybe the very fact that Kelly had been engaged, however briefly, would be enough to assure Gran that she didn't have to worry so much.

"Will you take a picture of your ring and send it to me?"

Oops. She looked at her naked ring finger and sighed.

"Um, I don't have a ring yet," Kelly said.

"The man thought of twinkle lights but didn't bother with a ring?" Linda asked.

The two women together were really hard to stand against. "Micah wants to wait until we go to New York so we can pick one out together."

"New York?" Linda's tone changed. "How exciting!"

"Hush, Linda," Gran told her sister. "When are you going to New York, sweetie? Can you send me pictures? I'd love to show the girls at bingo."

"Sure I can, Gran." *Oh, my God, stop talking, Kelly.*

But the lies kept piling on top of each other until any second now, she'd be buried beneath a mountain of them. There was no way to stop now. She'd started all of this and she had to follow through because admitting a lie to her grandmother was simply impossible.

"I don't know when we're going to New York though..." That was true, at least. "He's busy with work and I've got Halloween coming up and—"

Gran clucked her tongue and Kelly muffled a groan.

"Well, you both just have to take the time for each other," Gran told her firmly. "Work will always be there, but this is a special time for you two."

Oh, it was special, all right. And wait until she told Micah about all of this. That scene promised to be extra special.

"Why a New York ring?" Linda demanded. "They don't sell rings in Utah?"

"Well," Kelly said, making it up as she went along, "when I told Micah I'd never been to New York, he insisted on flying me out there in a private jet so he could show me around. So, we really want to wait on the ring until then."

"Oh, my goodness," Gran whispered. "Linda, can you imagine? Private jets."

"He must be rich," Linda said thoughtfully.

"Course he is," Gran told her. "Haven't we seen his books just everywhere? Don't tell him we don't read his books because they're too scary, though, all right dear?"

"Sure, I won't tell him," Kelly promised.

"You know," Aunt Linda said, "I saw a documentary on those private jets not long ago. They've got *bedrooms* on those jets. You could live on them, I swear."

Kelly couldn't sit still anymore. She lunged out of the chair, walked to her tiny, serviceable kitchen and threw open the fridge. Grabbing the bottle of chardonnay, she pulled out the cork and took a swig straight from the bottle. Oh, if Gran could see her at that moment. Sighing a little, Kelly got a wineglass from a cabinet and poured herself what looked like eight ounces. It might not be enough.

"Well," Gran continued to argue with her sister.

"They're not looking to live on the plane, for heaven's sake, and you just keep your mind out of bedrooms."

"Nothing wrong with a good romp," Linda told her sister. "It would do you good to try one."

Kelly took a big gulp of wine. She didn't want to know about her grandmother's sex life. Or her aunt's, for that matter. Actually, she didn't want to know they *had* sex lives.

"What's that supposed to mean?" Gran sounded outraged. "Just because you don't have standards…"

"I have standards," Linda countered, "but they don't get in the way of a good time."

This argument could go on all night, Kelly knew. The two women loved nothing better than arguing with each other. Drinking her wine, Kelly told herself that while they were arguing about their men friends, they weren't interrogating Kelly about *her* love life. That was something, anyway.

Halfheartedly listening to the two of them, Kelly had enough of a break from her lie fest that she had the time to start worrying about breaking all of this to Micah. How was she supposed to explain it to him when she could hardly figure out herself why she'd started all of this?

She stared out the kitchen window at the yard and the stately Victorian where the man she was using shamelessly was currently living, unaware that he'd just gotten engaged. Oh, boy.

"When's the wedding?" Linda asked suddenly.

"She's *my* granddaughter," Gran said tightly. "I'll ask the questions here. When Debbie gets engaged, then it'll be your turn. Kelly, when's the wedding, honey?"

Kelly's cousin Debbie had already insisted that she and her girlfriend were *never* getting married because

the two grans would drive her insane. Kelly could understand that. After all, she'd already lived through one
wedding where Gran had made and changed plans every
day. If she ever really did get married again one day, she'd
elope. Vegas sounded good.

But, for now, Gran was waiting for an answer and
since Kelly couldn't tell the truth, she told another lie. It
seemed she was on a roll.

"Oh, the wedding won't be for a while yet," she
hedged, and had another drink of wine. At this rate, she
was going to pass out in another few minutes. "I mean,
Micah's got this book he's working on and then he has to
do other writing stuff—" Oh, God, that sounded weak,
even to her. What did writers have to *do*? "Um, book
tours and research trips for the next book, so we probably won't be able to get married for at least another six
months, maybe even a year. It all depends on Micah's
work." There. That was reasonable, right?

"Wonderful," Gran said, and Kelly released a breath
she hadn't realized she'd been holding. "That gives us
plenty of time to *plan*. You'll have the wedding at the
Victorian, of course…"

"Oh, of course," Kelly agreed, rolling her eyes so hard
she heard them rattle.

"Or," Linda argued. "You could get married on the
beach right here in Florida. Next summer, maybe?"

"I don't know, Aunt Linda…"

"Why would you want to get married on a beach?"
Gran snorted. "All that sand in your shoes and the
wind ruining your hair and seagulls pooping all over
the place."

"It's romantic," Linda insisted.

"It's dirty," Gran countered.

"Oh, God," Kelly murmured, so quietly that the other two women on the line didn't hear her.

Completely wrapped up in their argument, the ladies didn't notice when Kelly went quiet and that was good. Carrying her wine back to the living room, Kelly dropped into a chair again and listened with only half an ear to her grandmother and aunt.

She didn't have to pay attention now. Kelly knew that she'd be hearing nothing but plans for the next four months—until Micah left and she could break this imaginary engagement. Supposing, of course, that she could talk Micah into going along with this in the first place. If she couldn't, then what? She'd have to claim insanity. That would be the only excuse accepted by her family.

Guilt was becoming such a familiar companion she hardly noticed when it dropped into the pit of her stomach and sat there like a ball of ice. Wine wouldn't melt it, either, though she gave it her best shot.

Her grandmother was talking about white dresses while Linda insisted that white was outdated and Kelly wasn't a virgin, anyway.

A snort of laughter escaped her throat and Kelly was half-afraid it would turn into hysteria. Shaking her head, she tried to figure out the best way to approach Micah about the story she'd created. Once she hung up the phone, Gran would be calling all of her friends in Banner to share the happy news, so Micah had to be prepared for questions. And for behaving like a man in love so she could keep her grandmother blissfully unaware for four short months.

Oh, boy. Lying got out of hand so quickly Kelly could only sit and stare blankly at the wall opposite her. Really, even when a lie seemed like the best idea, it wasn't. No one ever looked far ahead as to what that lie was going to look like once other people picked it up and ran with it. But it wasn't as if she'd had a whole lot of options. She wasn't dating anyone, so she'd had to name Micah. She couldn't let her grandmother give up her new life and sacrifice herself on the altar of Sad Lonely Granddaughter.

But, even though she knew she was doing the right thing, the hole she'd dug for herself was beginning to feel like a bottomless chasm.

At least, she *hoped* it was bottomless. Otherwise, the crash landing she was going to make would be spectacular.

Micah woke up irritated. Not surprising since what little sleep he had gotten had been haunted by images of Kelly Flynn.

"Your own damn fault," he muttered. "If you hadn't kissed her…"

The taste of her was still with him. The feel of her body, warm and pliant against his. Her eager response had fired his blood to the point that it had taken everything he had just to let her go and back off.

Hell, the woman had been making him nuts for the last two months. Sexy, smart and a wiseass, Kelly was enough to bring any man to his knees.

"But damned if I will," he muttered darkly, and got out of bed. Disgusted with himself *and* her, he stalked to the bathroom, turned the water on to heat up, then stood under the shower. He let the hot water slam into his head, hoping it might wash away the last of the dreams that had tormented him and had had him waking up hard as iron.

Naturally it didn't work. It was like her features were imprinted on his brain. Her wide green eyes, the way she had lifted one hand to her lips when their kiss ended. Her smile, her ridiculous insistence on keeping track of "points" scored.

Shaking his head, he saw her in the stupid pumpkin patch talking about her war with deer, of all things. Micah had never *seen* a deer. He closed his eyes and reminded himself that he didn't want or need a woman. But maybe that was wrong, too. If he was fantasizing this much about the landlady, it had clearly been too long since he'd been with a woman.

"Gotta be it," he murmured, shutting off the water and stepping out of the tiled, glassed-in shower. "That's the reason I can't stop thinking about a woman who doesn't even know when she has orange paint on her face."

He dried off, then walked into the bedroom, not bothering to shave. Hell, he'd gotten so little sleep he'd probably slit his own throat if he attempted it.

"What I need to do is put this out of my head and get to work." Losing himself in a grisly murder was just the thing to take his mind off finding Kelly and dragging her here to his bed.

He pulled on a pair of black jeans, then tugged a forest green T-shirt over his head. Micah didn't bother with shoes. It might be gray and cold outside, but inside the old house was toasty. All he wanted was some coffee and then some quiet so he could create another murder.

As soon as he opened the bedroom door, the unmistakable scent of fresh coffee hit him hard. But it wasn't just coffee. It was bacon, too. And toast. "What kind of burglar breaks into a house to make breakfast?"

He started down the long staircase, his bare feet silent on the sapphire-blue carpet runner. Two months here and he still felt like a stranger in this big old house with its creaky doors and polished, old-world style.

He couldn't complain about anything. The house had been updated over the years and boasted comfortable furniture, every amenity and a view from every window that really was beautiful. But it was a lot more space than he was used to. A lot more quiet than he was happy with. Being solitary was part of being a writer. After all, the bottom line was sitting by yourself at a computer. If you needed people with you every damn minute, then writing was not the job for you.

But even solitary creatures needed sensory input from time to time. And being on your own in a house built for a family of a couple dozen could be a little unsettling. Hell, as a mystery/horror writer, Micah could use this house, the solitude and the woods behind the property as the perfect setting for a book.

As that thought took root in his mind, he stopped at the bottom of the stairs, considered it and muttered, "Of course I should be using this house. Why the hell aren't I?"

He continued on through to the kitchen, his senses focused on the tantalizing scents dragging him closer even while his mind figured out how big a rewrite he was looking at. To move his heroine from a small apartment in town to this big house, he'd have to change a million little things. But, he told himself, the atmosphere alone would be worth it.

A cold winter night, the heroine closed up in her bedroom, a fire burning as the wind shrieked and sleet pelted the windows. Then over that noise, she hears something else. Someone moving downstairs—when she's alone in the house.

"Oh, yeah," he told himself, nodding, "that's good. I like it."

He hit the swinging door into the kitchen, stepped inside and stopped dead. Kelly stood at the stove, stirring scrambled eggs in a skillet. Morning sunlight danced in her hair, making the red and gold shine like a new penny. Her black yoga pants clung to her behind and hugged her legs before disappearing into the tops of the black boots on her feet. She half turned toward him when he came in. Her pale green long-sleeved shirt had the top two buttons undone, giving Micah just a peek at what looked like a lacy pink bra.

Instantly his body went hard as stone again. He swallowed the groan that rose in his throat. Wasn't it enough that she'd tormented him all damn night? Why was she here first thing in the morning? Cooking? God, he needed coffee.

And the only way to get it was to deal with the woman smiling at him.

Five

"What're you doing?"

"Cooking." She smiled at him and Micah felt every drop of blood drain from his brain and head south.

After turning the fire down under the pan, she walked to the coffeemaker, poured him a cup and carried it to him.

"I made breakfast." She sounded bright, cheerful, but her eyes told a different story. There was worry there and a hesitation that put Micah on edge.

Whatever was going on, though, would be handled best *after* coffee. He took his first sip of the morning and felt every cell in his body wake up and dance. How did people survive without coffee?

After another sip or two, he felt strong enough to ask, "Why?"

"Why what?"

One eyebrow lifted. "Why are you here? Why are you cooking?"

"Just being neighborly," she said, and he didn't believe a word of it.

"Yeah." He walked to the table, sat down and had another sip. "I've been here two months. This is the first time you've been 'neighborly.'"

"Well, then, shame on me." She stirred the eggs in the pan and neatly avoided meeting his gaze. Not, Micah told himself, a good sign.

"You're not really good at prevarication."

Her eyes widened. "Oh. Good word."

"And," Micah added wryly, "not very good at stalling, either."

She sighed heavily. "Okay, yes, there is something I need to talk to you about, but after breakfast, okay?"

He grabbed a slice of bacon, took a bite and chewed. When he'd swallowed, he sent her a hard look. "There. I ate. What's going on?"

Taking a deep breath, she turned the fire off under the eggs before facing him. "I need a husband."

Not enough coffee, he told himself. Not nearly enough. But he said only, "Good luck with that."

"No," she corrected quickly. "Not a husband, really. I just need a fiancé."

"Again. Happy hunting." He got up to refill his coffee and thought seriously about just chugging it straight from the pot.

"Micah, I need you to pretend to be my fiancé." After she blurted out that sentence, she grabbed her own cup and took a drink of coffee.

He leaned back against the granite counter, feeling the cold of the stone seep through his T-shirt and into his bones. He crossed his bare feet at the ankles, kept a tight grip on his coffee mug and looked at her. "That seems like an overreaction to one kiss."

"What?" She flushed, flipped her hair behind her shoulders and said, "For heaven's sake, this isn't about the kiss. Though, I admit, it gave me the idea…"

More confused than ever, he could only say, "What?"

"Oh, man, this is harder than I thought it would be." She dropped into a chair at the table, grabbed a slice of bacon and took a bite. "I don't even know how to say all of this without sounding crazy."

"I'll give you a clue," he said softly. "Just say it. Don't lie to me, either, trying to soften whatever it is that's going on. Just say it."

"I wasn't going to lie to you."

"Good. Let's keep it that way."

"Okay." She nodded, took another breath that lifted her breasts until he got another peek at that lacy bra, then started talking. "When I went home last night, my gran called and she started in on moving back again because I'm so alone, and before I knew what I was saying, I told her that she didn't have to worry about me being lonely anymore because I'm engaged. To *you*."

Well, he'd wanted the truth. Micah shook his head, walked to the table, sat down opposite her and waited. Objectively, as a writer, he couldn't wait to hear the rest of this story, because it promised to be a good one. As a man with zero interest in marrying *anyone*, he felt itchy enough that he snatched another piece of bacon and bit into it.

Her green eyes were flashing and her chin was up defiantly, but she chewed at her bottom lip, and that told him she was nervous. That didn't bode well.

"You have to understand, Micah. Gran's my only family and she was so sad after my grandfather passed away." She folded both hands around her coffee mug. "Then she moved to Florida with her sister, my aunt Linda, and she was happy again. Then Sean died and she came home to be with me and she started worrying and the sorrow crept back into her eyes, her voice, everything. It was like she was being *swallowed*, you know?"

No, he didn't know. He didn't have family. Didn't have the kind of deep connections she had, so he couldn't be sure if he'd have reacted the same way she did or not. But just looking at Kelly told him that she was emotionally torn in a couple of different directions.

"I finally convinced her to go back to her life by telling her I needed time alone—which wasn't a lie," she added. "And being away from here, the memories of Grandpa and Sean, helped her and she was happy again. Micah, she's determined to come back here and protect me. To sacrifice her own happiness on the altar of what she thinks of as my misery."

"*Are* you miserable?" he asked, interrupting the stream of words pouring from her.

"Of course not." She took a sip of coffee. "I mean, sure, I get lonely sometimes, but everybody does, right?"

He didn't say anything because what *could* he say? She was right. Even Micah experienced those occasional bouts when he wished there was someone there to talk to. To hold. But those moments passed, and he realized that his life was just as he wanted it.

"But when I told her I was engaged to you..." Kelly sighed helplessly. "She was so happy, Micah, that from there, I just grabbed the proverbial ball and ran with it."

"Meaning?"

"Oh." She put her head in her hands briefly, then looked up at him again. "I told her how romantic your proposal was—"

"What did I do?" Now he was just curious. He couldn't help it. This was all so far out there that it didn't even seem real. It was like watching a movie or reading a book about someone else.

Still worrying her bottom lip, she said, "You set up a candlelit dinner on the porch around back and you had roses everywhere and music playing and little twinkle lights strung over the ceiling…"

He could *see* it and thought she'd done a nice job of scene setting. "Well, I'm pretty good."

She gave a heavy sigh. "You're laughing at me."

"Trust me," he said. "Not laughing."

"Right." She nodded, swallowed hard and said, "Anyway, then you went down on one knee and asked me. But you didn't have a ring because you want to take me to New York to pick one out."

"That's thoughtful of me."

"Oh, stop." She tossed her slice of bacon onto her plate. "I feel terrible about all of this, but I was so worried that Gran was going to hop on the first plane out of Florida…" She plopped both elbows on the table and cupped her face in her palms again, making her voice sound weirdly muffled when she added, "Everything's just a mess now and if I call her back and tell her it never happened, she'll think I lied—"

"You *did* lie."

She looked up at him. "It was just a little lie."

"So now size *does* matter?" He shook his head.

"Oh, God. How can you even make jokes about this?"

"What should I do? Rant and rave? Won't change what

you told your grandmother. But I never understood," Micah said, watching her as misery crossed her face, "how people could convince themselves that *little* lies don't matter. Lies are never the answer."

"Oh." She smirked at him and Micah was pleased to see the snap and sizzle of her attitude come back. "Mr. Perfect never lies?"

"Not perfect," he told her tightly. "But, no, I don't."

"You've never had to tell a lie to protect someone you care about?"

Since he had only a handful of people he gave a flying damn about, the answer was an emphatic no. Micah didn't do lies. Hell, his mother's lie—*I'll come back for you. Soon...*—still rang in his ears. He would never do to someone what she had done to him with that one lie designed, no doubt, to make him feel better about being abandoned.

He scrubbed one hand across his face. It was too damn early to be hit with all of this and maybe that's why Micah wasn't really angry. Confused, sure. Irritated? Always. But not furious. A part of him realized he should be mad. He was used to people trying to use him to get what they wanted. It was practically expected when you were rich and famous. And those people he had no trouble getting rid of.

But Kelly was different. He looked across the table at her and noted the worry in her eyes. Why was he so reluctant to disappoint her? Why was he willing to give her the benefit of the doubt when he never did that for anyone else? She was *lying* to her grandmother. That wasn't exactly a recommendation for trustworthiness. And yet...

"Why me?" he asked abruptly. He got up, walked to the coffeepot and carried it back to the table. He filled both of their cups, then set the pot down on a folded towel. Staring at her from across the table, he said, "There have to be some local guys you could choose from. Pick someone you know. Someone who knows your grandmother and might want to help you out with this."

She took a gulp of coffee like it was medicinal brandy and she was swilling it for courage. "Why you? Who else could I tap for this? Gran knows everyone in town. She'd never believe a sudden engagement to Sam at the hardware store. Or Kevin at the diner. If anything romantic had been going on between me and someone in town, her friends would have told her about it already."

Irritating to realize she had a point.

"But you're a mystery," she continued, leaning toward him. "She knows I have a famous writer living here, but no one in town could have told her anything about you. You hardly ever leave the house, so, for all anyone knows, we could have been carrying on some torrid affair right here in the house for the last two months."

Torrid affair? Who even talked like that anymore? But as archaic as the words sounded, they were enough to make breathing a little more difficult and Micah's jeans a little tighter. Still, he shifted his mind away from what his body was feeling and forced it to focus on what she'd said.

Kelly wasn't doing this because he was rich. Or for the thrill of claiming a famous fiancé. He was her choice because no one in town knew him. Because her grandmother would believe her lie. So it wasn't *him* so much that she wanted. Probably any single renter would have done. That made him feel both better and worse.

"That's why I picked you. You're perfect."

Perfect, he thought wryly. *And handy.*

"Why should I go along with this?" Not that he was

considering it, he assured himself. But he was curious what she'd come up with.

"As a favor?" she asked, throwing both hands high. "I don't know—because you're a fabulous human being and I'm flawed and you feel sorry for me?"

He snorted.

She sighed and scowled at him. "Micah, I know it's a lot. But this is really important to me. Gran's happy in Florida. She has friends, a nice life with her sister. She's enjoying herself and I don't want her to give it all up for *me*."

He heard the sincerity in her voice, read it in her eyes and knew she meant every word. And he wondered what it would be like to love someone so much you were willing to do whatever it took to make them happy? But since he avoided all closeness with everyone, he'd never know.

Hell, he'd broken off his own real engagement because, bottom line, he couldn't bring himself to trust the woman he'd proposed to. He didn't believe she loved him—because she hadn't known the *real* him. He hadn't allowed her to peek behind that curtain, so he couldn't trust that she would still care for him if she ever found out that he was a man whose past haunted every minute of his present. So he'd ended it. Walked away and vowed he'd never do that again.

Yet here he was, actually considering another engagement? This one based on a lie?

"Micah, I don't want anything from you."

He laughed shortly. "Except an engagement to fool an old woman, the lies to keep the pretense going, and a trip to New York to pick out a ring..."

"Oh, God." She flushed and shook her head. "Okay, yes, I do want you to pretend to love me. But you won't have to lie to Gran—"

"Just everyone else you know."

"Okay, yes—" She winced a little as she admitted that. "But there won't be a trip to New York and there won't be a ring, either. I can keep postponing our *trip* when I talk to Gran and—"

"More lies."

"Not more lies, just a bit more emphasis on the original lie," she argued. Frowning, she met his gaze squarely and said, "If you think I *want* to be dishonest with my grandmother, you're wrong. I love her. I'm only doing this because it's the best thing for *her.*"

He drank his coffee and felt her steady gaze focus on him. As if she could will him to do this just by staring at him. And, hell, maybe it was working. He was still here and listening, right?

She must have sensed that he was weakening because she leaned toward him, elbows on the table. Did she know that the vee of her blouse gaped open wider, giving him a clear and beautiful view of the tops of her breasts?

"I'll sign anything you want, Micah," she said. "I know you probably have lots of people trying to get things from you—"

Surprised that she seemed to have picked that thought right out of his mind, he watched her carefully.

"But I'm not. Really. If you're worried I'll sue you or something, you don't have to. I don't want anything from you. Really. Just this fake engagement."

In his experience, everyone wanted something. But Micah was intrigued now. "And when I leave town? What then?"

"Then," she said, heaving a sigh as if she already dreaded it, "I'll tell Gran we broke up. She'll be upset, but this *engagement* will buy me some time. Gran will be able to stay in Florida without worrying and…" She took a breath, then lifted her coffee cup for another sip. "Maybe I'll think of a way to convince her to stay there even if I'm not engaged."

He didn't like it, but Micah couldn't see where this ploy was going to cost him anything, either. He'd only be in town four more months, and then he'd be gone and this would all be a memory. Including the fake engagement. And, he had to admit, the longer he looked at Kelly, seeing the worry in her eyes, hearing it in her voice, the more he wanted to ease it. He didn't explore the reasons he was wanting to help her out because he wasn't sure he'd like the answers.

"All right," he said, before he could think better of it.

"Whoop!" Kelly jumped out of her chair, delighted. She came around the table, bent to him and gave him a hard, quick hug. Then she stood up and smiled in relief. "That's so great. Thanks, Micah. Seriously."

That hug had sent heat shooting straight through him, so he needed a little space between him and Kelly. Fast.

"Yeah," he said, rising to put the coffeepot back on its burner. He turned around to face her. "So what do I have to do?"

"Nothing much," she assured him, and joined him at the counter, closing the distance he'd just managed to find. "Just, when we're around people in town you have to act like you're nuts about me."

"Oh." Well, he thought, that would be easy enough. Not that he was in love with her or anything. Sure, he liked her. But what he felt for her was more about extreme *lust*. So, he could sure as hell act like he *wanted* her, because he did. Now more than ever.

What he didn't want was a wife. Or a fiancée. But he'd

never wanted *anything* in his life more than he wanted Kelly in bed.

She looked insulted as she stared up at him. "Oh, come on," she said. "You don't have to look so horrified about pretending to love me. It won't be that hard to do."

Hard? Not a word Micah should be thinking about at the moment. Staring into her green eyes was almost hypnotic, so Micah shifted his gaze slightly. "Yeah," he said with just a hint of sarcasm, "I think I can handle it."

She laid one hand on his arm, and once again a flash of heat shot through him. "I really appreciate this, Micah. I know it's weird, but—"

"It's okay, I get it." He didn't. Not really. How the hell could he understand real family? He'd lost whatever family he had when he was six years old. But, as a writer, he did what he always did. He put himself in someone else's point of view. Tried to look at a situation through their eyes. Over the years, he'd been in the minds of killers and victims. Children and parents.

Yet, he was coming up blank when he tried to figure out what Kelly was thinking, feeling. In fact, she was the one woman he'd ever known who was as damn mysterious as the stories he created. Ironic, he told himself, since he made his living inventing mysteries—and now he was faced with an enigma he couldn't unravel.

It wasn't just Kelly confusing him. It was what being near her did to him that had him baffled.

And he didn't like the feeling.

A couple of hours later, Kelly was at Terry's house, wishing she was anywhere else.

"I tell you to have a steamy affair and you say no," Terry mused thoughtfully as she tapped one finger against her chin. "But you *do* get engaged. Sure that makes sense."

Kelly hung her head briefly, then lifted it to look at her best friend. Terry's place was just a block or two off Main Street. It was a small old brick house with a great backyard and what Terry called *tons of potential*. She and Jimmy were completely rehabbing the old place that Kelly had found for them, a little at a time. The living room was cozy, the kitchen was fabulous, the bathroom was gorgeous—and the rest of the house still needed work.

Sitting on her friend's couch sipping tea and eating cookies was pure comfort. Which Kelly really needed at the moment. In fact, it almost took the sting out of what Terry was saying.

"It's crazy," Kelly agreed. "I know that."

"Good for you," Terry said, injecting false cheer into her voice. "Always best to recognize when you've completely lost your mind."

"You're not helping."

"Of course I'm not helping." Terry shook her head, sending the silver hoops at her ears swinging. "For Pete's sake, Kelly, what were you thinking? You're setting yourself up for God knows what, and now there's no way out."

Kelly knew all of that, but hearing it made her feel worse somehow. Honestly, she still wasn't sure what had made her come up with this idea in the first place. And she sure didn't know why Micah had agreed.

Actually, when she'd first started talking to him that morning, she was positive he'd give her an emphatic no and tell her to get out. But the longer she talked, the more she saw him change, his features changing from irritated to sympathetic to amusement and finally acceptance.

Kelly still could hardly believe he'd agreed to this, but she was super grateful he had. Yes, it was a mess, but at least for the short term, her grandmother was happy and wasn't trying to give up her own happiness for Kelly.

"You should have heard Gran though, Terry," Kelly said softly, remembering. "She was so happy when I told her Micah and I were engaged."

Terry's concerned frown only deepened. "Sure, until you 'break up.'"

Okay, yes, that conversation with her grandmother wasn't one Kelly was looking forward to. But she'd find a way to soften the disappointment. "Yeah, but until then, I've got time to think of a way to keep her from worrying."

"Well, I hope your next plan is as entertaining as this one."

Scowling, Kelly picked up a lemon cookie drizzled with thin caramel stripes and took a bite. Seriously, nobody made better cookies than Terry. People clogged up her tiny coffee shop just to buy the baked goods. And they weren't wrong to do so.

"You're my best friend," Kelly said. "You're supposed to be on my side."

"And if you wanted to rob a bank or drive off a cliff, I should just pick up my pom-poms and cheer you on?"

"That's hardly the same thing as—"

Terry held up one hand. "I'm sorry. You refused a blind date, then got engaged, instead."

"Fake engaged."

"I stand corrected." Terry finished off her tea and set the cup on the coffee table in front of them. "Really, though, I'm on your side, Kelly. I'm just not sure what your side *is*."

"If it makes you feel any better, neither am I." It had all seemed so reasonable when she'd thought of it the night before. But facing Micah with it a couple of hours ago had shaken her a little. Still, Kelly knew this was the best thing to do. The *only* thing, as far as she could tell. Gran was happy, and Kelly didn't have to worry about the older woman giving up her new life.

Micah was fine with it—okay, maybe *fine* wasn't exactly right. *Resigned* might be better. Either way, though, Kelly was getting what she wanted: a reprieve for her worried grandmother.

As far as pretending feelings for the town's benefit, she could pretend to be in love with Micah. She would just have to keep reminding herself that it wasn't real.

Because, honestly, one kiss from that man had melted away every reservation she'd had. Every vow she'd ever made to *not* get involved with another man had simply melted under the incredible rush of heat enveloping her during that kiss. God, even remembering it could set her on fire.

So, okay, this pretense would be a little risky for Kelly. Micah Hunter was the kind of man who could slip past a woman's defenses if she wasn't careful. Even defenses as strong as hers. So Kelly would be *very* careful.

She popped the last of the cookie into her mouth, then said, "Okay, enough 'torture Kelly' time."

"Oh, I'm not nearly finished," Terry told her.

"Fine. We'll pick it up again later, but, for now, are you going to help me with the load of plywood I need to pick up or not?"

"Sure." Terry shrugged and pushed off the couch. "Get engaged, then build a haunted house. What could be more normal?"

Kelly reached for another cookie as Terry picked up the plate and cups to take back to the kitchen. Sighing, Terry said, "And I bet you want to take some cookies home with you."

"That'd be great," Kelly said. "Thank you, very-best-friend-in-the-world-who-is-always-on-my-side-and-only-wants-what's-best-for-me."

Laughing, Terry shook her head and said, "I'll put some in a bag for you."

Kelly grinned as she tugged on her sweatshirt. "Thanks. And to respond to your earlier statement… *normal* is way overrated."

But, while she waited for Terry, Kelly's smile faded and her brain raced. Images of Micah rose up in her mind, and instantly a curl of something dangerous spun in the pit of her stomach.

Yeah. Maybe this fake engagement wasn't such a great idea, after all.

Six

Micah came out of the house as soon as he saw the two women struggling to pull sheets of plywood out of the back of Kelly's truck.

"So much for getting any work done," he muttered, and made a mental note to tell Sam that if this book went in late, it would be *his* fault. How the hell was Micah supposed to get work done when Kelly was always interrupting? Even when she wasn't there, thoughts of her plagued him, interfering with his concentration and leaving him staring into space as he willed his body into submission.

Hell, how did *any* writer work when they had people coming in and out of their lives? There was just no way to concentrate on your fictional world when the *real* world kept intruding.

As he approached, he noticed for the first time that Kelly's truck had definitely seen better days. It had once been red, but now was an oxidized sickly pink. There were rust spots along the bottom of the body, no doubt caused by all the salt used on winter roads to prevent skidding. There was an old dent in the back right fender, and he had a feeling the inside of the damn thing was no prettier than the outside.

Frowning, he remembered that Kelly had said she plowed driveways and roads during the winter. Did she use this truck? Of course she did, and it probably hadn't even occurred to her that it looked as if it was on its last legs. He didn't like the idea of her out in some snowstorm in a broken-down truck, freezing to death in the cab while she waited for someone to dig her out of a snowdrift— and, yeah, sometimes being a writer was a bad thing. His mind was all too willing to make up the worst-possible scenario of any given situation just to torture him. He shook off the vague ideas and focused on the now.

He was down the front steps and headed across the lawn before either woman noticed him. Kelly had her back to him, but the tiny woman with dark hair and wide silver hoops at her ears spotted him.

Tipping her head back, she stared at the gray sky and shouted to whoever might be listening, "Thank you!"

Looking back at Micah, she grinned. "Well, hi, gorgeous. You must be the new fiancé. I'm the best friend, Terry."

"Good to meet you." It was impossible to *not* smile back at a woman who looked like a seductive elf. "I'm Micah."

Kelly jolted upright from where she was bent over trying to lift one end of the boards. Seductive elf or not, the only woman Micah could see was Kelly. Her hair was back in a ponytail, her gray sweatshirt was paint stained, and her worn denim jeans were ripped high on her right thigh. She must have changed into work clothes after she'd left him that morning. And even in what she was wearing right now, she looked amazing.

She dropped the plywood sheets she was trying to maneuver, and they clattered when they hit the truck bed. Straightening up, she smiled a little nervously. "Um, hi, Micah. This is Terry."

"Yeah, we met." He walked closer, looked into the truck bed, then up at Kelly. "What's all this for?"

She pushed one stray windblown lock of hair out of her face. "Every year I build a haunted house for the kids."

That didn't even surprise him. "Of course you do."

Kelly kept talking. "Last year Terry's husband, Jimmy, helped me out, but he's deployed this year."

Terry sat on the edge of the truck. "I think Kelly misses him almost as much as I do."

"Today I do," Kelly agreed. Her heart flipped over as Micah's gaze was fixed on her with the wariness of a man waiting to see if a suspicious package will explode. And of course she *had* to look absolutely hideous. "So, Micah, can you help carry these boards to the front of the house?"

"I can." He dropped both hands onto the side of the truck. "Does it get me a point?"

"A what?" Terry asked.

"No," Kelly said, smiling because he was acting as he always had around her. Things weren't awkward and she'd worried about that. Oh, she knew he was as good as his word and that he'd act like her lover in public. But she'd been afraid that asking him to do this for her might make things weird between them in private. "This is a favor. Not a point earner."

"What points are we talking about?" Terry looked from one to the other of them.

"Hmm," he mused, "seems to me I already did you a favor earlier. If I do this one, as well, that's two in one day. Is there any kind of payoff for a favor?"

"What'd you have in mind?" Kelly's stomach did a fast spin and roll. Honestly, the man's eyes were so dark that when they were fastened on her, as they were now, she could feel the earth beneath her feet slide and shift.

"Another kiss," he said.

All of her breath left her in a rush.

"Okay," Terry murmured. "This is getting interesting. Wait a minute. Did he say *another* kiss?"

Kelly paid no attention to Terry because she couldn't see anything but Micah. It took everything in Kelly not to vault over the side of the truck and lock her mouth onto his. Just the thought of being held close to him again made her want it more than anything. But she had a question first. "Why?"

He shrugged and his broad chest sort of rippled beneath his black T-shirt. "You said we needed to put on a show in front of people, right?"

"Yeah…" she said, "but Terry doesn't count."

"Thanks very much," Terry said, "however, since Jimmy's gone, I wouldn't mind seeing a red-hot kiss. A little vicarious living would do me worlds of good."

"Pay no attention to her," Kelly advised.

"I wasn't talking about Terry," Micah said, his gaze flicking briefly to a point over Kelly's shoulder. "I was talking about the two old women watching from their window."

"Oh, God…" Kelly murmured. She'd forgotten all about her neighbors, but the two sisters probably had their noses pressed to the glass.

"Hi!" Terry shouted as she turned to wave at Sally and Margie.

The curtains dropped instantly, blocking the women from view. But Kelly knew they were still there. Watching. Hoping to see something worth gossiping about.

"So? Is it a deal?" Micah asked.

Kelly sighed. This had been all her idea, after all. "Deal."

She moved to the side of the truck and Micah reached up to grab her at the waist. His hands were big and strong and hot enough to sear her skin right through the fabric of her shirt. He lifted her out of the truck bed as if she weighed nothing and then let her slide slowly along his body until she was standing on her own two feet again.

By the time her feet hit the ground, Kelly's insides were sizzling and her brain was fogging over. Her hands at his shoulders, she stared up into his brown eyes and read a wild mix of desire and amusement there. She couldn't have said why that particular combination appealed to her, but it did. "Well," she asked after a long minute of simply staring into each other's eyes, "are you going to kiss me?"

"Nope."

Surprised, she tried to pull away, but his hands only tightened on her waist. "Fine. But I thought you wanted a kiss for a favor."

"Yeah," he said, his gaze sliding over her face before meeting hers again, "but this time, *you* kiss *me.*"

Another swirl of hot nerves inside, but she had to admit it was only fair. He'd surprised her with their first kiss, and now she wanted to surprise him with just how hot a kiss could be if she knew it was coming. Giving him a faint smile, Kelly went up on her toes and slanted her mouth over his.

He held on to her but didn't take the lead. This show was all Kelly's. She parted his lips with her tongue, slid into his mouth and felt his breath catch in his throat. She explored his mouth, tasting, plundering. Spearing her fingers through his hair, she turned her head slightly to one side and groaned as he finally surrendered to the fire building between them. He clutched her tightly to him and tangled his tongue with hers until Kelly's mind splintered and floated out of her head to blow away in the cold breeze.

"Niiiiccceee…" Terry's voice was no more than a buzz that Kelly barely registered.

Kelly's heart banged against her ribs. She held on to Micah because if she didn't, she'd have keeled over from the rush of sensations pouring through her. His hands fisted at her back and held her so tightly to him she felt the hard length of him pressing into her belly. She rubbed against him, torturing them both. Knowing he felt what she felt, wanted what she wanted, only made her own feelings that much deeper. More intense.

God, she wanted to feel his skin beneath hers. She wanted to feel his heavy weight on top of her. Feel his hard body sliding into hers…

"Um, guys?" Terry's voice came again, hesitant but insistent. Then she got louder, demanding they hear her. "*Guys!* You realize you're about to get way out of control right in the front yard?"

In a daze, feeling a little drunk, Kelly pulled her head back and turned to look blearily at her friend. "What?"

"Damn." Terry fanned herself with both hands. "I think that's enough of a show for now or you'll kill Sally and Margie."

"What?" Kelly asked again, and then realization slammed into her, and she turned to Micah and dropped her forehead on his chest. She could hardly believe what had just happened. If Terry hadn't spoken up, who knows what might have happened? "Oh, God."

"Yeah," Micah said tightly as he struggled to even out his ragged breathing. "I think Terry's right. I'll just get those boards for you now. Where do you want them?"

"Okay, that's good. Um, right in front of the porch," she whispered, and he let her go. Amazing how *alone* she felt without the strength of his arms wrapped around her middle.

Still a little shaky, she leaned against the truck and watched while Micah lifted a few of the huge plywood sheets and, balancing them on his shoulder, carried them to the front of the Victorian. His muscles stretched and shifted beneath his shirt. His black jeans hugged his behind and his long legs, and her mouth went dry just watching him.

"Honest to God," Terry murmured in her ear, "if you don't jump that man immediately, you're not the brave, intrepid Kelly I know."

"It's not that easy," Kelly said, gaze locked on him.

"Why the hell not?" Terry gave Kelly's shoulder a nudge. "You want him. He clearly wants you. I almost went up in flames just watching, and I can tell you that after seeing that kiss, when I get home, I'm video chatting Jimmy and hoping he's alone."

"That's different," Kelly grumbled. "You're married."

"And you're *engaged*," Terry reminded her. "For God's sake, take advantage of it."

But that hadn't been part of their deal, Kelly told herself. Was it fair to try to alter their agreement now? Then she remembered the grinding pressure of his mouth on hers and knew that he'd be okay with changing the rules. The question was, could she keep her emotions separate from the physical desire engulfing her? And could she live with herself if she *didn't* act on what she was feeling?

Micah walked back across the yard for the next load and Kelly's gaze fixed on him. Black jeans. Black boots. Black T-shirt. Dark brown hair ruffling in the cold breeze. Brown eyes that met hers for one long, blistering moment.

And she knew that, complicated or not, deal or not, she had to have him.

Micah ignored the noise from the front of the house for the next two hours. He heard the constant hammering, the arguing between Kelly and Terry and told himself it had nothing to do with him. What did he care about haunted houses? Besides, he had work to do. If thoughts of Kelly and that kiss ever left him the hell alone.

Scowling, he glared at the computer screen, rereading what he'd just written. His heroine was in deep trouble and getting in deeper every second. She was wandering the woods, looking for a lost child, and had no idea there was a killer right behind her.

Grimly he kept typing, in spite of the fact that his jeans were so tight he felt he was going to be permanently injured. He kept tasting Kelly on his lips and told himself that it didn't matter. It had been for show. To impress the neighbors and show them that Kelly's fiancé was crazy about her. The fact that it had impacted *him* so much wasn't the point.

Points. Kelly and her points. What was it now, three to one with her in the lead? Hell, if she'd brought it up at the time, he'd have awarded her five more points for that kiss today. He felt like her mouth was permanently imprinted on his. If he lived to be a hundred, he'd still be able to bring back the taste of her and the feel of her in his arms while the cold wind danced around them.

"This isn't getting any work done," he muttered, and stood up from the desk. It wasn't until that moment that Micah realized how quiet it was. The hammering had stopped, and there was no more good-natured shouting from Kelly and Terry.

He walked to the window and looked out. At that angle, all he could see were the tops of plywood panels the two women were fixing together and standing in front of the porch. But it seemed that work on the haunted house was over for the day. Good. No noise meant not being reminded of Kelly. With no thoughts of Kelly, maybe he'd get some pages written.

"Where did she go?" he muttered an instant later, drumming his fingers on the window frame. "And why do you care?"

He didn't, of course. Curiosity didn't translate into *caring*.

Shaking his head, Micah walked to the desk and it felt like the computer screen was glaring at him, mocking him for stopping in the middle of a damn sentence. Well, he didn't have to be insulted by his own tools. He slammed the laptop shut and stalked out of the office. Work wasn't happening. Relaxing wasn't happening. So he'd try a beer, the game on TV and a chance to shut off his mind. Micah took the stairs, then turned and headed for the kitchen.

He never made it.

Kelly stepped through the swinging door from the kitchen into the dining room and stopped dead when she saw him. Everything in Micah tensed and eased at the same time.

Her hair tumbled wild and wavy around her face and down over her shoulders. Her eyes were bright and locked on him like laser beams. Micah's breath caught in his chest as a tight fist of need closed around his throat.

"Surprised to see me?" she whispered.

"Yeah." He nodded. "A little. But then you seem to be full of surprises."

"I'll take that as a compliment," she said, and moved a couple steps closer to him.

"You should." Micah walked toward her, too, one slow step at a time. "I never know from one minute to the next what you're going to do." He didn't admit how much he liked that about her. Didn't mention that he saw her *everywhere.* That images of her were dancing through his brain 24/7. Hell, he didn't even like admitting that to himself, let alone her.

Kelly's eyes flashed and his insides burned.

"Like being here now for instance," Micah said quietly. "What're you doing, Kelly?"

"I came to ask you a question."

He blew out a breath. "What is it?"

"Pretty simple, really," Kelly said, moving still closer.

He could have reached out and touched her, but Micah curled his hands into fists to keep from doing exactly that. After that kiss this afternoon, he was sure that if he held on to her now, he might not let her go again.

"There's a lot of…tension between us, Micah."

He snorted. "Yeah, you could say that."

She kept talking as if he hadn't spoken at all. "I mean, that kiss today? I thought the top of my head was going to blow off."

Micah reached up and rubbed the back of his neck. "I felt the same."

"Good," she said, nodding. "That's good."

"Kelly…" He was at the ragged edge of his near-legendary control. Her scent was reaching for him, and the look in her spring-green eyes was tempting him to just let go. "What're you getting at?"

"Well, we're both grown-ups, Micah," she said, tipping her head back to look at him.

"Yeah," he said tightly. "That might be part of the problem."

She laughed shortly. "True."

Her hair fell in a red-gold curtain behind her, and a light floral scent that clung to her skin seemed to surround him. "But, since we *are* adults, there's a simple way to take care of that tension." She took a breath and held it. When she spoke again, the words tumbled from her in a rush. "I think we should just go to bed together. Once we do that, we'll both be able to relax and—"

Control snapped at the suggestion he'd been hoping for. Micah grabbed her, speared his fingers through her hair and held her head still for his kiss. He poured everything he felt into it. The unbearable frustration that had tortured him for two months. The wild, frantic need that disrupted his sleep every night. The desire that pulsed inside him like an extra heartbeat.

She groaned, fueling the fire enveloping him, and kissed him back with the same fierce hunger that was clawing at him. Her hands moved up and down his back, up into his hair, then clutched at his shoulders.

Micah's brain simply shattered. He didn't need it anyway. The only thing either of them needed now was their own willing bodies. When Micah tore his mouth free of hers and gasped for air, Kelly grinned at him. "I guess that's a yes?"

Surprise after surprise.

"No, it's a *hell yes*," he corrected, then picked her up and slung her over one shoulder in a fireman's carry.

"Hey!" Hands against his back, she pushed up and swung her hair back in an attempt to see him. "What're you doing?"

He glanced back at her and rubbed one hand over her behind until she shifted in his grasp.

"This is faster. No time to waste," he told her, and headed for the stairs again.

"Right." She rubbed her own palms over his back, then down to his butt. "Hurry."

He took the stairs two at a time, his long legs making short work of the distance separating them from the nearest bed. He covered the hallway in a few long steps, walked into his bedroom and tossed her onto the mattress.

"Whoop!" She laughed as she bounced, then her gaze met his and all amusement fled. "Oh, I'm so glad you didn't say *thanks, but no thanks*."

"Not a chance of that," Micah assured her, and yanked his T-shirt off over his head.

Kelly smiled, licked her lips and toed off her shoes before immediately tugging at the button and zipper of her jeans. She squirmed out of them, making Micah's mouth water at his first peek at the tiny triangle of pink lace panties she had on under those jeans.

She kept her gaze locked on his as she worked on the buttons of her long-sleeved shirt and slowly let it slide down off her arms. The pink lace bra matched the panties and displayed more of her breasts than it hid.

He couldn't look away from her. Every breath came loud and harsh in the room. Micah felt like he was straining against a leash that had held him in place for two long months. Now that it was ready to snap, he didn't know what to do first. Where to touch. Where to kiss. Where to lick. He wanted it all. When she took off the bra and panties then tossed them over her head to the floor, the leash finally snapped.

She lay there, her pale skin luminous against the forest-green duvet. Her hair spilled out around her head like a red-gold halo of silk. Her breasts were fuller than he'd imagined, but delicate, too, her dark rose nipples rigid with the desire pumping through her.

His mind simply went blank. Like a starving man suddenly faced with a gourmet feast, Micah froze, helpless to look away from the woman laid out in front of him like a dream.

"Micah...you're wearing too many clothes," she murmured, licking her lips.

"Right. I am." He peeled out of his clothes, and in seconds he was naked and covering her body with his. Her hands slid up and down his back, across his shoulders to his chest and then up to cup his face. When Micah kissed her again, their bodies moved against each other as if they both were looking for that skin-to-skin contact. To revel in the heat. To drown in it. As if to assure each other that they were finally going to ease the raging desperation that had chased them both through torturous days and long, sleepless nights.

He swept one hand down the length of her as he shifted, dragging his mouth from hers to trail kisses along the line of her jaw, the slim column of her throat. She sighed, gasped and arched up into him. Her legs tangled with his, smooth to rough, adding new sensations to those already crashing down on them.

He slid his hand across her abdomen, down her belly to the center of her. To the heat he needed to claim, to bury himself in. She jerked helplessly. To drive her higher, faster, Micah took one hard nipple into his mouth.

Instantly, Kelly writhed in his arms as if trying to escape even while she held his head to her breast to keep him from stopping. "Micah… Micah, this is too much."

"No," he whispered, "not nearly enough." He covered her damp, hot core with his hand and slid first one, then two fingers inside her. She arched into him and his mind splintered at the feel of her generous, oh-so-eager body shaking and twisting in his arms.

His lips, teeth and tongue worked her nipple as his fingers continued to push her toward a release they both needed so badly.

"Stop, Micah," she whispered brokenly.

He lifted his head, questions in his eyes. "You want me to stop?"

Shaking her head, she choked out a short laugh. "Not on your life. I just want more than your hand on me." She was breathless, eyes a little wild, and she'd never looked more beautiful. "If you keep touching me like that, I'm going to climax and I don't want to. Not without you inside me."

Relief flooded him. He'd have had to back away if she'd changed her mind, and Micah knew without a doubt that stopping would have killed him. Knowing that she was simply trying to hold back an orgasm gave him the freedom to push her beyond the ability to fight it.

"One now," he said, stroking that one sensitive nub at her core with his thumb. "More later."

"Oh…my…goodness…" Her fingers dug into his shoulders. Her hips rocked frantically into his hand. She planted her feet and lifted herself higher, higher. He watched as Kelly's eyes glazed. "Micah—I… What are you doing to me? I've never…"

Micah had never been with anyone like her before. What she felt echoed inside him. The taste of her filled him, the scent of her swamped him, and the shattered, hungry look in her eyes fed the fires inside him like nothing he'd ever experienced before.

He hadn't been prepared for this, he thought, frantic himself as he watched her body bow and twist. He'd thought it would be a simple matter of bodies meeting, doing what came naturally. Feeling that sweet flash of release and moving the hell on. But no woman had ever affected him like this. No woman had slipped beneath his defenses, made him crave *her* release as much as his own. He didn't know what any of it meant, and now wasn't the time for trying to figure it out.

Micah felt the first shudder take her, body rippling with too much sensation all at once. She fought for breath, grasping at his shoulders, digging her head back into the mattress, struggling for air as she screamed his name like a prayer to an indifferent god.

His own breath caught in his chest. Mouth dry, heart hammering, body as tight as a bowstring, Micah set her down on the bed and shifted, reaching for the drawer of the nightstand. He pulled it open, grabbed a condom and ripped the foil packet. He had to have her. Now.

"Micah, that was—" She shook her head, at a loss for words. The smile that curved her lips shone in her eyes, as well. "I've never…" She stretched like a happy cat and damn near purred. Then she opened her eyes at the sound of foil tearing.

"Wow. You went out and bought condoms just in case?"

He shook his head. "Nope, had them with me."

"You *travel* with condoms?" she asked, surprise in her voice.

He glanced at her. "Doesn't everyone?"

"Hoping to get lucky, were you?"

"Babe," he admitted as he sheathed himself, "I'm a *guy*. I'm always hoping to get lucky."

Her grin spread as she held out her arms to him. "Well, since I think we're both pretty lucky at the moment, I can't really complain, can I?"

He returned her grin, and as he shifted to part her thighs and kneel before her, he quipped, "So, having a condom handy means a point for me, huh?"

"Oh," she teased, "I don't know about that. I mean *points* are serious business and—"

He slid into her heat, and she went instantly quiet as she shifted a little to accommodate him. Then she groaned and tipped her head back into the mattress.

"Yes," she said. "If you can keep making me feel like—*oh!*—this, definitely a point for you."

"I love a challenge," he whispered. Still smiling, he covered her mouth with his and tangled their tongues in a dance that mimicked the movements of their bodies. She gave as much as she took, Micah thought, and realized that for the first time he was with a woman who was completely herself. There was no pretense with Kelly.

Whatever she felt, she let him know. Her soft cries

and whimpered moans told him exactly what she liked. She was a little wild and he liked it. His mouth moved on hers as his hips rocked, slipping into a rhythm that had her kissing him hungrily, sliding her hands up and down his back, dragging her nails across his skin.

When he was strangling for air, he lifted his head to watch her expressive face as he claimed her completely. Her body held his in a tight, hot embrace, and he gritted his teeth to keep from giving in to the urge to let go. He wanted this to last. Wanted to make her crazy before he finally gave them both what they needed most.

Outside, twilight stained the sky a deep violet. Inside, the only light was in her eyes as she stared up at him, a look of wonder in her gaze. Their hands met, fingers linked, and he felt it when her climax slammed into her. Her body arched, her heels dug into his lower back. She screamed his name, and Micah watched the inner explosions ripple across her face and felt more satisfaction himself than he could ever remember. His heart raced, and his body continued to move in hers, and only when the last of the tremors coursed through her did he let himself go, finally giving up control and diving into the maelstrom, willingly letting it take him.

Seven

Kelly didn't know how much time had passed. And truthfully, she couldn't have cared less. Her whole body was humming as if her finger was somehow stuck in a light socket and electricity was pouring through her.

Finally, though, when she thought she could speak again, she said simply, "Wow."

"Agreed." Micah's voice was muffled because his face was buried in the curve of her shoulder.

She smiled to herself and stared blankly up at the ceiling. Good to know that he was as shattered as she felt. Micah's body pressed her into the bed and she knew she should ask him to move, but it was so lovely to feel the heavy press of a man's body on hers after so long on her own.

At that thought, Kelly felt a pang of sorrow that peaked and ebbed inside her in seconds. *Sean.* She closed her eyes briefly, as if thinking about him now was a breach of trust, somehow. Which was just stupid and she knew it. But, until today, Sean was the only man she'd ever been with. Hardly surprising that thoughts of her late husband would rise up.

Sean and Micah were so very different in so many ways. Micah's body was stronger, bigger—in every way, she thought with a tiny stab of guilt for the comparison. But it wasn't just their physical differences that set them apart.

With Micah there was laughter along with the sex. Kelly smiled, remembering the teasing about points and traveling condoms. With Sean, lovemaking had been a serious business. Instead of romance and fun, she'd always felt as if Sean had had a mental checklist. *Turn lights off, check. Kiss Kelly, check. Tongue, check. Touch breasts, check.* Their times in bed together had been almost clinical, more of a task to be accomplished.

God, she couldn't believe she was even having these disloyal thoughts. Kelly had never told anyone how unsatisfied she'd been in her marriage. Not even Terry. Though she had loved Sean, until now Kelly had believed that she simply wasn't capable of the kind of orgasms that Terry described—*blinding, mind-shattering, earthshaking.* Because in her husband's arms, Kelly had never felt more than a tiny blip of pleasure. Before today, sex had been just a sense of closeness.

She'd had absolutely no idea that there was a tsunami of sensations she'd never experienced.

Kelly opened her eyes and looked at the man she still held cradled to her. In the first few moments with Micah, Kelly had discovered more, *felt* more than she ever had with her husband. And maybe, Kelly thought for the first time, that was the reason she hadn't been interested in going on dates, finding another man. Because being with Sean hadn't been all that great.

She'd long blamed herself for the lack of spark between her and Sean, assuming that she just wasn't experienced enough to really make things heated between them. Now she had to admit that maybe the truth was that she and Sean had been friends too long to make the adjustment to lovers.

"I can hear you thinking," Micah murmured. "Keep it down."

Kelly grinned, grateful he'd interrupted her thoughts. Silently she let go of the past and returned to this amazing moment and the man she'd shared it all with. "Are you sleeping?"

"Yes," he muttered.

She laughed and the motion had his body, still locked inside her, creating brand-new ripples of expectation. Stunned, she couldn't believe she was ready to go again after what had been the most staggering orgasm of her life. Kelly slid her hands up and down his broad back and lifted her hips slightly to recreate that feeling. Instantly she was rewarded with another tiny current of electricity.

He hissed in a breath, lifted his head and looked down at her, one eyebrow arched high. "You keep moving like that and we're going to need a new condom."

Naturally she wriggled again, deliberately awakening a wave of fresh need. Reaching up, Kelly cupped his face in her palms and asked, "How many condoms do you have?"

He rocked his hips against her and she gasped.

One corner of his mouth lifted. "I'm thinking not nearly enough."

Was it bad that her heart did a slow roll and flip at

the sight of his smile? Was it dangerous that she wanted nothing more than to stay here, like this, with Micah smiling down at her, forever? Her heart pounded painfully in her chest and her whole body trembled as he sat back onto his heels, drawing her with him, keeping their bodies locked together.

"Oh, boy." She said it on a sigh as she settled onto Micah's lap. Face-to-face, their mouths only a kiss apart, Kelly was lost in the rich brown of his eyes. His body went deep. She *felt* him growing, thickening inside her, and she swiveled her hips, grinding her core against him to feel even more.

He bent his head to take her nipples, one after the other, into his mouth. Kelly looked blindly around the familiar room, trying to distract herself so she wouldn't climax as quickly this time. She wanted to draw this moment out as long as she could. So she looked at the forest-green walls, the white crown molding, the now-cold white-tiled fireplace and the chairs drawn up before it.

She'd lived here most of her life and knew every corner of the old Victorian; yet, she'd never been more alive than she was at that moment. Never been so in tune with her surroundings, with her own body and with the man currently setting her on fire with a desire sharper, richer than she'd known ever before.

He suckled at her as if trying to draw everything she was within him. Kelly surrendered to the moment, concentrating not on where she was but what was happening. His big hands scooped up her spine and into her hair, fingers dragging along her scalp. Kelly watched him at her breasts while that delicious tugging sensation shot through her body.

Another first. She'd never made love like this—sitting

atop a man so that every stroke of his body into hers was like a match struck. Kelly went up on her knees and slid down slowly, taking him as deep as she possibly could.

When Micah groaned and lifted his head, staring into her eyes, she felt stronger than she ever had. She moved on him again, picking up a rhythm that tormented both of them, and every time she rocked on him, she swore she could feel him touch her heart.

Her breath came in sharp, short puffs as she rode that crest of building pleasure again. How could she have not known all there was to *feel*? To *experience*?

Micah's jaw was tight as he fought for control. He looked into her eyes and dropped his hands to her hips to guide her into a faster rhythm. Bracing her hands on his broad shoulders, Kelly bit her bottom lip, tossed her hair back and stared deeply into Micah's steady gaze. She couldn't look away. Couldn't stop the growing wave of sensation inside her. Sliding her hands from his shoulders, she ran the flat of her palms across the sharply defined muscles of his chest. She ran her thumbnails across his nipples and watched him shudder and grind his teeth in response and she felt...powerful. Knowing what she was doing to this strong man made her feel sexy. Desired.

On his knees, he pushed into her and she twisted on his lap, grinding her pelvis against his, torturing them both, hurrying them along the path to a climax that would, she knew, completely shatter her. She wanted it. More than anything. She raced blindly toward it.

"Micah," she whispered, still scraping her nails across his nipples, still looking into his eyes. "Go faster. Go harder."

"You're killing me," he ground out, then flipped her

over onto her back. Still locked inside her, he drove himself into her, again and again, harder, higher, faster until neither of them could breathe easily. He lifted her legs, draped them across his shoulders and continued his relentless claiming of her.

Kelly shouted and fisted her hands in the duvet beneath her. The world was rocking wildly. He was so deep inside her she thought he might always be there. And she wanted that, too.

Again and again, they moved in a frantic dance designed to end in a splintering of souls, until the world shrank down to the bed alone and nothing outside the two of them mattered. He took her hard and fast and deep and she went with him eagerly.

Kelly called his name over and over again until it became a chant. Lifting her hands, she held on to his upper arms as he braced himself over her and dug her nails into his skin.

"It's coming. Come with me," she said brokenly, voice tearing like wisps of fog in a heavy wind. The tension inside her heightened unbearably. She moved into it, trying to throw herself at the pleasure waiting for her. "Now, Micah. Please, *now.*"

"Come then," he ground out, staring into her eyes. "Let me see your eyes when I take you."

Her release slammed into her like a freight train. She forced her eyes to stay open. She wanted him to see what he was doing to her. What only he had ever done. She quaked and shivered and finally screamed his name in desperation.

And, before the last of the tremors shuddered through her, he called out her name and stiffened as his body joined hers. Kelly held him as he took from her as much as he had given. Then he collapsed, bonelessly atop her, and, shattered, Kelly cradled him in her arms.

It was dark when Kelly woke up. She was a little stiff. A little sore. And a lot desperate for air. Micah was sound asleep on top of her. Couldn't really blame him for being wiped out, but as good as he felt on top of her, Kelly really needed to breathe easier. Shaking her head, she said, "Micah! Micah, roll over."

"What?" Groggy, he lifted his head and opened his eyes. Understanding instantly, he rolled to one side, keeping an arm locked around her middle. "I fell asleep."

"We both did." Taking a deep breath, she curled into his side and just managed to swallow a sigh of satisfaction. "What time is it, anyway?"

"Who cares?" He threw one arm across his eyes.

"Good point."

"Hey," he said. "Another point for me."

"That wasn't a point. That was just a figure of speech. So it's still three to two, my favor."

He smiled. "So I *did* get a point for all of this."

Kelly sighed. By rights she should have given him ten, twenty, even thirty points for everything he'd made her feel. "Oh, boy, howdy."

"I can live with that."

She laughed. "Okay, so, are you hungry? I'm hungry."

He opened one eye. "You're kidding."

"I never kid about food." She went up on one elbow and looked down at him. Oh, my, he was great looking when he was dressed, but *naked*? The man was drool-worthy. Kelly shook her head. If she kept going down that path, she would start something that wouldn't get her fed.

And if she didn't eat soon, she wouldn't have the strength for everything else she wanted to do with Micah. Now that was motivation. "Come on, you've got to be hungry, too."

"Not enough to move anytime soon."

"Really?" Kelly sat up and stretched, feeling looser and more limber than she had in years. "I'm not tired at all. In fact, I feel energized. We should have done this a long time ago."

He stared up at her and frowned.

"What?"

"Seriously?" He studied her as if she were on a slide under a microscope. "You feel great and you're hungry. That's all you have to say?"

Confused, Kelly laughed. "What were you expecting?"

Propping himself up on both elbows, Micah tipped his head to one side. "So you're not going to say that you've been doing some thinking and that we should talk?"

"About what?"

"About your feelings," he said. "And how sex changes things between us and we should figure out where our *relationship* goes from here."

She would have laughed again, but he looked so serious she just couldn't do it. Shaking her head, Kelly held up one hand. "Wait. Is that what most women do? Have sex with you and then ruin it with...*talk*?"

He frowned. "Well, generally, yeah."

She didn't know whether to be insulted that he'd expected her to be like every other woman he'd met in his life—or to feel bad that he had to protect himself against wily women looking to hook him into a relationship he didn't want. So she did neither.

Kelly smiled, bent down and planted a quick, hard kiss on his mouth. "Well, then, I'm happy to surprise you again. I came to you, remember? All of this was *my* idea—"

"Well," he said, "in my defense, I'd had the same idea—I just hadn't approached you with it yet."

"Even if you had, it wouldn't matter." She shrugged. "We're two adults, Micah. We can have sex—really *good* sex—without it meaning hearts and flowers, right?"

Confusion shone in his eyes. "Well, yeah, it's just—"

"What's wrong now?" Hadn't she eased his mind yet?

"Nothing," he said, a scowl tugging at his lips. "It's just, I'm the one who usually gives that little speech. It's weird being on the receiving end."

"Another first." Kelly took a deep breath then blew it out. "Well, I'm done talking. But I could really go for a sandwich."

She scooted off the bed, picked up his discarded T-shirt and pulled it over her head. God, she felt good. "You want one?"

"Sure," he said slowly, thoughtfully. "I could eat."

"Great. I'll see you in the kitchen." Kelly left the room and didn't stop walking until she was downstairs. Then she paused and looked back up toward the room where she'd left him.

She'd told him she didn't want to talk and that was true. What she didn't tell him was that she was starting to feel a lot more for him than she'd planned on. Maybe it was the way he was so hesitant about letting people in. Maybe it was the half smile that curved his mouth so unexpectedly. She didn't know exactly what it was that was growing inside her, but Kelly was pretty sure that she was headed for trouble.

* * *

For the next few days, Micah and Kelly developed a routine that worked for both of them.

Micah spent the mornings working, building his novel page by page while Kelly raced from one job to the next. In the afternoons, they worked together on her Halloween project.

And every night they were together at the Victorian in Micah's bed.

Micah glanced over at Kelly now as she showed three kids how to roll black paint onto the plywood sheets. A reddish-gold ponytail hung down between her shoulder blades and swung like a metronome with her every movement. She wore her favorite worn jeans with the rip on the right thigh, black work boots and a faded red sweatshirt with the slogan Women Do It Better scrawled across the front. There was black paint on her cheek and a smile on her face as she listened to some long, involved story one of the kids told her.

A sharp stab of desire hit Micah so hard, so fast he nearly lost his breath. Hell, the skies were gray and there was an icy wind sliding through the nearby canyon, and Micah felt like his insides were blazing.

He and Kelly had thought to ease the sexual tension between them by sleeping together. Instead, they'd poured gasoline on a smoldering fire and started an inferno. Micah wanted Kelly all the time now. She was constantly on his mind. Her image, her scent, the harsh cries she made when he was inside her, pushing her over the edge.

This had never happened to him before. He should have known, he told himself, that Kelly would be unlike any woman he'd ever met. That had to be why he found her so intriguing. It was the newness factor. Her unpredictable nature. Her ability to keep him guessing, always on his toes. Hell, she *still* hadn't started that whole *we should talk* conversation he kept expecting. And a part of him was waiting for that shoe to drop.

There was no one else in his life who could have gotten him to stand out in the cold putting up plywood walls for a neighborhood Halloween maze. Shaking his head, he didn't know whether to be impressed by her or ashamed of himself.

He emptied his mind and took a good look at what they were building. It wasn't really a haunted house, but more of a passageway kids would have to go through to collect candy on Halloween night. Black walls, fake spiderwebs, a recording of scary sounds and voices, there were also going to be black lights to cast weird shadows and a few ghoulish mannequins to finish it all off.

If anyone had told him a year ago that he'd be in a small town in Utah building scary Halloween stuff, he would have called them crazy. Yet, here he stood.

"How the hell did this happen?" he muttered.

"You said a bad word," Jacob said, frowning up at him.

He looked down at the little boy and sighed. For some reason, this one particular kid had adopted Micah. Apparently, since Micah had taken the kid to visit his pumpkin, that had forged a bond. At least in Jacob's mind.

"What?"

"A bad word," the boy said. "You said *hell*."

"Oh." He rolled his eyes. Really had to watch that, he supposed. But then he wasn't exactly accustomed to dealing with children, was he? Even when he was at Sam and Jenny's place, Micah didn't spend much time with their two kids. In his defense, Isaac was a baby, so the kid didn't have much to say. And Annie, he realized suddenly, was Jacob's age.

Funny. He'd always told himself that he didn't pay attention to Sam's kids because he had no idea how to act with them. But he and Jacob got along so well that the boy had unofficially adopted him. That made him wonder if maybe he should have tried harder to get to know Sam's daughter, Annie.

But at the same time, Micah remembered that he didn't *like* kids. He didn't ask Jacob to hang around all the time, did he? Micah didn't want to get close to anyone. Had, in fact, spent most of his life avoiding any kind of connection.

And how has that worked out for you?

He glanced at the little boy kneeling beside him and gave an inner sigh. Now he had to remember to watch his language because a child had decided the two of them were best friends.

"Yeah, well," Micah said finally. "I shouldn't have said the bad word. And don't you say it."

Jacob's eyes went wide. "Oh, I won't cuz once Jonah said *damn* and Mommy made him go sit in his room and he *cried*."

And the ten-year-old probably wouldn't appreciate his little brother sharing that bit of news. Still, nodding sagely, Micah said, "Learn from your brother's mistakes then. Now," he added, "hold the hammer in both hands and hit the nail."

Micah yanked his fingers out of the way just in time, as Jacob's aim was pretty bad. But the grin on the kid's face was infectious. He was clearly proud of himself and loved being thought of as big enough to help like the other kids. Micah smiled at the kid and wondered again just how this had happened to him.

"Can I do another one?" Jacob asked, turning his face up to Micah's.

"Sure," he said, glancing at the bent, smashed nail. Micah would fix them later. For now, let the kid feel important. Memories of his own childhood swept through Micah's mind in an instant. Ignored by adults, he'd taken advantage of their disinterest and learned how to become invisible. He didn't cause trouble. Didn't stand out for good or bad reasons. And because he'd spent every minute trying to not be seen, not once had he *ever* felt important. To anyone.

Micah held out another nail and watched Jacob situate it just right. "Be careful. If you smash your fingers Kelly will get mad."

Jacob laughed delightedly. "No, she won't. But I can be careful."

When his cell phone rang, Micah grabbed it from his back pocket and looked at the screen. "Can you be careful on your own?"

"I can do it. I'm not a baby."

"Right. I forgot." The phone rang again and Micah stood up. "I'll be right back," he told Jacob, then answered the phone as he stepped away from all the hammering and kids' high-pitched voices. "Hey, Sam."

"Hey, yourself," his agent countered. "You haven't called to whine in a few days so I figured you were dead."

Reluctantly Micah laughed. "That's not bad. Giving up the agent life to hit the stand-up circuit?"

"I could," Sam said. "Annie thinks I'm funny."

"Your daughter is three." Micah kept walking until he was ten feet from the small crowd gathered in front of the Victorian. The breeze was stronger out here, without the big house giving any shelter. "She thinks your evil cat is funny."

"Sheba's a perfectly nice cat," Sam pointed out. "With excellent judgment. She likes everyone but you."

"She knows I'm a dog person," Micah said, then frowned. Hell, he didn't know if he was a dog person. He'd never had a pet. Not that he cared. It was just odd to suddenly realize that. But he was always traveling. How was he supposed to take care of an animal if he didn't have a home?

"Great, I'll get you a puppy."

"Do it and die," Micah told him, though it surprised him to realize that a puppy didn't sound like such a bad idea. He scrubbed one hand over his face as if he could wipe away thoughts that had no business in his mind. "If you're calling about the book, it's still coming slowly."

Mostly because instead of just imagining what it might be like to have sex with Kelly, he was spending most of his free time remembering what they'd done together the night before. Hell, it was a wonder he got *any* work done.

"Yeah, this isn't about the book," Sam said. "I'm flying out to California in a couple days. I've got a Friday meeting with an indie publishing house."

Thanks to the internet, independent publishers were springing up all over the place. Most started and disappeared within a span of a few months—just long enough to fulfill and then crush would-be writers' dreams. But a few started small and built a strong list of writers and grew into houses with good reputations and steady sales.

Micah's gaze shifted to Kelly. She was bent over, helping Jacob's older brothers and a girl from down the street apply layers of black paint to plywood. The curve of her behind drew his gaze unerringly, and Micah had to look away for his own sanity.

He started paying attention again just in time.

"So," Sam was saying, "I thought you might want to fly out for the weekend. Take a break from small-town life and visit with an old friend."

It sounded like a great idea to Micah. He'd been here in Banner for more than two months and he could do with a good dose of city life. Plush hotel, room service, noise, people...

"Sold," he said abruptly, then looked at Kelly again. She tossed her ponytail and laughed as Jacob's big brothers started painting each other. Looking at her wide smile, he could only think about getting her away from her home ground. Into some plush, luxurious life where he could seduce her nonstop. "But I won't be coming alone."

"Yeah?" He actually heard the intrigued smile in Sam's voice.

"Thought I'd bring my fiancée with me." He grinned, anticipating Sam's reaction. He wasn't disappointed.

A couple of long seconds filled with stunned silence ticked past before Sam sputtered, "Your *what*?"

"Can't get into it right now. I'll explain when I see you," Micah said, and had to admit he was enjoying leaving Sam hanging on the information front. "Where do you want to meet?"

"I'm staying at the Monarch Beach Resort in Dana Point, and who is this fiancée and when did this happen?"

"Got it," Micah said, ignoring the questions. "When's your meeting?"

"I'm flying in early Friday for a meeting that afternoon. But I'll be staying until Sunday."

"Okay." Micah did some fast figuring. It was Tuesday now—he had plenty of time to arrange for a suite at the hotel and a private jet to get him and Kelly to Orange County. All he had to do was convince her to leave town for a few days. He had confidence in his ability there. "I'll see you then."

"You are *not* going to leave me hanging with no information," Sam complained. "Do you know what'll happen if I go home with this news and no details? Jenny will hound me."

Micah laughed. "Sounds perfect."

"You're gonna pay for this—"

Micah hung up and enjoyed it. Sure, Sam would find a way to get revenge, he told himself. But that's what good friends were for, right?

His gaze locked on Kelly. She must have felt him staring, and something inside him turned when she met his gaze and smiled at him. Her eyes were shining, the curve of her delicious mouth was tempting and when she turned back to the kids and bent down, his gaze locked on her behind again. The woman really had a world-class butt.

His body went tight and hard in an instant. Yeah. A few days away from here. No work interfering for either of them. Just relaxing and enjoying each other. What could be better?

Going online, Micah went to the hotel's website and reserved the Presidential Ocean Suite. He stayed there whenever he was in Southern California and he knew that Kelly would love it. The hotel was top-of-the-line, and this room in particular was damn impressive, with a private balcony that offered sweeping views of the Pacific. Micah smiled to himself as he imagined her on that terrace, the wind in her hair, moonlight making her bare breasts seem to glow. Naked with only the sky, the stars and the sea as witnesses. That's how he wanted her.

All he had to do now was find a way to convince her to take a break from her many responsibilities.

Kelly was flabbergasted.

One of her grandmother's favorite words, it was the *only* one that fit this situation, Kelly told herself. In fact, she was so stunned she couldn't think of a thing to say. And that was so unusual for her, she couldn't remember the last time it had happened.

Micah's invitation had come out of the blue and she'd instantly agreed. True, she had to rearrange the jobs she had lined up, but the chance to get away with Micah was one she didn't want to miss. Being with him was so important to her she was already worrying about what it would be like when he eventually left. But, until then, she wanted to be with him every minute she could be.

She and Terry had made an emergency shopping run to Salt Lake City. It had taken them hours, since Terry had insisted on hitting every single boutique and dress shop in the city, but it had been worth the trip. In her suitcase now, Kelly had clothes suited to a five-star resort.

As soon as Micah told her about the Monarch Bay Resort, Kelly had looked it up online so she'd have some idea of where she'd be staying. The hotel was lovely, elegant. And completely intimidating.

First there had been the limo ride to the airport, then they had been ushered to a private concourse and escorted onto the jet Micah had chartered. Kelly had felt like a queen, lounging in the supple blue leather chairs set into conversation areas. *So* much better than flying like a sardine in an overcrowded can.

She and Micah had sipped champagne and nibbled on strawberries during the short flight. The limo ride to the hotel hadn't flustered her and she'd idly wondered if she was already getting accustomed to being spoiled. But walking into this hotel, where the staff called Micah by name and rushed to do his bidding, and then this spectacular suite... Kelly was simply overwhelmed.

The Presidential Ocean Suite was breathtaking. There was a fireplace, several overstuffed couches and chairs in soft pastels. The carpet was thick and the color of sand. There were vases filled with fresh yellow roses, and there were French doors leading to the private terrace.

The bedroom was huge, with its own fireplace and another set of French doors leading to the balcony they shared with no one. There were crystal chandeliers over the dining table and the bathroom was bigger than her whole cottage back home, with a tub wide and deep enough to swim in and a shower built for a cozy party of five or six, with built-in benches that made Kelly think of any number of things she and Micah could do on them.

And *when* had she become so interested in sex?

Answer, of course—the first time Micah kissed her. He'd created a monster. Smiling to herself, Kelly said simply, "Micah, this is just...amazing. The whole day has been—" She broke off, at a loss for words for the first time in forever. "I wouldn't have missed this for anything."

She walked toward the open terrace doors and caught the shimmer of sunlight on the deep blue of the ocean as it stretched out into eternity. A soft sea breeze danced into the room, ruffling the sheer white curtains.

"I'm glad you came," he said.

"So am I."

Kelly turned to him. He wore black slacks, a dark red dress shirt with the collar open and a black sports coat. He looked comfortable in his surroundings and she realized that *this* was how he lived all the time. He'd told her that he moved from hotel to hotel when he was working, but somehow, even knowing he was rich and famous, she hadn't considered that the hotels he was talking about were really more like palaces.

Kelly tried to imagine living in a place like this and just couldn't do it. The thought of trying to fit into this kind of lifestyle on a daily basis was exhausting. For Kelly, this was an aberration. A step outside her own reality. Okay, more than a step. A *leap*. But the reality was this: as gorgeous as this place was, as glad as she was that she'd come away with Micah, Kelly felt like an interloper here. But, for the next few days, she was going to pretend that she *did* belong, because there was nowhere else she'd rather be.

His gaze locked on her. "Did I tell you before we left that you look beautiful today?"

Kelly flushed, relishing the heat that always raced through her when Micah was near. And now she was doubly glad she and Terry had done so much shopping. Her new black slacks, white silk blouse and deep green brocade vest looked good on her, she knew. And she didn't want to *look* as out of place here as she felt. "You did tell me. Thank you."

He walked across the room to her, took her hand and then led her to the French doors. Stepping onto the terrace, she took a quick look around at the earth-toned tile floor, the table and chairs in one corner and the pair of lounge chairs complete with deep blue cushions and red pillows.

"It just keeps getting better and better," she murmured, and, letting go of his hand, walked to the iron railing and looked out at the sea. The ocean was a deep blue with gold glints of sunlight shining on its surface. Boats with jewel-toned sails skimmed along the waves while surfers closer to shore rode their boards with a grace she envied.

A soft breeze tossed her hair across her eyes. She plucked it free and sighed. "It's like a fairy tale."

"I've pictured you here," he said, and when she turned to look at him, she found his gaze locked on her. "Standing just there, the wind in your hair, a smile on that incredible mouth."

Her heartbeat skittered. "And is the reality as good?"

"Almost," he said, moving in close.

"Only almost?" Her eyebrows lifted and she laughed softly.

"Well, when I pictured you standing there, I was seeing you naked in the moonlight," he admitted, pulling her up against him.

A curl of damp heat settled at her core, and Kelly lifted her head to meet his gaze. Hunger shone in his eyes as he slid his hands down to cup her bottom and hold her tight to his erection. What was it about this man that turned her into a puddle of desires she'd never known before? Why was it he could touch her and send her up in flames? How could one smile from him turn her heart upside down?

She was very much afraid she knew the answers to all of those questions. But now wasn't the time to explore it. The next few days were just for them. To be together. To revel in each other. She didn't want to waste a minute of it.

"Well," she said, when she could breathe past the knot

in her throat, "it's important to make dreams come true. So tonight…"

He hissed in a breath through gritted teeth and held her even tighter to him. "That's a date," he promised, then deliberately took a step back, groaning. "But if I want to show you anything of California, we'd better get going. How about we go down, pick up the car I've got waiting and drive up the coast?"

At that moment, she would have gone with him anywhere.

Eight

Micah took her up the coast to Laguna where they parked the car and walked along Pacific Coast Highway. They popped into art galleries, bought ice cream from a vendor and swayed in time to a street performer's smooth, slow saxophone performance.

Early October in California meant it was still warm, and with the sun shining down on them, the day couldn't have been more perfect. Then he spotted something in a shop window.

"Come with me," he said, taking Kelly's hand and pulling her into the cool quiet of the jewelry shop. The interior of the shop was cool and dimly lit so that the jewels in the glass display cases could shine like stars in the night beneath lights fixed to the underside of the cabinets. There was a dark red rug on the wood-plank floor, and a grandfather clock ticked loudly into the hushed quiet.

"Micah, what're you doing?"

"I saw something I want to get." He signaled an older man behind the gleaming glass cases filled with diamonds and gemstones.

"May I help you?" He wore round, wire-rimmed glasses. His gray hair was expertly trimmed, and his pin-striped suit complete with vest made him look as though he'd stepped out of the nineteen forties.

"Yeah." Micah glanced at Kelly as she wandered down the glass cases, admiring everything within. Turning back to the man in front of him, he said, "The emerald necklace in the window."

The man brightened. His eyes sparkled and a tiny smile curved his mouth. "One of our finest pieces, sir. One moment."

Kelly wandered back to Micah and leaned into him. "What're you buying?"

"A gift for someone," he said, leaving it at that as the man came back, laid the emerald necklace out on a black velvet tray and waited for their admiration.

"Oh, my, that's gorgeous," Kelly whispered, as if she were in church.

"It is, isn't it?" Micah liked the look of it himself, but he was more glad that Kelly approved of it, too. Square cut, the emerald was as big as his first thumb joint. The setting was simple, with platinum wire at the gemstone's corners and twin diamonds on either side of it, the stone hung on a delicate platinum chain. And the emerald itself, he thought, was exactly the color of Kelly's eyes. That's what had caught his attention in the first place. "Okay, I'll take it."

The older man's eyebrows lifted but, otherwise, he

remained cool and polite. "Of course. Would you like it gift wrapped?

"Not necessary," Micah said, reaching for his wallet and then his credit card. He didn't bother to ask the price. It didn't matter, anyway.

"I'll take care of it straight away," the man said, then looked at Kelly. "I hope you enjoy it." Then he scurried away to ring up the sale, clearly wanting the business done before Kelly talked Micah out of the purchase.

"Oh," she said to the man's back as he left, "it's not for me..."

Her voice trailed off as Micah lifted the necklace from the black velvet and turned to her.

Eyes wide, Kelly looked horrified as she took a step back. "Micah, no."

Again, she surprised him. She hadn't even considered the possibility that the necklace was for her. "You said you liked it."

"Well," she said, "I'd have to be blind *and* stupid to not like it. That's not the point."

"You're right," he said, pushing past her reservations. "The point is, I want you to have it." He stepped behind her, laid the jewel at the base of her neck and ordered, "Lift your hair."

She did, but all the while she was shaking her head. "You can't just buy me something like this out of the blue—"

"Well," he said, voice low and teasing, "you did tell your grandmother that we were going to New York for a ring, so..."

"Micah." She turned her head to look at him, and he smiled at her to ease the worried look in her eyes.

When the necklace was secured around her neck, he

moved to stand in front of her. The emerald shone like green fire on her skin and he felt a swift tug of satisfaction seeing her wearing it. "It looks perfect."

"It would look perfect on a three-legged troll," Kelly argued, but her fingers reached up to touch the stone and her gaze slipped to a mirror on the counter to admire it. "It's beautiful, Micah. Seriously. But you don't have to do this. Buy me things, I mean."

No, she wouldn't expect that from him and he found that…refreshing. Most of the women he'd ever been with had anticipated trinkets like this. They'd oohed and aahed over jewelry-store windows or even, on occasion, dragged him inside to let him know in no uncertain terms which piece they'd most like to have. But Kelly didn't want anything from him. Didn't demand anything. She was happy just being with him, and that had never happened before.

And maybe that was why Micah had felt compelled to buy her that damn necklace. He wanted her to have something to remember him by. In a few months, he'd be gone from her life, but every time she looked at that necklace, she'd remember today and she'd…what? *Miss him?* Had anyone, anywhere ever missed him? Had he ever wanted them to? Questions for another time, another place, he told himself.

"I wanted you to have it," he said simply. "It's the same color as your eyes."

"Oh, Micah…" Those big beautiful green eyes filled with tears and, just for a second, he panicked. But Kelly blinked the moisture back and lifted her chin. "You don't want to make me cry. I look hideous when I cry. I'm a sobber. I don't do delicate weeping."

Of course she wouldn't cry. He chuckled—how could

he not? Kelly was one in a million at everything. "Good to know. I'll make a note. No making Kelly cry."

A wry smile curved her mouth briefly, then her shoulders slumped and a defeated sigh escaped her. "I can't stop you from doing this, can I?" she asked, still touching the cold, green stone.

"Already done, so no."

Nodding, she took a breath, let it out again and said, "Fine. Am I allowed to thank you?"

"Only briefly," he told her warily.

"Thank you, Micah," she said, going up on her toes to lay a soft, slow kiss on his mouth. "I've never owned anything more lovely. Whenever I wear it, I'll think of you."

His heart jolted. It was just what he'd wanted, yet hearing her say it he could almost hear the "goodbye" in her voice. He hadn't thought it would bother him, but it did. For the first time in his adult life, he wasn't looking forward to moving on. Frowning, he told himself he would. He had to. Eventually. But Micah didn't want to think about endings today.

Looking at her, the pleasure in her eyes, an emerald at her throat and a smile on that fabulous mouth of hers, all he could say was, "I'll think of you, too."

And he knew he'd never meant anything more.

Later that night, Kelly did a quick spin in place on her three-inch heels, sending the skirt of her new black dress flying. Then she stopped and looked up at Micah. "Today was so lovely. Thank you, Micah."

He shrugged. "It was fun."

It was a revelation, she thought but didn't say. She'd seen Micah in a whole new light. He was famous. Rich. Important. Everywhere they went, people scrambled to please him. Fans—mostly women—had stopped him on the street to coo over him, completely ignoring Kelly's presence. And she'd seen his reaction to all of the notoriety. It all made him uncomfortable. Sure, he was polite to everyone, but there was a cool detachment in everything he did that told Kelly he'd much prefer going unnoticed.

Micah lived a life that was so far removed from Kelly's they might as well have been on different planets. But, for now anyway, they were together. And maybe that was all she should think about.

She strolled across the terrace to the railing and lifted her face into the sea breeze that was soft and cool. Turning her head to him, she said, "I thought the maître d' at dinner was going to cry when you signed his book for him."

Micah poured them each a glass of champagne and carried them to her. Handing her one, he had a sip of his own. "I couldn't believe he had it with him at work."

She laughed and took a drink of the really fabulous wine. Shaking her hair back from her face, she sighed. "I can't believe I'm here. Not just California," she amended. "But here… Here. In this beautiful hotel. With you."

"I'm glad you are," he admitted, then frowned slightly as if he'd like to call the words back.

But it was too late, because Kelly heard them and held them close in her heart. He might not want to care about her, but he did. For now, that was enough for her. Neither of them had gone into this expecting anything but a release of sexual tension. And if she was feeling… more, then she'd just keep that piece of info to herself. He wouldn't want to hear it and she wasn't ready to admit it, anyway.

Pushing those thoughts out of her mind, Kelly turned from the railing, walked to the table and set her champagne flute down. When she turned back to Micah, she smiled and reached behind her back for the zipper. "I think we made a date for this terrace tonight, didn't we?"

She saw his grip on the fragile stem of the flute tighten. "Yeah. We did, didn't we?"

The zipper slid down with a whisper and she lifted both hands to hold the deeply scooped bodice of the dress against her. "And you're sure no one can see us?"

He took a drink and speared her with a look that was so hot, so barely contained, his brown eyes burned with it. "Private terrace. No neighbors. Empty ocean."

"Okay then." Kelly took a breath and let the dress drop to pool at her feet. She'd never done anything like this, and she felt both excited and exposed. But Micah's gaze on her heated her through, and she forgot about feeling self-conscious and instead enjoyed what she was doing to him.

On that shopping trip with Terry, Kelly had indulged in some new lingerie, as well. His expression was all she'd hoped for.

Micah's gaze moved up and down her body before settling on her eyes again. "You're killing me."

"You like?" He more than liked and she knew it.

"Yeah," he ground out. "You could say so. One point for the black lace."

Kelly grinned. "Nice! That makes it four to two, my favor."

"You keep dressing like that, I'll give you all the points you want."

She shook her head slowly and said, "But didn't you say that in your dream I was naked?"

"So you *are* trying to kill me."

"No," she assured him. "Just torture you a little." Slowly she peeled out of the black lace bra, dropping it onto the nearest chair. And, leaving her high heels on, she slipped out of the matching scrap of her panties and stood there with the ocean breeze drifting across her skin like a lover's hands.

"Well," she asked softly, "as good as the dream?"

"Better," he told her, and bent to take a kiss while his hands cupped her breasts, rolling her nipples between his thumbs and forefingers.

Kelly groaned and leaned into him, loving the feel of his hands on her skin. The taste of his mouth on hers. She felt completely wicked and absolutely wonderful.

He dropped one hand to her core and she parted her thighs for his touch. Micah had shown her more about herself, what her body was capable of, than she'd ever have believed possible. And now she wanted him all the time. Craved what happened between them when they were together. He stroked her, explored her, and she whimpered with need as an oh-so-familiar tension crept through her.

His thumb moved over that one sensitive spot and she gasped, moving her hips, trying to feel more, faster. He pushed one finger, then two, inside her and Kelly groaned again, clutching his shoulders, holding on while her body went on another wild ride courtesy of Micah Hunter.

The cold air brushed against her while his warm hands stoked fires inside her. Over and over, he touched, caressed, until she was just on the brink of a shattering climax. Then he stopped and she nearly shrieked.

"Micah—don't—"

"Wait." He lifted her, plopped her onto the table then, as she watched, he parted her thighs and knelt in front of her.

"What're you— Oh, Micah…"

Beneath her, the heavy metal table was cold against her behind, but she didn't feel cold. She felt as if she were on fire. Then Micah covered her center with his mouth and Kelly cried out in surprised pleasure. His lips, tongue and teeth drove her crazy. She threaded her fingers through his hair and held him to her as he continued his delicious torment.

He licked and suckled at the very heart of her, and the sensations rising inside her were powerful. Overwhelming. She had to hold on to him or she was sure she would have simply fallen off the face of the earth. She rocked helplessly in place as he pushed her so high there was no higher to go. Then the crash came and Kelly cried his name in a broken voice and let the sound drift away into the night wind.

Still trembling, she locked her eyes on his as he stood up and looked down at her. "Point to you," she whispered. "That was—"

"Four to three then," he said, scooping her off the table to cradle her close. "I'm catching up."

She smiled because she felt so darn good, but Kelly looked up at him through glazed eyes as she admitted in a whisper, "I've never— I mean no one…"

"I know what you meant," he said softly, his gaze locked with hers. "And if you're interested, there are a lot more firsts headed your way."

"I love to learn," she said, reaching up to briefly cup his face in the palm of her hand. Kelly laid her head on his chest as he carried her through the spacious living area into their bedroom.

Whatever he had in mind, Kelly was ready for it.

The following night, Micah and Kelly had dinner with Sam and Jenny Hellman, then the four of them took a walk around the hotel property. Both women were strolling slowly ahead of the men, and Micah could only guess they were still bonding over their favorite romance author.

Since Sam and Jenny had arrived, the four of them had spent a lot of time together, and Micah was pleased at how well Jenny and Kelly were getting along. Though why it mattered, he told himself, he couldn't have said. It wasn't as if they were all going on vacation together. And unless Sam and Jenny rented the Victorian for ski season again, they wouldn't be seeing each other after this weekend. Once Micah had moved on, none of the others would have any reason to meet. So why did it matter to him that the people he was closest to were becoming friends?

Hell, he didn't know. But that was typical. Since meeting Kelly, Micah had felt off his game. Off balance. And she was doing it to him. Micah's gaze locked on Kelly. She wore a bright yellow dress that made her look like a lost sunbeam in the night. Her hair was long and loose and the wind kept lifting it, as if teasing her. Something inside him stirred and warmth spread through his chest.

"You're sleeping with her, aren't you?"

"None of your business," Micah said tightly, and he knew that was as good as saying *yes*.

"Ah, touchy." Sam nodded thoughtfully. "That's interesting."

"What're you talking about?" Micah kept his gaze straight ahead because looking at Kelly was more fun than looking at Sam.

"Just that you've never minded talking about your women before…"

Micah ground his teeth together. "She's not one of my women," he said. "She's Kelly."

"Also interesting." Sam smiled to himself. "Getting attached, huh?"

"No." He was definitely not getting attached. Of course he cared about her. But there was nothing more than that because he wouldn't allow it. "Leave it alone, Sam."

"Not gonna happen." His old friend punched him in the shoulder and said, "For the first time, you've brought a girl home."

Micah snorted. "Are you crazy?"

"Come on. We both know Jenny and I are as close to family as you've got, and here we are, the four of us, bonding nicely. So I think that says something."

"And I think you should stick to being an agent," Micah told him. "Because the fiction you dream up sucks."

Sam laughed and waved one hand at his wife when Jenny turned around to look at them. "Why not just admit that you and Kelly have something good together?"

Micah sighed and fixed his gaze on Kelly again. The way her hair fell around her shoulders. Her long legs, the way that yellow dress clung to her curvy body. Everything about her appealed to him. And that was enough to make him wary. She was the only woman he'd ever met who had tempted him to look deeper. That made her dangerous.

"Because what we have is temporary." Saying it aloud reinforced what he knew was pure truth. There was no future here.

"Well, I like her."

"Yeah," Micah said grimly. "So do I."

"Well, you don't sound too happy about it."

Micah scowled and wasn't sure if he was directing the expression at his friend or himself. "Why should I be? You know as well as I do I'll be leaving in a few more months."

Although, as he said it, Micah realized that moving on didn't sound as good as it usually did. Strange. Normally, after three months in one place, Micah was already getting restless. Making plans for where he would go next. Polishing up one book and already plotting the next. That was his life. Had been for years. And it worked for him, so why would he even consider changing it?

"And your point is…?"

"Don't say *point*."

"What?"

"Never mind." Micah shook his head. He'd never be able to hear that word again without thinking of Kelly. What were they now? Four to three. He remembered how he'd been awarded that last point and his body went hard as stone.

"This is *temporary*," he said again, emphasizing that last word, more for his own sake than for Sam's.

Sam stared at him as if he had three heads. "It doesn't have to be, that's what I'm saying. Hell, Micah, you're already engaged to her."

And this engagement would end just like the last one, he told himself. Sighing, Micah stuffed his hands into his slacks pockets. "We explained the whole thing to you. It's just a lie for Kelly's grandmother's sake."

"Lies can become truths."

Micah snorted. "No, they can't."

Sam shrugged. "Hey, look at it from my perspective. You guys get married, and Jenny, me and the kids have a place to stay every ski season."

"That's very thoughtful," Micah said wryly.

Sam smiled as he watched his wife stumble, catch herself and keep walking. "Jenny could trip over air, I swear." Sighing in exasperation, he said, "You and Kelly are good together, Micah. Why be in such a damn hurry to throw it away?"

Because he didn't know what to do with it.

"You don't buy gigantic emeralds for a woman you don't give a damn about—and thanks for that, by the way. Jenny's already reminded me that her favorite stone is a sapphire."

Micah laughed a little and it felt good to ease the tightness in his chest. "That's your problem. As for the emerald, I just wanted Kelly to have it. That's all."

They were walking through the hotel gardens and past the pool where a couple dozen people splashed in the aquamarine water. The sky was clear, the air was warm and the ocean breeze was cool and damp.

"Why?" Sam asked. "Why'd you want her to have it?"

"Because," Micah said in exasperation. "Just…because."

Sam laughed and Jenny turned around to look at him. He waved her off again and said, "Damn, Micah. No wonder I can get you so much money for your books. You've got a real way with words."

"Drop it, Sam."

Sam stopped. He was a couple inches shorter than Micah, a little heavier and a lot more patient. "Just admit it, man, she's got you. You care about her."

"Of course I care. What am I—a monster?" Micah stared out at the black ocean. "She's a nice woman." *Lame*, he thought. "We have a good time together." *They had a hell of a lot together.* "I like her." *Like. Care.* Hell, even he didn't believe him.

"Must be love."

Micah's head snapped around and his gaze burned into Sam's. "Nobody said anything about love."

Shaking his head, Sam mused, "Damn, you react to that word like a vampire does to a cross."

"I've got my reasons," Micah reminded him.

"Yeah, you do," Sam agreed. He leaned back against the railing behind him, folded his arms over his chest and said, "I'm the first to agree you had a crap time of it as a kid. So I get why you've closed yourself off up until now."

"I hear a 'but' coming," Micah mused.

Sam slapped his shoulder. "That's because you're a very smart man. So here it is. *But*, how long are you going to use that excuse?"

Micah shot him a look that would have had most people backing up with their hands in the air. Not Sam, though.

He gave Micah a bored smile. "Please. Don't bother giving me the Death Stare. It's never worked on me."

Micah rolled his eyes. True. "Fine. But my past is not an excuse, Sam. It's a damn *reason*."

"Because you had a miserable childhood you can't love anyone? That's just stupid." Shaking his head, Sam said, "It's like saying you never had a burger when you were a kid so now you can't have a Big Mac."

Micah scowled.

"Basically, buddy," Sam continued, "you're letting a crappy past mess with your present and future."

Micah ground his teeth together so hard it was a wonder they didn't turn into a mouthful of powder. Having his past reduced to a stupid analogy didn't help the situation any, and Micah felt compelled to defend his decisions on how he chose to run his life. If he wanted to be a footloose wanderer with no connections to anyone, that was his call, wasn't it? If it sounded lonely all of a sudden, that shouldn't be anyone's business but Micah's. And it had *never* mattered to him before, so he'd get over it. He liked being alone. Liked the freedom. Liked being able to pick up and move and have no one miss him. Right?

He frowned to himself over that last thought. Would Kelly miss him when he left? Would she think about him? Because he damn sure knew he would be thinking about her. *Just another reason to leave.*

"Wow," he said finally, "thanks for the analysis. How much do I owe you?"

"This one's on the house," Sam said, ignoring the sarcasm. "At some point," he paused. "Sorry. Used the word 'point' again, and someday you'll have to explain why we're not using it anymore."

Micah choked out a harsh laugh, but Sam wasn't finished.

"You have to decide if you want a life—or if you'd just rather be somebody else's victim for-freaking-ever."

"I'm not a damn victim," Micah muttered, insulted at the idea.

"Glad to hear it," Sam countered. "Now, what do you say we catch up with our women and go get a drink?"

"God, yes."

Sam hustled on ahead to catch up with Jenny and Kelly. Micah smiled in spite of everything as his friend offered each of them an arm and then led them off toward the hotel bar. Kelly turned her head to smile at him, and even at a distance Micah's heart gave a hard jolt.

He hadn't planned on any of this. All he'd wanted was a quiet place to work for six months. He hadn't asked to have Kelly come into his life. And now that she was there, he didn't know what to do about it. Sam meant well, but he couldn't understand what drove Micah. How the hell could he?

When you lived a life in the moment, tomorrows just never came into play. So, like always, Micah wouldn't look to the future—he'd just make the best of today.

Luxury hotels, limos and five-star restaurants made for a wonderful holiday, but after two weeks back at home, it all seemed like a pretty dream to Kelly.

As soon as they'd got home, she had stepped right back into her routine as if she'd never left, and that's how Kelly liked it. Her time away with Micah had been wonderful, but being here in her small town with him was perfect. She never took off the emerald necklace he'd given her so that, even when she was busy with her different jobs and Micah was shut away in the Victorian working on his book, it was like she had him with her everywhere she went.

Micah.

"You're doing it again."

Kelly jumped guiltily and grinned at Terry. "Sorry, sorry."

"Where were you?" Terry held up a hand. "Nope. Never mind. I know that look. I have it on my face constantly when Jimmy's home."

Kelly sighed a little, took a sip of her latte and scooted closer to where Terry was rolling out dough for the next batch of cookies for her shop. The kitchen smelled like heaven and, like Terry, was organized down to the last cookie sheet stacked carefully on its rack.

Kelly kept her voice down so the girls running the counter out front couldn't hear her. "Terry, I've never— I mean, I had no idea that— Why didn't you tell me how amazing sex is?"

Terry laughed and shook her head. She picked out a cookie cutter and quickly, efficiently, stamped out a dozen shapes in the dough. Then she carefully lifted each of them to put on a cookie sheet for baking. "Honey, you were married, I thought you knew."

Feeling disloyal again, Kelly said, "It was never like this with Sean. I didn't know feelings could be so *big.* I mean," she said, sighed heavily and closed her eyes briefly to bring back the magic of Micah's hands on her skin. "What he does to me, it's…" She couldn't even find the words to explain and maybe that was best. "I just never want him to stop touching me."

Terry took a moment to fan herself with her hands. "Good thing Jimmy's calling me tonight because I'm dying of jealousy here." Then she took another long look at Kelly and said, "You're feeling guilty, too, aren't you? About Sean, I mean."

"A little." A lot. She didn't mean to compare the two men, but it was inevitable when what she felt with Micah was so much more than anything she'd ever known.

"You don't have to." Terry patted her hand. "Sean was

a sweetie, but it's not like you two were legendary lovers or anything."

"I loved him," Kelly said softly.

"Of course you did," Terry agreed. "In a nice, comfortable, safe kind of way."

Was that what her marriage had been, Kelly wondered? Had she simply married Sean because he'd made her feel safe and settled? If Sean had lived, would they have stayed together? Would they have been happy? Kelly sighed again. There were no answers, and even if there were, they wouldn't change anything.

"He loved you, too," Terry said. "Enough, I think, to want you to be happy, Kelly. So, if Micah makes you happy, then yay him!"

Kelly picked up a finished cookie and took a bite, thinking about what Terry said. "He really does, you know? Every day, it just gets better between us. He's funny and crabby and kind and, God, the man has magic hands. In California, we were together all the time and... look." Leaning in, Kelly reached beneath the collar of her T-shirt and pulled out the emerald.

"Holy Mother of Cinnamon!" Terry all but leaped over the marble counter to lift the emerald with the tips of her fingers. She looked from the stone to Kelly and back again. "Is it real? Of course it's real. Rich guys don't buy junk. I didn't know emeralds *got* that big, for heaven's sake. And those are diamonds...

"Oh my God, I can't believe it took you two weeks to show me!"

Kelly laughed at her friend's reaction. "I just—it's kind of embarrassing. I mean, I told him not to buy it—"

"Of course you did." Terry sighed. "Why are you embarrassed to show me?"

"Because it sort of felt like bragging, I guess."

"Why wouldn't you want to brag about it?" Terry lifted the emerald and turned it back and forth so that the light caught and flashed off it. "That is amazing. If it was mine, I'd wear it stapled to my forehead so everyone would see it."

Laughing, Kelly realized she should have shown it to Terry as soon as she got home. But hiding the necklace wasn't just about not wanting to show off.

It was about the unshakable feeling she had that the emerald had been Micah's way of saying goodbye. Of letting her know that he would be leaving but he wanted her to have something to remember him by. Being Micah, it just had to be an emerald-and-diamond necklace, but the point was, she worried that he was already pulling away.

She'd noticed it more after Sam and Jenny had shown up. It was as if having his friends there had somehow made Micah shut down, go into self-defense mode. Jenny had told her that she'd never seen Micah happier than he was with Kelly. But since their weekend away, he'd drawn more into himself. It was nothing overt, but she *felt* the distance he was slamming down between them, and she had no idea how to get past it.

Yes, this had all started as a lie to make her grandmother feel better, but it had become so much more for Kelly. And maybe, she told herself, this was Karma's way of punishing her for the lie. Make her feel. Make her want. Then deny her. But even if it was, she told herself, she still had three months with Micah and she wouldn't let him leave her emotionally before he actually left.

Ruefully, Kelly admitted, "I can't bring myself to take the necklace off. It's like as long as I wear it, Micah's mine."

"Oh, sweetie, you've got it bad, don't you?"

"I love him." Her eyes went wide and she gasped a little before saying, "Oh, God. I love Micah." Kelly slapped both hands to her stomach as if she were going to be sick. "How could I do this?"

"Are you kidding?" Terry demanded. "Have you *looked* at him lately? It's a wonder it took you this long to fall for him. And that's not even counting the jewelry and the great sex."

Kelly laughed, but it sounded a little hysterical, even to her. She hadn't meant to fall in love, and she knew all too well that Micah would be horrified if she confessed what she felt for him. Heck, he'd probably be nothing more than a blur on his way out the door if he thought she was in love with him.

This had just slipped up on her. She hadn't meant to love him. And it wasn't the luxury vacations. Or the necklace. Or the sex—okay, maybe the sex was part of it. But she'd fallen in love with the *man*.

The man who could look so surprised when she didn't react the way he expected. The man who helped her with her haunted maze. The man who stood with a little boy so he could say good-night to his pumpkin.

"Oh, God," she whispered again. "This isn't good."

"Honey," Terry reached for her hand and squeezed it. "Maybe he loves you, too."

"Even if he did, he probably wouldn't tell me." Kelly shook her head. He'd been pretty clear, hadn't he? One engagement in his past and no desire for another. She could still hear him… *No wife. No girlfriend. No interest.* She closed her eyes and took a breath to try to steady herself. It didn't work.

"This wasn't supposed to be about love, Terry," she

said, and was talking to herself as much as her friend. "This was just…"

"An affair?" Terry shook her head. "You're just not the affair kind of person, sweetie. This was *always* going to end up with you in love."

"You might have warned me," Kelly said miserably.

"You wouldn't have listened," Terry assured her and carried the cookie sheet to the oven. She slid it inside, set the timer and came back again. "You might be upset over nothing. I've seen you guys together and he does feel something for you, Kelly. If it's not love, it's close. So, maybe he won't leave when his time here is done."

"I want to think that, but I can't." Kelly shook her head firmly. She'd already set herself up to have her heart broken. She wouldn't make it harder by holding on to the hope that things would change. "If I believe he'll stay, when he does eventually leave it'll only be worse on me."

"You could *try* to keep him here."

"No." Kelly had some pride, after all. She took another breath, squared her shoulders and lifted her chin. "If I had to *make* him stay then it wouldn't be worth it, would it?"

Terry sighed. "I hate when you're rational."

Kelly laughed sadly. "Thanks. Me, too." She finished off her latte. "He's going to leave, and I'll have to deal with that when it happens. For right now though, he's here. And I've got to go. Micah went to the university library today to do some research—"

"He's never heard of the internet?" Terry asked.

"He's a writer," Kelly said, with a sad smile. "He likes books. Anyway, I want to beat him home because I'm making dinner."

"I thought you said you loved him," Terry quipped.

"I'm not that bad," Kelly argued, though she could

admit that she wasn't the best cook in the world, no one had died from eating what she made.

"Right." Terry turned and headed to the cooling racks. "Why don't I send some cookies home with you and then at least you'll have dessert."

"You're the best."

"So I keep telling Jimmy," Terry said with a wink.

The drive home only took a few minutes, but even at that, her faithful truck wheezed and coughed like an old man forced to run when all he wanted was a nap. Kelly sighed a little, knowing she'd be buying a new one soon.

Micah's car wasn't in the driveway, so Kelly took that as a good sign. She wasn't completely ready to face him yet. The whole *I'm in love* revelation had hit her hard and she needed a bit more time to deal with it.

Grabbing the grocery bags from the passenger seat, she headed into the kitchen through the back door. She had steaks, potatoes for baking, a salad and now the world's best cookies. After she put everything away, she opened a bottle of wine so it could breathe. Because, boy, she needed a glass of wine. Or two. Maybe it would help her settle.

She'd been married, been in love and, yet, this feeling she had for Micah was so huge it felt as if she might drown in it. And she couldn't tell him. Kelly had absolutely no desire to hand him her heart only to have him hand it right back.

She looked around the familiar kitchen as if she were lost and looking for a signpost to guide her home. Micah had stormed into her life with the promise to leave again in six months. Now she was halfway through that timeline and Kelly knew that nothing in her life would be the same without him in it.

"Oh, stop it," she told herself, slapping both hands onto the cold granite counter. "You're feeling sorry for yourself. You're missing him even though he's not even gone yet. So cut it out already." Nodding, she reacted to the personal pep talk by tucking her feelings away. There'd be plenty of time to explore them all later. But for now... "Grab a shower, and put on something easy to take off."

Wow. She was thinking about sex. Again. And had been since... "Micah came into your life, that's when."

Her stomach swirled again as she headed for the stairs. Nerves? Anticipation? Worry? She frowned a little. "Please don't be getting sick, that's all. There's enough going on without that. Besides, it's almost Halloween and there's way too much to do."

Kelly climbed the stairs, walked down the hall, turned into the big bedroom and stopped dead. "Who are you?"

The completely naked stranger propped up against Kelly's pillows stared at her. "I'm Misty. Who're you? Where's Micah?"

Nine

"Micah?" Kelly stared blankly at the woman. Why was she naked? Why was she here? In *their* bed? And mostly Kelly's brain screamed, *Why are you just standing there talking to her? Why aren't you calling the police?* All very good questions. And still, Kelly started with, "How did you get in?"

"The doors weren't locked." Misty sat up higher in the big bed, clutching the duvet to her bare breasts. Thick black hair fell in tousled waves around her shoulders. She had too much makeup on her wide blue eyes and her lips had been slicked a bright red. As for the rest of her, Kelly didn't want to know.

"You need to get dressed and get out of my house." Kelly folded her arms across her chest and tapped the toe of her boot against the rug. She was hoping to look intimidating. If that didn't work, the sheriff was next.

"*Your* house?" The woman sniffed and settled back more comfortably against the bank of pillows. "Micah Hunter lives here and I don't know what you're trying to pull, but he won't be happy when he comes home to find you."

God, Micah would be home any minute, too. Good thing? Bad? Who could tell?

"How do you know Micah?" Kelly had to wonder at the woman's complete confidence. Was she a girlfriend Micah hadn't told Kelly about? An ex, maybe?

"He's my soul mate," Misty declared dramatically. "I knew it the first time I read his books. His words speak to my *heart*. He's been waiting for me to find him and he won't appreciate *you* being here and spoiling our reunion."

Kelly shook her head. "Reunion?"

"We've lived lifetimes together," Naked Misty intoned with another touch of drama. "In each incarnation, we struggle to find each other again. At last now, we can be together as we were meant."

Baffled, Kelly could only stare at the woman. She was clearly delusional and that might make her dangerous. And she was *naked*. What was going—and that's when the truth hit her.

Naked Misty had to be one of the crazed fans Micah had told her about. He'd said they tracked him down and sneaked into hotel rooms. Sneaking into an unlocked Victorian had to have been a snap. Kelly was now alone with a crazy person who might at any moment decide that Kelly was her competition. She had to get Misty out of the house and she wanted backup for that plan. Finally, she pulled her cell phone from her back pocket.

"I'm calling the police if you're not out of this house in the next minute."

"You can't make me leave." Misty pouted prettily. She probably practiced the look in a mirror. "I'm not going anywhere until I see Micah. He'll *want* to see me," she said, letting the duvet slip a little to display the tops of a pair of very large breasts.

Irritated, Kelly realized she was going to have to burn the sheets, the duvet…maybe the bed. First, however, she had to get rid of Naked Misty.

"Kelly?" Micah's voice came in a shout from downstairs. "Are you here?"

"Well, backup's arrived. It seems you're about to get your wish," Kelly told the woman who was still pouting and using one hand to further tousle her hair to make the best possible impression. Without taking her eyes off the woman, Kelly shouted, "I'm upstairs, Micah. Could you come up?"

The tone of her voice must have clued him in that something was wrong. Kelly heard him come upstairs at a dead run, and when he swung around the corner into the room, he stopped right behind her.

"What the hell?"

"Micah," Naked Misty cried, then sat up straight, threw her arms wide in welcome and let the duvet drop, displaying what had to be man-made breasts of monumental proportions.

Kelly slapped one hand across her eyes. "Oh, I didn't need to see those."

"Me, neither," Micah muttered.

"Who's *she*?" Naked Misty demanded with a finger point of accusation at Kelly.

Micah gritted his teeth, then gave Kelly an apologetic

look before saying, "Kelly's my fiancée. Who the hell are you? No," he corrected. "Never mind. Doesn't matter."

"You're *engaged*?" Misty sputtered and still managed to sound outraged. Betrayed.

"Yeah," Kelly said, then pointedly used Misty's own words in retaliation. "His words speak to my heart."

"How can you be engaged to *her*?"

Insulted, Kelly countered, "Hey, at least *my* breasts are real."

Honestly, she might have laughed at this mess, but the situation was just too weird.

"That's it," Micah ordered, stepping past Kelly to stride to the bed. "Get up whoever you are—"

"Misty."

"Of course you are." He huffed out a breath. "Well, Misty, get out of my bed, get dressed and get out."

"But I *love* you."

"Oh, boy," Kelly murmured. She didn't know whether to feel sorry for Misty or Micah or all three of them.

"No, you don't love me." Micah glared down at the woman until Misty seemed to shrink into the covers.

Kelly's stomach churned. Yes, Misty was crazy and an intruder, but she'd told Micah she loved him and he'd brushed it off coldly. And she knew that he probably wouldn't accept her declaration any better.

His features were cold, tight, as he stalked across the bedroom, scooping up the woman's discarded clothes. He tossed them at her and Naked Misty's pout deepened.

"You're mean."

"Damn straight." He stood beside the bed, legs braced, arms folded across his broad chest, and gave Misty a look that singed even as it iced. "If you're not out of this house in two minutes flat, I'll have you arrested."

"But—"

"If you ever come back," he added, "I'll have you arrested."

Naked Misty was pulling on a shirt as quickly as she could, thankfully tucking away those humongous breasts. "I only wanted to tell you how I feel. I do *love* you."

Kelly was watching now and saw the miserable resignation on Micah's face, and she didn't know how to help. She felt sorry for Misty, but she felt sorrier for herself. Loving Micah was hard. Knowing he wouldn't want her to was even harder.

"You don't even know me." He moved out of the woman's way when she leaped out of the bed and dragged her jeans on. Once she was dressed, Micah gave her enough time to scoop up her shoes and grab her purse from a chair. Then he took her by the arm and steered her out of the room.

Kelly heard them taking the stairs, but she didn't wait for Micah to come back. The only way to get a handle on the strangest situation she'd ever been in was to return things to normal. She immediately began stripping the bed. When Micah returned, he helped her take the sheets and duvet off and put on fresh sheets. Through it all he was silent, but the expression on his face told Kelly he wasn't happy.

"Did Misty get away all right?"

"Yeah." He huffed out a breath. "What the hell kind of name is Misty?" He smoothed the sheet, still avoiding her gaze. Well, Kelly wanted things back to normal between them, too.

"This wasn't your fault, Micah." She pulled the top sheet taut and folded the top back.

"She only came here because of me," he said, reaching for a replacement duvet, this one brick red, and flipping it out to cover the mattress.

"Still doesn't make it your fault." Kelly stacked pillows in fresh cases against the headboard. "How did she even find you?"

"Easy enough." Scowling, he too tossed a few pillows onto the bed. "Like I told you. Social media is everywhere. Someone in Banner probably put it out on Facebook or Twitter that I was here. That's enough to get every nut in the world moving." Shaking his head, he smoothed wrinkles that weren't there. "She shows up in town, talks to a few people, finds out where I am and bingo. Naked in my bed."

That was just beyond creepy. Living your life knowing there were thousands of would-be stalkers out there, ready to hunt you down and barge into your life? Kelly shuddered. "I don't know how you deal with this stuff all the time."

"It's why I don't stay anywhere for very long," he said, walking around the end of the bed to come to her side. "And now that one has found me, others will be coming too. I can't stay, Kelly."

Panic blossomed in the center of her chest and sent out tendrils of ice that wrapped around her heart and squeezed. This was what she'd been feeling since their holiday in California. If Naked Misty hadn't shown up, it would have been something else. For whatever reason, Micah wanted to get away from Banner. From Kelly. "But…you haven't finished your book yet."

"I'm close though," he said. "I can finish it somewhere else."

She was losing him. Standing right in front of him and

he was slipping away. "Why should you have to move out because of a crazy person?"

He sighed, dropped both hands onto her shoulders and met her eyes squarely. "It's not just her. Things have gotten…complicated between us, and I think it'd be easier if I left early."

"Easier? On who?"

"On both of us," he said, and stepped back. "Better to stop this before things get more tangled up."

But she wanted those three months. She wanted Micah here for the first snow, for Christmas. For New Year's Eve. She wanted him here *always.*

"Micah—" She broke off because anything she said now would sound like begging him to stay and she couldn't bring herself to do it. Couldn't make herself say *I love you*, either. He wouldn't believe her any more than he had Misty. Or, worse, he *would* believe her and feel sorry for her, and she refused to put herself in the position of having to accept either reaction.

"It's the best way, Kelly." His gaze locked with hers, and though she tried to read what he was feeling, thinking, it was as if he'd erected a barrier across his eyes to keep her out.

"Halloween's in a few days," he said. "I'll stay for that, okay? I'd like to see the kids go through that maze after spending so much time building the damn thing…"

A few days. That was all she had with him. So she'd take it and never let him know what it cost her to stay quiet. To let him go without asking him to stay.

"I'd like that, too," she said, and forced a smile that felt brittle and cold. "Where will you go?"

"I don't know," he admitted, stuffing his hands into his

jeans pockets. "There's a hotel in Hawaii I like. Maybe I'll go there for a few months."

"Hawaii." Well, that couldn't be farther from Utah, could it? He was so anxious to be apart from her, he was sticking an ocean between them. Couldn't be clearer than that. "Okay, then."

He reached for her again but let his hand fall before he touched her, and that, Kelly thought, was so sad it nearly broke her heart.

"It's best this way, Kelly."

"Probably," she said, agreeing with him if only to see a flicker of surprise flash across his face. "Don't worry about me, Micah. I was good before you got here and I'll be fine when you leave." She wondered idly if her tongue would simply rot and fall out of her head on the strength of those lies. She picked up the dirty sheets and the duvet and held them to her like a shield. "I'll just go start the washing."

Kelly felt his gaze on her as she left the room, so she didn't look back. There was only so much she was willing to put herself through.

The morning of Halloween, Kelly had the black lights up and ready, the CD of haunted house noises—growls, moans, chains rattling and a great witch's cackle—loaded up and a mountain of candy for all of the trick-or-treaters.

She also had the same unhappy stomach she'd been dealing with for days. She wasn't worse, but she wasn't getting better, either. Which was why she'd made a quick trip to the drugstore. Not being a complete idiot, she didn't go to the mom-and-pop shop in Banner, instead driving down to Ogden to shop anonymously. One thing Kelly didn't need was the gossips in town speculating on if she was pregnant or not before she knew herself. At that thought, her stomach did another quick spin.

Micah was in his office typing away—pretty much where he'd been since Naked Misty had crashed into their lives uninvited, precipitating his announcement that he was leaving early.

The only time Kelly saw him lately was at night in bed. And though he might be trying to keep distance between them during the day, in the darkness Micah turned to her. Sex was just as staggering, but shadowed now with a thread of sorrow that neither of them wanted to talk about.

Kelly wanted to be with him as much as she could, but at the same time, whenever they came together, another tiny piece of her heart broke off and shattered at her feet. Seconds, minutes, hours were ticking away. All of her life she'd loved Halloween, and now for the first time, she hated it. Because he'd be leaving in the morning and Kelly was already dreading it.

She looked into the mirror over the bathroom sink and saw the misery in her own eyes. Her face was paler than usual, her freckles standing out like gold dust on vanilla ice cream. Kelly lifted her fingers to touch the cold surface of Micah's emerald as it shone brightly in the overhead light.

The tick of her kitchen timer sounded like a tiny heartbeat in the bathroom. *Tiny heartbeat.* Was it possible? Was she pregnant? And if she was, what then? When the buzzer sounded, letting her know the three minutes were up, Kelly shut down the timer, picked up the early-pregnancy-test stick and held her breath, still unsure what she was hoping for.

"A plus sign." She released that breath and giddily took

another one. "Plus sign means *pregnant*." She laughed and suddenly she knew exactly how she felt about this. Kelly grinned at her reflection. All of her doubts and worries disappeared, washed away by a wave of pure joy. "You don't have the flu. You have a *baby. Micah's baby.*"

She couldn't stop smiling. The woman in the mirror looked like a fool, standing there with that wide grin on her face, but Kelly didn't mind. This was…amazing. The most amazing thing that had ever happened to her. When Sean died, Kelly had never intended to remarry, so she'd had to accept that she'd never have children. And that was painful.

Then along came Micah, who swept her off her feet and into a tangle of emotions that had left her reeling right from the first time he'd kissed her. The misery of the last few days, pretending she was all right with him leaving just slid off her shoulders. He was leaving, but he had also given her a gift. A wonderful gift. When Micah was gone, she'd still have a part of him with her. Always. She wouldn't be alone. She'd have her child and the memories of the man who'd given that child to her.

"I have to tell him," she said aloud, and looked down at the pregnancy test stick again as if to reassure herself that this was really happening. *It was.* Even though Micah was leaving, he had a right to know about his child. Her feelings were her own, but this baby, they shared.

Still smiling, she laid one hand over her belly in a protective gesture. "We'll be okay, you know. Just you and me, we'll be good."

Steeling herself, she nodded at her reflection, feeling new strength and determination fill her. When Micah left, her heart would be crushed. But she would have her baby to look after now and that was enough to keep her strong. "I'll tell him tonight. When Halloween's over. I'll tell him. And then I'll let him go."

Halloween was a rush of noise, laughter, shrieks and a seemingly never-ending stream of children. Micah had never done Halloween as a foster kid. And as an adult, he'd kept his distance from kids on general principle, so this holiday had never made much of an impact on him. Until celebrating it with Kelly.

Up and down the block, porch lights were on and pumpkins glowed. Even the two nosy sisters, Margie and Sally, were across the street sitting on their front porch. They were bundled up against the cold and sipping tea, but they clearly wanted to watch all the kids.

The pumpkins Micah had taken Kelly to buy on their first ride together were carved into faces and shining with glow sticks inside them. Orange lights were stretched out along the porch railing. Black crepe paper fluttered from the gingerbread trim on the house and twisted in the wind. Polyester spiderwebs were strung out everywhere, and ghosts were suspended from the big oak tree out front.

Kelly was dressed up, of course, as her idea of a farmer, in overalls, a long-sleeved plaid shirt and work boots. Her hair was in pigtails and the emerald peeked out from behind the collar of her shirt. From the porch Micah handed out candy to those who made it through the haunted maze. Kelly had stationed herself in front of the maze to walk the little kids through personally so they wouldn't be scared. Cries of "Trick or treat!" rang out up and down the block. Parents kept stopping to congratulate him on his engagement, and Micah had to go along with the lies because he'd promised.

He wondered, though, what all of these people would think of him tomorrow when he left town, supposedly walking out on Kelly? He frowned. Good thing he didn't care.

Passing out candy like it was about to be banned, Micah glanced around the yard and knew he was right to leave early. This wasn't his home. The sooner he got to a nice anonymous hotel the better. For everyone. Hell, he was handing out *candy*. He was carving pumpkins, for God's sake. Too much was changing and he didn't like it.

Even the tone of the book he'd been working on had changed. As if Kelly and what he'd found here with her had invaded even his fictional world. His heroine was now stronger, sexier, funnier than before. She stood up for herself and drove the hero as crazy as Kelly made Micah. Life was definitely imitating art. Or more the other way around.

"Micah!" A small hand tugged at the hem of Micah's coat, splintering his thoughts, which was just as well, since he had at least three hundred pounds of candy to give out.

Jacob, dressed like a lion, stared up at him. His lion's mane was yellow yarn and his nose had been colored black to match the whiskers drawn across his cheeks. "Are you scared cuz I'm a lion?"

"You bet." No point in dampening the excitement in the boy's eyes just because Micah was in a crap mood. "You make a good one."

"I can roar."

"I believe you."

"And you can come see my pumpkin all lit up, can't you? I put a happy face on it, but Daddy cut it cuz I'm too little to hold the knife."

"I will later," Micah said, wondering how he and this little boy had become friends. "Don't you have to go with your brothers to get more candy?"

"Yeah, and I can have lots my dad says even though Mommy says no cuz daddies are the boss when Mom's not looking my dad says and Mommy laughed at him but said okay."

Micah blinked. That was a lot of words for one sentence. He wondered what the kid would be like next year. Or the year after. The kid would grow up in this town, play football, fall in love, get married and start the whole cycle over again. But Micah wouldn't be there to see any of it. Soon Jacob would forget all about a friend named Micah. And wasn't that irritating? "No, it's not."

"What?"

He looked down at the tiny lion. "Nothing, Jacob. Go on. Find your brothers. Have fun."

"Okay!"

As he ran off, Micah looked around and realized that he didn't belong there. He wasn't a part of this town. He could pretend to be. But the truth was he didn't belong anywhere and that's how he liked it. Who the hell else could just pick up and take off for Hawaii at a moment's notice? He was damn lucky living just the way he wanted to, answering to no one. He liked his life just fine and it was time to get back to it.

Several minutes later, he saw Jacob's parents rush up to Kelly, talking fast, looking all around frantically. Something was wrong. Micah left the candy bowl on the porch and took the steps down through the crowd. "What's going on?"

Kelly looked at him, worry etched into her features. "Jacob's missing."

He snorted. "No, he's not. He was just here a few minutes ago."

Jacob's mother, Nora, shook her head. "Jonas saw Jacob run into the woods. He was following a deer and Jonas ran to get us instead of going in after him."

"It was the right thing to do," her husband said. "Or they'd both be lost. You stay here, Nora, in case he finds his way out on his own. I've got my cell. Call me if you see him." Then he looked at Kelly, Micah and a few of the other adults. "If we split up, we should be able to find him fast."

Kelly pulled her cell phone out of her overalls, hit the flashlight app and looked up at Micah. "He's only three."

Micah was already headed to the woods, fighting a hard, cold knot that had settled in his gut. "We'll find him."

The woods were thick and dark and filled with the kind of shadows that lived in Micah's imagination. It was the perfect setting for murder. Wisps of fog, moonlight trickling through bare branches of trees, the rustle of dead leaves on the ground and the quick, scuttling noise of something rushing through them. It was as if he'd written the scene himself. But it wasn't so good for a lost little boy. They moved as quickly as they could, their flashlights bobbing and dancing in the darkness. Roots jutted from the ground and Kelly tripped more than once as they hurried through the trees.

Kelly called for Jacob over and over, but there was no answer. The flashlight beams looked eerie, shining past the skeletons of trees to get lost in the pines. *Where the hell was he? He hadn't had enough time to go far.* Micah fought down his own sense of frustration and worry, but they came rushing back up. Anything could happen to a kid that size. His writer's mind listed every possibility and each was worse than the last.

He shouldn't have let the kid wander off to find his brothers alone.

"God," Kelly murmured, turning in a slow circle. "Where is he?"

"Hiding? Chasing the deer?" Micah strained his eyes, looking from right to left. "Who the hell knows?"

From a distance came the calls of the others searching for the little boy, and their flashlights looked like ghosts moving through the shadows. Micah had to wonder why Jacob wasn't answering. Was he hurt? God. Unconscious? In the next instant, Micah thought he heard something so he pulled Kelly to a stop.

"Listen. There it is again." He whipped his head around. "Over there."

"Jacob?" Micah shouted and this time he was sure he heard the little boy yell, "I'm lost."

"Thank God." Kelly ran right behind him and in seconds they'd found him. Jacob was scared and cold and his sneaker was caught under a tree root.

"The deer ran away," he said as if that explained everything.

Micah's heart squeezed painfully. "The deer doesn't matter. You okay, buddy? Are you hurt?"

"No," he said, "I'm stuck. And I'm cold. And I spilled my candy."

Kelly's flashlight caught his overturned pumpkin basket with the candy bars scattered around it. She quickly scooped them all up.

"See? Kelly's got your stuff and we can fix the rest," Micah said. "Kelly, call Jacob's dad. Tell him he's okay."

"Already on it," she said, and he heard her talking.

"Am I in trouble?" Jacob rubbed his eyes, smearing his whiskers.

Once he freed the boy's foot, Micah picked him up. "I don't think so. Your parents are probably going to be too happy to see you to be mad."

"Okay, good. I still need to get more candy." Jacob wrapped his arms around Micah's neck. "When we get back you wanna see my pumpkin?"

Kelly laughed. Micah caught her eye and grinned. Kids were damn resilient. More so than the adults they scared the life out of. He took a breath and slowly released it. With the boy's arms around his shoulders and Kelly smiling at him, Micah knew he'd become too attached. Not just to Kelly, but to this place. Even this little boy.

And as they left the shadows and stepped into the light again, Micah knew he'd stayed too long. He had to leave. While he still could.

A part of Kelly wanted to do just what he was sure she would. Cry, ask him to stay. But none of that would help. Just as she'd told Terry, if she had to force him to be with her, then what they had wasn't worth having.

She wouldn't tell him she loved him. He should know that already from the way they were together—and if he didn't, it was because he didn't *want* to know. So Kelly would keep her feelings to herself and remain perfectly rational.

Too bad it did nothing for the hole opening up in the center of her chest.

"I called for the jet," Micah said, stuffing his folded clothes into a huge black duffel. His suits were already in a garment bag laid out on the bed. Their bed.

"So you'll be in Hawaii late tonight."

"Or early in the morning, yeah." He zipped the bag closed, straightened up and faced her. His features were unreadable, his eyes shadowed. "Look, I know I said I was leaving tomorrow, but there's no reason to wait and I thought it would be easier this way."

Nothing about this was easy, but Kelly smiled. She would get through this. "Did you get everything?"

He glanced around the room, "Yeah. I did. Kelly…"

God, she didn't want him to say he was sorry. Didn't want to see sympathy in his eyes or hear it in his voice. She cut him off with the one sure way she knew to make him stop talking. "Before you go, I've got something you need to see."

His eyes narrowed on her suspiciously. "What is it?"

Kelly took a breath, pulled the test stick from her pocket and handed it to him. Still confused, he stared at her for another second or two, then his gaze dropped to the stick. "Is this—" He looked into her eyes. "You're pregnant?"

"I am. Thought I was getting sick, but no."

"We used protection."

"Apparently latex just isn't what it used to be." It was hard to smile, but she did it. Hard to keep her spirits up, but she was determined. Kelly took a step toward him. "Micah, I just thought you had a right to know about the baby. I—"

"How long have you known?"

"Since this morning."

"And you waited until I'm all packed and ready to go before you drop it on me?"

"Well," she said, her temper beginning to rise, "I didn't know you were leaving tonight, did I? Sprung that one on me."

"What's that supposed to mean?"

"Oh, come on, Micah." Her vow to remain rational was slowly unraveling. But then, she told herself, temper wasn't pitiful. "You know exactly what I mean. You wanted to catch me off guard so I wouldn't have time to plead with you not to go."

He stiffened. "That's not—"

"Relax. I'm not asking you to stay, Micah. Go ahead. Leave. I know you have to, or at least that you think you have to, which pretty much amounts to the same thing anyway. So go. I'm fine."

"You're pregnant," he reminded her.

Kelly laid both hands on her belly and for the first time that night gave him a real smile. "And will be, whether you're here or not. I'm *happy* about the baby. This is a gift, Micah. The best one you could have given me."

"A gift." He shook his head and paced the room, occasionally glancing down at the stick he still held. "Happy. My God, you and this place…"

"What're you talking about?" Now it was her turn to be confused, but she didn't like the cornered anger snapping in his eyes.

He shoved one hand through his hair. "You don't even see it, do you?" Muttering now, he said, "I told myself earlier that I didn't belong here and I know why. But you just don't get it."

"I don't appreciate being talked down to," Kelly snapped. "So if you've got something to say, just say it."

"You're pregnant and you're *happy* about it, even though I'm walking out and leaving you alone to deal with it."

"That's a bad thing? Micah—"

"You live in a land of kids and dogs." He choked out

a short laugh and shook his head as if even he couldn't believe all of this. "You paint pictures on windows, carve pumpkins." He threw up his hands. "You have nosy neighbors, deer in your garden and ghosts hanging from your tree, and none of that has anything to do with the real world. With the world I live in."

He was simmering. She could see frustration and anger rippling off him in waves and Kelly responded to it. If he was leaving, let them at least have truth between them when he did.

"Which world is that, Micah?" When he didn't speak, she prompted, "Go ahead. You're clearly on a roll. Tell me all about how little I know about reality."

He laughed, but there was no humor in the sound. Tossing the test stick onto the bed, he stalked to her side. "You want reality?" He looked down into her eyes and said, "I grew up in foster homes. My mother walked out when I was six and I never saw her again. I didn't have a damn friend until I met Sam in the navy, because I never stayed anywhere long enough to make one." His gaze bored into hers. "My world is hard and cruel. I don't have the slightest clue how to live in a land where everything is rosy all the damn time."

He was breathing fast, his eyes flashing, but he had nothing on Kelly. She could feel her temper building inside her like a cresting wave, and like a surfer at the beach, she jumped on board and rode it.

"Rosy?" Insult stained her tone as she poked him in the chest with her index finger. "You think my world is some cozy little space? That my life is perfect? My parents died when I was little and I came here to live when I was twelve. Then my grandfather died. My *husband* died. And my best friend's husband is in danger every day he's deployed."

He swiped one hand across his face. "God, Kelly…"

"Not finished," she said, tipping her head back to glare at him. "Life happens, Micah. Even in *rosy* little towns. People die. Three-year-olds get lost in the woods. And men who don't know any better walk away."

His jaw was tight and turmoil churned in his eyes. "Damn it, Kelly, I wasn't thinking."

She heard the contrition in his voice, but she couldn't let go of her anger. If she did, the pain would slide in and that might just finish her off. Thank God she hadn't told him she loved him—that would have been the capper to this whole mess.

"You're the one who doesn't get it, Micah," she said. "Bad things happen. You just have to keep going."

"Or you stop," he countered. "And back away." Micah shook his head. "I don't know how to do this, Kelly. You. This town. A *baby*, for God's sake. Trust me when I say I'm not the guy you think I am."

"No, Micah," she said, feeling sorrow swallow the anger. "You're not the guy *you* think you are."

He snorted and shook his head. "Still surprising me." He walked to the bed, picked up his bags and stood there, staring at her. "Anything you need, call me. You or the baby. You've got my cell number."

"I do," she said, lifting her chin and meeting his gaze steadily. "But I won't need anything, Micah. I don't want anything from you." All she wanted was *him*. But she realized now she couldn't have him. Her heart was breaking and that empty place in her heart was spreading, opening like a black hole, devouring everything in its path.

She felt hollowed out, and looking at him now only made that worse. He was close enough to touch and so far away she couldn't reach him.

"Goodbye, Kelly," he said, and, carrying his bags, he walked past her.

She heard him on the stairs. Heard the front door open and then close, and he was gone.

Dropping to the end of the bed, Kelly looked around the empty room and listened to the silence.

Ten

By the following afternoon, Kelly had most of the Halloween decorations down and stacked to be put away. This chore used to depress her, since the anticipation and fun of the holiday was over for another year. But today she already felt as low as she could go.

"I still can't believe he left, knowing you're pregnant."

Kelly sighed. She'd told her best friend the whole story and somehow felt better the more outraged Terry became. But it had been an hour and she was still furious. "Terry, he was always going to leave, remember?"

"Yeah, but *pregnant* changes things."

"No, it doesn't."

"Plus," Terry added, "I can't believe you're pregnant before me. Jimmy's got his work cut out for him when he gets home."

Kelly laughed as Terry had meant her to. What did

people without best friends do when the world exploded? Her mind wandered as she rolled up the orange twinkle lights from the porch and carefully stored them in a bag marked for Halloween.

She'd done a lot of thinking the night before—since God knows she hadn't gotten any sleep—and had come to the conclusion that she'd done the right thing. Kelly didn't want Micah to stay because of the baby. She wanted him to stay for *her*.

"If he had stayed because I'm pregnant," she told Terry, "sooner or later, he'd resent us both and *then* he'd leave." Shaking her head firmly, she said, "This way is better. Not great, but better."

"Okay, I get that, and I hate it when you're mature and I'm not," Terry said. "But I'd still feel better if Jimmy were here and I could tell him to go beat Micah up."

Kelly laughed, hugged her best friend and said, "It's the thought that counts."

Her cell phone rang and she cringed at the caller ID. Looking at Terry, she said, "It's Gran."

"Oh, boy." Shaking her head, Terry said, "Let's go inside. You can sit down and I'll make some tea."

As the phone continued to ring, Kelly mused, "It's a shame I can't have wine because, boy, after this conversation, I'm going to need some."

Kelly wasn't looking forward to breaking this news to her grandmother, but she might as well get it over with. She followed Terry into the house and answered the phone. "Hi, Gran."

"Sweetie, I found the prettiest wedding dress—it would be perfect on you. I'm going to send you the picture, okay, and I don't want to interfere, but—"

Kelly sat down at the table and winced at Terry, already moving around the kitchen. Bracing herself, she interrupted her grandmother's flow. "Gran, wait. I've got something to tell you."

"What is it, dear? Oh, hold on. Linda's here, I'm putting you on speaker."

Great. Kelly sighed and winced again. "Well, the good news is, I'm pregnant!"

Terry frowned at her and mouthed, *Chicken*, as she wandered the kitchen making tea. Kelly set the phone on the table, hit speaker and her grandmother's and Aunt Linda's voices spilled into the room.

"Oh, a baby!"

"That's so wonderful," Linda cooed. "You know my Debbie keeps telling me she's going to one of those sperm banks, but she hasn't done it yet. You should talk to her, Kelly."

Terry laughed and once again, Kelly felt bad for her cousin Debbie. First an engagement and now a baby. She was putting a lot of pressure on Debbie and Tara.

"Oh, Micah must be so excited," Gran said.

"Yeah," Terry threw in. "He's thrilled."

Kelly scowled at her. *Not helping.*

"That's the thing, Gran," Kelly said quickly. "The bad news is that Micah and I broke up."

"What?" Twin shrieks carried all the way from Florida, and Kelly had the distinct feeling she might have heard the two women without the phone.

Terry set out some cookies and brewed tea while Kelly went through the whole thing for the second time that day. A half hour later, Gran and Aunt Linda were both fuming.

"I'll get Big Eddie to go out there and give that boy a punch in the nose."

"Oh, for heaven's sake, Linda," Gran said. "Big Eddie's seventy-five years old."

"He's tough, though," Linda insisted. "Spry, too and I have reason to know."

"Spry or not, you can't ask the man to fly somewhere just to punch someone, no matter how badly he deserves it," Gran snapped.

Terry set cups of tea on the table, then gave two thumbs-ups in approval.

"No one needs to beat anybody up," Kelly said, sipping her fresh cup of tea. "I had no idea my family was so violent. Terry already offered to have Jimmy do the honors."

"Terry's a good girl, I always said so."

"Thanks, Gran," Terry called out.

"What are you going to do about all of this, Kelly?" Gran asked.

"I'm gonna have a baby," she said, then added quickly, "and I'm going to be fine, Gran. I don't want you rushing home to take care of me."

"She's got me right here," Terry said.

"This just doesn't seem right, though," Gran mumbled. "You shouldn't be alone."

Kelly ate a cookie and thought about another one.

"Get a clue, Bella," Linda told her. "The girl doesn't want you there hovering. She's got things to do, to think about, isn't that right, Kelly?"

If she'd been closer, Kelly would have kissed her aunt. "Thanks, Aunt Linda. Honest, Gran, I'm fine. Micah's doing what he has to do and so am I."

"I don't like it," her grandmother said, then sighed. "But you're a grown woman, Kelly, and I'll respect your decisions."

Terry's eyes went wide in surprise and Kelly stared at the phone, stunned. "Really?"

"You'll figure it out, honey," Gran said.

"You will," Linda added. "And if you need us for anything, you call and say so. A great-grandchild's something to celebrate, like I keep telling Debbie."

"This one's mine," Gran pointed out.

"Oh, you can share," Linda said. "I'll share when Debbie finally comes through."

Terry was laughing and Kelly almost cried. She'd been hit by a couple of huge emotional jolts in the last twenty-four hours, but the bottom line was that she had her family. She wasn't alone. She just didn't have Micah.

And that was going to hurt for a long time.

For a solid week, Micah holed up in his penthouse suite. He couldn't work. Couldn't sleep. Had no interest in eating. He lived on coffee and sandwiches from room service he forced down. A deep, simmering fury was his only companion and even at that, he knew it was useless. Hell, *he* was the one who left. Why was he so damn mad?

The second week gone was no better, though anger shifted to worry and that made him furious, too. He hadn't wanted any of this. Hadn't asked to care. Didn't want to wonder if Kelly was all right. If the baby was okay. And it was November and that meant snow for her, and he started thinking about her broken-down truck and her riding around in it, and that drove him even crazier.

Micah wasn't used to this. Once he moved on from a place, he wiped it from his mind as if it didn't even exist anymore. He was always about the next place. He didn't do the past. He moved around on his own and liked it.

He didn't *miss* people, so why the hell did he wake up every morning reaching for Kelly in that big empty bed?

"You Kelly Flynn?"

The burly man in a blue work shirt and khaki slacks held a clipboard and looked at her through a pair of black-framed glasses.

"Yes, I am. Who're you?"

"I'm Joe Hackett. I'm here to deliver your truck?"

"My what?" Kelly stepped onto the porch of the cottage and looked out at the driveway. Parked behind her old faithful truck was a brand-new one. November sunlight made the chrome sparkle against the deep glossy red paint. It was bigger than her old one, with a shorter bed but a longer cab with a back seat bench. It was shiny. And new. And beautiful. Kelly loved it. But it couldn't be hers. "There must be some mistake."

"No mistake, lady," Joe said. "Sign here and she's all yours. Paid for free and clear including tax and license."

She looked from the truck to the clipboard and saw her name and address on the delivery sheet. So not a mistake. Which could mean only one thing. Micah had sent it.

He'd been gone two weeks. The longest two weeks of her life. And, suddenly, here he was. Okay, not *him*, but his presence, definitely. Tears filled her eyes and she had to blink frantically to clear her vision. What was she supposed to think about this? He leaves but buys her a new truck? Why would he do it?

"Lady? Um, just sign here so we can get going?" He was giving her the nervous look most men wore around crying women.

"Right. Okay." She scrawled her name on the bottom line and took the keys Joe handed over. As he and another guy left in a compact car, Kelly walked to her new truck. She ran her hand across the gleaming paint, then opened the driver's-side door and got in. The interior sparkled just as brightly as the outside. Leather seats. Seat warmers. Backup camera. Four-wheel drive. She laughed sadly. The truck had so many extras it could probably drive itself.

"Micah, why?" She sat back and stared through the windshield at the Victorian. Her fingers traced across the surface of the emerald she still wore, and she wondered where he was now and if he missed her as much as she missed him.

Micah hated the hotel. He felt like a rat in a box.

The penthouse suite was huge, and still he felt claustrophobic. He couldn't just step outside and feel a cold fall breeze. No, he'd have to take an elevator down thirty floors and cross a lobby just to get to the damn parking lot.

He didn't keep the doors to the terrace open because they let in the muffled roar of the city far below. He'd gotten so used to the quiet at Kelly's place that the noise seemed intrusive rather than comforting.

Three weeks now since he'd left Kelly, and the anger, the worry, the outrage had all boiled down into a knot of guilt, which made him mad all over again.

What the hell did he have to feel guilty about? She'd known going in that he wasn't going to stay. And if she'd wanted him to stay why didn't she say so?

No. Not Kelly. *I'm fine. I have the baby. We don't need anything from you.*

"Perfect. She doesn't need me. I don't need her. Then we're both happy. *Right?*" Was she driving that new truck? Had it snowed yet? Had she gotten the plow blade attached to the new truck? Was she out plowing people's roads and drives? Was she doing it alone?

God, he hated this room.

Pregnant.

She was carrying *his* kid, and what the hell was he supposed to do about that? If she'd wanted his help, she would have said so. But she didn't beg him not to leave. Hell, she hadn't even watched him go. What the hell was that about? Did she just not give a damn?

Irritation spiking, he grabbed his cell phone, hit the speed dial and waited for Sam to answer.

"Hi, Micah. What's up?"

What *wasn't* up? Micah hadn't talked to Sam since leaving Utah mainly because he just hadn't wanted to talk to anyone, really. Now he'd been alone with his own thoughts for too long and needed…something. He pushed one hand through his hair, walked to the open terrace doors and stared out at the ocean. The last time he'd had an ocean view, he'd been on a different terrace. With Kelly. And *that* memory would kill him if he started thinking about it. So he didn't.

"Kelly's pregnant." He hadn't meant to just say it, but it was as if the words had been waiting for a chance to jump out.

"That's great. Congratulations, man."

He scowled. "Yeah, thanks I guess. Kelly told me about the baby the night I left."

"You left? Where the hell are you?"

"Hawaii." Paradise, his ass. There was too much sunshine here. People were too damn cheerful.

"Why?"

"Because it was time to go." Micah scrubbed one hand

across his jaw and remembered he hadn't shaved in a couple weeks. "I couldn't stay. Things were getting too—"

"Real?" Sam asked.

He frowned at the phone. "What's that supposed to mean?"

"It means that you've never lived an ordinary life, Micah. You went from your crap childhood to the navy to posh hotels."

Micah scowled into the wide mirror over the gas fireplace as he listened.

"You've never had a real woman, either. All those models and actresses? They weren't looking for anything more than you were—one night at a time." Sam paused. "Trust me when I say that has nothing to do with the real world."

God, hadn't he thrown practically the same accusation at Kelly that last night with her?

"What's your point?" God. *Points*. He rubbed his eyes tiredly. They felt like marbles in a bucket of sand.

"My point is—Kelly is *real*. What you had there mattered, Micah, whether you admit it or not, and I think it scared the crap out of you."

"I wasn't scared." He remembered telling little Jacob that everybody got scared sometimes. That included him, didn't it?

The realization was humbling.

"Sure you were," Sam said jovially. "Every guy is scared out of his mind when he meets the one woman who matters more than anything."

"I never said anything like that—"

"You didn't have to, Micah." He chuckled, which was damn irritating. "I've known you long enough to figure things out for myself. For example. When's the last time you left a hotel in the middle of a book?"

He blew out a breath. "Well…"

"Never, that's when," Sam told him. "You stay six months at every place you go. This time you bolt after three? Come on, Micah."

The man in the mirror looked confused. Worried. Was that it? Had he run from Kelly because she mattered? Because he was afraid? He turned away from the damn mirror because he couldn't stand to see the questions in his own eyes. "Look, I didn't call for advice. I just wanted you to know where I am."

"Great, but you get the advice anyway," Sam said. "Do yourself a favor and go back to Kelly. Throw yourself on her mercy and maybe she'll take your sorry ass back."

Micah glared at the room because it wasn't the Victorian. Because Kelly wasn't here with him. Because he was hundreds of miles away from her and he didn't know what she was doing. How she was feeling. "How the hell can I do that? What do I know about being somebody's father, for God's sake?"

"If nothing else," Sam said, "you know what *not* to do. And that's stay away from your own kid. You grew up without a father. That's what you want for your baby, too?"

Putting it like that gave Micah something to think about. He'd done to his kid exactly what his mother had done to him. "I'm no good at this stuff, Sam."

"Nobody is, Micah. We just figure it out as we go along."

"Well, that's comforting."

"Figure it out, Micah. Don't be an ass."

On that friendly piece of advice, Sam hung up, leaving Micah with too much to think about.

The first snow hit two days later, but it was a mild storm after warm days, so the snow wasn't sticking. Which meant Kelly didn't have to go out and clear any drives or private roads. Instead, she was cozy in the Victorian, enjoying the snap and hiss of the fireplace. She'd been staying in the cottage because she didn't want to torture herself with memories of Micah in the Victorian. But, with winter here, she wanted the fireplace, so she convinced herself that the only way to get past the pain of missing Micah was by facing it.

With a cup of tea, a book and the fire, the setting would have been perfect. If Micah were there.

The front door opened suddenly and Kelly's heart jolted. She jumped up, ran to the hall, and all of the air left her lungs as she stood there in shock staring at Micah. Snow dusted his shoulders and his hair. He dropped his duffel bag, slammed the front door and flipped the dead bolt. When he turned around and saw her, he scowled.

"Lock the damn door, Kelly. *Anybody* could just walk into the house."

She laughed shortly and seriously considered racing down the hall and throwing herself into his arms. It was only pride that kept her in place. "Anybody did."

"Very funny." Still scowling fiercely, he walked down the hall, took her arm and steered her into the living room.

"What're you doing, Micah?" She pulled her arm from his grip even though she wanted nothing more than to hold on to him. And she desperately wished she wasn't wearing her new flannel pajamas decorated with dancing pandas. "Why are you here?"

His gaze moved over her as if he were etching her image into his brain. Then he stepped back and stalked to the fireplace. Turning around to face her from a safe distance, he said, "You know, I thought I was doing the right thing."

"By leaving?"

"Yeah." He sighed heavily. Shaking his head, Micah stared down at the fire for a long minute before lifting his gaze to hers. "Kelly, I have no idea how to do *this*." He waved one hand to encompass the house, her, the baby and everything else that was so far out of his experience. "You know how I told you I was engaged once before? I said it didn't take?"

"Yes." She'd wondered about that woman in his past.

"I ended it because I didn't care enough. I figured I was incapable of caring enough," he ground out, and she could see that the words were costing him. "Then I met you."

Heat began to melt the ice that had been around her heart for weeks. Hope rose up in her chest, and Kelly clung to it but kept quiet, wanting him to go on. To say it all.

He threw his hands high, then snorted. "Hell, I've never known anyone like you. You made me nuts. Made me feel things I never have. Want things I never wanted."

"Thanks."

Micah laughed and shook his head. "See? Like that. You surprise me all the damn time, Kelly. I never know where I'm standing with you and, turns out, I like it."

"You do?"

"Gotta have it," he admitted, and swallowed hard. He

took a step toward her, then stopped. "The last three weeks I've been so bored I thought I was losing my mind. I was at a hotel I'd been in before and this time, I hated it. Hated that it was small and there was no damn yard with deer and kids running through it. Hated that it was so damn noisy—but the wrong kind of noise, you know?"

"No," she admitted, smiling. "What are you saying, Micah?"

"I'm saying—all I could think about was you. And the baby. And this place. But mostly *you.*"

Tears were coming and she couldn't stop them this time. Didn't even try. They rolled unheeded down her cheeks as Kelly kept her gaze fixed on the only man in the world for her.

"You love me," he said, pointing a finger at her.

"Do I?" she said, and her smile widened.

"Damn right you do." Micah started walking—well, *stalking* the perimeter of the room. "A woman like you… love shows. Not just the sex, though that was great, for sure."

"It was."

"But you were there. Every day. You laughed with me. You cooked with me." He glared at her. "Yet, when I tell you I'm leaving, you just say, have a nice trip and by the way I'm pregnant."

Kelly flushed. "Well, that's not exactly—"

"Basically," he snapped. "That was it. And I finally started wondering why you hadn't told me that you love me. Why didn't you use the baby as a lever to keep me here? Why didn't you beg me to stay?"

She stiffened and tried to look as dignified as possible in her panda pj's. "I don't beg."

"No," he said thoughtfully, his gaze locked with hers.

"You wouldn't. Just like you wouldn't coerce me to stay. You were way sneakier than that."

"Me?" Now Kelly laughed. "I am *not* sneaky."

"This time you were," he said, and walked across the room to her. "You let me go, knowing I'd be miserable without you. You didn't say you loved me because you knew I'd wonder about that. And you didn't tell me I loved you because you wanted me to figure it out for myself. You wanted me to be away long enough to realize I was being a damn fool."

"That was clever of me." Or would have been if she'd actually planned it. She swayed, bit her bottom lip and held her breath. "And did you? Figure it all out?"

"I'm here, aren't I?" He blew out a breath, grabbed her and pulled her in close to him. Wrapping his arms around her, he rested his chin on top of her head and whispered, "You feel so good. This—*us*—is so good. I love you, Kelly. Didn't know I *could* love. But maybe I was only waiting to find you."

"Oh, Micah…" She held on to him, nestled her head against his chest and listened to the steady beat of his heart. It was as if every one of her dreams was coming true. The last three weeks had been so painful. Now there was so much joy she felt as if she were overflowing. "I love you, too."

"I know."

She laughed and tipped her head back to stare at him. "Sure of yourself, are you?"

"I am now," he admitted. "And I'm sure about this, too. You're going to have to marry me for real. It's the only answer. I have to be here in this big old house with you. I need to be with you at Christmas. I have to help you run for mayor. And next year, Jacob and I will help

you plant the pumpkin patch. I want to meet Jimmy—
I think he and I can be friends when we bond over our
crazy women."

Kelly's heart was flying. "I'll have to give you a point
for that crazy proposal."

He grinned. "Not a proposal. Just an acceptance of
your earlier proposal. Remember?"

"You're right. So, no points."

"No more points at all," he said softly. "Say yes and
we *both* win."

Kelly laughed, delighted with him, with everything.
"Of course, yes."

"Good." He nodded as if checking things off a mental list. "That's settled. I've got to ride with you when
you start plowing and—" He stopped. "Did you like the
truck?"

She laughed again, a little wildly, but she didn't care.
"I love it, you crazy man."

"Huh. You plow snow, but I'm crazy." He shook his
head and stared down at her with hope and relief and *love*
shining in his eyes.

"I never should have left, Kelly," he whispered, "but
in a way I guess I had to, because I never learned how
to *stay.* But I want to stay now, Kelly. With you. With
our kids…"

"Kids?" she asked hopefully. "Plural?"

He grinned. "It's a big house. We should do our best
to fill it."

God, this was everything Kelly had ever wanted,
and more. The firelight threw dancing shadows across
Micah's face, making his eyes shine with hope and promise and love. "I love you so much, Micah. I'm so glad
you came home."

He cupped her face in his palms and kissed her tenderly. "The only home I ever want is wherever you are. For the first and last time in my life, I'm in love. And I never want to lose it."

"You won't," she promised. "*We* won't."

He blew out a breath and said, "Damn straight we won't. Now. For part two of my brilliant plan."

"You had a plan?"

"Still do and I think you'll like it," he said, sweeping her up in his arms, surprising a laugh out of her. He sat down in one of the overstuffed chairs and held her on his lap. He frowned at her pajamas. "What are those? Dogs?"

"Pandas."

"Sure. Why not?" Shaking his head, he said, "I'm thinking we hire a jet and fly to Florida tomorrow—"

"Tomorrow?"

"—pick up your grandmother and your aunt, and then all of us go to New York for a week. Maybe the Ritz-Carlton. I think they'd like that place."

"What?"

He shrugged. "I've never had a family before. I'd like to get to know them. Have them meet Sam and Jenny and the kids, because they're as close to family as I've ever known. And while we're there, your grandmother can help you pick out that ring we talked about."

"Oh, Micah!" Many more surprises and her head would simply spin right off her shoulders. She threw her arms around his neck and kissed him hard and fast. Then something occurred to her. "We'd better call first, though."

"Why?"

"I told Gran and Aunt Linda that we broke up and

they were arranging for one of the seniors to fly out and punch you in the nose."

"More surprises," Micah said, grinning. "I'll risk it if you will."

"Absolutely," she said.

"I love you, Kelly Flynn."

"I love you, Micah Hunter," she said, melting against him. As he bent his head to claim another kiss, Kelly whispered, "Welcome home."

* * * * *

ONE MONTH WITH THE MAGNATE

MICHELLE CELMER

To my editor Charles, who has been, and continues to be, an amazing source of support and encouragement. It has been a privilege, a joy and a lot of fun working with you.

One

This was, without a doubt, the lowest Isabelle Winthrop-Betts had ever sunk.

Not even the sting of her father's open palm across her cheek had caused the humiliation she was feeling now thanks to Emilio Suarez, a man she once loved with all her heart and had planned to marry.

Her father had made sure that never happened. And Isabelle couldn't blame Emilio for the bitterness in his eyes as he sat behind his desk in his corner office at Western Oil headquarters, like a king on a throne addressing a local peasant.

Thanks to her husband, Leonard, that was really all she was now. She had gone from being one of the richest women in Texas, to a pauper. Homeless, penniless, widowed and about to be thrown in prison for fraud. And all because she had been too naive and trusting. Because when her husband had put documents in front of her, instead of reading them, she had blindly signed. How could she question the man who had rescued her from hell? Who had probably saved her life?

And the son of a bitch had up and died before he could exonerate her.

Thanks, Lenny.

"You have a lot of nerve asking me for help," Emilio said in the deep, caramel-smooth voice that strummed every one of her frayed nerve endings, but the animosity in his tone curdled her blood. Not that he wasn't justified in his anger, not after the way she'd broken his heart, but she'd had no choice. She didn't expect him to understand that, she just hoped he would take pity on her.

His charcoal gray eyes bore through her, and she fought not to wither under their scrutiny. "Why come to me? Why not go to your rich friends?"

Because his brother, Alejandro, was prosecuting her case. Besides, she had no friends. Not anymore. They had all invested with Lenny. Some had lost millions.

"You're the only one who can help me," she said.

"Why would I want to? Maybe I want to see you rot in prison."

She swallowed the hurt his words caused, that he hated her that much.

Well, he would be happy to learn that according to her lawyer, Clifton Stone, nothing would prevent that now. The evidence against her was overwhelming and her best bet was a plea bargain. And while the idea of spending even another minute in jail terrified her, she was prepared to take full responsibility for her actions and accept any punishment they considered appropriate. Unfortunately, Lenny had gotten her mother involved in his scams, too. After suffering years of physical and emotional abuse from her husband, Adriana Winthrop deserved some happiness. Not to spend the rest of her life in prison. Not for something that was Isabelle's fault.

"I don't care what happens to me," Isabelle told him. "I want my mother's name cleared. She had no part in any of Leonard's scams."

"Leonard's and *your* scams," he corrected.

She swallowed hard and nodded.

One dark brow rose. "So, you're admitting your guilt?"

If blind trust was a crime, she was definitely guilty. "It's my fault that I'm in this mess."

"This is not a good time for me."

She'd seen coverage on the news about the accident at the refinery. The explosion and the injured men. She'd tried to visit him last week, but the front of the Western Oil headquarters building had been crawling with media. She would have waited another week or two, but she was running out of time. It had to be now. "I know it's a bad time and I'm sorry. This couldn't wait."

Arms folded across his chest, he sat back in his chair and studied her. In a suit, with his closely cropped hair combed back, he barely resembled the boy she'd known from her adolescence. The one she had fallen head over heels in love with the instant she'd laid eyes on him, when she was twelve and he was fifteen. Although, it had taken him until college to notice her.

His mother had been their housekeeper and in her father's eyes, Emilio would never be good enough for his precious daughter. That hadn't stopped her from seeing Emilio in secret, fully aware of the price she would pay if they were caught. But they had been lucky—until her father learned of their plans to elope.

Not only had he punished her severely, he'd fired Emilio's mother. He accused her of stealing from them, knowing that no one else would hire her.

She wished her father could see them now. Emilio sitting there like the master of the universe and her begging for his help. He would be rolling in his grave.

See Daddy, he was good enough for me after all. Probably even better than I deserved.

Emilio never would have hurt her, never would have sacrificed her reputation out of greed. He was honest and trustworthy and loyal.

And right now, seriously pissed at her.

"So you're doing this for your mother?" he asked.

Isabelle nodded. "My lawyer said that with all the media attention, it's unlikely that your brother will be willing to deal. She'll serve some time."

"Maybe I'd like to see her rot in prison, too," he said.

She felt her hackles rise. Adriana Winthrop had never been anything but kind to him and his mother. She had done *nothing* to hurt them. She'd only been guilty of being married to an overbearing, abusive bastard. And even that wasn't entirely her fault. She had tried to leave and he'd made her live to regret it.

"Your appearance," he said. "Is it supposed to make me feel sorry for you?"

She resisted the urge to look down at the outdated blouse and ill-fitting slacks she had rummaged from the bag of clothes her mother had been donating to charity. Obviously he'd expected her to be wearing an outfit more suited to her previous station, but when her possessions had been seized, she kept nothing. For now, this was the best she could do.

"I don't feel sorry for you, Isabelle. It seems to me you're getting exactly what you deserve."

That was one thing they could agree on.

She could see that coming here had been a waste of time. He wasn't going to help her. He was too bitter.

Oh, well. It had been worth a try.

She rose from the chair, limp with defeat. Her voice trembled as she said, "Well, thank you for seeing me, Mr. Suarez."

"Sit down," he snapped.

"For what? You obviously have no intention of helping me."

"I never said I wouldn't help you."

Something in his eyes softened the slightest bit and hope welled up inside of her. She lowered herself into the chair.

"I'll talk to my brother on your mother's behalf, but I expect something in return."

She had expected as much, but the calculating look he wore sent a cold chill down her spine. "What?"

"You will agree to be my live-in housekeeper for thirty days. You'll cook for me, clean my house, do my laundry. Whatever I ask. At the end of the thirty days, if I'm satisfied with your performance, I'll talk to my brother."

In other words, he would make her work for him the way his mother had worked for her. Clever. Obviously he saw her plea for help as an opportunity to get revenge. What had happened to the sweet and kindhearted boy she used to know? The one who never would have been capable of dreaming up such a devious plan, much less have the gall to implement it. He had changed more than she could ever have guessed, and it stung to know that it was probably her fault. Had she hurt him so much when she left that he'd hardened his heart?

And what of his *offer?* The day her father died she had vowed never to let a man control her again. But this wasn't about her. She was doing this for her mother. She *owed* her. Besides, she had swallowed her pride so many times since the indictment, she was getting used to the bitter taste.

Despite what Emilio believed, she was no longer the

shy, timid girl of her youth. She was strong now. Anything he could dish out, she could take.

"How do I know I can trust you?" she asked. "How do I know that after the thirty days you won't change your mind?"

He leaned forward, eyes flaming with indignation as they locked on hers. "Because I have never been anything but honest with you, Isabelle."

Unlike her, his tone implied. He was right. Even though she'd had a valid reason for breaking her word, but that hardly seemed worth mentioning. Even if she told him the truth she doubted he would believe her. Or care.

He leaned back in his chair. "Take some time to think about it if you'd like."

She didn't need time. She didn't have any to spare. Less than six weeks from now she and her lawyer would meet with the prosecutor, and her lawyer warned her that it didn't look good. For her or her mother.

This wasn't going to be a pleasant thirty days, but at least she knew Emilio wouldn't physically harm her. He may have become cold and callous, but he had never been a violent man. He'd never made her feel anything but safe.

What if he changed? a little voice in her head taunted, but she ignored it. The decision had already been made.

She sat straight, squared her shoulders and told him, "I'll do it."

Isabelle Winthrop was a viper.

A lying, cheating, narcissistic viper.

Yet Emilio couldn't deny that despite the fifteen years that had passed, she was still the most physically beautiful woman he had ever laid eyes on.

But her soul was as black as tar.

She'd had him duped, all those years ago. He thought

she loved him. He had believed, despite the fact that she was a Winthrop and he was the son of a domestic servant, they would be married and live happily ever after. She told him she didn't care about the money or the status. She would be happy so long as they had each other. And he had fallen for it, right up until the minute he read the article in the paper announcing her marriage to finance guru Leonard Betts. A multi*billionaire.*

So much for her not caring about money and status. What other reason would she have to marry a man twenty-five years older?

When all was said and done, his relationship with Isabelle hadn't been a total loss. She had taught Emilio that women were not to be trusted, and he'd learned from her deceit never to put his heart on the line again.

That didn't mean he wasn't ready to dish out a little good old-fashioned revenge.

As for her being a criminal like her husband, he wasn't sure what to believe. According to the law, if she signed it, she was legally responsible. Now that Leonard was dead, someone had to pay.

Guilty or not, as far as Emilio was concerned, she was getting exactly what she deserved. But he was not prepared to be dragged down with her.

"There's just one condition," he told her.

She nervously tucked her pale blond hair behind her ears. Hair that he used to love running his fingers through. It was once shiny and soft and full of body, but now it looked dull and lifeless. "What condition?"

"No one can know about this." If it got out that he was helping her, it could complicate his chances for the CEO position at Western Oil. He was in competition with COO Jordan Everett and his brother, Nathan Everett, Chief Brand Officer. Both were friends and worthy opponents.

But Emilio deserved the position more. He'd earned it through more hard work than either of them could ever imagine with their Harvard educations that Daddy footed the bill for.

Maybe he was a fool to risk everything he'd worked so hard for, but Isabelle was offering an opportunity for revenge that he just couldn't pass up. After his father died, his mother worked her fingers to the bone trying to provide for Emilio and his three brothers. It was years after being fired by the Winthrops when she finally admitted to her children the verbal abuse she'd endured from Isabelle's father. Not to mention occasional improper sexual advances. But the pay was good, so she'd had no choice but to tolerate it. And after he had fired her, accused her of stealing from them, no respectable family would even think of hiring her.

Now Emilio's mother, his entire family, would finally be vindicated.

"Are you sure you don't want to brag to all of your friends?" Isabelle asked him.

"I'm the chief financial officer of this company. It wouldn't bode well for me or Western Oil if people knew I was in business with a woman indicted for financial fraud. If you tell a soul, not only is the deal off, but I will see that you *and* your mother rot in prison for a very long time."

"I can't just disappear for thirty days. My mother will want to know where I am."

"Then tell her you're staying with a friend until you get back on your feet."

"What about the authorities? I'm out on bond. They need to know where I'm staying. I could go back to jail."

"I'll take care of it," he said. He was sure he could work something out with his brother.

She looked wary, like she thought maybe it was a trick, but clearly she had no choice. She needn't have worried though. Unlike her, he honored his word.

"I won't tell anyone," she said.

"Fine." He slid a pad of paper and a pen across the desk to her. "Write down where you're currently staying and I'll have my driver come by to get you tonight."

She leaned forward to jot down the address. He assumed she would be staying with her mother, or in a high-class hotel, but what she wrote down was the name and address for a motel in one of the seedier parts of town. She really must have been in dire straits financially. Or she was pretending to be.

Several million dollars of the money they had stolen had never been recovered. For all he knew, she had it stashed somewhere. Of course, if she had been planning to run, wouldn't she have done it by now? Or was she waiting to cut a deal for her mother, then intending to skip town?

It was something to keep in mind.

"Be ready at seven," he told her. "Your thirty days will start tomorrow. Agreed?"

She nodded, chin held high. She wouldn't look so proud when he put her to work. Isabelle had never lifted a finger to do a thing for herself. He was sorry he wouldn't be home to witness what he was sure would be a domestic disaster.

The thought almost made him smile.

"Do you need a ride back to the hotel?" he asked.

She shook her head. "I borrowed my mother's car."

"That must be a change for you. Having to drive yourself places. It's a wonder you even remember how."

He could tell that she wanted to shoot back a snarky comment, but she kept her mouth shut and her eyes all but dared him to give it his best shot. She was tough, but she had no idea who she was dealing with. He wasn't the naive, trusting man he'd been before.

He stood and she did the same. He reached out to shake on the deal, and she slipped her finely boned hand into his—her breath caught when he enclosed it firmly, *possessively.* Though she tried to hide it, being close to him still did something to her. Which was exactly what he was counting on. Because bringing her into his home as a housekeeper was only a ruse to execute his true plan.

When they were together, Isabelle had insisted they wait until they were married to make love, so he had honored her wishes for a torturous year. Then she left him high and dry. Now it was time for some payback.

He would seduce Isabelle, make her want him, make her *beg* for it, then reject her.

By the time he was through with her, prison would seem like Club Med.

TWO

"Is that who I think it was?"

Emilio looked up from his computer to find Adam Blair, the current CEO of Western Oil, standing in his office doorway. He should have known word of his *visitor* would get around fast. Her disguise—if that had been her intention with the ridiculous clothes, the straight, lifeless hair and absence of makeup—not to mention the fake name she had given the guards when she insisted on seeing him, obviously hadn't worked. When he saw her standing there in the lobby, her shoulders squared, head held high, looking too proud for her own good, he should have sent her away, but curiosity had gotten the best of him.

Emilio had warned Adam months ago, just before news of the Ponzi scheme became public, that he had a past connection to Isabelle. But he'd never expected her to turn up at his office. And he sure as hell hadn't considered that she would have the audacity to ask for his help. She was probably accustomed to getting exactly what she wanted.

"That was Isabelle Winthrop-Betts," he told Adam.

"What did she want?"

"My help. She wants her mother's name cleared, and she wants me to talk to my brother on her behalf."

"What about her own name?"

"She more or less admitted her guilt to me. She intends to take full responsibility for everything."

Adam's brows rose. "That's…surprising."

Emilio thought so, too. With a federal prosecutor for a sibling, he had heard of every scheme imaginable from every type of criminal. Freely admitting guilt wasn't usually one of them. Isabelle was clearly up to something. He just hadn't figured out what. He had considered that she and her mother were planning to take the unrecovered money and disappear, but why bother exonerating her first? Maybe he could gain her trust, encourage her to tell him her plans, then report her to the authorities.

"So, will you help her?" Adam asked.

"I told her I would talk to Alejandro." Which he still had to do, and he wasn't looking forward to it.

"Also surprising. The last time we talked about her, you seemed awfully bitter."

Not only was Adam a colleague, he was one of Emilio's closest friends. Still, he doubted Adam would even begin to understand his lust for revenge. He wasn't that kind of man. He'd never been betrayed the way Emilio had. Emilio would keep that part of his plan to himself. Besides, Adam would no doubt be opposed to anything that might bring more negative press to Western Oil.

What he didn't know wouldn't hurt him.

"Call me sentimental," Emilio said.

Adam laughed. "Sorry, but that's the last thing I would

ever call you. Sentimental isn't a word in your vocabulary, not unless it's regarding your mother. Just tell me you're not planning on doing something stupid."

There were many levels of stupid. Emilio was barely scratching the surface.

"You have nothing to be concerned about," he assured Adam. "You have my word."

"Good enough for me." Adam's cell buzzed, alerting him that he had a text. As he read it, he smiled. "Katy just got to the house. She's staying in El Paso for a few days, then we're driving back to Peckins together."

Katy was Adam's fiancée. She was also his former sister-in-law and five months pregnant with their first child. Or possibly Katy's dead sister's baby. They weren't sure.

"Have you two set a date yet?" Emilio asked.

"We're leaning toward a small ceremony at her parents' ranch between Christmas and New Year's. I'll let you know as soon as we decide. I'd just like to make it official before the baby is born." Adam looked at his watch. "Well, I have a few things to finish before I leave for the day."

"Send Katy my best."

Adam turned to leave, then paused and turned back. "You're sure you know what you're doing?"

Emilio didn't have to ask what he meant. Adam obviously suspected that there was more to the situation than Emilio was letting on. "I'm sure."

When he was gone, Emilio picked up the phone and dialed his brother's office.

"Hey, big brother," Alejandro answered when his secretary connected them. "Long time no see. The kids miss their favorite uncle."

Emilio hadn't seen his nephews, who were nine, six and two, nearly often enough lately. They were probably the closest thing he would ever have to kids of his own, so he tried to visit on a regular basis. "I know, I'm sorry. Things have been a little crazy here since the refinery accident."

"Any promising developments?"

"At this point, no. It's looking like it may have been sabotage. We're launching an internal investigation. But keep that between us."

"Of course. It's ironic that you called today because I was planning to call you. Alana had a doctor's appointment this morning. She's pregnant again."

Emilio laughed. "Congratulations! I thought you decided to stop at three."

"We did, but she really wanted to try for a girl. I keep telling her that with four boys in my family, we'd have better luck adopting, but she wanted to give it one more try."

Emilio couldn't imagine having one child now much less four. There had been a time when he wanted a family. He and Isabelle had talked about having at least two children. But that was a long time ago. "Are the boys excited?" he asked his brother.

"We haven't told them yet, but I think they'll be thrilled. Alex and Reggie anyway. Chris is a little young to grasp the concept."

"I don't suppose you've heard from Estefan," Emilio asked, referring to their younger brother. Due to drugs, gambling and various other addictions, they usually only heard from him when he needed money or a temporary place to crash. Their mother lived in fear that one day the phone would ring and it would be the coroner's office asking her to come down and identify his body.

"Not a word. I'm not sure if I should feel worried or relieved. I did get an email from Enrique, though. He's in Budapest."

Enrique was the youngest brother and the family nomad. He'd left for a summer backpacking trip through Europe after graduating from college. That was almost three years ago and he hadn't come home yet. Every now and then they would get a postcard or an email, or he would upload photos on the internet of his latest adventures. Occasionally he would pick up the phone and call. He kept promising he'd be home soon, but there was always some new place he wanted to visit. A new cause to devote his life to.

Emilio and Alejandro talked for several minutes about family and work, until Emilio knew he had to quit stalling and get to the point of his call. "I need a favor."

"Anything," Alejandro said.

"Isabelle Winthrop will be checking out of her motel this evening. As far as your office is concerned, she's still staying there."

There was a pause, then Alejandro muttered a curse. "What's going on, Emilio?"

"Not what you think." He told his brother about Isabelle's visit and his "agreement" with her. Leaving out his plan to seduce her, of course. Family man that Alejandro was, he would never understand. He'd never had his heart broken the way Emilio had. Alana had been his high school sweetheart. His first love. Other than a short break they had taken in college to explore other options—which lasted all of two weeks before they could no longer stand to be apart—they had been inseparable.

"Are you completely out of your mind?" Alejandro asked.

"I know what I'm doing."

"If Mama finds out what you're up to, she's going to kill you, then she's going to kill *me* for helping you!"

"I'm doing this for Mama, for *all* of us. For what Isabelle's father did to our family."

"And it has nothing to do with the fact that Isabelle broke your heart?"

A nerve in his jaw ticked. "You said yourself that she's guilty."

"On paper, yes."

"She all but admitted her guilt to me."

"Well, there've been developments in the case."

Emilio frowned. "What kind of developments?"

"You know I can't tell you that. I shouldn't be talking to you about this, period. And I sure as hell shouldn't be helping you. If someone in my office finds out what you're doing—"

"No one will find out."

"My point is, it won't just be your job on the line."

He hadn't wanted to pull out the big guns, but Alejandro was leaving him no choice. "If it weren't for me, little brother, you wouldn't be in that cushy position."

Though Alejandro had planned to wait until his career was established for marriage and kids, Alana had become pregnant with Alex during Alejandro's last year of law school. With a wife and baby to support, he couldn't afford to stay at the top-notch school he'd been attending without Emilio's financial help.

Emilio had never held that over him. Until now.

Alejandro cursed again and Emilio knew he had him. "I hope you know what you're doing."

"I do."

"I'll be honest though, and you did not hear this from me, but with a little more pressure from her lawyer, we would have agreed to a deal on her mother's charge. She would have likely come out of this with probation."

"Isabelle's lawyer told her you wouldn't deal."

"It's called playing hardball, big brother. And maybe her lawyer isn't giving her the best advice."

"What do you mean?"

"I'm not at liberty to say."

"Is he a hack or something?"

"Not at all. He was Betts's lawyer. Clifton Stone. A real shark. And he's representing her *pro bono*."

"Why?"

"She's broke. All assets were frozen when she and Betts were arrested, and everything they owned was auctioned off for restitution."

"Everything?"

"Yeah. It was weird that she didn't fight for anything. No clothes or jewelry. She just gave it all up."

"I thought there was several million unrecovered."

"If she's got money stashed somewhere, she's not touching it."

That could have simply meant that the minute her mother's name was cleared, she would disappear. Why pay for a top-notch defense when she wouldn't be sticking around to hear the verdict? The crappy motel and the outdated clothes could have all been another part of the ruse.

"So why is her lawyer giving her bad advice?"

"That's a good question."

One he obviously had no intention of answering. Not that it mattered to Emilio either way.

"Are you sure this is about revenge?" Alejandro asked.

"What else would it be?"

"All these years there hasn't been anyone special in your life. What if deep down you still have feelings for her? Maybe you still love her."

"Impossible." His heart had been broken beyond repair, and had since hardened into an empty shell. He had no love left to give.

* * *

Emilio had a beautiful house. But Isabelle wouldn't have expected any less. The sprawling stucco estate was located in one of El Paso's most prestigious communities. She knew this for a fact because, until she married Lenny, she used to live in the very same area. Her parents' home had been less than two blocks away. Though she was willing to bet from the facade that this was even larger and more lavish. It was exactly the sort of place Emilio used to talk about owning someday. He'd always set his sights high, and it looked as though he'd gotten everything he ever wanted.

She was happy for him, because he deserved it. Deep down she wished she could have been part of his life, wished she still could be, but it was too late now. Clearly the damage she had done was irreparable. Some people weren't meant to have it all, and a long time ago she had come to terms with the fact that she was one of those people.

Not that she was feeling sorry for herself. In fact, she considered herself very lucky. The fifteen years she had been married to Lenny, she'd had a pretty good life. She had never wanted for a thing. Except a man who loved and desired her, but Lenny had loved her in his own way. If nothing else, she had been safe.

Until the indictment, anyway.

But she would have years in prison to contemplate her mistakes and think about what might have been. All that mattered now was clearing her mother's name.

The limo stopped out front and the driver opened the door for her. The temperature had dipped into the low fifties with the setting sun and she shivered under her light sweater. She was going to have to think about getting herself some warmer clothes and a winter jacket.

It was dark out, but the house and grounds were well lit. Still, she felt uneasy as the driver pulled her bag from the back. He set it on the Spanish tile drive, then with a tip of his hat he climbed back into the limo. As he drove off, Isabelle took a deep breath, grabbed her bag and walked to the porch, a two-story high structure bracketed by a pair of massive white columns and showcased with etched glass double doors. Above the door was an enormous, round leaded window that she imagined let in amazing morning light.

Since Emilio knew what time she was arriving, she'd half expected him to be waiting there to greet her, but there was no sign of him so she walked up the steps and rang the bell. A minute passed, then another, but no one came to the door. She wondered if maybe the bell was broken, and knocked instead. Several more minutes passed, and she began to think he might not be home. Was he held up at the office? And what was she supposed to do? Sit there and wait?

She had a sudden sinking feeling. What if this was some sort of trick? Some sick revenge. What if he'd never planned to let her in? Hell, maybe this wasn't even his house.

No, he wouldn't do that. He may have been angry with her, he may have even hated her, but he could never be that cruel. When they were together he had been the kindest, gentlest man she had ever known.

She reached up to ring the bell one last time when behind her someone said, "I'm not home."

Her heart slammed against her rib cage and she spun around to find Emilio looking up at her from the driveway. He wore a nylon jacket and jogging pants, his forehead was dotted with perspiration and he was out of breath.

Still a jogger. Back in college, he'd been diligent about

keeping in shape. He'd even convinced her to go to the gym with him a few times, but to the annoyance of her friends, her naturally slim build never necessitated regular exercise.

He stepped up to the porch and stopped so close to her that she could practically feel the heat radiating off his body. He smelled of a tantalizing combination of aftershave, evening air and red-blooded man. She was torn between the desire to lean close and breathe him in, or run like hell. Instead she stood her ground, met his penetrating gaze. He'd always been tall, but now he seemed to tower over her with the same long, lean build as in his youth. The years had been good to him.

He looked at her luggage, then her. "Where's the rest?"

"This is all I brought."

One dark brow rose. A move so familiar, she felt a jab of nostalgia, a longing for the way things used to be. One he clearly did not share.

"You travel light," he said.

Pretty much everything she owned was in that one piece of luggage. A few of her mother's fashion rejects and the rest she'd purchased at the thrift store. When the feds had seized their home, she hadn't tried or even wanted to keep any of the possessions. She couldn't stand the thought of wearing clothes that she knew had been purchased with stolen money.

The clothes, the state of the art electronic equipment, the fine jewelry and priceless art had all been auctioned off, and other than her coffee/espresso machine, she didn't miss any of it.

Leaving the bag right where it was—she hadn't really expected him to carry it for her—Emilio turned and punched in a code on the pad beside the door. She heard a click as the lock disengaged, and as he opened the door the lights automatically switched on.

She picked up her bag and followed him inside, nearly gasping at the magnificence of the interior. The two-story foyer opened up into a grand front room with a curved, dual marble stairway. In the center hung an ornately fashioned wrought iron chandelier that matched the banister. The walls were painted a tasteful cream color, with boldly colored accents.

"It's lovely," she said.

"I'll show you to your quarters, then give you a tour. My housekeeper left a list of your daily duties and sample menus for you to follow."

"You didn't fire her, I hope."

He shot her a stern look. "Of course not. I gave her a month paid vacation."

That was generous of him. He could obviously afford it. She was thankful the woman had left instructions. What Isabelle knew about cooking and cleaning could be listed on an index card with lines to spare, but she was determined to learn. How hard could it be?

Emilio led her through an enormous kitchen with polished mahogany cabinets, marble countertops and top-of-the-line steel appliances, past a small bathroom and laundry room to the maid's quarters in the back.

So, this was where she would spend the next thirty days. It was barely large enough to hold a single bed, a small wood desk and padded folding chair, and a tall, narrow chest of drawers. The walls were white and completely bare but for the small crucifix hanging above the bed. It wasn't luxurious by any stretch of the imagination, but it was clean and safe, which was more than she could say for her motel. Checking out of that hellhole, knowing she would no longer wake in the middle of the night to the sound of roaches and rodents scratching in the walls, and God only knows what sort of illegal activity just outside her door, had in itself almost been worth a month of humiliation.

She set her bag on the faded blue bedspread. "Where is your housekeeper staying while I'm here?" she asked. She hoped not in the house. The idea of someone watching over her shoulder made her uneasy. This would be humiliating enough without an audience.

"She's not a live-in. I prefer my privacy."

"Yet, you're letting *me* stay," she said.

Up went the brow again. "I could move you into the pool house if you'd prefer. Although you may find the lack of heat less than hospitable."

She was going to have to curb the snippy comments. At this point it probably wouldn't take much for him to back out of their deal.

He nodded toward the chest. "You'll find your uniform in the top drawer."

Uniform? He never said anything about her wearing a uniform. For one horrifying instant she wondered if he would seize the opportunity to inflict even more humiliation by making her wear a revealing French maid's outfit. Or something even worse.

She pulled the drawer open, relieved to find a plain, drab gray, white collared dress. The same kind his mother wore when she worked for Isabelle's parents. She almost asked how he knew what size to get, but upon close inspection realized that the garment would be too big.

She slid the drawer closed and turned to face Emilio. He stood just inside the doorway, arms folded, expression dark—an overwhelming presence in the modest space. And he was blocking the door.

She felt a quick jab of alarm.

She was cornered. In a bedroom no less. What if his

intentions were less than noble? What if he'd brought her here so he could take what she'd denied him fifteen years ago?

Of course he wouldn't. Any man who would wait a year to be with a woman knew a thing or two about self-control. Besides, why would he want to have sex with someone he clearly hated? He wasn't that sort of man. At least, he never used to be.

He must have sensed her apprehension. That damned brow lifted again and he asked, with a look of amusement, "Do I frighten you, Izzie?"

Three

Izzie. Emilio was the only one who ever called her that. Hearing it again, after so many years, made Isabelle long to recapture the happiness of those days. The sense of hopefulness. The feeling that as long as they had each other, they could overcome any obstacles.

How wrong she had been. She'd discovered that there were some obstacles she would never overcome. At least, not until it was too late.

She squared her shoulders and told Emilio, "You don't scare me."

He stepped closer. "Are you sure? For a second there, I could swear you looked nervous."

She resisted the urge to take a step back. But not from fear. She just didn't appreciate him violating her personal space. She didn't like the way it made her feel. Out of control. Defenseless. His presence still did something to her after all this time. He would never know how hard it had been to tell him no back then, to wait. So many times she had come *this close* to giving in. If he had pushed a little harder, she probably would have. But he had been too much of a gentleman. A genuinely good guy. He had respected her.

Not anymore.

"I know you," she said. "You're harmless."

He moved even closer, so she had to crane her neck to look into his eyes. "Maybe I've changed."

Unlikely. And she refused to back down, to let him intimidate her.

She folded her arms and glared up at him, and after a few seconds more he backed away, then he turned and walked out. She assumed she was meant to follow him. A proper host would have given her time to unpack and freshen up. He might have offered her something to drink. But he wasn't her host. He was her employer. Or more appropriately, her warden. This was just a prison of a different kind. A prison of hurt and regret.

On the kitchen counter lay the duty list he'd mentioned. He handed it to her and when she saw that it was *eight* pages single-spaced she nearly swallowed her own tongue. Her shock must have shown, because that damned brow quirked up and Emilio asked, "Problem?"

She swallowed hard and shook her head. "None at all."

She flipped through it, seeing that it was efficiently organized by room and listed which chores should be performed on which day. Some things, like vacuuming the guest rooms and polishing the chrome in the corresponding bathrooms, were done on a weekly basis, alternating one of the five spare bedrooms every day. Other duties such as dusting the marble in the entryway and polishing the kitchen counters was a daily task. That didn't even include the cooking.

It was difficult to believe that one person could accomplish this much in one day. From the looks of it, she would be working from dawn to dusk without a break.

"I'm putting a few final touches on the menus, but you'll have them first thing tomorrow," Emilio said. "I'm assuming you can cook."

Not if it meant doing much more than heating a frozen dinner in the microwave or boiling water on a hot plate. "I'll manage."

"Of course you'll be responsible for all the shopping as well. You'll have a car at your disposal. And you're welcome to eat whatever you desire." He gave her a quick once-over, not bothering to hide his distaste. "Although from the looks of you, I'm guessing you don't eat much."

Eating required money and that was in short supply these days. She refused to sponge off her mother, whose financial situation was only slightly less grave, and no one was interested in hiring a thief six weeks from a twenty-to-life visit to the slammer. Besides, Isabelle had been such a nervous wreck lately, every time she tried to eat she would get a huge lump in her throat, through which food simply refused to pass.

She shrugged. "Like they say in Hollywood, there's no such thing as too thin."

"I see you still have the same irrational hang-ups about your body," he snapped back, his contempt so thick she could have choked on it. "I remember that you would only undress in the dark and hide under the covers when I turned the light on."

Her only hang-up had been with letting Emilio see the scars and bruises. He would have wanted an explanation, and she knew that if she'd told him the truth, something bad would happen. She'd done it to protect him and he was throwing it back in her face.

If this was a preview of what she should expect from the next thirty days, it would be a long month. But she could take it. And the less she said, the better.

The fact that she remained silent, that she didn't rise to her own defense, seemed to puzzle him. She waited for his next attack, but instead he gestured her out of the kitchen. "The living room is this way."

If he had more barbs to throw, he was saving them for another time.

She could hardly wait.

Though Emilio's hospitality left a lot to be desired, his home had all the comforts a person could possibly need. Six bedrooms and eight baths, a state of the art media room and a fitness/game room complete with autographed sports memorabilia. He had a penchant for Mexican pottery and an art collection so vast he could open a gallery. The house was furnished and decorated with a lively, southwestern flair.

It was as close to perfect as a home could be, the apotheosis of his ambitions, yet for some reason it seemed…empty. Perfect to the point of feeling almost unoccupied. Or maybe it simply lacked a woman's touch.

When they got to the master suite he stopped outside the door. "This room is off-limits. The same goes for my office downstairs."

Fine with her. That much less work as far as she was concerned. Besides, his bedroom was the last place she wanted to be spending any time.

He ended the tour there, and they walked back down to the kitchen. "Be sure you study that list, as I expect you to adhere to those exact specifications."

Her work would be exemplary. Now that she'd had a taste of how bitter he was, it was essential that she not give him a single reason to find fault with her performance. Too much was at stake. "If there's nothing more, I'll go to my room now," she said.

"No need to rush off." He peeled off his jacket and tossed it over the back of a kitchen chair. Underneath he wore a form-fitting muscle shirt that accentuated every plane of lean muscle in his chest and abs, and she was far from immune to the physical draw of an attractive man. Especially one she had never completely fallen out of love with. Meaning the less time she spent with him, the better.

He grabbed a bottled water from the fridge, but didn't offer her one. "It's early. Stick around for a while."

"I'm tired," she told him. "And I need to study that list."

"But we haven't had a chance to catch up." He propped himself against the counter, as though he was settling in for a friendly chat. "What have you been up to the past fifteen years? Besides defrauding the better part of Texas high society."

She bit the inside of her cheek.

"You know what I find ironic? I'll bet if your parents had to guess who they thought was more likely to go to federal prison, you or me, they would have chosen the son of Cuban immigrants over their precious daughter."

Apparently his idea of catching up would consist of thinly veiled insults and jabs at her character. *Swell.*

"No opinion?" he asked, clearly hoping she would retaliate, but she refused to be baited. Others had said much worse and she'd managed to ignore them, too. Reporters and law officials, although the worst of it had come from people who had supposedly been her friends. But she wouldn't begrudge a single one of them their very strong opinions. Even if the only thing she was truly guilty of was stupidity.

"It's just as well," Emilio said. "I have work to catch up on."

Struggling to keep her face devoid of emotion so he wouldn't see how relieved she was, she grabbed the list and walked to her quarters, ultra-aware of his gaze boring into her back. Once inside she closed the door and leaned against it. She hadn't been lying, she was truly exhausted. She couldn't recall the last time she'd had a decent night's sleep.

She gazed longingly at the bed, but it was still early, and she had to at least make an effort to familiarize herself with her duties before she succumbed to exhaustion.

She hung her sweater on the back of the folding chair and sat down, setting the list in front of her on the desk.

According to the housekeeper's schedule, Emilio's car picked him up at seven-thirty sharp, so Isabelle had to be up no later than six-thirty to fix his coffee and make his breakfast. If she was in bed by ten, she would get a solid eight and a half hours' sleep. About double what she'd been getting at the motel if she counted all the times she was jolted awake by strange noises. The idea of feeling safe and secure while she slept was an enticing one, as was the anticipation of eating something other than ramen noodles for breakfast, lunch and dinner.

If she could manage to avoid Emilio, staying here might not be so bad after all.

Usually Emilio slept like a baby, but knowing he wasn't alone in the house had him tossing and turning most of the night.

It had been odd, after so many years apart, to see Isabelle standing on his front porch waiting for him. After she married Betts, Emilio had intended never to cross paths with her again. He'd declined invitations to functions that he knew she would be attending and chose his friends and acquaintances with the utmost care.

He had done everything in his power to avoid her, yet here she was, sleeping in his servants' quarters. Maybe the pool house would have been a better alternative.

He stared through the dark at the ceiling, recalling their exchange of words earlier. Isabelle had changed. She used to be so subdued and timid. She would have recoiled from his angry words and cowered in the face of his resentment, and she never would have dished out any caustic comments of her own. A life of crime must have hardened her.

But what had Alejandro said? She was guilty on paper, but there had been new developments. Could she be innocent?

That didn't change what she had done to him, and what her father had done to Emilio's family. She could have implored him to keep his mother on as an employee, or to at least give her a positive recommendation. She hadn't even tried.

In a way, he wished he had never met her. But according to her, it was destiny. She used to say she knew from the first moment she laid eyes on him that they were meant to be with one another, that fate had drawn them together. Although technically he had known her for years before he'd ever really noticed her. His mother drove them to school in the mornings, he and his brothers to public school and Izzie to the private girls' school down the road, and other than an occasional "hi," she barely spoke to him. To him, she had never been more than the daughter of his mother's employer, a girl too conceited to give him the time of day. Only later had she admitted that she'd had such a crush on him that she'd been too tongue-tied to speak.

During his junior year of high school he'd gotten his own car and rarely saw her after that. Then, when he was in college, she had shown up out of the blue at the house he'd rented on campus for the summer session. She had just graduated from high school and planned to attend classes there in the fall. She asked if he would show her around campus.

Though it seemed an odd request considering they had barely ever spoken, he felt obligated, since her parents paid his mother's salary. They spent the afternoon together, walking and chatting, and in those few hours he began to see a side of her that he hadn't known existed. She was intelligent and witty, but with a childlike innocence he found compelling. He realized that what he had once mistaken for conceit and entitlement was really shyness and self-doubt. He found that he could open up to her, that despite their vast social differences, she understood him. He liked her, and there was no doubt she had romantic feelings toward him, but she was young and naive and he knew her parents would never approve of their daughter dating the son of the hired help. He decided that they could be friends, but nothing more.

Then she kissed him.

He had walked her back to her car and they were saying goodbye. Without warning she threw her arms around his neck and pressed her lips to his. He was stunned—and aroused—and though he knew he should stop her, the scent of her skin and the taste of her lips were irresistible. They stood there in the dark kissing for a long time, until she said she had to get home. But by then it was too late. He was hooked.

He spent every minute he wasn't at work or in class that summer with her, and when they were apart it was torture. They were only dating two weeks when he told her he loved her, and after a month he knew he wanted to marry her, but he waited until their six month anniversary to ask her formally.

They figured that if they both saved money until the

end of the school year they would have enough to get a small place together, then they would elope. He warned her it would be tight for a while, maybe even years, until he established his career. She swore it didn't matter as long as they were together.

But in the end it *had* mattered.

Emilio let out an exasperated sigh and looked at the clock. Two-thirty. If he lay here rehashing his mistakes he was never going to get to sleep. These were issues he'd resolved a long time ago. Or so he'd thought.

Maybe bringing Isabelle into his home had been a bad idea. Was revenge really worth a month of sleepless nights? He just had to remind himself how well he would sleep when his family was vindicated.

Emilio eventually drifted off to sleep, then roused again at four-fifteen wide-awake. After an unsuccessful half hour of trying to fall back to sleep, he got out of bed and went down to his office. He worked for a while, then spent an hour in the fitness room before going upstairs to get ready for work. He came back down at seven, expecting his coffee and breakfast to be waiting for him, but the kitchen was dark.

He shook his head, disappointed, but not surprised. His new housekeeper was not off to a good start. Her first day on the job could very well be her last.

He walked back to her quarters and raised his hand to knock, then noticed the door wasn't latched. With his foot he gave it a gentle shove and it creaked open. He expected to find Isabelle curled up in bed. Instead she sat slumped over at the desk, head resting on her arms, sound asleep. She was still wearing the clothes from last night, and on the desk, under her arms, lay the list of her duties. Her bag sat open but unpacked on the bed, and the covers hadn't been disturbed.

She must have dozed off shortly after going to her room, and she must have been pretty exhausted to sleep in such an awkward position all night.

He sighed and shook his head. At least one of them had gotten a good night's rest.

A part of him wanted to be angry with her, wanted to send her packing for neglecting her duties, but he had the feeling this had been an unintentional oversight. He would give her the benefit of the doubt. Just this once. But he wouldn't deny himself the pleasure of giving her a hard time about it.

Four

"Isabelle!"

Isabelle shot up with such force she nearly flung the chair over, blinking furiously, trying to get her bearings. She saw Emilio standing in the doorway and her eyes went wide. "Wh-what time is it?"

"Three minutes after seven." He folded his arms, kept his mouth in a grim line. "Were you expecting breakfast in bed?"

Her skin paled. "I was going to set the alarm on my phone. I must have fallen asleep before I had the chance."

"And you consider that a valid excuse for neglecting your duties?"

"No, you're right. I screwed up." She squared her shoulders and rose stiffly from the chair. "I'll pack my things and be out of here before you leave from work."

For a second he thought she was playing the sympathy

card, but she wore a look of resigned hopelessness that said she seriously expected him to terminate their agreement.

He probably should have, but if he let her go now he would be denying himself the pleasure of breaking her. Lucky for her, he was feeling generous this morning. "If you leave, who will make my coffee?"

She gazed up at him with hope in her eyes. "Does that mean you're giving me a second chance?"

"Don't let it happen again. Next time I won't be so forgiving."

"I won't, I promise." She looked over at the dresser. "My uniform—"

"Coffee first."

"What about breakfast?"

"No time. I only have twenty-five minutes until the company car is here to pick me up."

"Sorry." She edged past him through the door and scurried to the kitchen.

He went to his office to put the necessary paperwork in his briefcase, and when he walked back into the kitchen several minutes later the coffee was brewed. Isabelle wasn't there, so he grabbed a travel mug and filled it himself. He took a sip, surprised to realize that it was actually good. A little stronger than his housekeeper, Mrs. Medina, usually made it, but he liked it.

Isabelle emerged from her room a minute later wearing her uniform. He looked her up and down and frowned. The oversize garment hung on her, accentuating her skeletal physique. "It's too big."

She shrugged. "It's okay."

It was an old uniform a former employee had left so he hadn't really expected it to fit. "You'll need a new one."

"It's only for thirty days. It's fine."

"It is not *fine*. It looks terrible. Tell me what size you wear and I'll have a new one sent to the house."

She chewed her lip, avoiding his gaze.

"Are you going to tell me, or should I guess?"

"I'm not exactly sure. I've lost weight recently."

"So tell me your weight and height and they can send over the appropriate size."

"I'm five foot four."

"And...?"

She looked at the floor.

"Your weight, Isabelle?"

She shrugged.

"You don't know how much you weigh?"

"I don't own a scale."

He sighed. Why did she have to make everything so difficult?

"Fitness room," he said, gesturing to the doorway. "I have a scale in there."

She reluctantly followed him and was even less enthusiastic about getting on the digital scale. As she stepped on she averted her eyes.

The number that popped up was nothing short of disturbing. "Considering your height, you have to be at least fifteen or twenty pounds underweight."

Isabelle glanced at the display, and if her grimace was any indication, she was equally unsettled by the number. Not the reaction he would have expected from someone with a "there's no such thing as too thin" dictum.

"Am I correct in assuming this weight loss wasn't intentional?" he asked.

She nodded.

It hadn't occurred to him before, but what if there was something wrong with her? "Are you ill?"

She stepped down off the scale. "It's been a stressful couple of months."

"That's no excuse to neglect your health. While you're here I expect you to eat three meals a day, and I intend to make you climb on that scale daily until you've gained at least fifteen pounds."

Her eyes rounded with surprise.

"Is that a problem?" he asked.

For an instant she looked as though she would argue, then she pulled her lip between her teeth and shook her head.

"Good." He looked at his watch. "I have to go. I'll be home at six-thirty. I expect dinner to be ready no later than seven."

"Yes, sir."

There was a note of ambivalence in her tone, but he let it slide. The subject of her weight was clearly a touchy one. A fact he planned to exploit. And he had the distinct feeling there was more to the story than she would admit. Just one more piece to this puzzle of a woman who he thought he knew, but wasn't at all what he had expected.

Though Isabelle wasn't sure what her father had paid Emilio's mother, she was positive it wasn't close to enough.

She never imagined taking care of a house could be so exhausting. The dusting alone had taken nearly three hours, and she'd spent another two and a half on the windows and mirrors on the first floor. Both tasks had required more bending and stretching than any yoga class she'd ever attended, and she'd climbed the stairs so many times her legs felt limp.

Worse than the physical exhaustion was how inept she was at using the most basic of household appliances. It had taken her ten minutes to find the "on" switch on the vacuum, and one frayed corner on the upstairs runner to learn that the carpet setting didn't work well for fringed rugs. They got sucked up into the spinny thing inside and ripped off. She just hoped that Emilio didn't notice. She would have to figure out some way to pay to get it fixed. And soon.

Probably her most puzzling dilemma was the cupboard full of solutions, waxes and paraphernalia she was supposed to use in her duties. Never had she imagined there were so many different types of cleaning products. She spent an hour reading the labels, trying to determine which suited her various tasks, which put her even further behind in her duties.

Her new uniforms arrived at three-thirty by messenger. Emilio had ordered four in two different sizes, probably to accommodate the weight he was expecting her to gain. The smallest size fit perfectly and was far less unflattering than the oversize version. In fact, it fit better and looked nicer than most of the street clothes she currently owned. Too bad it didn't contain magic powers that made her at least a little less inept at her duties.

When she heard Emilio come through the front door at six-thirty, she hadn't even started on the upstairs guest room yet. She steeled herself for his latest round of insults and jabs and as he stepped into the kitchen, travel cup in one hand, his briefcase in the other, her heart sailed up into her throat. He looked exhausted and rumpled in a sexy way.

He set his cup in the sink. Though she was probably inviting trouble, she asked, "How was work?"

"Long, and unproductive," he said, loosening his tie. "How was your day?"

A civilized response? Whoa. She hadn't expected that. "It was…good."

"I see you haven't burned the house down. That's promising."

So much for being civil.

"I'm going to go change," he said. "I trust dinner will be ready on time."

"Of course." At least she hoped so. It had taken her a bit longer to assemble the chicken dish than she'd anticipated, so to save cooking time, she'd raised the oven heat by one hundred degrees.

He gave her a dismissive nod, then left the room. She heard the heavy thud of his footsteps as he climbed the stairs. With any luck he wouldn't look down.

A minute passed, and she began to think that she was safe, then he thundered from the upstairs hallway, "Isabelle!"

Shoot.

It was still possible it wasn't the rug he was upset about. Maybe he'd checked the guest room and saw that she hadn't cleaned it yet. She walked to the stairs, climbing them slowly, her hopes plummeting when she reached the top and saw him standing with his arms folded, lips thinned, looking at the corner of the runner.

"Is there something you need to tell me?" he asked.

It figured that he would ignore all the things she had done right and focus in on the one thing she had done wrong. "The vacuum ate your rug."

"It *ate* it?"

"I had it on the wrong setting. I take full responsibility." As if it could somehow *not* be her fault.

"Why didn't you mention this when I asked how your day went?"

"I forgot?"

One dark brow rose. "Is that a question?"

She took a deep breath and blew it out. "Okay, I was hoping you wouldn't notice."

"I notice *everything*."

Apparently. "I'll pay for the damage."

"How?"

Good question. "I'll figure something out."

She expected him to push the issue, but he didn't.

"Is there anything else you've neglected to mention?"

Nothing she hadn't managed to fix, unless she counted the plastic container she'd melted in the microwave, but he would never notice that.

She shook her head.

Emilio studied her, as if he were sizing her up, and she felt herself withering under his scrutiny.

"That's better," he said.

She blinked. "Better?"

"The uniform. It actually fits."

Did he just compliment her? Albeit in a backhanded, slightly rude way. But it was a start.

"You ate today?" he asked.

"Twice." For breakfast she'd made herself fried eggs swimming in butter with rye toast slathered in jam and for lunch she'd heated a can of clam chowder. It had been heavenly.

He looked down at the rug again. "This will have to be rebound."

"I'll take care of it first thing tomorrow."

"Let me know how much it will be and I'll write a check."

"I'll pay you back a soon as I can." She wondered what the hourly wage was to make license plates.

"Yes, you will." He turned and walked into his bedroom, shutting the door.

Isabelle blew out a relieved breath. That hadn't gone

nearly as bad as she'd expected. With any hope, dinner would be a smashing success and he would be so pleased he would forget all about the rug.

Though she had the sneaking suspicion that if it was the most amazing meal he'd ever tasted, he would complain on principle.

Dinner was a culinary catastrophe.

She served him overcooked, leathery chicken in lumpy white sauce with a side of scorched rice pilaf and a bowl of wilted salad swimming in dressing. He wouldn't feed it to his dog—if he had one. But what had Emilio expected from someone who had probably never cooked a meal in her entire life?

Isabelle hadn't stuck around to witness the aftermath. She'd fixed his plate, then vanished. He'd come downstairs to find it sitting on the dining room table accompanied by a highball glass *full* of scotch. Maybe she thought that if she got him good and toasted, he wouldn't notice the disastrous meal.

He carried his plate to the kitchen and dumped the contents in the trash, then fixed himself a peanut butter and jelly sandwich and ate standing at the kitchen sink. Which he noted was a disaster area. Considering all the dirty pots and pans and dishes, it looked as though she'd prepared a ten course meal. He hoped she planned to come out of hiding and clean it up.

As he was walking to his office, drink in hand, he heard the hum of the vacuum upstairs. Why the hell was she cleaning at seven-thirty in the evening?

He climbed the stairs and followed the sound to the first guest bedroom. Her back was to him as she vacuumed around the queen-size bed. He leaned in the doorway and watched her. The new uniform was a major improvement, but she still looked painfully thin. She had always been finely boned and willowy, but now she looked downright scrawny.

But still beautiful. He used to love watching her, even if she was doing nothing more than sitting on his bed doing her class work. He never got tired of looking at her. Even now she possessed a poise and grace that was almost hypnotizing.

She turned to do the opposite side of the bed and when she saw him standing there she jolted with alarm. She hit the Off switch.

"Surprised to see me?" he asked.

She looked exhausted. "Did you need something?"

"I just thought you'd like to know that it didn't work."

She frowned. "What didn't work?"

"Your attempt to poison me."

He could see that he'd hurt her feelings, but she lifted her chin in defiance and said, "Well, you can't blame a girl for trying. Besides, now that I think about it, smothering you in your sleep will be so much more fun."

He nearly cracked a smile. "Is that why you're trying to incapacitate me with excessive amounts of scotch?"

She shrugged. "It's always easier when they don't fight back."

She'd always had a wry sense of humor. He just hadn't expected her to exercise it. Unless she wasn't joking. It might not be a bad idea to lock his bedroom door. Just in case.

"Why are you up here cleaning?" he asked.

She looked at him funny, as though she thought it was a trick question. "Because that's what you brought me here to do?"

"What I mean is, shouldn't you be finished for the day?"

"Maybe I should be, but I'm not."

It probably wasn't helping that he'd instructed Mrs. Medina to toss in a few extra tasks on top of her regular duties, though he hadn't anticipated it taking Isabelle quite this long. He'd just wanted to keep her busy during the day. Apparently it had worked. A little *too* well.

"I have work to do and the noise is distracting," he told her.

She had this look, like she wanted to say something snotty or sarcastic, but she restrained herself. "I'll try to keep the noise down."

"See that you do. And I hope you're planning to clean the kitchen. It's a mess."

He could tell she was exasperated but struggling to suppress it. "It's on my list."

He wondered what it would take to make her explode. How far he would have to push. In all the time they were together, he'd never once seen her lose her temper. Whenever they came close to having a disagreement she would just…shut down. He'd always wondered what it would be like to get her good and riled up.

It was an intriguing idea, but tonight he just didn't have the energy.

He turned to leave and she said, "Emilio?"

He looked back.

"I'm really sorry about dinner."

This was his chance to twist the knife, to put her in her place, but she looked so damned humble he didn't have the heart. She really was trying, holding up her end of the bargain. And he…well, hell, he was obviously going soft or something. He'd lost his killer instinct.

"Maybe tomorrow you could try something a little less complicated," he said.

"I will."

As he walked away the vacuum switched back on.

Despite a few screwups, her first day had been less of a disaster than he'd anticipated.

Emilio settled at his desk and booted his computer, and after a few minutes the vacuum went silent. About forty-five minutes later he heard her banging around in the kitchen. That continued for a good hour, then there was silence.

At eleven he shut down his computer, turned off the lights in his office and walked to the kitchen. It was back to its previous, clean state, and his travel cup was washed and sitting beside the coffeemaker. He dumped what was left of his drink down the drain, set his glass in the sink and was about to head upstairs when he noticed she'd left the laundry room light on. He walked back to switch it off and saw that Isabelle's door was open a crack and the desk lamp was on.

Maybe he should remind her to set her alarm, so he didn't have to get breakfast in the coffee shop at work again tomorrow.

He knocked lightly on her door. When she didn't answer, he eased it open. Isabelle was lying face down, spread-eagle on her bed, still dressed in her uniform, sound asleep. She hadn't even taken off her shoes. She must have dropped down and gone out like a light. At least this time she'd made it to the bed. And on the bright side, she seemed in no condition to be smothering him in his sleep.

The hem of her uniform had pulled up, giving him a nice view of the backs of her thighs. They were smooth and creamy and he couldn't help but imagine how it would feel to touch her. To lay a hand on her thigh and slide it upward, under her dress.

The sudden flash of heat in his blood, the intense pull of arousal in his groin, caught him off guard.

Despite all that had happened, he still desired her.

Maybe his body remembered what his brain had struggled to suppress. How good they had been together.

Though they had never made love, they had touched each other intimately, given each other pleasure. Isabelle hadn't done much more than kiss a boy before they began dating. She had been the most inexperienced eighteen-year-old he'd ever met, but eager to learn, and more than willing to experiment, so long as they didn't go all the way. He had respected her decision to wait until marriage to make love and admired her principles, so he hadn't pushed. Besides, it hadn't stopped them from finding other ways to satisfy their sexual urges.

One thing he never understood though was why she had been so shy about letting him see her body. Despite what he had told her yesterday, he'd never believed it had anything to do with vanity. Quite the opposite. For reasons he'd never been able to understand, she'd had a dismally low opinion of herself.

After she left him, he began to wonder if it had all been an act to manipulate him. Maybe she hadn't been so innocent after all. To this day he wasn't sure, and he would probably never know the truth. He was long past caring either way.

He shut off the light and stepped out of her room, closing the door behind him. The lack of sleep was catching up to him. He was exhausted. What he needed was a good night's rest.

Everything would be clearer in the morning.

Five

Isabelle hated lying. Especially to her mother, but in this case she didn't have much choice. There was no way she could admit the truth.

They sat at the small kitchen table in her mother's apartment, having tea. Isabelle had been avoiding her calls for three days now, since she moved into Emilio's house, but in her mother's last message her voice had been laced with concern.

"I went by the motel but they told me you checked out. Where are you, Isabelle?"

Isabelle had no choice but to stop by her mother's apartment on her way home from the grocery store Thursday morning. Besides, she'd picked up a few things for her.

"So, your new job is a live-in position?" her mother asked.

"Room and board," Isabelle told her. "And she lets me use her car for running errands."

"What a perfect position for you." She rubbed Isabelle's arm affectionately. "You've always loved helping people."

"She still gets around well for her age, but her memory isn't great. Her kids are afraid she'll leave the stove on and burn the house down. Plus she can't drive anymore. She needs me to take her to doctor appointments."

"Well, I think it's wonderful that you're moving on with your life. I know the last few months have been difficult for you."

"They haven't been easy for you, either." And all because of Isabelle's stupidity. Not that her mother ever blamed her. She'd been duped by Lenny, too, and held him one hundred percent responsible.

"It's really not so bad. I've made a few new friends in the building and I like my job at the boutique."

Though her mother would never admit it, it had to be humiliating selling designer fashions to women she used to socialize with. But considering she had never worked a day in her life, not to mention the indictment, she had been lucky to find a job at all. Even if her salary was barely enough to get by on. It pained Isabelle that her mother had to leave the luxury of her condo to live in this dumpy little apartment. She'd endured so much pain and heartache in her life, she deserved better than this.

"This woman you work for...what did you say her name is?" her mother asked.

She hadn't. That was one part of the lie she'd forgotten about. "Mrs. Smith," she said, cringing at her lack of originality. "Mary Smith."

Why hadn't she gone with something really unique, like Jane Doe?

"Where does Mrs. Smith live?"

"Not too far from our old house."

Her brow crinkled. "Hmm, the name isn't familiar. I thought I knew everyone in that area."

"She's a very nice woman. I think you would like her."

"I'd like to meet her. Maybe I'll come by for a visit."

Crap. Wouldn't she be shocked to learn that Mrs. Smith was actually Mr. Suarez.

"I'll talk to her children and see if it's okay," Isabelle told her. She would just have to stall for the next month.

"Have you been keeping up with the news about Western Oil?" her mother asked, and Isabelle's heart stalled. Did she suspect something? Why would she bring Emilio up out of the blue like that?

"Not really," she lied. "I don't watch television."

"They showed a clip of Emilio and his partners at a press conference on the news the other day. He looks good. He's obviously done well for himself."

"I guess he has."

"Maybe you should...talk to him."

"Why?"

"I thought that maybe he would talk to his brother on your behalf."

"He wouldn't. And it wouldn't matter if he did. I'm going to prison. Nothing is going to stop that now."

"You don't know that."

"Yes, I do."

She shook her head. "Lenny would never let that happen. He may have been a thief, but he loved you."

"Lenny is dead." Even if he had intended to absolve her of guilt, he couldn't do it from the grave. It was too late.

"Something will come up. Some new evidence. Everything will be okay."

She looked so sad. Isabelle wished she could tell her

mother the truth, so at least she wouldn't have to worry about her own freedom. But she'd promised Emilio.

Isabelle glanced at her watch. "I really have to get back to work."

"Of course. Thank you for the groceries. You didn't have to do that."

"My living expenses are practically nonexistent now, and as you said, I like helping people."

She walked Isabelle to the door.

"That's a nice car," she said, gesturing to the black Saab parked in the lot.

It was, and it stuck out like a sore thumb amidst the vehicles beside it. "I'll drop by again as soon as I can."

Her mother hugged her hard and said, "I'm very proud of you, sweetheart."

The weight of Isabelle's guilt was suffocating. But she hugged her back and said, "Thanks, Mom."

Her mother waved as she drove away, and Isabelle felt a deep sense of sadness. Hardly a week passed when they didn't speak on the phone, or drop by for visits. They were all the other had anymore. What would her mother do when Isabelle went to prison? She would be all alone. And she was fooling herself if she really believed Isabelle could avoid prison. It was inevitable. Even if Emilio wanted to help her—which he obviously didn't—there was nothing he could do. According to her lawyer, the evidence against her was overwhelming.

Isabelle couldn't worry herself with that right now. If she did the dread and the fear would overwhelm her. She had a household to run. Which was going more smoothly than she had anticipated. Her latest attempts in the kitchen must not have been too awful, either, because Emilio hadn't accused her of trying to poison him since Monday, though he'd found fault with practically everything else she did.

Okay, maybe not *everything*. But when it came to his home, he was a perfectionist. Everything had its place, and God help her if she moved something, or put it away in the wrong spot. Yesterday she'd set the milk on the refrigerator shelf instead of the door and he'd blown a gasket. And yeah, a couple of times she had moved things deliberately, just for the satisfaction of annoying him. He did make it awfully easy.

Other than a few minor snafus, the housekeeping itself was getting much easier. She had settled into a routine, and some of her chores were taking half the time they had when she started. Yesterday she'd even had time to sit down with a cup of tea, put her feet up and read the paper for twenty minutes.

In fact, it was becoming almost *too* easy. And she couldn't help but wonder if the other shoe was about to drop.

Emilio stood by the window in Adam's office, listening to his colleagues discuss the accident at the refinery. OSHA had released its official report and Western Oil was being cited for negligence. According to the investigation, the explosion was triggered by a faulty gauge. Which everyone in the room knew was impossible.

That section had just come back online after several days of mandatory safety checks and equipment upgrades. It had been inspected and reinspected. It wasn't negligence, or an accident. Someone *wanted* that equipment to fail.

The question was why?

"This is ridiculous," Jordan said, slapping the report down on Adam's desk. "Those are good men. They would never let something like this happen."

"Someone is responsible," Nathan said from his seat opposite Adam's desk, which earned him a sharp look from his brother.

Somber, Adam said, "I know you trust and respect every man there, Jordan, but I think we have to come to terms with the fact that it was sabotage."

Thankfully the explosion had occurred while that section was in maintenance mode, and less than half the men who usually worked that shift were on the line. Only a dozen were hurt. But one injured man was too many as far as Emilio was concerned. Between lawsuits and OSHA fines, financially they would take a hit. Even worse was the mark on their good name. Until now they'd had a flawless safety record. Cassandra Benson, Western Oil's public relations director, had been working feverishly to put a positive spin on the situation. But their direct competitor, Birch Energy, owned by Walter Birch, had already taken advantage of the situation. Within days of the incident they released a flood of television ads, and though they didn't directly target Western Oil, the implication was clear— Birch was safe and valued their employees. Western Oil was a death trap.

Western Oil was firing back with ads boasting their innovative techniques and new alternative, environmentally friendly practices.

"I don't suppose you'll tell me how the investigation is going," Jordan said.

Adam and Nathan exchanged a look. When they agreed to launch a private investigation, it was decided that Jordan wouldn't be involved. As Chief Operations Officer he was the one closest to the workers in the refinery. They trusted him, so he needed a certain degree of deniability. A fact Jordan was clearly not happy about.

They had promised to keep him in the loop, but

privately Adam had confided in Emilio that he worried Jordan wouldn't be impartial. That he might ignore key evidence out of loyalty to the workers.

Jordan would be downright furious to know that two of the new men hired to take the place of injured workers were in reality undercover investigators. But the real thorn in Jordan's side was that Nathan was placed in charge of the investigation. That, on top of the competition for the CEO position, had thrust their occasional sibling rivalry into overdrive. Which didn't bode well for either of them. And though Emilio considered both men his friends, there had been tension since Adam announced his intention to retire.

"All I can say is that it's going slowly," Nathan told Jordan. "How is morale?"

"Tom Butler, my foreman, says the men are nervous. They know the line was thoroughly checked before the accident. Rumor is someone in the refinery is to blame for the explosion. They're not sure who to trust."

"A little suspicion could work to our advantage," Nathan said. "If the men are paying attention to one another, another act of sabotage won't be so easy."

Jordan glared at his older sibling. "Yeah, genius. Or the men will be so busy watching their coworkers they won't be paying attention to their own duties and it could cause an accident. A real one this time."

Emilio stifled a smile. Normally Jordan was the most even-tempered of the four, but this situation was turning him into a bona fide hothead.

"Does anyone have anything *constructive* to add?" Adam asked, looking over at Emilio.

"Yeah, Emilio," Jordan said. "You've been awfully quiet. What's your take on this?"

Emilio turned from the window. "You feel betrayed,

Jordan. I get that. But we *will* get to the bottom of this. It's just going to take some time."

After several more minutes of heated debate between Nathan and Jordan that ultimately got them nowhere, Adam ended the meeting and Emilio headed out for the day. He let himself in the house at six-thirty, expecting to find Izzie in the kitchen making what he hoped would be an edible meal. She'd taken his advice to heart and was trying out simpler recipes. The last two nights, dinner hadn't been gourmet by any stretch of the imagination. To call it appetizing had been an even wider stretch, but he'd choked it down.

Tonight he found two pots boiling over on the stove—one with spaghetti sauce and the other noodles—and a cutting board with partially chopped vegetables on the counter. Izzie was nowhere to be found. Perhaps she didn't grasp the concept that food could not cook itself. It required supervision.

Grumbling to himself, he jerked the burner knobs into the Off position, noting the sauce splattered all over the stove. Shedding his suit jacket, he checked her room and the laundry room, but she wasn't there, either. Then he heard a sound from upstairs and headed up.

As soon as he reached the top and saw that his bedroom door was open, his hackles rose. She knew damned well his room was off-limits.

He charged toward the door, just as she emerged. Her eyes flew open wide when she saw him. He started to ask her what the hell she thought she was doing, when he noticed the blood-soaked paper towel she was holding on her left hand.

"I'm sorry," she said. "I didn't mean to invade your privacy. I was looking for a first-aid kit. I thought it might be in your bathroom."

"What happened?"

"I slipped with the knife. It's not a big deal. I just need a bandage."

A cut that bled enough to soak through a paper towel would require more than a bandage. He reached for her hand. "Let me see."

She pulled out of his reach. "I told you, it's not a big deal. It's a small cut."

"Then it won't hurt to let me look at it." Before she could move away again, he grabbed her arm.

He lifted away the paper towels and blood oozed from a wound in the fleshy part between the second and third knuckle of her index finger. He wiped it away to get a better look. The cut may have been small, but it was deep.

So much for a relaxing night at home. He sighed and said, "Get your jacket. I'll drive you to the E.R."

She jerked her hand free. "No! I just need a bandage."

"A bandage is not going to stop the bleeding. You need stitches."

"I'll butterfly it."

"Even if that did work, you still should see a doctor. You could get an infection."

She shook her head. "I'll wash it out and use antibiotic ointment. It'll be fine."

He didn't get why she was making such a big deal about this. "This is ridiculous. I'm taking you to the hospital."

"*No,* you're not."

"Izzie, for God sakes, you need to see a doctor."

"I can't."

"*Why?*"

"Because I have no way to pay for it, okay? I don't have health insurance and I don't have money."

The rush of color to her cheeks, the way she lowered her eyes, said that admitting it to him mortified her.

He assumed she had money stashed somewhere for emergencies, but maybe that wasn't the case. Was she really that destitute?

"Since it was a work-related accident, I'll pay for it," he said.

"I'm not asking for a handout."

"You didn't ask, I offered. You hurt yourself in my home. I consider it my responsibility."

She shook her head. "No."

"Isabelle—"

"I am not going to the doctor. I just need a first-aid kit."

"Obstinado," he muttered, shaking his head. The woman completely baffled him. Why wouldn't she just accept his help? She'd had no problem sponging off her rich husband for all those years. Emilio would have expected her to jump at his offer. Had she suddenly grown a conscience? A sense of pride?

Well, he wasn't going to sit and argue while she bled all over the place. He finally threw up his hands in defeat. "Fine! But I'm wrapping it for you."

For a second he thought she might argue about that too, but she seemed to sense that his patience was wearing thin. "Fine," she replied, then grumbled under her breath, "and you call *me* stubborn."

Six

Isabelle followed Emilio through his bedroom to the bathroom and waited while he grabbed the first-aid kit from the cabinet under the sink. He pulled out the necessary supplies, then gestured her over to the sink and turned on the cold water.

"This is probably going to hurt," he told her, but as he took her hand and placed it under the flow, she didn't even flinch. He gently soaped up the area around the cut with his thumb to clean it, then grabbed a bottle of hydrogen peroxide. Holding her hand over the sink, he poured it on the wound. As it foamed up, her only reaction was a soft intake of breath, even though he knew it had to sting like hell.

He grabbed a clean towel from the cabinet and gently blotted her hand dry. It was starting to clot, so there was hope that a butterfly would be enough to stop any further bleeding if he wrapped it firmly enough. Although he still thought stitches were warranted. Without them it could leave a nasty scar.

He sat on the edge of the counter and pulled her closer, so she was standing between his knees. She didn't fight him, but it was obvious, by the tension in her stance as he spread ointment on the cut, that she was uncomfortable being close to him.

"Something wrong?" he asked, glancing up at her. "You seem…tense."

She avoided his gaze. "I'm fine."

If she were fine, why the nervous waver in her voice? "Maybe you don't like being so close to me." He lifted his eyes to hers, running his thumb across her wrist. The slight widening of her eyes, when she was trying hard not to react, made him smile. "Or maybe you do."

"I definitely don't."

Her wildly beating heart and the blush of her cheeks said otherwise. There was a physical reaction for him, as well. A pull of desire deep inside of him. Despite everything she had done, she was still a beautiful, desirable woman. And he was a man who hadn't been with a woman in several months. He just hadn't had the time for all the baggage that went along with it.

"Are you almost finished?" Isabelle asked.

"Almost." Emilio took his time, applying the butterfly then smoothing a second, larger bandage over the top to hold it in place.

"That should do it," he said, but when she tried to pull her hand free, he held on. "How about a kiss, to make it feel better?"

Her eyes widened slightly and she gave another tug. "That's really not necessary."

"I think it is." And perhaps she did, too, because she didn't try to pull away as he lifted her hand to his mouth and pressed his lips to her palm. He felt her shiver, felt her skin go hot. He kissed her palm again, then the inside of her wrist, breathing warm air against her skin. "You like that."

"Not at all."

"Your body says otherwise."

"Well, obviously it's confused."

That made him smile. "You still want me. Admit it."

"You're delusional," she said, but there was a hitch in her voice, a quiver that belied her arousal. She was hot for him.

This was going to be too easy.

Izzie gently pulled from his grasp. "I have to finish dinner."

She turned, but before she could walk away he slipped his arms around her waist and pulled her close to him. She gasped as her back pressed against his chest, her behind tucked snugly against his groin. When she felt the ridge of his erection, she froze.

He leaned close, whispered in her ear, "What's your hurry, Isabelle?"

All she had to do was tell him to stop and he would have without question, but she didn't. She stood there, unmoving, as if she were unsure of what to do. He knew in that instant she was as good as his. But not until she was begging for it. He wanted total submission. The same unconditional and unwavering devotion he had shown her fifteen years ago.

He nuzzled her neck and her head tipped to the side. He couldn't see her face, but he sensed that her eyes were closed.

"You smell delicious, Isabelle." He caught her earlobe between his teeth and she sucked in a breath. "Good enough to eat."

"We can't do this," she said, her voice uneven, her breathing shallow.

He brushed his lips against her neck. "Are you asking me to stop?"

She didn't answer.

He slid his hands up, over her rib cage, using his thumbs to caress the undersides of her breasts. They were as full and supple as they had been fifteen years ago. He wanted to unbutton her dress and slip his hands inside, touch her bare skin. Taste her.

But all in good time.

"My bed is just a few steps away," he whispered in her ear, wondering just how far she was willing to let this go. He didn't have to wait long to find out.

"Stop."

He dropped his hands and she whirled away from him, her eyes wide. "Why did you do that? You don't even like me."

A grin curled his mouth. "Because you wanted me to."

"I most certainly did not."

"We both know that isn't true, Isabelle." He pushed off the edge of the counter and rose to his feet. He could see that she wanted to run but she stood her ground. "You like it when I touch you. I know what makes you feel good."

"I'm not stupid. You don't really want me."

"I would say that all evidence points to the contrary."

Her gaze darted to his crotch, then quickly away. "I have to go finish dinner."

"Don't bother. I had a late lunch. Save the sauce for later."

"Fine."

"But that doesn't mean you should skip dinner. I want to see another pound on the scale in the morning." She had only gained two so far this week, though she swore she'd been eating three meals a day. "And take something for your hand. It's going to hurt like hell."

"I will," she said, but his concern clearly confused her.

And it was a sensation she would be experiencing a lot from now on, he thought with a smile.

Isabelle headed downstairs on unsteady legs, willing her heart to slow its frantic pace, her hands to stop trembling.

What the *hell* had she been thinking? Why had she let Emilio touch her that way? Why had she let him touch her at all? She had been perfectly capable of bandaging her own finger. She should have insisted he let her do it herself. But she foolishly believed he was doing it because he cared about her, cared that she was hurt.

When would she learn?

He didn't care about her. Not at all. He was just trying to confuse her. This was just some twisted plot for revenge.

And could she blame him? Didn't she deserve anything he could dish out? Put in his position, after the way she'd hurt him, would she have done things any differently?

She'd brought this on herself. That's what her father used to tell her, how he justified his actions. She'd spent years convincing herself that it wasn't her fault, that he was the one with the problem. What if she was wrong? What if she really had deserved it back then, and she was getting exactly what she deserved now? Maybe this was her penance for betraying Emilio.

She heard him come downstairs and braced herself for another confrontation, but he went straight to his office and shut the door.

Limp with relief, she cleaned up the mess from the unfinished meal then fixed herself a sandwich with the leftover roast beef from the night before, but she only managed to choke down a bite or two. She covered what was left with plastic wrap and put it in the fridge—if there was one thing she had learned lately, it was to not waste food—then locked herself in her room. It was still early, but she was exhausted so she changed into her pajamas and curled up in bed. Her finger had begun to throb, but it didn't come close to the ache in her heart. Maybe coming here had been a mistake. In fifteen years she hadn't figured out how to stop loving Emilio.

Maybe she never would.

"How's the finger?" Emilio asked Isabelle the next evening as he ate his spaghetti. He usually sat in the dining room, but tonight he'd insisted on sitting at the kitchen table. If that wasn't awkward enough, he kept *watching* her.

At least he hadn't complained about dinner, despite the fact that the noodles were slightly overdone and the garlic bread was a little singed around the edges. He seemed to recognize that she was trying. Or maybe he thought if he complained she might make good on her threat and smother him in his sleep.

"It's fine," she said. It still throbbed, but the ibuprofen tablets she'd been gobbling like candy all day had at least taken the sharp edge off the pain.

"We'll need to redress it."

We? As if she would let him anywhere near her after last night.

"I'll do it later," she said.

He got up to carry his plate to the sink, where she just happened to be standing, loading the dishwasher. She couldn't move away without looking like she was running from him, and she didn't want him to know he was making her nervous. He already held most of the cards in this game he'd started. And she had little doubt that it was a game.

The key was not letting him know that he was getting to her, that she even cared what he thought.

He put his plate and fork in the dishwasher. "I should check it for signs of infection."

He reached for her arm but she moved out of his grasp. "I can do it myself."

"Suit yourself," he said, wearing a cocky grin as he turned to wash his hands.

Ugh! The man was insufferable. Yet the desire to lean into him, to wrap her arms around him and breathe in his scent, to lay her cheek against his back and listen to the steady thump of his heart beating, was as strong now as it had been all those years ago. She'd spent more than half her life fantasizing about him, wishing with all her heart that they could be together, and for one perfect year he had been hers.

But she had made her choice, one that up until a few days ago, she'd learned to accept. Now her doubts had begun to resurface and she found herself rehashing the same old *what ifs.* What if she had been stronger? What if she stood up to her father instead of caving to his threats?

What if she'd at least had the courage to tell Emilio goodbye?

She had tried. She went to see him, to tell him that she had decided to marry Lenny. She knew he would never understand why, and probably never forgive her, but she owed him an explanation. Even if she could never tell him the truth.

But the instant she'd seen his face, how happy he was to see her, she'd lost her nerve and, because she couldn't bear to see him hurting, she pretended everything was okay. She hadn't stopped him when he started kissing her, when he took her hand and led her to his room. And because she couldn't bear going the rest of her life never knowing what it would be like to make love to him, she'd had every intention of giving herself to him that night.

Emilio had been the one to put on the brakes, to say not yet. He had been concerned that she would regret giving in so close to their wedding day. She hadn't had the heart, or the courage, to tell him that day would never come.

Would things have been different if she had at least told him she was leaving? For all she knew, they might have been worse. He might have talked her into telling him the truth, and that would have been a disaster.

She never expected him to forgive her—she hadn't even forgiven herself yet—but she had hoped that he would have moved on by now. It broke her heart to know how deeply she had hurt him. That after all this time he was *still* hurting. If he wasn't why would he be so hell-bent on hurting her back?

Maybe she should give him what he wanted, allow him his vengeance if that was what it would take to reconcile the past. Maybe she owed it to him—and to herself. Maybe then she could stop feeling so guilty.

After last night she could only assume he planned to use sex to get his revenge. If she slept with him, would he feel vindicated? And was she prepared to compromise her principles by having sex with a man who clearly hated her? Or did the fact that she still loved him make it okay?

Before she could consider the consequences of her actions, she stuck her hand out.

"Here," she said. "Maybe you should check it. Just in case."

He looked at her hand, then lifted his eyes to her face. There was a hint of amusement in their smoky depths. "I'm sure you can manage on your own."

Huh?

He dried his hands, then walked out of the kitchen.

She followed him. "What do you want from me, Emilio?"

He stopped just outside his office door and turned to her. "Want?"

He knew exactly what she meant. "I know I hurt you, and I'm *sorry*. Just tell me what you want me to do and I'll do it."

His stormy gaze leveled on her and suddenly she felt naked. How did he manage to do that with just a look? How did he make her feel so stripped bare?

He took a step toward her and her heart went crazy in her chest. She tried to be brave, to stand her ground, but as he moved closer, she found herself taking one step back, then another, until she hit the wall. Maybe offering herself up as the sacrificial lamb hadn't been such a hot idea, after all. Maybe she should have worked up to this just a little slower instead of jumping right into the deep end of the pool. But it was too late now.

In the past he had always been so sweet and tender, so patient with her. Now he wore a look that said he was about to eat her alive. It both terrified and thrilled her, because despite the years that had passed, deep down she still felt like the same naive, inexperienced girl. Way out of her league, yet eager to learn. And in all these years the gap seemed to widen exponentially.

Emilio braced a hand on one side of her head, leaning in, the faint whisper of his scent filling her senses—familiar, but different somehow. If she were braver she would have touched him. She *wanted* to. Instead she stood frozen, waiting for him to make the first move, wondering how far he would take this, and if she would let him. If she *should*.

Emilio dipped his head and nuzzled her cheek, his breath warm against her skin, then his lips brushed the column of her throat and Isabelle's knees went weak.

Thank goodness she had the wall to hold her steady. One kiss and she was toast. And it wasn't even a *real* kiss.

His other hand settled on the curve of her waist, the heat of his palm scorching her skin through the fabric of her uniform. She wanted to reach up and tunnel her fingers through the softness of his hair, slide her arms around his neck, pull him down and press her mouth to his. The anticipation of his lips touching hers had her trembling from the inside out.

He nipped the lobe of her ear, slid his hand upward and as his thumb grazed the underside of her breast she had to fight not to moan. Her nipples tingled and hardened. Breath quickened. She wanted to take his hand and guide it over her breast, but she kept her own hands fisted at her sides, afraid that any move she made might be the wrong one.

His lips brushed the side of her neck, her chin. This was so wrong, but she couldn't pull away. Couldn't stop him. She didn't *want* him to stop.

His lips brushed her cheek, the corner of her mouth, then finally her lips. So sweet and tender, and when his tongue skimmed hers she went limp with desire. In that instant she stopped caring that he was using her, that he didn't even like her, that to him this was just some stupid game of revenge. She didn't even care that he would probably take her fragile heart and rip it all to pieces. She was going to take what she wanted, what she needed, what she'd spent the last fifteen years *aching* for.

One minute her arms were at her sides and the next they were around his neck, fingers tunneling through his hair, and something inside Emilio seemed to snap. He shoved her backward and she gasped as he crushed her against the wall with the weight of his body. The kiss went from sweet and tender to deep and punishing so fast it stole her breath.

He cupped her behind, arched against her, and she could feel the hard length of his erection against her stomach. If not for the skirt of her dress, she would have wound her legs around his hips and ground into him. She wanted him to take her right there, in the hallway.

But as abruptly as it had begun, it was over. Emilio let go of her and backed away, leaving her stunned and confused and aching for more.

"Good night, Isabelle," he said, his voice so icy and devoid of emotion that she went cold all over. He stepped into his office and shut the door behind him and she heard the lock click into place. She had to fight not to hurl herself at it, to keep from pounding with her fists and demand he finish what he started.

She had never been so aroused, or so humiliated, in her life. She wasn't sure what sort of game he was playing, but as she sank back against the wall, struggling to make sense of what had just happened, she had the sinking feeling that it was far from over.

Damn.

Emilio closed and locked his office door and leaned against it, fighting to catch his breath, to make sense of what had just happened.

What had gone wrong?

Things had been progressing as planned. He had been in complete control. He'd had Isabelle right where he wanted her. Then everything went to hell. Their lips touched and his head started to spin, then she wrapped her arms around his neck, rubbed against him and he'd just...*lost* it.

He'd been seconds from ripping open that god-awful uniform and putting his hands on her. He had been this-close to shoving up the skirt of her dress, ripping off her panties and taking her right there in the hallway, up against the wall. He wanted her as much now as he had fifteen years ago. And putting on the brakes, denying himself the pleasure of everything she offered, had been just as damned hard.

That hadn't been part of the plan.

On the bright side, making Isabelle bend to his will, making her beg for it, was clearly not going to be a problem.

He crossed the room to the wet bar and splashed cold water on his face. This had just been a fluke. A knee-jerk reaction to the last vestiges of a long dormant sexual attraction. It was physical and nothing more. So from now on, losing control wasn't going to be an issue.

Seven

Isabelle stood at the stove fixing breakfast the next morning, reliving the nightmarish events of last night. How could she have been so stupid? So naive?

Just tell me what you want and I'll do it.

Well, she'd gotten her answer. He hadn't come right out and said it, but the implications of his actions had been crystal clear. He wanted to make her want him, get her all hot and bothered, then reject her. Simple yet effective.

Very effective.

As much as she hated it, as miserable and small as he'd made her feel, didn't she deserve this? Hadn't she more or less done the same thing to him fifteen years ago? Could she really fault him for wanting revenge?

She had gotten herself into this mess, she'd asked for his help, now she had to live with the consequences. She could try to resist him, try to pretend she didn't melt when

MICHELLE CELMER 75

he touched her, but she had always been a terrible liar. And honestly, she didn't have the energy to fight him.

The worst, most humiliating part was knowing that if she told him no, if she asked him to stop, he would. He would never force himself on her. He'd made that clear the other night. The problem was, she didn't *want* to tell him no.

Unlike Emilio, she couldn't switch it off and on. Her only defense was to avoid him as often as possible. And when she couldn't? Well, she would try her hardest to not make a total fool of herself again. She would try to be strong.

She would hold up her end of the bargain, and hopefully everyone would get exactly what they wanted. She just wished she didn't feel so darned edgy and out of sorts, and she knew he was going to sense it the second he saw her.

According to Mrs. Medina's "list," Emilio didn't leave for work until nine-thirty on Saturdays, so Isabelle didn't have to see him until nine when he came down for breakfast. If she timed it just right, she could feed him right when he walked into the kitchen, then hide until his ride got there.

Of course he chose that morning to come down fifteen minutes early. She was at the stove, trying not to incinerate a pan of hash brown potatoes, when he walked into the room.

"Good morning," he said, the rumble of his voice tweaking her already frayed nerves.

She took a deep breath and told herself, *You can do this.* Pasting on what she hoped was a nothing-you-do-can-hurt-me face, she turned…and whatever she had been about to say died the minute she laid eyes on him.

He wasn't wearing a suit. Or a tie. Or a shirt. Or even shoes. All he wore was a pair of black silk pajama bottoms slung low on his hips. That was it. His hair was mussed from sleep and dark stubble shadowed his jaw.

Oh boy.

Most men declined with age. They developed excess flab or a paunch or even unattractive back hair, but not Emilio. His chest was lean and well-defined, his shoulders and back smooth and tanned and he had a set of six-pack abs to die for. He was everything he had been fifteen years ago, only better.

A lot better.

Terrific.

She realized she was staring and averted her eyes. Was it her fault she hadn't seen a mostly naked man in a really long time? At least, not one who looked as good as he did.

Lenny had had the paunch, and the flab, and the back hair. Not that their relationship had ever been about sex.

Ever the dutiful housekeeper, she said, "Sit down, I'll get you coffee." Mostly she just wanted to keep him out of her half of the kitchen.

He took a seat on one of the stools at the island. She grabbed a mug from the cupboard, filled it and set it in front of him.

"Thanks."

Their eyes met and his flashed with some unidentifiable emotion. Amusement maybe? She couldn't be sure, and frankly she didn't want to know.

Make breakfast, run and hide.

She busied herself with cutting up the vegetables that would go in the omelet she planned to make, taking great care not to slice or sever any appendages. Although it was tough to keep her eyes on what she was doing when Emilio was directly in her line of vision, barely an arm's reach away, looking hotter than the Texas sun.

And he was *watching* her.

She would gather everything up and move across to the opposite counter, where her back would be to him instead, but she doubted his probing stare would be any less irritating. She diced the green onions, his gaze boring into her as he casually sipped his coffee.

"Don't you have to get ready for work?" she asked.

"You trying to get rid of me, Isabelle?"

Well, *duh.* "Just curious."

"I'm working from home today."

She suppressed a groan. Fantastic. An entire day with Emilio in the house. With any luck, he would lock himself in his office and wouldn't emerge until dinnertime. But somehow she doubted she would be so lucky. She also doubted it was a coincidence that he chose this particular day to work at home. She was sure that every move he made was calculated.

She chopped the red peppers, trying to ignore the weight of his steely gray stare.

"I want you to clean my bedroom today," he said, reaching across to the cutting board to snatch a cube of pepper.

Of course he did. "I thought it was off-limits."

"It is. Until I say it isn't."

She stopped chopping and shot him a glance.

He shrugged. "My house, my rules."

Another calculated move on his part. He was just full of surprises today. He was manipulating her and he was good at it. He knew she had absolutely no recourse.

He sipped his coffee, watching her slice the mini bella mushrooms. But he wasn't just watching. He was *studying* her. She failed to understand what was so riveting about seeing someone chop food. Which meant he was just doing it to make her uncomfortable, and it was working.

When she couldn't take it any longer, she said in her most patient tone, "Would you please stop that?"

"Stop what?"

"Watching me. It's making me nervous."

"I'm just curious to see what you're going to cut this time. The way you hold that knife, my money is on the tip of your thumb. Although I'm sure if we keep it on ice, there's a good chance they can reattach it."

She stopped cutting and glared at him.

He grinned, and for a second he looked just like the Emilio from fifteen years ago. He used to smile all the time back then. A sexy, slightly lopsided grin that never failed to make her go all gooey inside. And still did.

She preferred him when he was cranky and brooding. She had a defense for that. When he did things like smile and tease her, it was too easy to forget that it was all an act. That he was only doing it to manipulate her.

Although she hoped someday he would show her a smile that he actually meant.

"Despite what you think, I'm not totally inept," she said.

"No?"

"No."

"So the pan on the stove is supposed to be smoking like that?"

At first she thought he was just saying it to irritate her, then she remembered that she'd been frying potatoes. She spun around and saw that there actually was black smoke billowing from the pan.

"Damn it!" She darted to the stove, twisted off the flame, grabbed the handle and jerked the pan off the burner. But she jerked too hard and oil sloshed over the side. She tried to jump out of the way, but she wasn't fast enough and molten hot oil splashed down the skirt of her dress, soaking through the fabric to the top of her thigh.

She gasped at the quick and sharp sting. She barely had time to process what had happened, to react, when she felt Emilio's hands on her waist.

He lifted her off her feet and deposited her on the edge of the counter next to the sink. And he wasn't smiling anymore. "Did you burn yourself?"

"A—a little, I think."

He eased the skirt of her uniform up her thighs. So far up that she was sure he could see the crotch of her bargain bin panties, but protesting seemed silly at this point since he obviously wasn't doing it to get fresh with her. And she knew there was something seriously wrong with her when all she could think was *thank God I shaved my legs this morning*.

The middle of her right thigh had a splotchy red spot the size of a saucer and it burned like the devil.

Emilio grabbed a dish towel from the counter and soaked it with cool water, then he wrung it out and laid it against her burn. She sucked in a breath as the cold cloth hit her hot skin.

"Are you okay?" he asked, his eyes dark with concern. "Do you feel light-headed or dizzy?"

She shook her head. What she felt was mortified.

Not totally inept, huh?

She couldn't even manage fried potatoes without causing a disaster. Although, this was partially his fault. If he'd worn a damn shirt, and if he hadn't been *looking* at her, she wouldn't have been so distracted.

Emilio got a fresh towel from the drawer and made an ice pack large enough to cover the burn, while she sat there feeling like a complete idiot.

"I guess I was wrong," she said.

He lifted the towel to inspect her leg and it immediately began to sting. "About what?"

"I am inept."

"It was an accident."

Huh?

He wasn't going to rub this in her face, try to make her feel like an even bigger idiot? He wasn't going to make fun of her and call her incompetent?

Was this another trick?

"It's red, but it doesn't look like it's blistering. I think your uniform absorbed most of the heat." He laid the ice pack very gently on the burned area. The sting immediately subsided. He looked up at her. "Better?"

She nodded. With her sitting on the counter they were almost eye to eye and, for the first time that morning, she really *saw* him.

Though he looked pretty much the same as he had fifteen years ago, there were subtle signs of age. The hint of crow's-feet branded the corners of his eyes, and there were a few flecks of gray in the stubble on his chin. The line of his jaw seemed less rigid than it used to be, and the lines in his forehead had deepened.

He looked tired. Maybe what had happened at the refinery, compounded by his deal with her, was stressing him out. Maybe he hadn't been sleeping well.

Despite it all, to her he was the same Emilio. At least, her heart thought so. That was probably why it was hurting so much.

But if Emilio really hated her, would it matter that she'd hurt herself? Would he have been so quick to jump in and take care of her? Would he be standing here now holding the ice pack on her leg when she could just as easily do it herself?

He may have been hardened by life, but maybe the sweet, tender man she had fallen in love with was still in

•

there somewhere. Maybe he would be willing to forgive her someday. Or maybe she was fooling herself.

Maybe you should tell him the truth.

At this point it would be a relief to have it all out in the open. But even if she tried, she doubted he would believe her.

"You're watching me," he said, and she realized that he'd caught her red-handed. Oh well, after last night he had to know she still had feelings for him. That she still longed for his touch.

She averted her eyes anyway. "Sorry."

"Did you know that you cursed? When you saw the pan was smoking."

Had she? It was all a bit of a blur. "I don't recall."

"You said 'damn it.' I've never heard you swear before."

She shrugged. "Maybe I didn't have anything to swear about back then."

It wasn't true. She'd had plenty to swear about. But she had been so terrified of slipping up in front of her father, it was safer to not swear at all. He expected her to be the proper Texas debutant. His perfect princess. Though she somehow always managed to fall short.

She still didn't swear very often. Old habits, she supposed. But sometimes a cuss or two would slip out.

He lifted the ice pack and looked at her leg again. "It's not blistered, so it's not that bad of a burn. How does it feel?"

"A little worse than a sunburn."

"Some aloe and a couple of ibuprofen should take care of the pain." He set the pack back on her leg. "Hold this while I go get it."

She was about to tell him that she could do it herself, but she sort of liked being pampered. He would go back to hating her soon, and lusting for revenge. She figured she might as well enjoy it while she could.

Isabelle heard his footsteps going up the stairs, then coming back down and he reappeared with a bottle of aloe and a couple of pain tablets. He got a glass down from the cupboard and filled it with water from the dispenser on the fridge. He gave her that and the tablets and she dutifully swallowed them. She assumed he would hand over the bottle of aloe so she could go in her room and apply it herself. Instead he squirted a glob in his palm and dropped the ice pack into the sink.

There was nothing overtly sexual about his actions as he spread the aloe across her burn, but her body couldn't make the distinction. She felt every touch like a lover's caress. And she wanted him. So badly.

So much for trying to resist him. He wasn't even trying to seduce her and she wanted to climb all over him.

"Why are you being so nice to me?" she asked.

He braced his hands on the edge of the counter on either side of her thighs and looked up at her. "Truthfully, Izzie, I don't know."

It was the probably the most honest thing he had said to her, and before she could even think about what she was doing, she reached up and touched his cheek. It was warm and rough.

His eyes turned stormy.

She knew this was a bad idea, that she was setting herself up to be hurt, but she couldn't stop. She wanted to touch him. She didn't care that it was all an illusion. It felt real to her, and wasn't that all that mattered? And who knows, maybe this time he wouldn't push her away.

She stroked his rough cheek, ran her thumb across his full lower lip. He breathed in deep and closed his eyes. He was holding back, gripping the edge of the countertop so hard his knuckles were white.

She knew she was playing with fire and she didn't care. This time she *wanted* to get burned.

Eight

Isabelle leaned forward and pressed a kiss to Emilio's cheek. The unique scent of his skin, the rasp of his beard stubble, was familiar and comfortable and exciting all at once. Which was probably why her heart was beating so hard and her hands were trembling. The idea that he might push her away now was terrifying, but she wanted this more than she'd ever wanted anything in her life.

She kissed the corner of his mouth, then his lips and he lost it. He wrapped his hands around her hips and tugged her to the edge of the countertop, kissing her hard. Her breasts crushed against his chest, legs went around his waist. This would be no slow, sensual tease like last night.

She had always fantasized about their first time being sweet and tender, and preferably in a bed. There would be candles and champagne and soft music playing. Now none of that seemed to matter. She wanted him with a desperation she'd never felt before. She wanted him to rip off her panties and take her right there in the kitchen, before he changed his mind.

She tunneled her fingers through his hair, fed off his mouth, his stubble rough against her chin. He slid his hands up her sides to her breasts, cupping them in his palms, capturing the tips between his fingers and pinching. She gasped and tightened her legs around him, praying silently, *Please don't stop.*

He tugged at the top button on her uniform, and when it didn't immediately come loose he ripped it open instead. The dress was ruined, anyway, so what difference did it make? And it thrilled her to know that he couldn't wait to get his hands on her.

He peeled the dress off her shoulders and down her arms, pinning them to her sides, ravaging her with kisses and bites—her shoulders and her throat and the tops of her breasts. Then he yanked down one of her bra cups, took her nipple into his mouth, sucking hard, and she almost died it felt so good.

Please, *please* don't stop.

She felt his hand on her thigh, held her breath as it moved slowly upward, the tips of his fingers brushing against the crotch of her panties…

And the doorbell rang.

Emilio cursed. She groaned. Not now, not when they were *so* close.

"Ignore it," she said.

He cursed again, dropping his head to her shoulder, breathing hard. "I can't. A courier from work is dropping off documents. I need them." He glanced at the clock on the oven display. "Although he wasn't supposed to be here until *noon.*"

This was so not fair.

He backed away and she had no choice but to drop her legs from around his waist.

This was *so* not fair.

"You're going to have to get it," he said.

"Me?" Her uniform was in shambles. Ripped and stained and rumpled.

"Consider the alternative," he said, gesturing to the tent in the front of his pajama pants.

Good point.

He lifted her off the counter and set her on her feet. She wrestled her dress back up over her shoulders and tugged the skirt down over her thighs as she hurried to the door. With the button gone she would have to hold her uniform together, or give the delivery guy a special tip for his trouble.

She started to turn and Emilio caught her by the arm.

"Don't think for a second that I'm finished with you."

Oh boy. The heat in his eyes, the sizzle in his voice made her heart skip a beat. Was he going to finish what he started this time? No, what *she* had started.

The idea of what was to come made her knees weak.

The doorbell rang again and he set her loose. "Go."

She dashed through the house to the foyer, catching a glimpse of herself in the full-length mirror by the door. She cringed at her rumpled appearance, convinced that the delivery person would know immediately that she and Emilio had been fooling around. Well, so what if he did? As long as he didn't recognize her, who cared?

Holding the collar of her dress closed, she yanked the door open, expecting the person on the other side to be wearing a delivery uniform. But the man standing on Emilio's porch was dressed in faded jeans, cowboy boots and a trendy black leather jacket. His dark hair was shoulder length and slicked back from his face, and there was something vaguely familiar about him.

He blatantly took in Isabelle's wrinkled and stained uniform, the razor burn on her chin and throat, her mussed hair. One brow tipped up in a move that was eerily familiar, and he asked with blatant amusement, "Rough morning, huh?"

Emilio cursed silently when he recognized the voice of the man on the other side of the door. After three months without so much as a phone call, why did his brother have to pick now to show his face again?

Talk about a mood killer.

He just hoped like hell that Estefan didn't recognize Isabelle, or this could get ugly.

Emilio rounded the corner to the foyer and pushed his way past Isabelle, who didn't seem to know what to say.

"I've got this," he said, and noted with amusement that as she stepped back from the door, she shot a worried glance at his crotch.

"I'll go change," she said, heading for the kitchen.

"Hey, bro," Estefan said, oozing charm. "Long time no see."

He looked good, and though he didn't appear to be under the influence, he was a master at hiding his addictions. Estefan was a handsome, charming guy, which was why people caved to his requests after he let them down time and time again. But not Emilio. He'd learned his lesson.

"What do you want, Estefan?"

"You're not going to invite me inside?"

With Isabelle there? Not a chance. If he had the slightest clue what Emilio was doing, he would exploit the situation to his own benefit.

"I don't even know where you've been for the past three months. Mama has been worried sick about you."

"Not in jail, if that's what you're thinking."

No, because if he'd been arrested, Alejandro would have heard about it. But there were worse things than incarceration.

"I know you probably won't believe this, but I'm clean and sober. I have been for months."

He was right, Emilio didn't believe it. Not for a second. And even if he was, on the rare occasions he'd actually stuck with a rehab program long enough to get clean, it hadn't taken him long to fall back into his old habits.

"What do you want, Estefan?"

"Do I need a reason to see my big brother?"

Maybe not, but he always had one. Usually he needed money, or a place to crash. Occasionally both. He'd even asked to borrow Emilio's car a couple of times, because his own cars had a habit of being repossessed or totaled in accidents that were never Estefan's fault.

He wanted something. He always did.

"Unless you tell me why you're here, I'm closing the door."

The smile slipped from Estefan's face when he realized charm wasn't going to work this time. "I just want to talk to you."

"We have nothing to talk about."

"Come on, Emilio. I'm your baby brother."

"Tell me where you've been."

"Los Angeles, mostly. I was working on a business deal."

A shady one, he was sure. Most of Estefan's "business" deals involved stolen property or drugs, or any number of scams. The fact that he was a small-time criminal with a federal prosecutor for a brother was the only thing that had kept him from doing hard time.

"You're really not going to let me in?" he asked, looking wounded.

"I think I already made that clear."

"You know, I never took you for the type to do the hired help. But I also never expected to see Isabelle Winthrop working for you. Unless the maid's uniform is just some kinky game you play."

Emilio cursed under his breath.

"Did you think I wouldn't recognize her?"

He had hoped, but he should have known better.

"I don't suppose Mama knows what you're doing."

He recognized a threat when he heard one. He held the door open. "Five minutes."

With an arrogant smile, Estefan strolled in.

"Wait here," Emilio said, then walked to the kitchen. Isabelle had changed into a clean uniform and was straightening up the mess from breakfast. She'd fixed her hair and the beard burns had begun to fade.

He should have waited until he shaved to kiss her, but then, he hadn't been expecting her to make the first move. And he hadn't meant to reciprocate. So much for regaining his control. If Estefan hadn't shown up, Emilio had no doubt they would be in his bed right now. Which would have been a huge mistake.

This wasn't working out at all as he'd planned. He wasn't sure if it was his fault, or hers. All he knew was that it had to stop.

She tensed when he entered the room, looking past him to the doorway. He turned to see that his brother had followed him. Figures. Why would he expect Estefan to do anything he asked?

"It's okay," Emilio told Isabelle. "We're going to my

office to talk. I just wanted to tell you to forget about breakfast."

She nodded, then squared her shoulders and met Estefan's gaze. "Mr. Suarez."

"Ms. Winthrop," he said, the words dripping with disdain. "Shouldn't you be in prison?"

The old Isabelle would have withered from his challenge, but this Isabelle held her head high. "Five more weeks. Thanks for asking. Can I offer you something to drink?"

"He's not staying," Emilio said, gesturing Estefan to follow him. "Let's get this over with."

When they were in his office with the door closed, Estefan said, "Isabelle Winthrop, huh? I had no idea you were that hard up."

"Not that it's any of your business, but I'm not sleeping with her." Not yet, anyway. And he was beginning to think making her work as his housekeeper might have to be the extent of his revenge. There were consequences to getting close to her that he had never anticipated.

"So, what is she doing here?"

"She works for me."

"Why would you hire someone like her? After what her family did to our mother. After what she did to you."

"That's my business."

A slow smile crossed his face. "Ah, I get it. Make her work for you, the way our mother worked for her. Nice."

"I'm glad you approve."

"What does she get out of it?"

"She wants Alejandro to cut a deal for her mother, so she won't go to prison."

"So, Alejandro knows what you're doing?"

Emilio took a seat behind his desk, to keep the balance

of power clear. "Let's talk about you, Estefan. What do *you* want?"

"You assume I'm here because I want something from you?"

Emilio shot him a look, putting a chink in the arrogant facade. Estefan crossed the room to look out the window. He didn't even have the guts to look Emilio in the face. "I want you to hear me out before you say anything."

Emilio folded his arms across his chest. *Here we go.*

"There are these people, and I owe them money."

Emilio opened his mouth to say he wouldn't give him a penny, but Estefan raised a hand to stop him. "I'm not asking you for a handout. That's not why I'm here. I have the money to pay them. It's just not accessible at the moment."

"Why?"

"Someone is holding it for me."

"Who?"

"A business associate. He has to liquidate a few assets to pay me, and that's going to take several days. But these men are impatient. I just need a place to hang out until I get the funds. Somewhere they won't find me. It would only be for a few days. Thanksgiving at the latest."

Which was *five* days away. Emilio didn't want his brother around for five minutes, much less the better part of a week.

"Suppose they come looking for you here?" Emilio asked.

"Even if they did, this place is a fortress." He crossed the room, braced his hands on Emilio's desk, a desperation in his eyes that he didn't often let show. "You have to help me, Emilio. I've been trying so hard to set my life straight. After I pay this debt I'm in the clear. I have a friend in rodeo promotions who is willing to give me a job. I could start over, do things right this time."

He wanted to believe his brother, but he'd heard the same story too many times before.

Estefan must have sensed that Emilio was about to say no because he added, "I could go to Mama, and you know she would let me stay, but these are not the kind of people you want anywhere near your mother. There's no telling what they might do."

Leaving Emilio no choice but to let him stay. And Estefan knew it. Emilio should have guessed he would resort to emotional blackmail to get his way. He also suspected that if he refused, it was likely everyone would find out that Isabelle was in his home.

He rose from his chair. "Five days. If you haven't settled your debt by then, you're on your own."

Estefan embraced him. "Thank you, Emilio."

"Just so we're clear, while you're staying in my house there will be no drinking or drugs."

"I don't do that anymore. I'm clean."

"And you won't tell anyone that Isabelle is here."

"Not a soul. You have my word."

"And you will *not* give her a hard time."

Estefan raised a brow.

"My house, my rules."

He shrugged. "Whatever you say."

"I'll have Isabelle get a room ready for you."

"I have a few things to take care of. But I'll be back later tonight. Probably late."

"I'll be in bed by midnight, so if you're not back by then, you're in the pool house for the night."

"If you give me the alarm code—"

Emilio shot him a *not-in-this-lifetime* look.

He shrugged again. "I'll be back by midnight, then."

Estefan left and Emilio went to find Isabelle. She was kneeling on the kitchen floor, cleaning up the oil that spilled by the stove. Only then did he remember that she'd burned her leg, and wondered if it still hurt.

Maybe he should have considered that before he put the moves on her. Of course, he hadn't started it this time, had he? Seducing her had been the last thing on his mind.

Okay, maybe not the *last* thing…

She saw him standing there and shot to her feet. "I'm so sorry. If I had known it was him at the door—"

"I told you to answer it, Isabelle. It's not your fault."

"He won't tell anyone, will he?"

"He promised not to. He's going to be staying here for a few days. Possibly until Thanksgiving."

"Oh."

"It won't change anything. Except maybe you'll be feeding one more person."

"There are always leftovers, anyway."

"What he said to you, it was uncalled for. It won't happen again. I told him that he's not allowed to give you a hard time."

"Because you're the only one allowed to make disparaging comments?"

Something like that. Although now when he thought about saying something rude, it just made him feel like a jerk. He kept thinking about what Alejandro said, about the new developments. That she might be innocent. And even if she was involved somehow, was he so beyond reproach that he felt he had the right to judge her?

That didn't change what she had done to him, and what her father did to his family. For that she was getting exactly what she deserved.

"I'm sorry I ruined breakfast," she said. "I guess hash browns are a little out of my league."

Or maybe it was the result of him distracting her. He never would have done it if he had known she would get hurt. "So you'll make easier things from now on."

"I don't think frying potatoes would be considered complicated. I think I'm just hopeless when it comes to cooking. But thanks for taking care of me. It's been a really long time since someone has done something nice for me. Someone besides my mom, anyway."

"Your husband didn't do nice things for you?" He didn't mean to ask the question. He didn't give a flying fig what her husband did or didn't do. It just sort of popped out.

"Lenny took very good care of me," she said, an undercurrent of bitterness in her voice. "I didn't want for a single thing when I was married to him."

But she wasn't happy, her tone said.

Well, she had made her own bed. Emilio would have given her anything, *done* anything to make her happy. But that hadn't been enough for her.

Her loss.

She pulled off her gloves, wincing a bit when it jostled her bandaged finger.

"It still hurts?" he asked, and she shrugged. "Any signs of infection?"

"It's fine."

That was her standard answer. It could be black with gangrene and she would probably say it was fine. "When was the last time you changed the dressing?"

"Last night…I think."

From the condition of the bandage he would guess it was closer to the night before last. Clearly she wasn't taking care of it. He didn't want to be responsible if it got infected.

He held out his hand. "Let's see it."

She didn't even bother arguing, she just held her hand out to him. He peeled the bandage off. The cut itself had closed, but the area around it was inflamed. There's no way she could not have known it was infected. "Damn, Isabelle, are you *trying* to lose a finger?"

"I've been busy."

"Too busy to take care of yourself?" He dropped her hand. "You still have the antibiotic ointment?"

She nodded.

"Use it. I want you to put a fresh dressing on it three times a day until the infection is cleared up."

"I will. I promise."

"I need you to get one of the guest rooms ready. Preferably the one farthest from mine. Estefan will be back later tonight."

"So, he's not here?"

"He just left."

She was watching him expectantly. He wasn't sure why, but then he remembered what he'd told her when the doorbell rang, that he wasn't finished with her.

"About what happened earlier. I think it would be best if we keep things professional from now on."

"Oh," she said, her eyes filled with confusion. And rejection. He shouldn't have felt like a heel, but he did. Isn't this what he'd wanted? To get her all worked up, then reject her? Well, the plan had worked brilliantly. Even better than he'd anticipated. What he hadn't counted on was how much he would want her, too.

"Well, I had better get the room ready," she said. She paused, as though she was waiting for him to say something, and when he didn't, she walked away, leaving him feeling like the world's biggest jerk.

The last few weeks had been stressful to say the least. He would be relieved when Isabelle was gone, and the investigation at the refinery came to a close, and he was securely in the position of CEO. Life would be perfect.

So why did he have the sneaking suspicion it wouldn't be so simple?

Nine

So much for hoping Emilio might forgive her, that he still wanted her. He wanted to keep their relationship *professional.* And they had come so close this afternoon. If it hadn't been for Estefan showing up...

Oh, well. Easy come, easy go.

Clearly he didn't want Estefan knowing he was involved with someone like her. It was bad enough she was living in his house. And could she blame him for feeling that way? Aside from the fact that her father had ruined their mother's reputation, Isabelle was a criminal.

Alleged criminal, she reminded herself.

Unfortunately, now Emilio seemed to be shutting her out completely. He hadn't come out of his office all day, or said more than a word or two to her. No insults or wry observations. He'd even eaten his dinner at his desk. Just when she'd gotten used to him sitting in the kitchen making fun of her.

Isabelle loaded the last of the dinner dishes in the dishwasher and set it to run. It was only eight and all her work for the day was finished, but the idea of sitting around feeling sorry for herself on a Saturday night was depressing beyond words. Maybe it was time she paid her mom another visit. They could watch a movie or play a game of Scrabble. She could use a little cheering up, and she knew that no matter what, her mother was there for her.

If Emilio would let her go. The only way she could get there, short of making her mother come get her, or taking a cab, was to use his car. She could lie and say she was going grocery shopping, but when she came home empty-handed he would definitely be suspicious. And would he really buy her going shopping on a Saturday night? Besides, she didn't like lying.

She could just sneak out without telling him, and deal with the consequences when she got back.

Yeah, that was probably the way to go.

She changed out of her uniform, grabbed her purse and sweater and when she walked back into the kitchen for the car keys Emilio was there, getting an apple from the fridge. He looked surprised to see her in her street clothes.

Well, shoot. So much for sneaking out.

"Going somewhere?" he asked.

"I finished all my work so I thought I would go see my mother. I won't be late."

"Did Estefan get back yet?"

"Not yet."

"You're taking the Saab?"

She nodded, bracing for an argument.

"Well, then, drive safe."

Drive safe? That was *it?* Wasn't he going to give her a hard time about going out? Or say something about her taking his car for personal use? Instead he walked out of the kitchen and a few seconds later she heard his office door close.

Puzzled, she headed out to the garage, wondering what had gotten into him. Not that she liked it when he acted like an overbearing jerk. But this was just too weird.

The drive to her mother's apartment was only fifteen minutes. Her car was in the lot, and the light was on in her living room. Isabelle parked and walked to the door. She heard laughter from inside and figured that her mother was watching television. She knocked, and a few seconds later the door opened.

"Isabelle!" her mom said, clearly surprised to see her. "What are you doing here?"

"Mrs. Smith didn't need me for the night and I was bored. I thought we could watch a movie or something."

Normally her mother would invite her right in, but she stood blocking the doorway. She looked nervous. "Oh, well…now isn't a good time."

Isabelle frowned. "Is something wrong?"

"No, nothing." She glanced over her shoulder. "It's just…I have company."

Company? Though Isabelle hadn't noticed at first, her mother looked awfully well put together for a quiet night at home. Her hair was swept up and she wore a skirt and blouse that Isabelle had never seen before. She looked beautiful. But for whom?

"Adriana, who is it?" a voice asked. A *male* voice.

Her mother had a *man* over?

As far as Isabelle knew, she hadn't dated anyone since her husband died three years ago. She had serious trust issues. And who wouldn't after thirty-five years with a bastard like Isabelle's father?

But was he a boyfriend? A casual acquaintance?

Her mother blushed, and she stepped back from the door. "Come in."

Isabelle stepped into the apartment and knew immediately that this was no "friendly" social call. There were lit candles on the coffee table and an open bottle of wine with two glasses. The good crystal, Isabelle noted.

"Isabelle, this is Ben McPherson. Ben, this is my daughter."

Isabelle wasn't sure what she expected, but it sure wasn't the man who stood to greet her.

"Isabelle!" he said, reaching out to shake her hand, pumping it enthusiastically. "Good to finally meet you!"

He was big and boisterous with longish salt-and-pepper hair, dressed in jeans and a Hawaiian shirt. He looked like an ex-hippie, with a big question mark on the *ex,* and seemed to exude happiness and good nature from every pore. He was also the polar opposite of Isabelle's father.

And though she had known him a total of five seconds, Isabelle couldn't help but like him.

"Ben owns the coffee shop next to the boutique where I work," her mother said.

"Would you like to join us?" Ben asked. "We were just getting ready to pop in a movie."

The fact that she almost accepted his offer was a testament to how low her life had sunk. The last thing her mother needed was Isabelle crashing her dates. Being the third wheel was even worse than being alone.

"Maybe some other time."

"Are you sure you can't stay for a quick glass of wine?"

"Not while I'm driving. But it was very nice meeting you, Ben."

"You, too, Isabelle."

"I'll walk you to your car," her mother said, and she told Ben, "I'll be right back."

Isabelle followed her mother out the door, shutting it behind them.

"Are you upset?" her mother asked, looking worried.

"About what?"

"That I have a man friend."

"Of course not! Why would I be upset? I want you to be happy. Ben seems very nice."

A shy smile tilted her lips. "He is. I get coffee in his shop before work. He's asked me out half a dozen times, and I finally said yes."

"So you like him?"

"He still makes me a little nervous, but he's such a nice man. He knows all about the indictment, but he doesn't care."

"He sounds like a keeper." She nudged her mom and asked, "Is he a good kisser?"

"Isabelle!" she said, looking scandalized. "I haven't kissed anyone but your father since I was sixteen. To be honest, the idea is a little scary."

They got to the car and Isabelle turned to face her. "Are you physically attracted to him?"

She smiled shyly and nodded. "I think I just need to take things slow."

"And he understands that?"

"We've talked. About your father, and the way things used to be. He's such a good listener."

"How many times have you seen him?"

"This is our third date."

She'd seen him *three* times and hadn't said anything? Isabelle thought they told each other everything.

And who was she to talk when she'd told her mother she worked for the fictional Mrs. Smith?

"You're upset," her mother said, looking crestfallen.

"No, just a little surprised."

"I wanted to tell you, I was just…embarrassed, I guess. If that makes any sense. I keep thinking that he's going to figure out that I'm not such a great catch, and every date we go on will be our last."

She could thank Isabelle's dad for that. He'd put those ideas into her head.

"He's lucky to have you and I'm sure he knows it."

"He does seem to like me. He's already talking about what we'll do next weekend."

"Well, then, I'd better let you get back inside." She gave her mother a hug. "Have fun, but not *too* much fun. Although after three dates, I would seriously consider letting him kiss you."

Her mother smiled. "I will."

"I'll see you Thursday, then. Is there anything you need me to bring?"

"Oh, I was thinking…well, the thing is, my oven here isn't very reliable, and…actually, Ben invited me to Thanksgiving dinner with him and a few of his friends. I thought you could come along."

That would be beyond awkward, especially when his friends found out who she was. But she could see that her mother really wanted to go, and she wouldn't out of guilt if Isabelle didn't come up with a viable excuse.

"Mrs. Smith's family asked me to have dinner with them," she lied. "They've been so kind to me, the truth is I felt bad telling them no. So if you want to eat with Ben and his friends, that's fine."

"Are you sure? We always spend Thanksgiving together."

Not after this year, unless her mother wanted to eat at the women's correctional facility. It was good that she was making new friends, getting on with her life. To fill the void when Isabelle was gone.

She forced a smile. "I'm sure."

She gave her one last hug, then got in the car. Her mother waved as she drove off. It seemed as if she was finally getting on with her life. Isabelle wanted her to be happy, so why did she feel like dropping her head on the steering wheel and sobbing?

Probably because, for a long, long time, Isabelle and her mom had no one but each other. They were a team.

Her mother had someone else now. And who did Isabelle have? Pretty much no one.

But she was not going to feel sorry for herself, damn it. What would be the point of creating new relationships now anyway, when in five weeks she would be going to prison?

She didn't feel like going back to Emilio's yet, so instead she drove around for a while. When she reached the edge of town, she was tempted to just keep going. To drive far from here, away from her life. A place where no one knew her and she could start over.

But running away never solved anything.

It was nearly eleven when she steered the car back to Emilio's house. She parked in the garage next to his black Ferrari and headed inside, dropping her purse and sweater in her room before she walked out to the kitchen to make herself a cup of tea. She put the kettle on to boil and fished around the cupboard above the coffeemaker on her tiptoes for a box of tea bags.

"Need help?"

She felt someone lean in beside her. She looked up, expecting to find Emilio, but it was Estefan standing there.

She jerked away, feeling...violated. He was charming, and attractive—although not even close to as good-looking as Emilio—but something about him always gave her the creeps. Even when they were younger, when his mother would drive them to school, Isabelle didn't like the way he would look at her. Even though he was a few years younger, he made her nervous.

He still did. She had to dig extra deep to maintain her show-no-fear attitude.

Estefan flashed her an oily smile and held out the box of tea bags. She took it from him. "Thank you."

"No problem." He leaned against the counter and folded his arms. *Watching* her.

"Did Emilio show you to your room?" she asked, mainly because she didn't know what else to say.

"Yep. It's great place, isn't it?" He looked around the kitchen. "My brother did pretty well for himself."

"He has."

"Probably makes you regret screwing him over."

So much for Estefan not giving her a hard time. She should have anticipated this.

"It looks like you've got a pretty sweet deal going here," Estefan said.

She wondered how much Emilio had told him. From the tone of their conversation at the front door—yes, she'd eavesdropped for a minute or two—Emilio hadn't been happy to see his brother. Would he confide in someone he didn't trust? And what difference did it make?

"You get to live in his house, drive his cars, eat his food. It begs the question, what is he getting in return?"

Housekeeping and cooking. But clearly that wasn't what he meant. He seemed certain there was more to it than that. Why didn't he just come right out and call her a whore?

The kettle started to boil so she walked around the island to the stove to fix her tea. Emilio had belittled and insulted her, but that had been different somehow. Less… sinister and vindictive. She just hoped that if she didn't give him the satisfaction of a reaction, Estefan would get bored and leave her alone.

No such luck.

He stepped up behind her. So close she could almost feel his body heat. The cloying scent of his aftershave turned her stomach.

"My brother is too much of a nice guy to realize he's being used."

She had the feeling that the only one using Emilio was Estefan, but she kept her mouth shut. And as much as she would like to tell Emilio how Estefan was treating her, she would never put herself in the middle of their relationship. She would only be around a few weeks. Emilio and Estefan would be brothers for life.

She turned to walk back to her room, but Estefan was blocking her way. "Excuse me."

"You didn't say *please*."

She met his steely gaze with one of her own, and after several seconds he let her through. She forced herself to walk slowly to her room. The door didn't have a lock, so she shoved the folding chair under the doorknob—just in case. She didn't really think Estefan would get physical with her, especially with his brother in the house. But better safe than sorry.

Life at Emilio's hadn't exactly been a picnic, but it hadn't been terrible, either, and she'd always felt safe. She had the feeling that with Estefan around, those days were over.

Ten

Though he wouldn't have believed it possible, Emilio was starting to think maybe his brother really had changed this time. Good to his word, he hadn't asked Emilio for a penny. Not even gas money. He'd spent no late nights out partying and, as far as Emilio could tell, had remained sober for the three days he'd been staying there. The animosity that had been a constant thread in their relationship for as many years as Emilio could remember was gradually dissolving.

When they were growing up, Estefan had always been jealous of Emilio, coveting whatever he had. The cool after-school jobs, the stellar grades and college scholarships. He just hadn't wanted the hard work that afforded Emilio those luxuries. But now it seemed that Estefan finally got it; he'd figured out what he needed to do, and he was making a valiant effort to change.

At least, Emilio hoped so.

Though things at Western Oil were still in upheaval, and

he had work he could be doing, Emilio had spent the last couple of evenings in the media room watching ESPN with his brother. He felt as if, for the first time in their lives, he and Estefan were bonding. Acting like real brothers. Besides, spending time with him was helping Emilio keep his mind off Isabelle.

Since he told her that he wanted to keep things professional, he hadn't been able to stop thinking about her. The way she tasted when he kissed her, the softness of her skin, the feel of her body pressed against his. She was as responsive to his touch, as hot for him now, as she had been all those years ago. And now that he knew he couldn't have her, he craved her that much more. This time it had nothing to do with revenge or retribution. He just plain wanted her, and he could tell by the way she looked at him, the loneliness and longing in her eyes, that she wanted him, too. And so, apparently, could Estefan.

"She wants you, bro," Estefan said Tuesday evening after dinner, while they were watching a game Emilio had recorded over the weekend.

"Our relationship is professional," he told his brother.

"Why? You could tap that, then kick her to the curb. It would be the ultimate revenge. Use her the way she used you."

Which was exactly what Emilio had planned to do, but for some reason now, it just seemed...sleazy. Maybe he was ready to let go of the past. Maybe all this time he'd just been brooding. He wasn't the only man to ever get his heart broken. Maybe it was time he stopped making excuses, stopped attaching ulterior motives to her decision and face facts. She left him because she'd fallen in love with someone else, and it was time he stopped feeling sorry for himself and got on with his life.

"Honestly, Estefan, I think she's getting what she has

coming to her. She's widowed, broke and a month away from spending the rest of her life in prison. She's about as low as she can possibly sink, yet she's handling it with grace and dignity."

"If I didn't know better, I might think you actually *like* her."

That was part of the problem. Emilio wasn't sure how he felt about her. He didn't hate her, not anymore. But he couldn't see them ever being best pals. Or even close friends. As the saying went, fool me once, shame on you…

Once she was in prison, he doubted he would ever see her again. It wasn't as if he would be going to visit her, or sending care packages.

If she actually went to prison, that is. The new lead his brother had mentioned could prove her innocence. And if it did? Then what?

Then, nothing. Innocent or guilty, sexually compatible or not, there was nothing she could say or do that would make up for the past. Not for him, and not for his family. Even if he wanted to be with her, his family would never accept it. Especially his mother. And they came first, simple as that.

Estefan yawned and stretched. "I have an early start in the morning. I think I'll turn in."

Emilio switched off the television. "Me, too."

"By the way," Estefan said, "I talked to my business associate today. He hit a snag and it's looking like I won't get that money until a few days after Thanksgiving. I know I said I would be out of here—"

"It's okay," Emilio heard himself say. "You can stay a few extra days."

"You're sure?"

"I'm sure."

"Thanks, bro."

They said good-night and Emilio walked to the kitchen to pour himself a glass of juice to take up to bed with him. By the light of the range hood he got a glass down from the cupboard and the orange juice from the fridge. He emptied the carton, but when he tried to put it in the trash under the sink, the bag was full.

He sighed. Mrs. Medina had specifically instructed Izzie to take the kitchen trash out nightly. He couldn't help but wonder if she'd forgotten on purpose, just to annoy him. If that was the case, he was annoyed.

He considered calling her out to change it, on principle, but it was after eleven and she was usually in bed by now. Instead he pulled the bag out, tied it and put a fresh one in. He carried the full bag to the trash can in the garage, noting on his way the dim sliver of light under Isabelle's door. Her lamp was on. Either she was still awake, or she'd fallen asleep with the light on again.

He dropped the bag in the can, glancing over at the Saab. Was that a *scratch* on the bumper?

He walked over to look, and on closer inspection saw that it was just something stuck to the paint. He rubbed it clean, made a mental note to tell Isabelle to take it to the car wash the next time she was out, then headed back inside. He expected to find the kitchen empty, but Isabelle was standing in front of the open refrigerator door. She was wearing a well worn plaid flannel robe and her hair was wet.

"Midnight snack?" he asked.

She let out a startled squeak and spun around, slamming the door shut. "You scared me half to death!"

He opened his mouth to say something sarcastic when his eyes were drawn to the front of her robe and whatever he'd been about to say melted somewhere into the recesses of his brain. The robe gaped open at the collar, revealing the uppermost swell of her bare left breast. Not a huge deal normally, but in his present state of craving her, he was transfixed.

Look away, he told himself, but his eyes felt glued. All he could think about was what it felt like to cup it in his palm, her soft whimpers as he took her in his mouth and how many years he had wondered what it would be like to make love to her.

Where was his self-control?

Isabelle followed his gaze down to the front of her robe. He expected her to pull the sides together, maybe get embarrassed.

She didn't. She lifted her eyes back to his and just stood there, daring him to make a move.

Nope, not gonna do it.

Then she completely stunned him by tugging the tie loose and letting the robe fall open. It was dark, but he could see that she wasn't wearing anything underneath.

Damn.

You are not going to touch her, he told himself. But Isabelle clearly had other ideas. She walked over to him, took his hand and placed it on her breast.

Damn.

He could have pulled away, could have told her no. He *should* have. Unfortunately his hand seemed to develop a mind of its own. It cupped her breast, his thumb brushing back and forth over her nipple. Isabelle's eyes went dark with arousal.

She reached up and unfastened his belt.

If he was planning to stop her, now would be a good time, but as she undid the clasp on his slacks, he just stood there. She tugged the zipper down, slipped her hand inside…

He sucked in a breath as her hand closed around his

erection, and for the life of him he couldn't recall why he thought this was a bad idea. In fact, it seemed like a damned good idea, and if he was going to be totally honest with himself, it had been an inevitability.

But not here. Not with Estefan in the house. His bedroom wouldn't be a great idea, either.

"Your room," he said, so she took his hand and led him there.

The desk lamp was on, and he half expected her to shut it off, the way she used to. Not only did she leave the light on, but the minute the door was closed, she dropped her robe. Standing there naked, in the soft light… *Damn.* He'd never seen anything so beautiful, and he'd only had to wait fifteen years.

"You have to promise me you won't stop this time," she said, unfastening the buttons on his shirt.

Why stop? If they didn't do this now, it would just happen later. A day, or a week. But it would happen.

He took his wallet from his back pocket, pulled out a condom and handed it to her. "I promise."

Isabelle smiled and pushed his shirt off his shoulders. "You'll never know how many times I thought of you over the years."

Did you think of me when you were with him? He wanted to ask, but what if he didn't like the answer?

She pushed his pants and boxers down and he stepped out of them. "Do you know what I miss more than anything?" she said.

"What do you miss?"

"Lying in bed with you, under the covers, wrapped around each other, kissing and touching. Sometimes we were so close it was like we were one person. Do you remember?"

He did, and he missed it, too, more then she could

imagine. There had been a lot of women since Izzie, some who had lasted weeks, and a few who hung around for months, but he never felt that connection. He'd never developed the closeness with them that he'd felt with her.

She pulled back the covers on the bed and lay down. Emilio slipped in next to her, but when she tried to pull the covers up over them, he stopped her. "No covers this time. I want to look at you."

She reached up to touch his face and he realized that her hands were shaking. Could she possibly be nervous? This woman who, a few minutes ago, seemed to know exactly what she wanted and wasn't the least bit afraid to go after it?

He put his hand over hers, pressing it to his cheek. "You're trembling."

"I've just been waiting for this for a really long time."

"Are you sure you want to do this?"

"Emilio, I have never been more sure of anything in my life." She wound her arms around his neck and pulled him down, wrapped herself around him, kissed him. It was like…coming home. Everything about her was familiar. The feel of her body, the scent of her skin, her soft, breathy whimpers as he touched her.

He felt as if he was twenty-one again, lying in his bed in his rental house on campus, with their entire lives ahead of them. He remembered exactly what to do to make her writhe in ecstasy. Slow and sweet, the way he knew she liked it. He brought her to the edge of bliss and back again, building the anticipation, until she couldn't take it anymore.

"Make love to me, Emilio." She dug her fingers through his hair, kissed him hard. "I can't wait any longer."

He grabbed the condom and she watched with lust-glazed eyes as he rolled it on. The second he was finished she pulled him back down, wrapping her legs around his waist.

He centered himself over her, anticipating the blissful wet heat of that first thrust, but he was barely inside when he met with resistance. She must have been tense from the anticipation of finally making love. He couldn't deny he was a bit anxious himself. He put some weight into it and the barrier gave way. Isabelle gasped, digging her nails into his shoulders and she was *tight.* Tighter than any wife of fifteen years should be.

He eased back, looking down where their bodies were joined, stunned by what he saw. Exactly what he would have expected…if he'd just made love to a virgin.

No way. "Isabelle?"

It was obvious by her expression that she had been hoping he wouldn't figure it out. How was this even possible?

"Don't stop," she pleaded, pulling at his shoulders, trying to get him closer.

Hell no, he wasn't going to stop, but if he had known he could have at least been more gentle.

"I'm going to take it slow," he told her. Which in theory was a great plan, but as she adjusted to the feel of him inside her, she relaxed. Then "slow" didn't seem to be enough for her. She began to writhe beneath him, meeting his downward slide with a thrust of her hips. He was so lost in the feel of her body, the clench of her muscles squeezing him into euphoria, that he was running on pure instinct. When she moaned and bucked against him, her body fisting around him as she climaxed, it did him in. His only clear thought as he groaned out his release was *perfect.* But as he slowly drifted back to earth, reality hit him square between the eyes.

He and Isabelle had finally made love, after all these years, and he was her first. Exactly as it was meant to be.

So why did he feel so damned…guilty?

"You know, I must have imagined what that would be like about a thousand times over the past fifteen years," she said. "But the real thing is way better than the fantasy."

Emilio tipped her face up to his. "Izzie, why didn't you tell me?"

She didn't have to ask what he meant. She lowered her eyes. "I was embarrassed."

"Why?"

"You don't run across many thirty-four-year-old virgins."

"How is this even possible? You're young and beautiful and sexy. Your husband never wanted to…?"

"Can we not talk about it?" She was closing down, shutting him out, but he wanted answers, damn it.

"I want to know how you can be married to a man for fifteen years and never have sex with him."

She sat up and pulled the covers over her. "It's complicated."

"I'm a reasonably intelligent man, Izzie. Try me."

"We…we didn't have that kind of relationship."

"What kind of relationship did you have?"

She drew her knees up and hugged them. "I really don't want to talk about this."

"Did you love him?"

She bit her lip and looked away.

"Isabelle?"

After a long pause she said, "I…respected him."

"Is that your way of saying you were just in it for the money?"

She didn't deny it. She didn't say anything at all.

If she loved Betts, Emilio would understand her leaving

him. It sucked, but he could accept it. Knowing it was only about the money, seeing the truth on her face, knowing that she'd really been that shallow, disturbed him on too many levels to count.

"This was a mistake," he said. He pushed himself up from the bed and grabbed his pants.

"Emilio—"

"No. This never should have happened. I don't know what the hell I was thinking."

She was quiet for several seconds, and he waited to see what she would do. Would she apologize and beg him to stay? Tell him she made a horrible mistake? And would it matter if she did?

"You're right," she finally said, avoiding his gaze. "It was a mistake."

She was agreeing with him, and she was right, so why did he feel like putting his fist through the wall?

He tugged his pants on.

"So, what now?" she asked.

"Meaning what?"

"Are you going to back out on our deal?"

He grabbed his shirt from off the floor. "No, Isabelle, I won't. I keep my word. But I would really appreciate if you would stay out of my way. And I'll stay out of yours."

He was pretty sure he saw tears in her eyes as he jerked the door open and walked out. And just when he thought this night couldn't get any worse, his brother was sitting in the kitchen eating a sandwich and caught him red-handed.

Damn it.

When he saw Emilio his eyes widened, then a wry smile curled his mouth.

Emilio glared at him. "Don't say a word."

Estefan shrugged. "None of my business, bro."

Emilio wished Estefan had walked into the kitchen

before Isabelle started her stripping routine, then none of this would have happened.

But one thing he knew for damned sure, it was not going to happen again.

Eleven

This was for the best.

At least, that was what Isabelle had been trying to tell herself all day. She would rather have Emilio hate her, than fall in love and endure losing her again. That wouldn't be fair. Not to either of them. She was tired of feeling guilty for hurting him. She just wanted it to be over. For good.

She should have left things alone, should never have opened her robe, offered herself to him, but she'd figured for him it was just sex. She never imagined he might still have feelings for her, but he must have, or it wouldn't have matter if she loved Lenny or not.

She ran the vacuum across the carpet in the guest room, cringing at the memory of his stunned expression when he realized she was a virgin. She didn't know he would be able to tell. A testament to how naive and inexperienced she was. But as first times go, she was guessing it had been way above average. Everything she had ever hoped, and she couldn't regret it. She loved Emilio. She'd wanted him to be her first. As far as she was concerned, it was meant to be.

Except for the part where he stormed off mad.

When he'd asked her about Lenny, she had almost told him the truth. It had been sitting there on the tip of her tongue. Now she was relieved she hadn't. It was better that he thought the worst of her.

She turned to do the opposite side of the room, jolting with alarm when she realized Estefan was leaning in the bedroom doorway watching her.

His mere presence in the house put her on edge, but when he watched her—and he did that a lot—it gave her the creeps. When she dusted the living room he would park himself on the couch with a magazine, or if she was fixing dinner he would come in for a snack and sit at one of the island stools. Occasionally he would assault her with verbal barbs, which she generally ignored. But most of the time he just stared at her.

It was beyond unsettling.

Estefan raised the beer he was holding to his lips and took a swallow. Isabelle had distinctly heard him tell Emilio that he was clean and sober, yet the second he rolled out of bed every day, which was usually noon or later, he went straight to the fridge for a cold one.

The breakfast of champions.

It wasn't her place to tattle on Estefan, and even if she told Emilio what he was doing, she doubted he would believe her. It was also the reason she didn't tell him that she'd caught Estefan in his office going through his desk. He claimed he'd been looking for a pen, when she knew for a fact he'd been trying to get into the locked file drawer.

He was definitely up to something.

She turned off the vacuum. She knew she should keep

her mouth shut, but she couldn't help herself. "Would you care for some pretzels to go with that?"

"Funny." His greasy smile made her skin crawl. "Where are the keys for the Ferrari?"

"Why?"

"I need to borrow it."

"I have no idea. Why don't you call Emilio and ask him?"

"I don't want to bother him."

No, he knew his brother would say no, so it was easier to take it without his permission.

"I guess I'll have to take the Saab instead."

"Why don't you take your bike?"

"No gas. Unless you want to loan me twenty bucks. I'm good for it."

She glared at him. Even if she had twenty bucks she wouldn't give it to him. He shouldn't even be driving. He would be endangering not only himself, but everyone else on the road.

He shrugged. "The Saab it is, then."

It wasn't as if she could stop him. Short of calling the police and reporting him, she had no recourse. And in her experience, the police never really helped anyway.

Besides, she had enough to worry about in her own life without sticking her nose into Estefan's business.

"So, this arrangement not working out the way you planned it?" Estefan asked.

She wondered what Emilio had told him, if anything.

"Still a virgin at thirty-four." He shook his head. "Let me guess, was your husband impotent, or did you just freeze him out?"

The humiliation she felt was matched only by her anger at Emilio for telling Estefan her private business. She knew he was mad, but this was uncalled for. Was that his way of getting back at her?

Estefan flashed her that greasy smile again. "If you needed someone to take care of business, all you had to do was ask. I'm twice the man my brother is."

The thought of Estefan coming anywhere near her was nauseating. "Not if you were the last man on earth."

His expression darkened. "We'll see about that," he said, then walked away.

She wasn't sure what he meant by that, but the possibilities made her feel uneasy. He wouldn't have the nerve to try something, would he?

Tomorrow was Thanksgiving and he was supposed to be leaving. She would just have to watch her back until then.

Emilio's Thanksgiving was not going well so far.

He stood in his closet, fresh out of a shower, holding up the shirt Isabelle had just ironed for him, noting the scorch mark on the left sleeve. "This is a three hundred dollar silk shirt, Isabelle."

"I'm sorry," she said, yet she didn't really look sorry.

"I just wanted it lightly pressed. Not burned to a crisp."

"I didn't realize the iron was set so hot. I'll replace it."

"After you pay me back for the rug? And the casserole dish you broke. And the load of whites that you dyed pink. Not to mention the grocery bill that has mysteriously risen by almost twelve percent since you've been here."

"Maybe I could stay an extra week or two and work off what I owe you."

Terrific idea. But she would inevitably break something else and wind up owing him even more. Besides, he didn't want her in his house any longer than necessary. If there was any way he could get his housekeeper back today and let Isabelle go on time served, he would, but he'd promised her a month off.

He balled the shirt up and tossed it in the trash can in the corner. "It would probably be in everyone's best interest if you avoided using the iron."

She nodded.

He turned to grab a different shirt and a pair of slacks. He was about to drop his towel, when he noticed she was still standing there.

He raised a brow. "You want to watch me get dressed?"

"I wasn't sure if you were finished."

"Finished what?"

"Yelling at me."

"I wasn't *yelling.*"

"Okay, disciplining me."

"If I were disciplining you, it would have involved some sort of punishment." Not that he couldn't think of a few. Putting her over his knee was one that came to mind. She could use a sound spanking. But he'd promised himself he was going to stop thinking of her in a sexual way and view her as an employee. Tough when he couldn't seem to stop picturing her naked and writhing beneath him.

"How about…chastising?" she said. "Dressing-down?"

"Exaggerate much? I was *talking* to you."

"If you say so."

Why the sudden attitude? If anyone had the right to be pissed, it was him.

"Is there anything else you need?" she asked.

"Could you tell my brother to be ready in twenty minutes?"

She saluted him and walked out.

He'd like to know what had gotten her panties in such a twist. Maybe she just didn't like the fact that he'd called her out on her marriage being a total sham. That he'd more or less made her admit she married Betts for his money. In which case she was getting exactly what she deserved.

He got dressed, slipped on his cashmere jacket and grabbed his wallet. Estefan was waiting for him in the kitchen. He wore jeans and a button-down shirt that was inappropriately open for a family holiday gathering, and the thick gold chain was downright tacky, but Emilio kept his mouth shut. Estefan was trying. He'd been on his best behavior all week.

Almost *too* good.

"Ready to go?"

"I'll bet you want to let me drive," Estefan said.

Reformed or not, he was not getting behind the wheel of a car that cost Emilio close to half a million dollars. "I'll bet I don't."

Estefan grumbled as they walked out to the garage. Emilio was about to climb in the driver's seat of the Ferrari when he glanced over at the Saab. "Son of a—"

"What's the matter?" Estefan asked.

The rear quarter panel was buckled. For a second he considered that someone had hit it while it was parked, but then he looked closer and noticed the fleck of yellow paint embedded in the black. Not car paint. More like what they used on parking barriers.

He shook his head. "Damn it!"

"Bro, go easy on her. I'm gonna bet she's used to having a driver. It's a wonder she even remembers how to drive."

He walked to the door, yanked it open and yelled, "Isabelle!"

She emerged from her room, looking exasperated. "What did I do this time?"

"Like you don't already know." He gestured her into the garage.

She stepped out. "What?"

"The *car*."

She looked at the Saab. "What about it?

Why was she playing dumb? She knew what she did. "The other side."

She walked around, and as soon as she saw the damage her mouth fell open. "What happened?"

"Are you telling me you don't recall running into something?"

She looked from Emilio, to Estefan, then back to the car. She didn't even have the courtesy to look embarrassed for lying to him. She squared her shoulders and said, "Put it on my tab."

That was it? That was all she had to say? "You might have mentioned this."

"Why? So you could make bad driver jokes about me?"

"What the hell has gotten into you, Isabelle?"

She shrugged. "I guess I'm finally showing my true colors. Living up to your expectations. You should be happy."

She turned and walked back into the house, slamming the door behind her.

"Nice girl," Estefan said.

No, this wasn't like her at all. "Get in the car."

When they were on the road Estefan said, "Dude, she's not worth it."

He knew that, in his head. Logically, they had no future together. The trick was getting the message to his heart. The protective shell he'd built around it was beginning to crumble. He was starting to feel exposed and vulnerable, and he didn't like it.

"Make her leave," Estefan said.

"I can't do that. I gave her my word." Besides, he didn't think she had anywhere else to go.

"Dude, you don't owe her anything."

He'd promised to help her, and in his world, that still meant something. Estefan hadn't kept a promise in his entire life.

They drove the rest of the way to Alejandro's house in silence.

When they stepped through the door, the kids tackled them in the foyer, getting sticky fingerprints all over Emilio's cashmere jacket and slacks, but he didn't care.

"Kids! Give your uncles a break," Alejandro scolded, but he knew they didn't mind.

Chris, the baby, was clinging to Emilio's leg, so he hoisted him up high over his head until he squealed with delight, then gave him a big hug. Reggie, the six-year-old, tugged frantically on his jacket.

"Hey, Uncle Em! Guess what! I'm going to be big brother again!"

"Your dad told me. That's great."

"Jeez, dude," Estefan said with a laugh. "*Four* kids."

Alejandro grinned and shrugged. "Alana wanted to try for a girl. After all these years I still can't tell her no."

"I think she should make a boy," Reggie said. "I don't want a sister."

Emilio laughed and ruffled the boy's hair. "I think she'll get what she gets."

"Hey, Uncle Em, guess who's here!" Alex, the nine-year-old said, hopping excitedly.

"Alex." Alejandro shot his oldest a warning look. "It's supposed to be a surprise."

"Who's here?" Emilio asked him, and from behind him he heard someone say, "Hey, big brother."

He spun around to see his youngest brother, Enrique, standing in the kitchen doorway. He laughed and said, "What the hell are you doing here? I thought you were halfway around the world."

"Mama talked me into it and Alejandro bought my ticket." He hugged Emilio, then Estefan.

"You look great," Estefan told him. "But I'll bet Mama's not very happy about the long hair and goatee."

"She's not," their mama said from the kitchen doorway, hands on her hips, apron tied around her slim waist. She was a youthful fifty-eight, considering the hard life she'd lived. First growing up in the slums of Cuba, then losing her husband so young and raising four boys alone.

"He does look a little scruffy," Alana teased, joining them in the foyer.

"But I finally have all my boys together," their mama said. "And that's all that matters."

Emilio gave his sister-in-law a hug and kiss. "Congratulations, sis."

She grinned. "I'm crazy, right? In this family I'm probably more likely to give birth to conjoined twins than a girl."

Emilio shrugged. "It could happen."

"Why are we all standing around in the foyer?" Alejandro said. "Why don't we move this party to the kitchen?"

For a day that had begun so lousy, it turned out to be the best Thanksgiving in years. The food was fantastic and it was great to have the whole family together again. The best part was that his mama was so excited to have Enrique home, it took her several hours to get around to nagging Emilio about settling down.

"It's not right, you living alone in that big house," she said, as they all sat in the living room, having after dinner drinks. Except Estefan, who was on the floor wrestling with the nephews. He'd been on his best behavior all day.

"I like living alone," Emilio told her. "And if I ever feel the need to have kids, I can just borrow Alejandro's."

"You need to fill it with niños of your own," she said sternly.

"Why don't you nag Enrique about getting married?" Emilio said.

She rubbed her youngest son's arm affectionately. "He's still a baby."

Emilio laughed. "So what does that make me? An old man?"

"You are pretty damn old," Enrique said, which got him plenty of laughs.

Chris climbed into Emilio's lap and hugged him, staring up at him with big brown eyes. And Emilio was thinking that maybe having a kid or two wouldn't be so bad, just as Chris threw up all down the front of his shirt.

"Oh, sweetie!" Alana charged over, sweeping him up off Emilio's lap. "Emilio, I'm so sorry!"

"It's okay," Emilio said, using the tissues his brother handed him to clean himself up.

"Honey, take your brother up and get him a clean shirt. You're the same size, right?"

"I'm sure I have something that will work," Alejandro said, and Emilio followed him upstairs to his bedroom.

Alejandro handed him a clean shirt and said, "While I've got you here, there's something I wanted to ask you."

He peeled off his dirty shirt and gave it to his brother. "What's up?"

"How much do you know about Isabelle's father?"

He was having such a good day, he didn't want to ruin it by thinking about Isabelle and her family. "I'm not sure what you mean. Other than the fact that he was a bastard, not too much I guess."

"Did you know he had a serious gambling problem?"

"So he was an even bigger bastard than we thought. So what?"

"He'd also had charges filed against him."

"For what?"

"Domestic abuse."

Emilio frowned. "Are you sure?"

"Positive. And he must have had friends in high places because I had to dig deep."

Emilio shrugged into the shirt and buttoned it. It was slightly large, but at least it didn't smell like puke. "So he was an even *bigger* bastard."

"There's something else." His grim expression said Emilio probably wasn't going to like this. "There were also allegations of child abuse."

Emilio's pulse skipped. Had Izzie been abused? "Allegations? Was there ever any proof?"

"He was never charged. I just thought you would want to know."

"Can you dig deeper?"

"I could, if it were relevant to my case."

"Are you suggesting I should investigate this further?"

Alejandro shrugged. "That would be a conflict of interest. Although I can say that if it were me, I would try to get a hold of medical records."

"Could this exonerate her?"

"I'm not at liberty to say."

"Damn it, Alejandro."

He sighed. "Probably not, but it might be relevant in her defense."

"I thought she was taking a plea."

"She is, on the advice of counsel, and I think we've already established that she may not be getting the best advice."

So in other words, Alejandro wanted him to dig deeper. He couldn't deny that the idea she might have been mistreated was an unsettling one. He could just ask her, but if she hadn't told him by now, what were the odds she would admit it? And if she had been, wouldn't he have noticed? Or maybe it was something that happened when she was younger.

"I'll look into it."

"Let me know what you find."

He followed his brother back downstairs, but he'd lost his holiday spirit. He felt…unsettled. And not just about the possible abuse. It seemed as though quite a few things lately weren't…adding up. Like why her husband kept her in the lap of luxury and expected nothing in return, and Isabelle's sudden change of personality to Miss Snarky.

"You ready to go?" he asked Estefan an hour later.

"I think I'm going to crash here tonight. Get some quality time with the nephews."

He glanced over at Alejandro, who nodded.

His mama protested him leaving so early, so he used exhaustion from work as an excuse. Everyone knew things had been hectic since the explosion.

He said his goodbyes and headed home. When he pulled into the garage just before nine, he was surprised to find the Saab there. He figured Isabelle would have taken it to her mother's. Or maybe she thought he wouldn't want her driving it now.

He crouched down to look at the dent. He didn't doubt that it was caused by backing into something. She probably wasn't paying attention to where she was going. If she had just fessed up when it happened, it wouldn't have been a big deal. Although it wasn't like her to lie. Every time she screwed up, she owned up to it, and she had looked genuinely surprised when he pointed it out.

Curious, he walked around to the driver's side and got in. He stuck the key in and booted the navigation system, going through the history until he found what he was looking for.

Damn it. What the hell had she been thinking?

Shaking his head, he got out and let himself in the house. There was an empty wine bottle on the counter by the sink. Cheap stuff that Isabelle must have picked up at the grocery store.

He checked the dishwasher and found a dirty plate, fork, cup and pan inside. She hadn't gone to her mother's. She'd spent the holiday alone.

Twelve

Isabelle wasn't in her bedroom, so Emilio went looking for her. He found her asleep in the media room, curled up in a chair in her pajamas, another bottle of wine on the table beside her, this one three quarters empty, and beside it the case for the DVD *Steel Magnolias*. The movie whose credits were currently rolling up the screen. There was a tissue box in her lap and a dozen or so balled up on the seat and floor.

Far as he could tell, she'd spent her Thanksgiving watching chick movies, crying and drinking herself into a stupor with cheap wine.

"Isabelle." He jostled her shoulder. "Isabelle, wake up."

Her eyes fluttered open, fuzzy from sleep, and probably intoxication. "You're home."

"I'm home."

She smiled, closed her eyes and promptly fell back to sleep.

He sighed. Short of dumping a bucket of cold water over her head—which he couldn't deny was awfully tempting—he didn't think she would be waking up any time soon. He just wished she would have told him she was spending Thanksgiving alone.

And he would have…what? Invited her to his brother's? Stayed home with her and ignored his family? He wouldn't have done anything different, other than feel guilty all day.

He picked her up out of the chair and hoisted her into his arms. Her eyes fluttered open and her arms went around his neck. "Where are we going?" she asked in a sleepy voice.

"I'm taking you to bed."

"Oh, okay." Her eyes drifted closed again and her head dropped on his shoulder. He started to walk in the direction of her quarters, but the thought of leaving her in there, alone, isolated from the rest of the house in that uncomfortable little bed…he just couldn't do it.

He carried her upstairs instead, to the spare bedroom beside his room. He pulled the covers back and laid her down, unhooking her arms from around his neck. It was dark, but he could see that her eyes were open.

"Where am I?"

"The guest room. I thought you would be more comfortable here."

"I had too much to drink."

"I know."

She curled up on her side, hugging the pillow. "I don't usually drink, but I didn't think it would be so hard."

"What?"

"Being alone today."

Damn. "Why didn't you go to your mother's?"

"She wanted to be with Ben and his friends."

He had no idea who Ben was. Maybe a friend or boy-friend. "You couldn't go with her?"

"She needs to meet people, make new friends, so it won't be as bad when I'm gone."

By gone he assumed she meant in prison. So she'd spent the day alone for her mother's sake. Not the actions of a spoiled, selfish woman.

He thought about the news his brother had sprung on him tonight and wondered if it could be true, if Isabelle had been abused as a child.

He sat on the edge of the bed. "Isabelle, why didn't you tell me the truth about the car?"

"I told you why."

"What I mean is, why didn't you tell me that it wasn't you who caused the damage?"

She blinked. "Of course I did."

More lies. "I looked in the navigation history. Unless you spent the afternoon at a strip joint downtown, it was Estefan who took the car." He touched her cheek. "Why would you take the fall for him?"

Looking guilty, she shrugged. "You're brothers. I didn't want to get between you."

"You're right, we are brothers. So I know exactly what he's capable of." He brushed her hair back, tucked it behind her ear. "Is there anything else? Anything I should know?"

She gnawed her lip.

"Isabelle?"

"He's been drinking."

Emilio cursed. "How much?"

"As soon as he gets up, pretty much until you get home." She took his hand. "I'm sorry, Emilio."

"I'm disappointed, but not surprised. I've been through this too many times with him before."

"But it sucks when people let you down."

She would know.

"I have a confession to make," she said.

"About Estefan?"

She shook her head. "I ruined your shirt on purpose."

Oddly enough, his first reaction was to laugh. "Why?"

"I was mad at you. For telling Estefan that I was a virgin."

What? "I never told him that. I never told him anything about us, other than it was none of his business."

"So how did he know? He made a remark about it yesterday."

"He was in the kitchen when I walked out of your room. Maybe he heard us talking?"

"All the way from the kitchen? We weren't talking *that* loud."

She was right. He would have had to be listening at the door.

She must have reached the same conclusion, because she made a face and said, "Ew."

"He's staying at Alejandro's tonight, and tomorrow he's out of here."

"No offense, but he's always given me the creeps. Even when he was a kid. I didn't like the way he stared at me."

Then she probably wouldn't want to know that Estefan used to have a crush on her. Apparently he thought that someday they would be together, because he had been furious when he found out that Emilio was dating her. He accused Emilio of stealing her from him.

"Emilio?" she said, squeezing his hand.

"Huh?"

"I didn't marry Lenny for his money. That isn't why I left you. You can think whatever horrible things about me that you want, but don't think that. Okay?"

"I don't think you're horrible. I wanted to, but you're making it really hard not to like you."

"Don't. I don't want you to like me."

"Why?"

"Because I'm going to prison and I don't want to hurt you again. It's better if you just keep hating me."

"Do you hate me?"

"No. I *love* you," she said, like that should have been perfectly obvious. "I always have. But we can't be together. It's not fair."

He didn't even know what to say to that. How could he have ever thought she was selfish? The truth is, she hadn't changed at all. She was still the sweet girl he'd been in love with fifteen years ago. And if her leaving him really had nothing to do with Betts's money, why did she do it?

He knew if he asked her, she wouldn't tell him. He could only hope that the medical records would be the final piece to the puzzle. But there was still one thing he'd been wondering about.

"How was it your mother wound up indicted?"

"After my father died, she knew virtually nothing about finances. She didn't even know what she and my father were worth, and it was a lot less than she expected. He was heavily in debt, and nothing was in my mother's name. After the debts were paid, there wasn't much left. Lenny said he could set up a division of the company in her name. He would do the work and she would reap the benefits, only it didn't turn out that way. She's in trouble because of me."

"I fail to see how that's your fault."

"I encouraged her to sign. I trusted Lenny."

"Does she blame you?"

"Of course not. If she knew I was planning to take a plea in exchange for her freedom, she would have a fit. But my lawyer said that was the only way. She's been through enough."

Izzie's mother had always been kind to him and his brothers, and his mother never had a negative thing to say about her. If she wasn't involved, he didn't want to see her go to jail, either, but if Isabelle was innocent she shouldn't be serving herself up as the sacrificial lamb. She should be trying to fight this.

"I'm sleepy," she said, yawning.

After all that wine, who wouldn't be? "And you're probably going to have one hell of a hangover in the morning."

"Probably."

"Scoot over," he said.

"Why?"

He unbuttoned his shirt. "So I can lie down."

"But—"

"Just go to sleep." The one thing they had never done was spend the night together. He figured it was about time.

And drunk or not, he'd be damned if he was going to let her spend the rest of her Thanksgiving alone.

Isabelle woke sometime in the night with her head in a vise, in a strange room, curled up against Emilio's bare chest.

Huh?

Then she remembered that he had carried her to bed, and the conversation they'd had. Though that part was a little fuzzy. She was pretty sure the gist of it was that Emilio wasn't mad at her anymore. Which was the exact opposite of what she had wanted.

She considered getting up and going to her own bed, but she must have fallen asleep before she got the chance. The next time she woke, Emilio was gone, and someone was inside her skull with a jackhammer.

She crawled out of bed and stumbled downstairs to the kitchen. Emilio was sitting at the island dressed for work, eating a bowl of cereal. When he heard her walk in he turned. And winced.

She must have looked as bad as she felt.

"Good morning," he said.

Not. "Shoot me and put me out of my misery."

"How about some coffee and ibuprofen instead?"

Honestly, death sounded better, but she took the tablets he brought to her and choked down a few sips of coffee.

"Why are you up so early?" he asked.

"I'm supposed to be up. It's a work day."

"Not for you it isn't." He took her coffee cup and put it in the sink, then he took her by the shoulders and steered her toward the stairs. "Back to bed."

"But the house—"

"It can wait a day."

He walked her upstairs to the guest room and tucked her back into bed. "Get some sleep, and don't get up until you're feeling better. Promise?"

"Promise."

He kissed her forehead before he left.

She must have conked right out, because when she woke again, sunshine streamed in through the break in the curtains, and when she sat up she felt almost human. She looked over at the clock on the dresser and was stunned to find it was almost noon. After a cup of coffee and a slice of toast and a few more ibuprofen, she was feeling almost like her old self, so she showered, dressed in her uniform and got to work. She wouldn't have time to do all her chores, but she could make a decent dent in them.

She was polishing the marble in the foyer when Estefan came in, looking about as bad as she felt this morning.

"Rough night?" she asked.

He smirked and walked straight to the kitchen. She heard the fridge open and the rattle of a beer bottle as he pulled it out. Figures. The best thing for a hangover was more alcohol, right?

She went back to polishing, but after several minutes she got an eerie feeling and knew he was watching her.

"Is there something you needed?" she asked.

"Have you got eyes in the back of your head or something?"

She turned to him. "Are you here for your things?"

His eyes narrowed. "Why?"

She just assumed Emilio would have called him by now. Guess not.

His eyes narrowed. "What did you tell Emilio?"

She squared her shoulders. "Nothing he didn't already know."

"You told him about the car?"

"I didn't have to. He looked up the history on the GPS. He knows it was you driving."

He cursed under his breath and mumbled, "It's okay. I can fix this."

She knew she should keep her mouth shut, but she couldn't help herself. "He knows about the drinking, too, and the fact that you were listening outside my bedroom door the other night."

He cut his eyes to her, and with a look that was pure venom, tipped his half-finished beer and dumped it onto her newly polished floor.

Nice. Very mature.

He walked up the stairs to his room. Hopefully to pack.

Isabelle cleaned up the beer with paper towels then repolished the floor. She cleaned all the main floor bathrooms next, buffing the chrome fixtures and polishing the marble countertops.

When she was finished she found Estefan in the living room, booted feet up on the glass top coffee table, drinking Don Julio Real Tequila straight from the bottle.

"You're enjoying this, aren't you?" he asked. "That I have to go, and you get to stay. That once again you mean more to him than his own brother."

Once again? What was that supposed to mean?

"You're leaving him no choice, Estefan."

"What the hell do you know? Emilio and I, we're family," he said, pounding his fist to his chest. "He's supposed to stand behind me. This is all your fault."

She knew his type. Everything was always someone else's fault. He never took responsibility for his own actions.

He took another swig from the bottle. "I loved you, you know. I would have done anything to have you. Then Emilio stole you from me."

Stole her?

So in his mind they had been embroiled in some creepy love triangle? Well, that wasn't reality. Even if there had been no Emilio, she never would have been attracted to Estefan.

He shoved himself up from the couch, wavering a second before he caught his balance. "I'm tired of coming in second place. Maybe I should take what's rightfully mine."

Meaning what?

He started to walk toward her with a certain look, and every instinct she had said *run*.

First thing when he got to work, Emilio called the firm Western Oil had hired to investigate the explosion and explained what he needed.

"Medical records are privileged," the investigator told him.

"So you're saying you can't get them?"

"I can, but you can't use the information in court."

"I don't plan to."

"Give me the name."

"Isabelle Winthrop."

There was a pause. "The one indicted for fraud?"

"That's the one." There was another pause, and he heard the sound of typing. "How long will this take?"

"Hold on." There was more typing, then he said, "Let me make a call. I'll get back to you in a couple of hours."

The time passed with no word and Emilio began to get impatient. He ate lunch at his desk, then forced himself to get some work done. By three o'clock, he was past impatient and bordering on pissed. He was reaching for the phone to call the firm back when his secretary buzzed him.

"Mr. Blair would like to see you in his office."

"Tell him I'll be there in a few minutes."

"He said right now."

He blew out a breath. "Fine."

When he got there Adam's secretary was on the phone, but she waved him in.

Adam stood at the window behind his desk, his back to the door.

"You wanted to see me, boss?"

He didn't turn. "Close the door and sit down."

He shut the door and took a seat, even though he preferred to stand, wondering what he could have done to earn such a cool reception. "Something wrong, Adam?"

"You may not know this, but due to the sensitive nature of the information we receive from the investigators in regard to the refinery accident, the mail room has implicit instruction to send any correspondence directly to my office."

Oh hell.

"So," he said, turning and grabbing a thick manila envelope from his desk, "When this arrived with your name on it, it came to me."

Emilio could clearly see that the seal on top had been broken. "You opened it?"

"Yeah, I opened it. Because for all I know you were responsible for the explosion, and you were trying to reroute key information away from the investigation."

The accusation stung, but put in Adam's place, he might have thought the same thing. He never should have used the same agency. He had just assumed they would call him, at which point he would have told them to send the files to his house.

"You want to explain to me why you need medical records for Isabelle Winthrop?"

"Not really."

Adam sighed.

"It's personal."

"How personal?"

"I just...needed to know something."

He handed Emilio the file. "You needed to know if someone was using her as their own personal punching bag?"

Emilio's stomach bottomed out. He hoped that was an exaggeration.

He pulled the file out of the envelope. It was thorough. Everything was there, from the time she was born until her annual physical the previous year. He flipped slowly through the pages, realizing immediately that Adam was not exaggerating, and what he read made him physically ill.

It seemed to start when she was three years old with a dislocated shoulder. Not a common injury for a docile young girl. From there it escalated to several incidences of concussions and cracked ribs, and a head injury so severe it fractured her skull and put her in the hospital for a week. He would venture to guess that there were probably many other injuries that had gone untreated, or tended by a personal physician who was paid handsomely to keep his mouth shut.

He scraped a hand through his hair. Why hadn't anyone connected the dots? Why hadn't someone *helped* her?

What disturbed him the most, what had him on the verge of losing his breakfast, was the hospital record from fifteen years ago. That weekend had been engraved in his memory since he opened the morning paper and saw the feature announcing Isabelle and Betts's wedding. Four days earlier Isabelle had been treated for a concussion and bruised ribs from a "fall" on campus. Emilio had seen her just two days later and he hadn't had a damned clue.

In the year they had been together what else hadn't he seen?

Then he had a thought that had bile rising in his throat. He was pretty sure that last concussion and the bruised ribs were his fault.

"Son of a bitch."

"Emilio," Adam said. "What's going on?"

Emilio had forgotten Adam was standing there.

"My brother thinks she might be innocent." In fact, he was ninety-nine point nine percent sure she was. "She's... she's been staying with me the last couple of weeks."

Adam swore and shook his head. "You said you wouldn't do anything stupid."

"If she's innocent, she needs my help. That's more clear now than ever."

"Just because someone knocked her around, it doesn't mean she's not a criminal."

"If you knew her like I do, you would know she isn't capable of stealing anything."

"Sounds like your mind is already made up."

It was. And he was going to help her. He had to.

"Emilio, if it gets out to the press what you're doing—"

"It's not going to."

"And if it does? Is she worth decimating your career? Your reputation?"

He was stunned to realize that the answer to that question was yes. Because it would only be temporary, then everyone would know she didn't do it. He would spend his last penny to get to the truth if that's what it took.

"If the press gets hold of this, I'll take full responsibility. As far as I'm concerned, Western Oil is free to hang me out to dry."

"Wow. You must really care about this woman."

"I do." But what really mattered was that fifteen years ago he'd failed her. In the worst possible way. He refused to make that mistake again.

Thirteen

Emilio left work early, and when he opened the front door he heard shouting and banging.

What the hell?

He dropped his briefcase by the door, followed the sound and found Estefan outside his office. The door was closed and Estefan was pounding with his fist shouting, "Let me in, you bitch!"

"What the hell is going on?"

Estefan swung around to face him. He was breathing hard, his eyes wild with fury. "Look what she did to me!"

Deep gouges branded his right cheek. Nail marks.

"*Isabelle* did that? What happened?"

"Nothing. She just attacked me."

That didn't sound like her at all. She'd never had a violent bone in her body. "Move out of the way," he said. "I'll talk to her."

He reluctantly stepped back.

"Wait in the living room."

"But—"

"In the living room."

"Fine," he grumbled.

Emilio waited until his brother was gone, then knocked softly. "Isabelle, it's Emilio. Let me in."

There was a pause, then he heard the lock turn. He opened the door and stepped into the room, and Isabelle launched herself into his arms. She clung to him, trembling from the inside out.

"Let me look at you. Are you okay?" He held her at arm's length. Her uniform was ripped open at the collar and she had what looked liked finger impressions on her upper arms.

He didn't have to ask her what happened. It was obvious. "Son of a bitch."

"He said he was going to take what was rightfully his," she said, her voice trembling. "He was drinking again."

Son of a bitch.

"I kind of accidentally told him that you were going to make him leave. He was really mad."

"I'm going to go talk to him. I want you to go upstairs, in my bedroom, shut the door and wait for me there. Understand?"

She nodded.

If this got out of hand he wanted her somewhere safe. He watched as she dashed up the stairs, waited until he heard the bedroom door close, then walked to the living room, where his brother was pacing by the couch. "What the hell did you do, Estefan?"

Outraged, his brother said, "What did *I* do? Look at my face!"

"You forced yourself on her."

"Is that what she told you? She's a liar. Man, she *wanted* it. She's been coming on to me for days. She's a whore."

Teeth gritted, Emilio crossed the room and gave his brother a shove. Estefan staggered backward, grabbing the couch to stop his fall. He righted himself, then listed to one side, before he caught his balance.

He *was* drunk.

"What's the matter with you, Emilio?"

"What's the matter with *me? You tried to *rape* her!"

Estefan actually laughed. "If you wanted to keep her all to yourself you should have said so."

Emilio swung, connecting solidly with Estefan's jaw. Estefan jerked back and landed on the floor.

"Emilio, what the hell!"

It took every ounce of control Emilio possessed not to beat the hell out of his brother. "You've crossed the line. Get your stuff and get out."

"You would choose that lying bitch over your own flesh and blood?"

"Isabelle has more integrity in the tip of her finger than you've ever had in your entire miserable excuse for a life."

His expression went from one of outrage to pure venom. This was the Estefan that Emilio knew. The one he had hoped he'd seen the last of. "I'll make you regret this."

Regret? He was already full of it. He thought about what might have happened if he hadn't come home early and he felt ill. What if Estefan had gotten into his office? "The only thing I regret is thinking that this time you might have changed."

"She's using you. Just like she did before."

"You know nothing, Estefan."

"I know her daddy wasn't very happy when I told him about your so-called engagement."

"You told him?"

"You should be thanking me. You were too good for her."

"You stupid son of a bitch. You have no clue what you did."

"I saved your ass, that's what I did."

He'd never wanted to hurt someone as much as he wanted to hurt Estefan right now. Instead he took a deep, calming breath and said, "Pack your things, and get out. As far as I'm concerned, we are no longer brothers."

While his brother packed, Emilio stood watch by the door and called him a cab. Estefan was too drunk to drive himself anywhere. Emilio didn't care what happened to him, but he didn't want him hurting someone else.

Estefan protested when Emilio snatched his keys away.

"Call me and tell me where you are, and I'll have your bike delivered to you."

He slurred out a few more threats, then staggered to the cab. Emilio watched it drive away, then he grabbed his case and headed up to his bedroom. Isabelle was sitting on the edge of his bed. She shot to her feet when he stepped in the room.

"He's gone," Emilio said. "And he isn't coming back."

She breathed a sigh of relief.

Emilio dropped his case on the floor by the bed, pulled her into his arms and held her. "I am so sorry. If I even suspected he would pull something like this I never would have let him stay here. And I sure as hell wouldn't have left you alone with him."

"I guess it was a case of unrequited love," she said, her voice still a little wobbly. "Who knew?"

He had, but he never imagined Estefan was capable of rape. He had been raised to respect women. They all had. There was obviously something wrong in Estefan's head.

"When I think what might have happened if I hadn't come home early…" He squeezed her tighter.

"He's going to tell people that I'm staying here, isn't he?"

"You can count on it." Definitely the family. With any luck he wasn't smart enough to go to the press, or they wouldn't listen.

She looked crestfallen. "If I leave today, right now, maybe it won't be so bad. You can deny I was here at all. And I will, too. No one has to know."

She was nearly raped, and she was worried about *him*. It was sickening how he had misjudged her, how he thought she could have anything to do with her husband's crimes. "You're not going anywhere, Izzie."

"But—"

"I don't care if anyone knows you're here."

"Why?"

"Because you're innocent."

"How do you know that?"

He shrugged. "Because I do."

She didn't seem to know what to say.

"There's something we need to talk about, something I need to know."

She frowned, as though she knew she wasn't going to like what was coming next.

"What did your father do when he found out we were eloping?"

"What makes you think he knew?"

"Because Estefan told him."

She sucked in a quiet breath.

"He did it to get back at me. He said he did it to help me, but I know he was just jealous."

"I always wondered how my father found out."

"Is that why he did it?"

"Did what?"

He opened his briefcase, pulled out the file and handed it to her. She started to read the top page and the color leeched from her face. She sank to the edge of the bed.

He sat beside her. "The concussion, the bruised ribs. He did that because of me, didn't he?"

She flipped through the pages, then looked up at him, eyes wide. "Where did you get this?"

"Why didn't you tell me, Izzie? Why didn't you tell me what he did to you?"

She shrugged, setting the file on the bed beside her. "Because that's not the way it works."

"I could have helped you."

She shook her head. "No one could help us."

Us? "Your mother, too?"

"My father was a very angry man. But if there's any justice in this world, I can rest easy knowing he's rotting in hell for what he did to us."

He could barely wrap his head around it. How could he have been so blind? Why didn't he see?

"I know you don't like to talk about it, but I have to know. Why did you do it? Why did you leave me for Betts?"

"It was the only way to keep her safe."

"Your mother?"

She nodded.

"Tell me what happened."

She bit her lip, wringing her hands in her lap.

He took her hand in his and held it. "Please, Isabelle."

"My father found out about us and *punished* me. When he was finished, he told me that if I ever saw you again he was going to disown me. I would be completely cut off. I was so sick of it, I told him I didn't care. I said I didn't want his money, and I didn't care if I ever saw him again.

I said I was going to marry you, and my mother was going to come live with us and nothing he could do would stop me." She took a deep, unsteady breath. "And he said…he said that if I married you, something terrible would happen to my mother. He said she would have an 'accident.'" She looked up at him. "My father did not make idle threats, and the look in his eyes…I knew he would kill her just to spite me. And to prove his point he punished her, too, and it was even worse than what he did to me. She couldn't get out of bed for a week."

Sick bastard. If Isabelle had a concussion and bruised ribs, he couldn't even imagine what he must have put her mother through.

Emilio felt sick to his stomach, sick all the way to his soul. "Did he force you to marry Betts?"

"Not exactly. Usually he was good about hiding the marks, but this time he didn't even try. My parents had been friends with Lenny for years. Long story short, he happened to stop by and saw the condition we were in. He was horrified. He'd suspected that my father was abusive, but he had no idea how bad it was. He wanted to call the police, but my mom begged him not to."

"Why? They could have helped you."

"Because she tried that before. My father was a very powerful man. The charges had a way of disappearing."

Alejandro had said as much.

"Lenny figured if he couldn't help my mother, he could at least get me out of there. He knew my father would agree to a marriage."

"A marriage between his nineteen-year-old daughter and a man in his forties?"

"My father saw it as a business opportunity. He had debts, and Lenny promised to make them go away."

The gambling Alejandro had mentioned. Just when

Emilio didn't think he could feel more disgust, her father sank to a whole new level of vile. "He *sold* you."

She shrugged. "More or less."

"So what was the going rate for a nineteen-year-old virgin?"

She lowered her eyes. "Lenny wouldn't tell me. Hundreds of thousands. Maybe millions. Who knows."

"If you had told me then, I would have taken you away. You and your mother. I would have killed your father if that's what it took to keep you both safe. I would kill him now if he wasn't already dead."

"And that's exactly why I couldn't tell you. If you only knew how many times she tried to leave. But he always found us and brought us back. He would have hurt you if you had tried to help. Look what he did to your mother just to spite me. At least Lenny had been able to take me away from it. And you were safe and free to live your life."

It was hard to fathom that Izzie's husband, a man that Emilio had despised for so many years, had really saved her life.

Only to turn around and ruin it again, he reminded himself.

"The sad fact is, I never should have come to see you that day on campus," Izzie said. "I should have known he would never let it happen, not if there wasn't something in it for him."

"I've never said this about another human being, but I'm glad your father is dead."

Her smile was a sad one. "No more than my mother and I."

"I'm sorry I've been such a jerk."

She shrugged. "I hurt you."

"That doesn't make it right."

She reached up, stroked his cheek. "Emilio, not a day

has gone by when I didn't miss you, and wished it were you I had married. It's going to sound silly, but I never stopped loving you. I still haven't."

A sudden surge of emotion caught him completely by surprise. He slipped his arms around her and pulled her against him, pressed his face against the softness of her hair. He wanted to hold her close and never let go, yet he couldn't help thinking he didn't deserve her love. He'd failed her, and all because he couldn't see past his own wounded pride. He should have trusted her. When he read in the papers that she was marrying Betts, he should have known something was wrong, that she would never willingly betray him.

He had promised to take care of her, to protect her and he'd let her down when she needed him most.

"Isabelle—"

She put her fingers over his lips to shush him. "No more talking."

She slid her arms around his neck and kissed him. And kept kissing him, until the past ceased to matter. All he cared about was being close to her. They would start over today, this very minute, and things would be different this time. He would take care of her and protect her. The way it should have been fifteen years ago.

Though there was no rush, Isabelle seemed in a hurry to get them both naked. She shoved his jacket off his shoulders, then undid the buttons on his shirt and pushed that off, too. Then she unbuttoned her dress and pulled it up over her head. Her bra was next to go, until all that was left was her panties.

She took those off, then pulled back the covers and stretched out on the bed, summoning him with a smile and a crooked finger.

"I like that you're not shy anymore," he said rising to take off his pants.

"There are no bruises or marks to hide now."

He hadn't even considered that. "Is that why you never let me see you undressed?"

"I wanted to, but I knew there would be questions."

"Isabelle."

"No more talking about the past. Let's concentrate on today. On right now. Make love to me, and nothing else will matter."

That was by far the best idea she'd had all day.

Fourteen

Emilio stripped out of his clothes and climbed into bed with Isabelle. Since Tuesday she hadn't stopped thinking about making love to him again. Only this time she wasn't nervous. This time she had nothing to hide. He knew her secrets. She could relax and be herself. Until the weight of everything she had hidden from him was finally gone, she hadn't realized what a heavy load she'd carried. And when Emilio took her in his arms and kissed her, she knew he was back to being the man he used to be. Sweet and tender and thoughtful.

Ironically that wasn't what she wanted now. She was eager to experiment. She wanted it to be crazy and exciting. There were hundreds of different ways to make love and she wanted to try as many as she could before she had to go. She wanted it to be fun.

"Emilio, I'm not going to break."

He gazed down at her, brow furrowed. "I just don't

want to hurt you again. And after what happened to you today…if you want to wait, we can take a few days."

They had so little time left, she didn't want to waste any of it. And she didn't want him to feel as if he had to treat her with kid gloves. "First of all, if you're referring to Tuesday night, you did not hurt me."

Up went the brow.

"Okay, maybe it hurt a little, but only for a minute. And it wasn't a bad hurt, if that makes sense. And after that it was…*amazing.* And as far as what happened today, yeah it scared the hell out of me, but that has nothing to do with us. I know you would never hurt me."

"But I did." He stroked her hair back from her face, touched her cheek. "I've been a total jerk the last couple weeks, and you've done absolutely nothing to deserve it."

"Except the rug, and the casserole dish, and the pink laundry. And of course the scorched shirt."

"That doesn't count. I put you in a position to fail so I could throw it back in your face."

"And I've forgiven you."

He sighed and rolled onto his back. "Maybe that's part of the problem. Maybe I feel like I don't deserve your forgiveness."

She sat up beside him. "In that case, you have to forgive *yourself.* You've got to let it go. Trust me on this one. If I hadn't made peace with my father, and Lenny, I would probably be in a padded room by now."

"How? How do you let it go?"

She shrugged. "You just do."

"I'm just so…*mad.*"

"At yourself?"

"At myself, and at your father. For what he did to you, and everything he stole from us. Everything that we could have been. If it wasn't for him, we would be married, we would probably have kids." He pushed himself up on his elbows. "I'm pissed at Estefan for ratting us out, and Alejandro for prosecuting you when I'm pretty sure he knows damn well that you're innocent. I'm pissed at every person who suspected your father was abusive and did nothing about it. I feel like I'm mad at the whole damned world!"

"So let it out."

"I can't."

"Yes, you can." She reached over and pinched his left nipple. Hard.

"Hey!" He batted her hand away, looking stunned, as if he couldn't believe she would do something like that. Sweet, nonconfrontational Isabelle. "What was that for?"

He was going to have to accept that she had changed. "Did it hurt?"

"Yeah, it hurt."

"Good." She did the same thing to the right side.

"Ow! Stop that!"

She pinched the fleshy skin under his bicep next and he jerked away.

"Izzie, stop it."

She climbed into his lap, straddling his thighs. "Make me."

She moved to pinch him again and his hand shot out to manacle her wrist, and when she tried to use her other hand, he grabbed that wrist, too. She struggled to yank free, but he held on tighter, almost to the point of pain. But that was good, that was what she wanted. She didn't want him to look at her as some frail flower he needed to protect. She wanted him to know how tough she was.

Since her hands were restrained, she leaned in and bit him instead, on his left shoulder. Not hard enough to break the skin, but enough to cause pain.

He jerked away. "Isabelle! What's gotten into you?"

"Are you pissed?"

"Yes, I'm pissed!"

"Good." She leaned in to do it again, but he'd apparently had enough. Finally. He pulled her down on top of him then rolled her onto her back, pinning her wrists over her head.

She'd never thought of herself as the type who would be into anything even remotely kinky, but she was so hot for him, she was afraid she might spontaneously combust. Emilio settled between her thighs, holding her to the mattress with the weight of his body, and it was clear that he liked it, too. A lot.

She hooked her legs around his, arching against him. He groaned and his eyes went dark, breath rasped out. So she did it again, bucking against him.

"Izzie." His voice held a warning, stop or else, but she *wanted* the "or else."

Lifting her head, she scraped her teeth across his nipple. She would keep biting and pinching and bucking until he gave her what she wanted. Only this time he turned the tables on her. He dipped his head and took her nipple in his mouth, sucked hard.

She cried out, pushing against his hands, digging her nails into her palms. *"Yesss."*

"You *like* this," he said.

His eyes said that he'd finally figured it out. He knew what she wanted.

It was about damned time.

She knew Emilio liked to be composed at all times, but she wanted him to lose control, to do something crazy.

He kissed her, like he never had before. A hard, punishing kiss. He started to work his way down, to her neck and her shoulders, kissing and nipping. Then he slipped lower still, letting go of her wrists so he could press her thighs wide. She thought they would make love right away, but clearly he had other ideas.

She held her breath in anticipation, gasping as he took her in his mouth. Oral sex had been a regular routine for them, and it was always good, but never like this. He was *devouring* her. She clawed her nails through his hair, so close to losing it…then he thrust a finger inside of her, then another, then a third, slow and deep, and pleasure seized her like a wild animal.

Emilio rose up and settled between her thighs, thrusting hard inside of her, and the orgasm that had begun to ebb slowly away suddenly picked up momentum again, only this time from somewhere deep inside. Somewhere she'd never felt before. Maybe her soul. It erupted into a sensation so beautiful and perfect, so exactly what she ever hoped it could be, tears welled in her eyes. And she was so utterly lost in her own pleasure she didn't realize he had come, too, until he flopped onto his back beside her.

"Wow," he said, breathing hard.

"So, are you still mad?"

He laughed—a genuine honest to goodness laugh. A sound she hadn't heard out of him in a very long time. "Not at all. In fact, I can't recall the last time I was so relaxed."

She smiled and curled up against his side. "Good."

"I didn't hurt you?"

"Are you kidding? That was *perfect*." And it must have been really good for him, too, because he was still mostly hard. Then she realized something that made her heart drop. "Emilio, you didn't use a condom."

"I know."

She shot up in bed. "You *know*? You did it *deliberately*?"

He didn't even have the decency to look remorseful.

"Not exactly. I realized the minute I was inside of you, but I didn't think you would appreciate me stopping to roll one on."

"Did it occur to you that I could get pregnant?"

"Of course."

"What did you think? That me being pregnant with his brother's baby will stop Alejandro from putting me in prison? They put pregnant women in prison all the time. Are you prepared to raise a baby alone? To be a single dad for the next twenty-to-life? Maybe if I get out early on good behavior I'll see him graduate high school."

"You're not going to prison."

She groaned and dropped her head in her hands. The man was impossible.

"Do you think you could be pregnant?" he asked.

"My period is due soon, so I'd say it's unlikely."

He actually looked disappointed. How had he gone from hating her one day, to wanting to have babies with her the next? This was crazy. Even if she didn't go to prison his family would never accept her.

"Can I ask you a question?" he said.

"Sure."

"Since you've told me everything else, would you explain how you never slept with Lenny? Because I really don't get it. I can't go five minutes without wanting to rip your clothes off."

"He had a heart condition and he was impotent. Ultimately he did screw me, just not in the bedroom."

"After your father died you could have divorced him."

"There didn't seem to be much point. There was only one other man I wanted." She touched his arm. "And I knew he would never take me back, never forgive me."

"I guess you were wrong."

"It would probably be better if you hadn't."

"You're *not* going to prison."

"Yes, I am. Nothing is going to stop that now."

"I just got you back, Izzie. I'm not letting you go again."

But he was going to have to. He couldn't keep her out of prison by sheer will. He was going to have to accept that they were living on borrowed time.

"Things are going to change around here," he said.

"What things?"

"First off, I'm calling my housekeeper back."

"You can't do that. You gave her the month off. It's not fair."

"So I'll hire a temp."

"But I like doing it."

He raised a brow at her.

"I do. And it gives me something to do. A way to pass the time, since I doubt all those charities I used to volunteer for would be interested in my services any longer."

"Are you sure?"

"Positive."

"Okay, but you're not allowed to wear the uniform anymore. And I'm buying you some decent clothes."

"There's no point."

"There sure as hell is. The ones you have are awful."

"And I'll only need them for another few weeks. Getting anything new would be a waste of money."

She could tell he wanted to argue, but he probably figured there was no point. She was not going to budge on this one. Besides, the last thing she wanted was for him to spend money on her. She didn't deserve it.

"You're obviously not staying in the maid's quarters any longer. You're moving in here with me. If you want to."

"Of course I do." It was probably a bad idea. The closer they got, the harder it would be when she had to go, but she had the feeling nothing would prevent that now. They might as well spend all the time they could together.

"You have a say in this, too," he said. "Is there anything you'd like to add? Anything you want?"

There were so many things she wanted. She wanted to marry him, and have babies with him. She wanted to do everything they had talked about before. It's all she had ever wanted. But why dwell on a future that wasn't meant to be?

The phone rang, so she grabbed the cordless off the bedside table and handed it to him. He looked at the display and cursed under his breath. "Well, that didn't take long."

He sat up and hit the talk button. "Hello, Mama."

Isabelle winced. Estefan hadn't wasted any time running to his mother, had he?

He listened for a minute, then said, "Yes, it's true."

She could hear his mother talking. Not what she was saying, but her tone came through perfectly. She was upset.

"I know he was drunk. Are you really surprised?"

More talking from his mother's end, then Emilio interrupted her. "Why don't I come over there right now so we can talk about this?"

She must have agreed, because then he said, "I'll be over as soon as I can."

He hung up and set the phone back on the table. "I guess you got the gist of that."

"Yeah."

"I shouldn't be too long."

"Take your time." He wasn't the only one who needed to talk to their mother. "I was thinking maybe I could go talk to my mother, too. I'd hate for her to hear it from someone besides me."

"I think that's a good idea. I'll pick up Chinese food on my way home."

"Sounds good." Although after dealing with their parents, she wondered if either of them would have much of an appetite.

Fifteen

Emilio parked in the driveway of his mother's condo. The year he'd made his first million he'd bought it for her. He'd wanted to get her something bigger and in a more affluent part of the city, but she had wanted to live here, in what was a primarily Hispanic neighborhood. Not that this place was what anyone would consider shabby. It had been brand-new when he bought it, and he made sure it had every upgrade they offered, and a few he requested special. After sacrificing so much for Emilio and his brothers, she deserved the best of everything.

He walked to the front door and let himself inside. "Mama?"

"In the kitchen," she called back.

He wasn't surprised to find her at the counter, apron on, adding ingredients to a mixing bowl. She always baked when she was upset or angry.

"What are you making?"

"Churros, with extra cinnamon, just the way you like them." She gestured to the kitchen table. "Sit down, I'll get you something to drink."

She pulled a pitcher of iced tea from the fridge and poured him a glass. He would have preferred something stronger, but she never kept alcohol of any kind in the house.

Handing it to him, she went back to the bowl, mixing the contents with a wooden spoon. "I guess you saw your brother's face."

"I saw it."

"He said she attacked him. For no good reason."

"Attempted rape is a pretty good reason."

She cut her eyes to him. "Emilio! Your brother would never do that. He was raised to respect women."

Emphatically as she denied it, something in her eyes said she was afraid it might be true.

"If you had seen Isabelle, the ripped uniform and the bruises on her arms… She was terrified."

She muttered something in Spanish and crossed herself.

"He needs help, Mama."

"I know. He told me that bad people are after him. He asked to stay here. I told him no."

"Good. We can't keep trying to save him. We have to let him hit rock bottom. He has to want to help himself."

"You told him you're no longer brothers. You didn't mean it."

"I did mean it. He hurt the woman I love."

"How can you love her after what she did to you? She left you for that rich man. She only cared about money. That's the only reason she's back now."

"She came to me because she wanted help for her mother, not herself. And she didn't marry Betts for his money. The only reason she left me for him is because her father threatened to hurt her mother."

He waited for the shock, but there was none, confirming what he already suspected. "You knew about the abuse, didn't you? You knew that Isabelle's father was hurting them. You *had* to."

She didn't answer him.

"Mama."

"Of course I knew," she said softly. "The things that man did to them." She closed her eyes and shook her head, as if she were trying to block the mental image. "It made me sick. And poor Mrs. Winthrop. Sometimes he beat her so badly, she would be in bed for days. And Isabelle, she always stayed right by her mother's side. I never speak ill of the dead, but that man did the world a favor when he died."

"You should have told me. I could have helped her."

She shook her head. "No. He would have hurt you, too. I was always afraid that something bad would happen if he found out about you and Isabelle."

"Well, he found out." He almost told her that Estefan was the one who ratted him out, but he didn't want to hurt her any more than necessary.

"You had the potential to go so far, Emilio. I was relieved when she left you."

"Even though you knew how much I loved her?"

"I figured you would get over her eventually."

"But I didn't. As bitter as I was, I never stopped loving her."

Was that guilt in her eyes? "What difference does it make now? Alejandro said she's going to prison."

"Not if I can help it."

She set the spoon down and pushed the bowl aside. "She stole money."

"No, she didn't. She's innocent."

"You know that for a fact?"

"I know it in my heart. In every fiber of my being. She's not a thief."

"Even if that's true, everyone thinks she's guilty."

He shrugged. "I don't care what everyone thinks."

"Emilio—"

"Mama, do you remember what you told me when I asked you why you never remarried? You said Papa was your one true love, and there could be no one else. I finally understand what you meant. I was lucky enough to get Izzie back. I can't lose her again."

"Even if it means ruining everything you've worked so hard for?"

"That's not going to happen. First thing Monday, I'm hiring a new attorney."

"People will find out."

"They probably will."

"And I could argue with you until I'm blue in the face and it won't do any good, will it?"

He shook his head.

She drew in a deep breath, then blew it out. "Then I will pray for you, Emilio. For you and Isabelle."

"Thank you, Mama." At this point, he would take all the help he could get.

Isabelle called her mother Friday, but she was out with Ben. They went to dinner with friends, then they left Saturday morning for an overnight trip to Phoenix to see an old college buddy of Ben's. Isabelle didn't get a chance to talk to her until Monday morning. She took the news much better than Isabelle expected. In fact, she suspected all along that Isabelle had been "bending" the truth.

"Sweetheart," she said, fixing them each a cup of tea

in her tiny kitchenette. "You know I can always tell when you're lying. And, *Mrs. Smith?*"

Isabelle couldn't help but smile. "Not very creative, huh?"

"I thought it was awfully coincidental that you were working in the same neighborhood where Emilio lived. Then I mentioned him and you got very nervous."

"And people think I'm capable of stealing millions of dollars." She sighed. "Not only am I a terrible liar, but I don't even know how to balance a checkbook."

Her mother walked over with their tea and sat down at the table.

"I'm sorry I lied to you, but I promised Emilio I wouldn't tell anyone I was staying there. It was part of our deal."

"Emilio is going to help you, right?"

"He's going to talk to his brother on your behalf. You won't be serving any time."

"But what about you?"

They had been through this so many times. "There isn't anything he can do. You know what Lenny's lawyer said. The evidence against me is indisputable."

"There has to be something Emilio can do. Can't he talk to his brother? Make some sort of deal?"

She was just as bad as Emilio, refusing to accept reality. She wished they would both stop being so stubborn. But she didn't want her mother to worry so she said, "I'll ask him, okay?"

Her mother looked relieved.

"So, tell me about this weekend trip. Did you have fun?"

She lit up like a firefly. "We had a *wonderful* time. Ben has the nicest friends. The only thing that was a little unexpected was that they put us in a bedroom together."

Her brows rose. "Oh really?"

"Nothing happened," she said, then her cheeks turned

red and she added, "Well, nothing much. But he is a very nice kisser."

"Only nice?"

Her smile was shy, with a touch of mischief. "Okay, better than nice."

They talked about her trip with Ben and what they had planned for the coming weekend. He clearly adored her mother, and the feeling was mutual. Isabelle was so happy she had found someone who appreciated her, and made her feel good about herself. At the same time she was a little sad that she wouldn't be around to see their relationship grow. Of course, they could always write letters, and her mother could visit.

Maybe she was a little jealous, too, that she had finally found her heart's desire, and it had to end in only a few weeks. They wouldn't even get to spend Christmas together.

She drove back to Emilio's fighting the urge to feel sorry for herself. When she pulled in the driveway there was an unfamiliar car parked there. A silver Lexus. She considered pulling back out. What if it was someone who shouldn't know she was staying there? But hadn't Emilio said he didn't care who knew?

She pulled the Saab in the garage and let herself in the house. Emilio met her at the door. "There you are. I was about send out a search party."

"I went to see my mother."

"Is everything okay? She wasn't angry?"

"Not at all."

"I need to get you a cell phone, so I can reach you when you're out."

For less than a month? What was the point? "Is there something wrong?"

"Nothing. In fact, I have some good news. Come in the living room, there's someone I want you to meet."

There was a man sitting on the couch, a slew of papers on the table in front of him. When they entered the room, he stood.

"Isabelle, this is David Morrison."

He was around Emilio's age, very attractive and dressed in a sharp, tailored suit. "Ms. Winthrop," he said, shaking her hand. "It's a pleasure to meet you."

"You, too," she said, shooting Emilio a questioning look.

"David is a defense attorney. One of the best. He's going to be taking over your case."

"What?"

"We're firing Clifton Stone."

"But…why?"

"Because he's giving you bad advice," Mr. Morrison said. "I've been going over your case. The evidence against you is flimsy at best. We'll take this to trial if necessary, but honestly, I don't think it will come down to that."

"I was using Lenny's lawyer because he was representing me pro bono. I can't afford a lawyer."

"It's taken care of," Emilio said.

She shook her head. "I can't let you do this."

"The retainer is paid. Nonrefundable. It's done."

"But I can't go to trial. The only way my mother will avoid prison is if I plead out." She turned to her "new" attorney. "Mr. Morrison—"

"Please, call me David."

"David, I really appreciate you coming to see me, but I can't do this."

"Ms. Winthrop, do you want to spend the next twenty years in prison?"

Was this a trick question? Did anyone *want* to go to prison? "Of course not."

"If you stick with your current attorney, that's what will happen. I've seen lawyers reprimanded and in some cases disbarred for giving such blatantly negligent counsel. Either he's completely incompetent, or he has some sort of agenda."

Agenda? How could he possibly benefit from her going to prison? "What about my mother? What happens to her?"

"Alejandro already told me they wouldn't ask for more than probation," Emilio said.

"When did he say that?"

He hesitated, then said, "The day you came to see me in my office."

So all this time she'd been working for him for no reason? She should be furious, but the truth was, it was a million times better here than at that dumpy motel. And if she hadn't come here, Emilio would have gone the rest of his life hating her. Maybe now they even had some sort of future together. Marriage and family, just like they had planned. Hope welled up with such intensity she had to fight it back down. She was afraid to believe it was real.

"You really think you could keep me and my mother out of prison?" she asked David.

"Worst case you may end up with probation. It would go a long way if the last few million of the missing money were to surface."

"If I knew where it was I would have handed it over months ago. I gave them everything else."

"I'm going to do some digging and see what turns up. In the meantime, I need you to sign a notice of change of counsel to make it official."

She signed the document, but only after thoroughly reading it—she had learned her lesson with Lenny—then David packed up his things and left.

"I told you I wouldn't let you go to prison," Emilio said,

sounding smug, fixing himself a sandwich before he went back to work.

"I still don't like that you're paying for it. What if someone finds out?"

"I've already said a dozen times—"

"You don't care who finds out. I know. But I do. Until I know for sure that I'm not going to prison, I don't want anyone to know. Even if that means waiting through a trial."

"I suppose that means we'll have to wait to get married."

Married? She opened her mouth to speak, but nothing came out. She knew he wanted to be with her, but this was the first time he had actually mentioned marriage.

"I was hoping we could start a family right away," he said, putting the turkey and the mayo back in the fridge. "If we haven't already, that is. But we've waited this long. I guess a few more months won't kill me. Just so long as you know that I love you, and no matter what happens, I'm not letting you go again."

He loved her, and wanted to marry her, and have a family with her. She threw her arms around him and hugged him tight. This was more than she ever could have hoped for. "I love you, too, Emilio."

"This is all going to work out," he told her, and she was actually starting to believe it.

"So, do you have to go back to work?" she asked, sliding her hands under his jacket and up his chest.

He grinned down at her. "That depends what you have in mind."

Though they had spent the better part of the weekend making love in bed—and on the bedroom floor and in the shower, and even on the dining room table—she could never get enough of him. "We haven't done it in the kitchen yet."

He lifted her up and set her on the counter, sliding her skirt up her thighs. "Well, that's an oversight we need to take care of immediately."

Sixteen

Isabelle never imagined things could be so wonderful. She and Emilio were going to get married and have a family—even though he hadn't officially asked her yet—and she and her mother weren't going to prison. Her life was as close to perfect as it could be, yet she had this gut feeling that the other shoe was about to drop. That things were a little *too* perfect.

Emilio wasn't helping matters.

He called her from work Thursday morning to warn her that a package would be arriving. But it wasn't one package. It was a couple dozen, all filled with clothes and shoes from department stores and boutiques all over town. It was an entire wardrobe, and it was exactly what she would have picked for herself.

Her first instinct was tell him to send it back, but now that she wasn't going to prison she did need new clothes.

"How did you know what I would like?" she asked Emilio when she called to thank him.

"I had help."

"What kind of help?"

"A personal shopper, so to speak. I swore her to secrecy."

Her? Who would know her exact taste, that Emilio knew to contact? There was really only one person. "My *mother?*"

"I knew you wouldn't get the clothes yourself, and who better to know what you like?"

"I talked to her this morning and she didn't say a word."

"She wanted it to be a surprise. If there's anything that you don't like just put it aside and I'll have it returned."

"It's all perfect."

"There should be something coming later this afternoon, too. A few things I picked out."

Isabelle called her mother to thank her, but she wasn't home so she left a message. After that she waited, very impatiently, until the package with Emilio's purchases arrived later that afternoon. She carried it into the living room where she had been sorting and folding all the other things.

Sitting on the couch, she ripped it open. It was lingerie. The first two items she pulled out were soft silk gowns in pink and white. When she saw what was underneath the gowns she actually blushed. Sexy items of silk and lace that were scandalously revealing. She'd never owned anything so provocative. There had never been any point.

She called Emilio immediately to thank him.

"I wasn't sure if they would be a little too racy," he said.

"No, I love them!"

"You'll have to try them on for me later."

"I might just be wearing one when you walk in the door," she said, and could practically feel his sexy smile right through the phone line.

"In that case I may just have to come home early."

After they hung up Isabelle was gathering all her new clothes to take upstairs when the doorbell rang again.

More new clothes?

She walked to the foyer and pulled the door open, expecting another delivery man, but when she saw who was standing there her heart plummeted. "Mrs. Suarez."

"May I come in?" Emilio's mother asked.

"Of course," she said, stepping aside so she could come inside. "Emilio isn't here."

"I came to talk to you."

The last time she had seen Mrs. Suarez, Isabelle's father had been accusing her of stealing from them. And after threatening to have her arrested, and her younger children taken away by Social Services, he'd fired her.

The phone started to ring. "Let me grab that really fast," Isabelle said, dashing to the living room where she'd left the cordless phone, answering with a breathless, "Hello?"

It was her mother. "Hi honey, I just got your message. I'm so glad you like the clothes. Wasn't that a sweet thing for Emilio to do?"

"Yes, it was. Mom, can I call you back?"

"Is everything okay?"

"Everything is fine." She glanced over and realized Mrs. Suarez had followed her. She was looking at the piles of clothes strewn over the furniture, specifically the lingerie, and she did not look happy.

Oh, hell.

"I'll call you soon." She disconnected and turned to Mrs. Suarez. "Sorry about that."

"How is your mother?"

"Really good." She gestured to the one chair that wasn't piled with clothes. "Please, sit down. Can I get you something to drink?"

His mother sat. "No, thank you."

Isabelle moved some of the clothes from the end of the couch and sat down.

"It looks like you've been shopping." With her son's money her look said. Talk about awkward.

"Actually, Emilio had my mother pick them out and they were delivered a little while ago."

"He's a very generous man." Her tone suggested that generosity was wasted on someone like Isabelle. Or maybe Isabelle was being paranoid. Put in his mother's position, she might not trust her, either.

There was an awkward pause, and Isabelle blurted out, "I'm so sorry for what happened with Estefan."

She looked puzzled. "Why are *you* sorry? Emilio said Estefan forced himself on you. You had every right to defend yourself. I see the bruises are fading."

Isabelle glanced down at her arms. The marks Estefan had left there had faded to a greenish-yellow. "I still feel bad for scratching him."

"Estefan is part of the reason I'm here. I wanted to apologize on his behalf. I felt it was my duty as his mother."

"Is he okay?"

"I don't know. He disappeared again. It could be months before I see him." Isabelle must have looked guilty because Mrs. Suarez added, "This is not your fault."

Logically she knew that, but she felt responsible.

"I also wanted to talk to you about Emilio."

She'd assumed as much.

"He says you're innocent."

"I have a new attorney. He says he thinks I'll be acquitted, or let off with probation."

"And Emilio is paying for this new lawyer?"

"I didn't want him to, but he insisted. And if he hadn't, I would have spent the next twenty years in prison."

"Emilio has done you many favors. Now I want you to do him a favor."

"Of course. Anything."

"Leave."

Leave? She didn't know what to say.

"Only until you are found innocent." Her eyes pleaded with Isabelle. "My son has worked so hard to get where he is, and because he loves you, he would risk throwing it all away. If you love him, you won't allow that to happen."

"And if I'm not acquitted? If I wind up with probation?"

Mrs. Suarez didn't say anything, but it was written all over her face. She wanted Isabelle to leave him for good. And her reasoning was totally logical.

The CFO of a company like Western Oil couldn't be married to a woman out on probation for financial fraud. They would have no choice but to fire him, and he would never find another job like it. At least, not one that would pay him even a fraction of what he was worth. Not to mention that he would lose all his friends.

Because of her, he would be a pariah.

He said he loved her and didn't care what people thought, but with his life in shambles he might feel differently. He would begin to resent her, and they would be right back to where they were before, only this time he would hate her not for leaving, but for staying. She couldn't do that to him.

Just once she had wanted something for herself, she

had wanted to be happy. For the first time in her life she wanted to do something selfish.

But Mrs. Suarez was right. It was time for her to go.

"I had an interesting talk with Cassandra," Adam said from Emilio's office doorway.

He glanced up from his computer screen. He had just a few things he needed to finish up before he went home for the night. "Is there another public relations nightmare on the horizon?"

"You tell me."

"Meaning what?"

He stepped into his office and shut the door. "Cassandra got a call from a reporter asking if it was true that there was a connection between Isabelle Winthrop-Betts and the CFO of Western Oil."

He sighed. *Here we go.*

"What did she tell them?"

"That she knows of no association, then she came and asked me about it. So I'm asking you, what's the status of her case? Someone is digging, and I get the feeling something big is about to break."

"I hired a new attorney. He wants to take it to trial. He thinks he can get an acquittal."

"But it will take some time."

"Probably."

Adam shook his head.

"If you have something to say, just say it, Adam."

"If she goes to trial and the story breaks about the two of you… Emilio, the damage will be done. You'll never make CEO. The board would never allow it. I can't guarantee they won't vote to terminate you immediately."

"Let me ask you something. Suppose Katy was accused

of a crime, and you knew she was innocent. Would you stand behind her, even if it meant making sacrifices?"

Adam took a deep breath and blew it out. "Yes, of course I would."

"Then why is everyone so surprised that I'm standing behind Isabelle? Do I want to be CEO? Do I think I'm the best man for the job? You're damn right I do. But what kind of CEO, what kind of *man* would I be if didn't stand up for the things I believe in? If I abandoned Isabelle when she needs me most?"

"You're right," Adam said. "I admire what you're doing, and I'll back you as long as I can."

"I know you will. And when it comes to the point that you can't help me, don't lose a night's sleep over it. This is my choice."

His secretary buzzed him. "I'm sorry to interrupt, Mr. Suarez, but your brother is on line one. He says it's important."

"Which brother?"

"Alejandro."

"Go ahead and take it," Adam said. "We'll talk later."

Adam left, and Emilio hit the button for line one. "Hey, Alejandro, what's up?"

"Hey, big brother, I was wondering if you're going to be home this evening."

"This was so important you would interrupt a meeting with my boss?"

"Actually, it is. I need to talk to you. In person."

"What time?"

"The earlier the better. Alana doesn't like it when I come home too late."

Emilio thought about Isabelle's promise to model the new lingerie. If he met with Alejandro early, then he and Isabelle would have the rest of the evening.

"Why don't you meet me at my house in an hour?"

"Sounds good. Will Isabelle be there?"

"Of course. Is that a problem?"

"No, I'll see you in an hour."

Seventeen

As his driver took him home, Emilio got to thinking about what Alejandro could possibly need to discuss that was so urgent. It couldn't have anything to do with Isabelle's case, because he wasn't allowed to question her without her lawyer present.

His driver dropped him at the front door and Emilio let himself inside—and nearly tripped over the suitcases sitting there. "What the hell?"

Isabelle appeared at the top of the stairs, and she was clearly surprised to see him. She was dressed in what he was guessing were her new clothes. She looked young and hip and classy. So different from the scrawny, desperate woman who had come to see him in his office.

"You're home early," she said, her tone suggesting that wasn't a good thing.

"Yeah, I'm home." He set his briefcase on the floor next to the open door. "What the hell is going on?"

She walked down the stairs, met him in foyer. "I was going to leave you a note."

"You're going somewhere?"

"I'm moving out."

"Why?"

"Because I have to. I can't let you risk your career for me."

"Isabelle—"

"I'm not talking forever. As soon as I'm acquitted we can be together again. But until then, we can't see each other. Not at all. If your career was ruined because of me, your family would never forgive me, and I would never forgive myself."

"And what if you aren't acquitted? David said you might possibly get probation."

She bit her lip, and he could guess the answer.

"I'm not losing you again, Isabelle."

"Hopefully you won't have to. I'm going to fight it Emilio. I will do anything I have to for an acquittal. But if I don't get it…I'm not sure how, but I'll pay you back for the lawyer's fee."

"I don't give a damn about the lawyer's fees. And I'm not letting you do this."

"You don't have a choice."

He could see by her expression that she meant it. She was really leaving, whether he liked it or not. His heart started to race and suddenly he couldn't pull in enough air. The thought of losing her again filled him with a sense of panic that seemed to well up from the center of his being.

This could not be happening. Not again.

"Knock, knock," someone said, and they both turned to see Alejandro standing on the porch at the open door. He stepped inside, saw the suitcases and asked Isabelle, "Going somewhere?"

"Nowhere out of your jurisdiction, if that's what you're worried about. I'm going to stay at my mother's for a while."

"No, she isn't," Emilio said.

She cut her eyes to him. "*Yes,* I am."

"Can I ask why?" Alejandro said.

"She's worried that her being here is going to damage my career, despite the fact that I keep telling her I don't give a *damn* about my career."

"I think you both need to listen to what I have to say."

"If has to do with my case, I can't talk to you without my lawyer present," Isabelle said.

"Trust me, you're going to want to hear this."

"I won't answer any questions."

"You won't have to." He handed her a white 6x9 envelope Emilio hadn't even noticed he was holding. "Open it."

She did and dropped the contents into her hand, looking confused. "My passport?"

"I don't get it," Emilio said. "Are you suggesting she should leave the country?"

Alejandro laughed. "I thought she might like it back, now that all the charges against her have been formally dropped."

Emilio was certain he misheard him. "Say again?"

"All the charges against Isabelle have been dropped."

Emilio looked over at Isabelle and realized she was practically hyperventilating.

"And my mother?" she asked.

"Your mother, too."

"You're serious?" she said. "This isn't just some twisted joke?"

"It's no joke."

She pressed her hand over her heart and tears welled in her eyes. She turned to Emilio. "Oh, my God, it's over."

He held out his arms and she walked into them, hugging him hard, saying, "I can't believe it's really over."

"What the hell happened?" Emilio asked his brother.

Isabelle turned in his arms and said, "Yeah, what the hell happened?"

Alejandro grinned. "You want the full story, or the condensed version?"

"Maybe we should go for the condensed version," she said. "Since you'll have to explain it all to me again when my head stops spinning."

"It was your husband's lawyer, Clifton Stone. He had the missing money."

"Stone?" Isabelle said, looking genuinely shocked. "I had no idea he was involved. I never even considered it."

"Is that why he wanted her to take a plea?" Emilio asked. "To take the attention off himself?"

"Yeah. Dumb move on his part. It's what made us suspicious in the first place, but we knew he wouldn't cooperate. We had to flush him out. We figured if we were patient he would do something stupid."

"So you knew all along that she was innocent?" Emilio asked.

"If I thought she was guilty do you think I would have dropped you all those bread crumbs, Emilio? I wanted you to get curious, to take matters into your own hands. And it worked. When you hired the new defense attorney, Stone panicked. He was going to run, and he led us right to the money."

"And he told you I wasn't involved?" Isabelle asked.

"He must have been paranoid about being caught because he saved every piece of correspondence between himself and your husband. Phone calls, emails, texts, you name it. He offered them up in exchange for a plea. He said they would exonerate you and your mother."

"And they did?" Emilio asked.

"Oh yeah. They were full of interesting information. If Betts hadn't died, I'm sure Stone would have flipped on him to save his own neck."

"So that's it?" Isabelle asked. "It's done?"

"The case is officially closed."

Emilio shook his brother's hand. "Thank you, Alejandro."

"Yes, thank you," Isabelle said.

"Well, I'm going to get out of here. I get the feeling you two have a lot to talk about." He started out the door, then stopped and turned back. "How about dinner at my place this weekend? Just the four of us. And the kids, of course."

That was an olive branch if Emilio had ever seen one.

"I'd like that," Isabelle said.

"Great. I'll have Alana call you and you can figure out a time." He shot his brother one last grin then left, shutting the door behind him.

Isabelle turned to Emilio and wrapped her arms around him. "I still can't believe it's really over. It feels like a dream."

"Does this mean you'll stay now?"

She looked up at him. "Only if you want me to."

He laughed. "You think? I had only reduced myself to *begging*."

She smiled up at him. "Then yes, I'll stay."

"We need to celebrate. We should open some champagne."

"Definitely."

"Or we could go out and celebrate."

She rose up on her toes to kiss him. "I think I'd rather

stay in tonight. I seem to recall a promise to model some lingerie."

A smile spread across his face. "I think I like the sound of that. But there's something I need to do first. Something I should have done a long time ago."

"What?"

He had hoped to do this in a more romantic setting, but he couldn't imagine a better time than now. "Isabelle, I never thought we would get a second chance together, and I don't want to spend another day without knowing that you'll be mine forever." He dropped down on one knee and took her hand. "Would you marry me?"

Tears welled in her eyes. "Of course I'll marry you."

He rose and pulled the ring box from his jacket pocket. "This is for you."

She opened it, and her look of surprise, followed by genuine confusion, was understandable.

"At this point you're wondering why a man of my means would give you a 1/4 carat diamond ring of questionable quality."

She was too polite to say he was right, but he could see it in her face.

"When I asked you to marry me before, I couldn't afford a ring, and you couldn't wear one anyway, because your father would find out. We decided that we would look for one together the day before we eloped. Remember?"

"I remember."

"Well, I couldn't wait. I saved up for months and bought this for you."

"And you kept it all this time?"

He shrugged. "I just couldn't let it go. I guess maybe deep down I hoped we'd get a second chance. I know it's small, and if you don't want to wear it I completely understand. I thought you might want to turn it into a necklace, or—"

"No." She took the ring from him, tears rolling down her cheeks, and slipped it on her finger. "You could offer me the Hope Diamond and it would never come close to meaning as much to me as this does."

"Are you sure?"

"Absolutely. I'll wear it forever."

He touched her cheek. "I love you, Isabelle."

"I love you so much." She rose up on her toes and kissed him, then she touched his face, as if she couldn't believe it was real. "Is this really happening?"

"Why do you sound so surprised?"

"Because I always thought I wasn't supposed to be this happy, that it just wasn't in the cards for me. That for some reason I didn't deserve it. And suddenly I've got everything I ever hoped for. I keep thinking it has to be a dream."

"It's very real, and you do deserve it." And he planned to spend the rest of his life proving it to her.

* * * * *

MISS PRIM AND
THE BILLIONAIRE

LUCY GORDON

PROLOGUE

As THE soft light of dawn crept into the room the young man looked down on the girl, asleep beside him, her long blonde hair cascading across the pillow, her face soft and sweet. He kissed her lips gently and she stirred, murmuring, 'Marcel.'

'Shh,' he said. 'I just want to tell you—'

'Mmm?'

'—lots of things. Some of them I can't say when you're awake. When I look at you I'm struck dumb. I can't even find the words to tell you how lovely you are—but then, you already know that.'

He drew the sheet back to reveal her glorious form, both slender and voluptuous.

'There are plenty of people to praise your beauty, those photographers, and so many other men who'd take you from me if they could. But you don't let them. Bless you, my darling, my sweet Cassie.'

Without opening her eyes, she gave a sleepy smile that made Marcel's heart turn over. He was in his early twenties with a face that was still boyish, and as gentle as her own. His naked body was lean, almost too much so. Time would fill out his shape and bring maturity to his features, but perhaps he would never be better than he was now, his dark eyes full of adoration as he gazed down at her.

'Can you hear me? I have something to tell you. You may

be cross with me for concealing it, but you'll forgive me, I know you will. And then I'll ask—no, I'll *beg* you to become my wife. What we have now is wonderful, but I want more. I want to claim you in the sight of the world, to climb to the top of the highest tower and cry aloud that you belong to me. To *me!* Nobody else. We'll marry as soon as possible, won't we, my darling? And all the world will know that you're mine as completely as I am yours.

'That time will come soon, but first I have to explain what I've been hiding. The fact is that I—no, let me keep my secret a little longer. In truth I'm a coward. I'm so afraid that you'll be angry with me when you know that I deceived you, just a little, that I let you think—never mind. I'll tell you when the right moment comes.

'For this moment I just want to say that I love you, I belong to you, and nothing will ever part us. My darling, if you knew how I long to call you my wife. I pray that our wedding will happen soon.

'But sleep now, just a little longer. There'll be time later. We have all our lives to love each other.'

CHAPTER ONE

'THE trouble with weddings is that they bring out the idiot in people.'

The cynical remark made Marcel Falcon glance up, grinning with agreement. The man who'd come to sit beside him was a business associate with whom he was on cordial terms.

'Good to see you, Jeremy,' he said. 'I'll get the drinks. Waiter!'

They were at a table in the bar of the Gloriana Hotel, one of the most luxurious establishments in London, providing not only rooms but wedding facilities for those who could afford them. Marcel gave his order, signed for it to go onto his bill and turned back to his companion, saying, 'You're right about weddings. No good to anyone. I'd just as soon have avoided this one, but my brother, Darius, is the bride's ex-husband.'

Jeremy stared. 'And he's a guest at her wedding to another man? I've heard of sophisticated, but that takes the biscuit.'

'It's for the children, Frankie and Mark. They need to see their parents acting friendly despite the divorce.'

'And I'll bet your father had a hand in the decision.'

'There aren't many decisions my father doesn't have a hand in,' Marcel agreed wryly. 'He actually got them to delay the wedding until a certain date had passed, so that he could come to England without incurring a huge tax bill.'

Amos Falcon was so extravagantly wealthy that he'd had to flee to the tax haven of Monaco where he lived for most of the time, venturing back to England for only ninety days of the year.

'Frankie and Mark are his only grandchildren,' Marcel said, 'so he's determined to stay part of their lives.'

'Strange, that. A man with five sons and only one of them has carried on the line so far.'

'He says the same thing. He's always urging us to marry, preferably Freya.'

'Who's Freya?'

'His stepdaughter, the closest thing to a daughter that he has, and he's set on marrying her to one of us, and so binding her into the family.'

'Don't any of you get a say in your choice of wife?'

'Are you kidding? This is my father we're talking about. Since when did anyone ever get a say?' Marcel spoke cynically but with wry affection.

'Failing Freya,' he went on, 'then some other wife to continue the great Falcon dynasty. But except for Darius we've all disappointed him. Jackson seems to find wild animals more interesting than people, Leonid is a man we hardly ever see. He could have a dozen wives, but since he seldom leaves Russia we wouldn't know. And Travis doesn't dare marry. He'd lose all his fans.'

He spoke of his younger half-brother, born and raised in America, and a successful television actor with an army of adoring female followers.

'No man could be expected to risk his fortune just for marriage,' Jeremy agreed solemnly. 'That just leaves you, the amorous Frenchman.'

Marcel grimaced. 'Enough!' he said. 'If you knew how that stereotype bores me.'

'And yet you make use of it. The life in Paris, the endless

supply of women—all right, all right.' He broke off hastily, seeing Marcel's face. 'But since you have what most men would give their eye teeth for, the least you can do is enjoy it.'

The waiter arrived with their drinks. When he'd gone Jeremy raised his glass.

'Here's to being a bachelor. I'd give a lot to know how you've managed to stay single so long.'

'A sense of reality helps. You start off regarding all women as goddesses, but you soon see reason.'

'Ah! Let you down with a crash, did she?'

'I can't remember,' Marcel said coldly. 'She no longer exists.'

She never really did, said the voice in his head. *A figment of your imagination.*

'Well, I reckon you've got it right,' Jeremy said. 'All the women you want, whenever you want.'

'Stop talking nonsense.'

'I'm not. Look at those girls. They can't keep their eyes off you.'

It was true. Three young women were at the bar, buying drinks then glancing around, seeming to take stock of the men, form opinions about them, each pausing when they came to Marcel. One of them drew a long breath, one put her head on one side, and the third gave an inviting smile.

You couldn't blame them, Jeremy reckoned, Marcel was in his thirties, tall, dark-haired and well built but without a spare ounce on him anywhere. His face was handsome enough to make the girls swoon and the men want to commit murder.

But it was more than looks. Marcel had a charm that was delightful or deadly, depending on your point of view. Those who'd encountered only that charisma found it hard to believe in the ruthlessness with which he'd stormed the heights

of wealth and success—until they encountered that ruthlessness for themselves. And were floored by it.

But the willing females at the bar knew nothing of this.
They saw Marcel's looks, the seemingly roguish gleam in his
eyes, and they responded. Soon, Jeremy guessed, at least one
of them would find an excuse to approach him. Or perhaps
all three.

'Have you made your choice?' he asked caustically.

'I don't like to rush it.'

'Ah yes, of course. And there are some more just coming
in. Hey, isn't that Darius?'

The door of the bar led into the hotel lobby, where they
could just see Marcel's half-brother, Darius Falcon, pressing
the button at the elevator. A young woman stood beside him,
talking eagerly.

'Who's she?' Jeremy asked.

'I don't know,' Marcel replied. 'I think she comes from the
island he's just acquired. A man who owed him money used
it to pay the debt, and he's living there at the moment while
he decides what to do. He told me he'd be bringing someone,
but he didn't say a lot about her.'

By now Darius and his companion had stepped into the
elevator and the doors had closed.

'I must go up and greet them,' Marcel said, draining his
glass. 'See you later.'

It was an excuse. Before visiting Darius he meant to call on
their father, who'd arrived an hour ago. But instead of heading straight for the main suite, he strolled about, inspecting
his surroundings with the eye of a professional. The Gloriana
might be among the top hotels in London but it couldn't com-
pete with La Couronne, the hotel he owned in Paris.

He'd named it La Couronne, the crown, to let the world
know that it was the queen of hotels, and his own pride and
joy. He had personally overseen every detail of an establish-

ment that offered conference facilities as well as luxurious accommodation, discretion as well as flamboyance. Anybody who was anybody had stayed there: top level businessmen, politicians, film stars. It was a place of fashion and influence. But most of all money.

Money was the centre of his life. And from that centre it stretched out its tentacles to every distant detail. He'd started his business with loans guaranteed by his father, who also added money of his own, to be repaid in due course. Marcel had returned every penny.

At the back of the hotel he found a huge room that would be used for the wedding next day. It was a grandiose place, decorated to imitate a church, although the ceremony would be a civil one. Flowers were being piled everywhere, suggesting a romantic dream.

'We'll marry as soon as possible, won't we, my darling? And all the world will know that you're mine as completely as I am yours.'

The voice that echoed in his head made him stiffen and take an involuntary step back, as though seeking escape.

But the voice was his own and there was nowhere to flee.

'If you knew how I long to call you my wife.'

Had he really said that? Had he actually been that stupid? Young, naïve, believing what he longed to believe about the girl he adored, until his delusions were stripped away in pain and misery.

But that was long past. Now he was a different man. If only the voice would stop tormenting him.

He left the wedding venue quickly and almost at once bumped into his father. They had last met several weeks ago when Amos had suffered heart trouble, causing his sons to hurry to his bedside in Monaco. Now, to Marcel's relief, the old man seemed strong again. His face had aged with the strain of his illness, but he was both vigorous and alert.

'Good to see you better,' he said, embracing his father unselfconsciously.

'Nothing wrong with me,' Amos declared robustly. 'Just a lot of fuss. But I was glad to have you all there for a while. Now you must come up and visit Janine and Freya. They're looking forward to seeing you again.'

Amos's private life might politely be described as colourful. Marcel's mother had been his second wife. Janine was his third. Freya, her daughter by a previous husband, was also part of the family. Amos, a man with five sons and no daughters, had particularly welcomed her as a plan formed in his mind.

'Let's go up slowly,' he suggested now. 'We can take a look at the place and get some ideas. It's not a bad hotel but you could do better.'

'I've been thinking of expanding,' Marcel mused. 'A change of scene might be interesting.'

'Then London's the place to look. Property prices have plunged and you could pick up a bargain. I've got some good banking contacts who'll help, and I can loan you some money myself, if needed.'

'Thanks. I might take you up on that.'

They toured the hotel, each making notes.

'The one thing this place has got that La Couronne hasn't is the wedding facility,' Amos observed. 'You might try that. Money to be made.'

'I doubt if it would increase my profit,' Marcel said coolly. There were many reasons why weddings didn't appeal to him, but none that he was prepared to discuss.

They finished on the eighth floor where there was a bar with magnificent views of London. Sitting by the window, Amos indicated a tall building in the distance.

'See that? Headquarters of Daneworth Estates.'

'I've heard of them,' Marcel mused. 'Things not going too well, I gather.'

'That's right. They're having to sell assets.'

Amos's tone held a significance that made Marcel ask, 'Any asset in particular?'

'The Alton Hotel. It was bought with the idea of development but the money ran out and it's ripe for takeover at a knock-down price.'

He quoted a figure and Marcel's eyebrows rose. 'As little as that?'

'It's possible, if someone with a certain amount of influence twisted the screw on Daneworth so that the sale became more urgent.'

'You don't happen to know anyone with that kind of influence?' Marcel asked satirically.

'I might. How long will you be in England?'

'Long enough to look around.'

'Excellent.' Amos made a noise that sounded like 'Hrmph!' adding, 'It's good to know I have one son I can be proud of.'

'Are you still mad at Darius because he gave his wife too generous a deal over the divorce? I thought you liked Mary. You've come to her wedding.'

'I won't quarrel with the mother of my only grandchildren. But sense is sense, and he hasn't shown any. Do you know anything about the girl he's bringing with him today?'

'I saw them arrive. She looks attractive and pleasant. I'm going to visit them in a minute.'

'While you're there take a good look at her. See if Darius is falling into her trap.'

'Thus spoiling your scheme to marry him to Freya?' Marcel said ironically.

'I'd like to have Freya as my daughter-in-law, I make no secret of it. And if Darius won't come up to the mark—'

'Forget it,' Marcel interrupted him.

'Why should I? It's time you were putting down roots.'

'There are plenty of others to do that.'

Amos snorted. 'Five sons! Five! You'd think more than one of you would have settled down by now.'

But Amos himself was hardly an advertisement for domesticity, Marcel thought cynically. Of the five sons, only two had been born to the woman he'd been married to at the time. His own mother hadn't married Amos until several years after his birth. Travis and Leonid were bastards and proud of it. But he didn't want to quarrel with his father, so he merely shrugged and rose to go.

'Tell Janine and Freya I'll be up as soon as I've been to see Darius,' he said.

As he approached his brother's room he was barely conscious of adjusting his mask. He donned it so often that it was second nature by now, even with a brother with whom he was on cordial terms. When he arrived his charming smile was firmly in place.

The door was already open, giving him a clear view of a pretty young woman, done up in a glamorous style, and Darius regarding her with admiration, his hands on her shoulders.

'Am I interrupting anything?' he asked.

'Marcel!' Darius advanced to thump his brother with delight, after which he turned and introduced his companion as Harriet.

'You've been keeping this lady a big secret,' Marcel said, regarding her with admiration. 'And I understand why. If she were mine I would also hide her away from the world.'

His father was in for a shock, he reckoned. Harriet was definitely a threat to his plans for Darius's next wife.

He chatted with her for a few moments, flirting, but not beyond brotherly limits.

'So Darius has warned you about the family,' he said at last, 'and you know we're a load of oddities.'

'I'll bet you're no odder than me,' she teased.

'I'll take you up on that. Promise me a dance tonight.'

'She declines,' Darius said firmly.

Marcel chuckled and murmured in Harriet's ear, 'We'll meet again later.'

After a little more sparring, he blew her a kiss and departed, heading for his father's suite. He greeted his stepmother cordially but he couldn't help looking over her shoulder at the window, through which he could see the building Amos had pointed out to him.

Daneworth Estates. Assets ripe for an offer. Interesting.

In an office on the tenth floor of a bleakly efficient building overlooking the River Thames, Mr Smith, the manager of Daneworth Estates, examined some papers and groaned before raising his voice to call, 'Mrs Henshaw, can you bring the other files in, please?'

He turned back to his client, a middle-aged man, saying, 'She'll have all the details. Don't worry.'

He glanced up as a young woman appeared in the doorway and advanced with the files.

'I've made notes,' she said. 'I think you'll find I've covered everything.'

'I'm sure you have,' he replied.

The client regarded her with distaste. She was exactly the kind of woman he most disliked, the kind who could have looked better if she'd bothered to make the best of herself. She had the advantage of being tall and slim, with fair hair and regular features. But she scraped her hair back, dressed severely, and concealed her face behind a pair of large steel-rimmed spectacles.

'It's nearly six o'clock,' she said.

Mr Smith nodded. 'Yes, you can go.'

She gave the client a faint nod and left the office. He shivered. 'She terrifies me,' he admitted.

'Me too, sometimes,' Mr Smith agreed. 'But if there's one person whose efficiency I can rely on it's Mrs Henshaw.'

'It always sounds odd to me the way you call her "Mrs". Why not just Jane?'

'She prefers it. Familiarity is something she discourages.'

'But you're her boss.'

'Sometimes I wonder which of us is the boss. I hesitate between valuing her skills and wanting to get rid of her.'

'She reminds me of a robot.'

'She certainly doesn't have any "come hither" about her,' the manager agreed. 'You'd never think she'd once been a fashion model.'

'Get away!'

'Really. She was called "Cassie" and for a couple of years she was headed for the very top. Then it all ended. I'm not sure why.'

'She could still look good if she tried,' the client observed. 'Why scrape her hair back against her skull like a prison wardress? And when did you last see a woman who didn't bother with make-up?'

'Can't think! Now, back to business. How do I avoid going bankrupt and taking your firm down with me?'

'Can't think!' the client echoed gloomily.

Neither of them gave a further thought to Mrs Henshaw on the far side of the door. She heard their disparaging comments and shrugged.

'Blimey!' said the other young woman in the room. 'How do you stand them being so rude about you?'

Her name was Bertha. She was nineteen, naïve, friendly and a reasonably good secretary.

'I ignore it,' Mrs Henshaw said firmly.

'But who was that Cassie they keep on about? The gorgeous model.'

'No idea. She was nothing to do with me, I know that.'

'But they said it was you.'

'They were wrong.' Mrs Henshaw turned to look at Bertha with a face that was blank and lifeless. 'Frankly,' she said, 'Cassie never really existed. Now hurry off home.'

The last words had an edge of desperation. She urgently needed to be alone to think about everything that was happening. She knew the company was in dire straits, and it would soon be time to move on.

But to what? Her life seemed to stretch before her, blank, empty. Just as it had done for the last ten years.

The days when she could afford a car were over, and she took a bus to the small block of apartments where she lived in a few rooms one floor up. Here everything was neat, restrained, unrevealing. A nun might have lived in this place.

Tonight was no different from any other night, she assured herself. The name Cassie, suddenly screaming out of the darkness, had thrown the world into chaos, but she'd recovered fast. Cassie was another life, another universe. Cassie's heart had been broken. Mrs Henshaw had no heart to break.

She stayed up late studying papers, understanding secrets about the firm that were supposed to be hidden. Soon there would have to be decisions but now she was too weary in her soul to think about them.

She was asleep as soon as her head hit the pillow, but it wasn't a peaceful sleep. The dreams she'd dreaded were waiting to pounce. There was Cassie, gloriously naked, madly in love, throwing herself into the arms of the handsome boy who'd worshipped her. There were his eyes, gazing at her with adoration, but then with hate.

'I loved you—I trusted you—now I can't bear the sight of you!'

In sleep she reached out her hands to him, crying, 'Marcel, you don't understand—please—please—'

'Get out of my sight! *Whore!*'

She screamed and awoke to find herself thrashing around in bed, throwing her head from side to side.

'No,' she cried. 'It isn't true. *No, no, no!*'

Then she was sitting up, staring into the darkness, heaving violently.

'Leave me alone,' she begged. 'Leave me alone.'

Wearily she got out of bed and stumbled into the bathroom. A shambling wreck of a woman looked back at her from the mirror. Now the severe barriers of the day were gone, leaving no trace of the steely 'prison wardress'. The tense stillness of her face was replaced by violent emotion that threatened to overwhelm and destroy her. Her hair, no longer scraped back, flowed over her shoulders, giving her a cruel resemblance to Cassie, the beautiful girl who had lived long ago. That girl had vanished into the mists, but suddenly her likeness taunted Mrs Henshaw from the mirror. Tears streamed from her eyes and she covered them with her hands, seeking oblivion.

'No,' she wept. 'No!'

But it was too late to say no. Years too late.

CHAPTER TWO

'I JUST hope I don't regret this,' Mr Smith said heavily. 'The Alton Hotel is worth twice what he's offering, but it's still the best offer we've had.'

Mrs Henshaw was frowning as she studied the figures. 'Surely you can drive him up a little?'

'I tried to but he just said "Take it or leave it." So I took it. We have to sell off properties fast, before we go under.'

'Is that your way of telling me to find another job?'

'Yes, but I may be able to help you. I've told him you'll meet him to discuss details. Marcel needs an assistant with local knowledge, so I'm sure you can impress him. Why are you looking like that?'

'Nothing—nothing—what did you say his name was?'

'Marcel Falcon. He's one of Amos Falcon's sons.'

She relaxed, telling herself to be sensible. The Marcel she had known had been Marcel Degrande, and obviously no connection with this man. It was absurd to be still reacting to the name after so long.

'Play your cards right and you'll come out on top,' Mr Smith advised.

'When do I go?'

'Right now. He's staying at the Gloriana Hotel, and he's expecting you there in half an hour.'

'Half a—? *What?* But that doesn't give me time to research the background or the man—'

'You'll have to play it by ear. And these papers—' he thrust some at her '—will give you the details of his offer. Yes, I know we don't usually do it like this, but things are moving fast and the sooner we get the money the better.'

She took a taxi and spent the journey memorising facts and figures, wishing she'd had time to do some online research. She'd heard of Amos Falcon, whose financial tentacles seemed to stretch halfway across the world, but it would have been useful to check his son out too.

Never mind, she thought. A heavy evening's work lay ahead of her, and she would tackle it with the meticulous efficiency that now ruled her whole life.

At last she entered the Gloriana and approached the reception desk. 'Please tell Mr Falcon that Mrs Jane Henshaw is here.'

'He's over there, madam.'

Turning, she saw the entrance door to the bar and just inside, a man sitting at a table. At that moment he turned his head, revealing just enough of his face to leave her stunned.

'No,' she whispered. 'No…no…'

The world went into chaos, thundering to a halt, yet still whirling mysteriously about her.

Marcel. Older, a little heavier, yet still the man whose love had been the glorious triumph of her life, and whose loss had brought her close to destruction. What malign chance had made their paths cross again?

She took a step back, then another, moving towards the door, desperate to escape before he saw her. She managed to get into the hotel garden where there was a small café, and sat down. She was shaking too violently to leave now. She must stay here for a while.

If only he hadn't seen her.

If only they had never seen each other in the beginning, never met, never loved, never hated, never shattered each other.

Who were those two youngsters who seemed to stand before her now? Naïve, innocent, ignorant, perhaps a little stupid, but only with the stupidity of children who knew they could conquer the world with their beauty, talent and enthusiasm.

Jane Agnes Cassandra Baines had always known she was destined to be a model.

'Nobody could be that beautiful and waste it,' her sister had said. 'Go for it, girl. And choose a better name. Jane will make people think of plain Jane.'

Rebecca was eight years her senior, and had been almost her mother since their parents died in their childhood. These days Rebecca's misfortunes meant that she was the one who needed caring for, and much of Jane's money went in helping her.

'Cassandra,' Rebecca had said back then. 'Mum loved that name because she said it meant "enticer of men". Dad was outraged. I can still remember them squabbling, him saying, "You can't call her that. It's not respectable." In the end Mum managed to squeeze it in as your third name.'

'Enticer of men,' she'd murmured in delight. 'Cassandra. Yes—I'm Cassandra.'

Her agent had partly agreed. 'Not Cassandra, Cassie,' he said. 'It's perfect. You're going to be a star.'

She'd climbed fast. Jane no longer existed. Cassie's picture was everywhere and so were her admirers. Wealthy men had laid their golden gifts at her feet, but she'd cared only for Marcel Degrande, a poor boy who lived in a shabby flat.

He'd been earning a pittance working for a grocery store, and they'd met when he'd delivered fruit to her door. One look at his smile, his teasing eyes, and she'd tossed aside two millionaires like unwanted rubbish. From then on there was only him.

For Marcel it had been the same. Generous, passionate, he had offered himself to her, heart and soul, with nothing held back.

'I can't believe this is happening,' he said. 'You could have them and their money, but me—you've seen how I live. I can't take you to posh restaurants or buy you expensive presents.'

'But you give me something no other man can give,' she assured him, laying her hand over his heart. 'Who cares about money? Money's boring.'

'Yes. Money is boring,' he said fervently. 'Who needs it?'

'Nobody.' She threw herself back on the bed and wriggled luxuriously. 'But there's something I do need, and I'm getting impatient.'

'Your wish is my command,' he said just before his mouth came down on hers, his hands explored her willing body, and they quickly became one.

Returning his love had been the greatest joy of her life, a joy that she knew instinctively could never be repeated. It had lasted a few months, then ended in cruelty.

Jake, a rich, powerful man with criminal connections, used to getting his own way, had made it plain that he wanted her. She'd told him he had no chance. He'd departed without a word, and she'd congratulated herself on having dealt with the situation.

Marcel had been away making a long-distance delivery. When he called she said nothing about Jake, not wanting to worry him. Time enough to tell him everything when he returned.

He never did return. On the evening she expected him the hours passed without a word. She tried to call, but his phone was dead. At last there was a knock on her door and there was Jake.

He thrust a photograph into her hands. It showed Marcel in bed, bloodied, bandaged and barely alive.

'He had an accident,' Jake said, smirking. 'A van knocked him over in the street.'

'Oh, heavens, I must go to him. Which hospital is he in?'

'You don't need to know that. You're not going to see him again. Are you getting the message yet? I could have him killed in a moment, and I will if you don't see sense. And don't even try to find the hospital and visit him because I'll know, and he'll pay the price.'

He pointed to the picture. 'A doctor who works there owes me a favour. She took this. I'm sure you don't want him to suffer any more…misfortunes.'

She was left with the knowledge that not only was Marcel badly hurt and she could never see him again, but that he would think she had deserted him. That thought nearly destroyed her.

She risked writing him a letter, telling everything, swearing her love, begging him not to hate her, and slipped it through the door of his dingy apartment. He would find it when he returned from the hospital.

For days she waited, certain that Marcel would contact her, however briefly. But he never did, and the deafening silence blotted out the world. His phone stayed dead. In desperation, she called his landlady, who confirmed that she'd seen him arrive home and collect mail from the carpet.

'Ask him to call me,' she begged.

'I can't. He's vanished, just packed his bags and left. I think he still has some family in France, so maybe he's gone there. Or maybe not. His mobile phone's dead and it's like he never existed.'

But it was the other way around, she thought in agony. Marcel had wiped *her* out as though she'd never existed. Obviously he didn't believe her explanation that she had done it for him. Or if he did believe, it made no difference. He hated her and he would not forgive.

Now his voice spoke in her memory.

'It's all or nothing with me, and with you it's all, my beloved Cassie. Everything, always.'

And she'd responded eagerly, *'Always, always—'*

But he'd warned her, all or nothing. And now it was nothing.

Sitting in the hotel garden, she tried to understand what she'd just learned. The 'poor boy' with barely a penny had actually been the son of a vastly wealthy man. But perhaps he hadn't known. He might have been illegitimate and only discovered his father later. She must try to believe that because otherwise their whole relationship had been based on a lie. The love and open-heartedness, so sweet between them, would have been an illusion.

She shivered.

It was time to flee before he found her. She couldn't bear to meet him and see his eyes as he discovered her now, her looks gone. How he would gloat at her downfall, how triumphant he would be in his revenge.

But as she neared the building she saw that it was already too late. The glass door into the garden was opening. Marcel was there, and with him the receptionist, saying, 'There's the lady, sir. I was sure I saw her come out here. Mrs Henshaw, here is Mr Falcon.'

'I'm sorry I kept you waiting,' Marcel said smoothly.

'No…it was my fault,' she stammered. 'I shouldn't have come outside—'

'I don't blame you at all. It's stifling in there, isn't it? Why don't we both sit out in the fresh air?'

He gestured towards the garden and she walked ahead, too dazed to do anything else.

He hadn't reacted.

He hadn't recognised her.

It might be the poor light. Twilight was settling, making everything fade into shadows, denying him a clear view of her face. That was a relief. It would give her time to take control of the situation.

But she was shaken with anguish as they reached a table and he pulled out a chair for her. He had loved her so much, and now he no longer recognised her.

'What can I get you to drink?' Marcel asked. 'Champagne?'

'Tonic water, please,' she said. 'I prefer to keep a clear head.'

'You're quite right. I'll have the same since obviously I'd better keep a clear head too. Waiter!'

A stranger might be fooled by this, she thought wryly, but the young Marcel had had an awesome ability to imbibe cheap wine while losing none of his faculties. After a night of particular indulgence she'd once challenged him to prove that he was 'up to it'. Whereupon he'd tossed her onto the bed, flung himself down beside her and proved it again and again, to the delight and hilarity of them both.

Hilarity? Yes. It had been a joy and a joke at the same time—exhausting each other, triumphing over each other, never knowing who was the winner, except that they both were.

'Cassie, my sweet beloved, why do you tease me?'

'To get you to do what I wanted, of course.'

'And did I do it to your satisfaction?'

'Let's try again and I'll let you know.'

'You clearly believe that business comes before pleasure,' he told her now in a voice that the years hadn't changed. He spoke English well, but with the barest hint of a French accent that had always enchanted her.

How many women, she wondered, had been enchanted by it since?

'Smith recommended you to me in the highest possible terms,' Marcel continued. 'He said nobody knew as much about my new property as you.'

'I hope I can live up to Mr Smith's praise,' she said primly.

'I'm sure you will.' His reply was courteous and mechanical.

'Do you mean to make the hotel similar to La Couronne?'

'I see you've been doing your homework. Excellent. There will be similarities. I aim to provide many facilities, like a conference centre.'

'I wonder if the building is big enough for that.'

'I agree. There will need to be expansion. I want the best firm of builders you can recommend.'

For a while he continued to talk about his plans, which were ambitious, and she made notes, not even raising her head when the waiter appeared with their tonic water.

Her hand, and one part of her brain, were working automatically. There was nothing in him to suggest recognition, no tension, no brightening of the eyes. His oblivion was so total that she even wondered if she was mistaken and he wasn't her Marcel after all. But when she stole a sideways glance she knew there had been no mistake. The shape of his head, the curve of his lips, the darkness of his eyes; all these she knew, even at a distance of years.

This was her Marcel.

Yet no longer hers.

And no longer really Marcel.

The same was true of her. Cassie was gone for ever and only Mrs Henshaw remained.

He moved and she hastened to bury herself in her work. When she dared to look up he had filled her glass. In her best businesslike voice she said, 'I happen to know that the owner of the building next door has been thinking of selling.'

'That would be useful for my expansion. Give me the details and I'll approach him. Do you have any more information?'

She scribbled some details and passed them to him.

'Excellent. I'm sure Smith told you that I need an assistant to work with me on this project. You'd do better than anyone.'

'That's very impulsive. Don't you need more time to think about it?'

'Not at all. The right decisions are very quickly made. And so they should be.'

For a moment she was fired with temptation. To take the job, be with him day after day, with him not knowing who she was. The prospect was so enticing as to be scary.

But she could not. She *must* not.

'It's impossible,' she said reluctantly.

'Why? Would your husband object? He doesn't mind you working for Smith.'

'I'm divorced.'

'So you're the mistress of your own destiny and can do as you choose.'

She almost laughed aloud. Once she'd imagined exactly the same, and been shown otherwise in the most brutal fashion.

'Nobody chooses their own destiny,' she said. 'We only think we do. Wise people remember that.'

He gave her a curious look. 'Are you wise, Mrs Henshaw?'

'Sooner or later we all become wise, don't we?'

'Some of us.'

As he said it he looked directly at her. She met his eyes, seeking recognition in them, but seeing only a blank. Or merely a weariness and disillusion that matched her own.

'Things are moving fast in the property world,' he said, 'as I'm sure you know. When I tell Smith that I've decided to employ you I'm sure he'll release you quickly.'

He'd decided, she noted. No suggestion that she had a decision to make.

'I need a little time to think,' she hedged.

'I'll pay you twice what you're getting now.'

'I could lie about the amount.'

'And I could check with him. I won't, though, I trust you. Don't worry, I'm a hard taskmaster. I'll get full value from you.'

'Now, look—'

'I won't take no for an answer. Fine, that's settled.'

'It is not,' she said, her temper rising. 'Please don't try to tell me what to do.'

'As your employer I shall expect to.'

'But you're not my employer.'

'I soon will be.'

He'd always liked his own way, she recalled, but he'd used charm. Now charm was gone, replaced by bullying. Perhaps she couldn't entirely blame him after the way he'd suffered. But still she knew she had to escape.

'Mr Falcon, I think it's time you understood—'

'Well, well, well. Who'd have thought it?'

The words, coming out of nowhere, startled them both. Approaching them was a large man with an air of pathological self-satisfaction.

'Oh, no,' she groaned. 'Not him.'

'You know this man?'

'He's Keith Lanley, part financial journalist, part muckraker. He spends his days scurrying around trying to work out who's going to go bankrupt next.'

'What a thing to happen!' Lanley exclaimed, coming up to them. 'So the rumours are true, Jane. You're a sly character, getting out of Daneworth while the going's good. Aren't you going to introduce me to your friend? Of course I already know who he is. Everyone's ears pricked up when the Falcon family came to town.'

'I'm here for a wedding,' Marcel said coldly. 'So are the other members of my family.'

'Of course, of course. But no Falcon ever passed up the chance of making money, now, did he? And a lot depends on how you present it to the world. Suppose we three—'

But she'd had enough.

'Goodbye,' she said, rising to her feet.

'Now, wait—'

Lanley reached to grab her but she evaded him and fled deeper into the garden. Trying to follow her, Lanley found himself detained by Marcel, his face dark with rage.

'Leave her alone,' he said furiously.

'Hey, no need to get irate. I could do you a favour.'

'The only favour you could do me is to vanish off the face of the earth. Now, get out before I have you arrested.'

'I suppose you could, too,' Lanley said in a resigned voice. 'All right, I'll go—for now.' He began to go but turned. 'You couldn't just give me a quote about your father?'

'Get out!'

When the man had departed Marcel looked around. He was breathing hard, trying to force himself to be calm when all he wanted to do was roar to the heavens. Anguish possessed him, but more than anguish was rage—terrifying anger at her, at himself, at the cruel fate that had allowed this to happen.

Where was she? Vanished into thin air?

Again!

He began to run, hunting her here and there until at last he came across her leaning against a tree, her back to him. He touched her and her reaction was instant and violent.

'No, leave me alone. I won't talk to you.'

'It's not Lanley, I've sent him away.'

But she didn't seem to hear, fending him off madly until she lost her balance and fell, knocking her head against the tree. He tried to catch her but could only partly break her fall, steadying her as she slid to the ground.

'Your head,' he said hoarsely. *'Cassie.'*

People were approaching, calling out.

'She's collapsed,' he called back. 'She needs a doctor.'

Lifting her in his arms, he hurried the hundred yards back to the hotel. Word had gone ahead and the hotel doctor was waiting for them.

Her eyes were closed but she was aware of everything, especially Marcel's arms holding her firmly. Where their bodies touched she could feel his warmth, and just sense the soft thunder of his heart.

Cassie. He'd called her Cassie.

Hadn't he?

Her mind was swimming. Through the confusion she could hear his voice crying 'Cassie,' but had he said it or had she imagined it through the fog of her agitation? Had he known her all the time and concealed it? What would he do now?

She felt herself laid down and heard voices above her. She gave a soft gasp and opened her eyes.

'I think Mrs Henshaw's coming round,' the doctor said.

Marcel's face hovered over her.

'I'm all right, honestly,' she murmured. 'I just bumped my head against the tree and it made me dizzy for a moment.'

'Let's do a check,' the doctor said.

She barely heard. Her eyes were seeking Marcel's face, desperate to know what she could read in it.

But it was blank. There was nothing there.

For a moment she fought the truth, but then she forced herself to accept it. He hadn't recognised her, hadn't spoken her name. She'd simply imagined what she wanted to believe.

No!

A thousand voices screamed denial in her head. That wasn't what she wanted. She wouldn't think it or allow him to think it.

The doctor finished checking her, cleaned the graze and pronounced himself satisfied. 'But I'd recommend an early night,' he said. 'Are you staying here?'

'No.'

'Does anyone live at home with you?'

'No.'

'Pity. I'd rather you weren't alone tonight.'

'She won't be,' Marcel intervened. 'She'll stay in my suite, with a woman to watch out for her.'

'Oh, will I?' she said indignantly.

'Yes, Mrs Henshaw. You will. Please don't waste my time with further argument.'

He walked out, leaving her seething. *'Cheek!'*

'Be fair,' said the doctor. 'He obviously cares a lot about you.'

'Not at all. I've only just met him.'

In a few minutes it was clear that Marcel had gone to make arrangements. He returned with a wheelchair.

'I don't need that,' she said, aghast.

'Yes, you do. Take my hand.'

This was the moment to hurry away, put the whole disastrous evening behind her and forget that Marcel had ever existed. But he had firm hold of her, ushering her into the chair in a manner that brooked no refusal.

Since arguing was useless she sat in silence as he took her into the elevator and upstairs to his suite, where a pleasant-looking young woman was waiting.

'This is my sister Freya,' he said.

'I've brought you a nightdress,' Freya said.

'I'll leave you.' Marcel departed quickly.

'This is the bedroom and bathroom,' Freya told her. 'I'll

look in often to make sure you're all right. Let me help you undress.'

As they worked on it Freya asked, 'Whatever did Marcel do to you?'

'It wasn't his fault. I fell against a tree.'

'Well, he obviously feels responsible.'

'He has no need.'

'Perhaps he's just a very generous and responsible man. I'm still getting to know him.'

'I thought he said you were his sister.'

'His stepsister.' Freya laughed. 'He keeps calling me his sister so that he doesn't have to marry me.'

'What?'

'Amos wants me to marry one of his sons so that I'll really be part of the family. His first choice is Darius but Darius is no more keen than I am. So then Marcel is "next in the firing line" as he puts it. That "sister" business is his way of protecting himself.'

'How do you feel about that?'

Freya chuckled. 'I'm not weeping into my pillow. He's not my style at all. Too much like his father. Oh, it's rotten of me to say that when Amos has been so kind to me, but now I can still escape. The thought of being married to a man like that—' She gave a melodramatic shudder.

'Like what?'

'Money, money, money. That and always being one step ahead of his enemies.'

'Does Marcel have a lot of enemies?'

'I've no idea. I don't think he has many friends. There's a coldness in him that it's hard to get past. There now, you're ready for bed. Would you like me to stay?'

'No, thank you. You've been very kind.'

She was desperate to be alone. As soon as the door closed

she pulled the covers over her head and tried to sort out her confused mind.

Freya had spoken of his coldness, but the young man she'd known and loved had been incapable of coldness. Somehow, one had become the other.

This isn't happening. It can't be. I'll wake up and find it was a dream. At least, I hope so. Or do I hope so? Is that what I really want? Did he recognise me or not? Is he just pretending not to? What am I hoping for?

But thinking was too troubling, so at last she gave up and fell asleep.

CHAPTER THREE

SHE awoke suddenly in the dark. Listening intently, she could make out the sound of footsteps nearing her room. Marcel. She slid further down the bed, pulling the duvet over her, not sure that she wanted to see him.

The door opened, someone came in and stood looking down at her. Her heart was thundering as the moment of truth neared. Last night he'd seemed not to know her, but then she'd heard her name whispering past. Surely that had come from him and now everything was different. What would he say to her? What could she say to him?

She gasped as a hand touched her.

'It's only me,' said Freya. 'I'm sorry, did I wake you?'

'No, no, I…I'm all right.' She didn't know what she was saying. Everything was spinning in chaos.

Freya switched on the lamp and sat down on the bed, placing a cup on the sidetable.

'I'm going now, but I brought you a cup of tea first.'

'Thank you.'

'Jane—do you mind if I call you Jane? Or should it be Mrs Henshaw?'

'Oh, please, no.' She shuddered. 'I've had enough of Mrs Henshaw.'

'Jane, then?'

'Yes, Jane. Although I think I've had enough of Jane too.'

'Goodness, what does that mean?' Freya's friendliness was charming.

'Suddenly I seem to be a lot of different people and none of them is really me. Does that sound crazy?'

'Not in this family,' Freya said wryly. 'You have to be a bit crazy to get your head around the way they all live. Sometimes I worry for my mother. She's Amos's third wife and he wasn't faithful to either of the others.'

'Where does Marcel come in the picture?' Jane Henshaw asked, careful to drink her tea at once to hide her face.

'When Amos was married to Elaine, Darius's mother, he travelled abroad a lot, and while he was doing business in France he met Laura, set up home with her and they had Marcel.'

'While he was still married to Elaine?'

'While he was still actually living with her in England. He divided his time between London and Paris, and even had another son by his wife. That's Jackson. A couple of years later Elaine found out about his infidelity and left him. He brought Laura and Marcel over to England and married her as soon as his divorce was through.'

'So Marcel grew up in England?' Jane said slowly.

'I think he was about eleven when he moved here. Of course it didn't last. When he was fifteen Laura discovered that Amos had been "at it" again, and she returned to Paris, taking Marcel with her. He came back seven years later, but not to Amos. He resented the way his mother had been treated, and he even stopped using the name Falcon and went back to using Laura's name, Degrande.

'He had a rebellious streak and set up home with some other lads, living from day to day, doing any job they could get. He enjoyed it for a couple of years, then went back to France. Eventually he and Amos were reconciled, and he returned to England and became a Falcon again. Actually I think that was bound to happen. In his heart he was always a chip off the old block. Those two years being free and easy were fun, but it was never going to last.'

'They might have done. Perhaps something happened to send that side of him into hiding.'

'Kill it off for good, more like,' Freya said robustly. 'Marcel is Amos's son through and through—hard, implacable, money-minded. Will it pay? What will I get out of it, and how can I squeeze more? That's how his mind works.'

'You don't like him, do you?'

'He's all right, always pleasant to me, but Amos can forget about me marrying him. I'd sooner marry the devil.'

'I'm surprised he isn't married already. Rich men don't tend to be short of women.'

'Oh, he's never been short of women,' Freya agreed. 'Just not the kind he's likely to marry, if you see what I mean. They serve their purpose, he pays them off. I believe his 'leaving tips' are quite generous. But he doesn't fall in love.' She gave a brief laugh. 'Don't take me too seriously. I'm only warning you that he'll be tough to work for. After all, you're not likely to want to marry him, are you?'

'Not if I've got any sense,' she said lightly.

'Right, I must be going, but first I need to take some of Marcel's clothes from the wardrobe. He's sleeping out there on the sofa and he says don't worry, he won't trouble you.'

'He's very kind.'

'He can be. Not always. Now I'm off.'

'Goodbye. And thank you.'

Freya slipped out of the door.

Cassie lay in silence, trying to come to terms with the storm of feeling inside her. It had started when she'd glimpsed him tonight, but now it had a new aspect. The woman who now convulsively clenched and unclenched her hands was no longer lovelorn and yearning, but possessed by a bitter anger.

Marcel had known all the time that he was Amos Falcon's son. And he'd deceived her, pretending to be poor as a joke, because it boosted his pride to think she'd chosen him over rich men. It might have started as an innocent game, but the result had been catastrophic.

If I'd known you had a wealthy, powerful father, I wouldn't have given in to Jake. I'd have gone to Amos Falcon, seeking his protection for you. He could have punished Jake, scared him off, and we'd have been safe. We could have been to-gether all these years, and we lost everything because you had to play silly games with the truth. You stupid...stupid...

She pounded the pillow as though trying to release all the fury in her heart, until at last she lay still, exhausted, shocked by the discovery that she could hate him, while the tears poured down her face.

Finally she slept again, and only then did the door open and a figure stand there in silence, watching the faint light that fell from the hallway onto the bed, just touching the blonde hair that streamed across the pillow.

He moved closer to the bed, where he could see her face, relaxed in sleep and more like the face he had once known. In the first moments of their meeting he'd denied the truth to himself, refusing to admit that the evil witch who'd wrecked his life could possibly have returned.

But a witch didn't die. She rose again to laugh over the de-struction she had wrought. With every blank word and silent laugh, every look from her beautiful dead eyes, she taunted him.

A wise man would have refused to recognise her, but he'd never been wise where this woman was concerned. Fate had returned her to him, freeing him to make her suffer as he had suffered. And the man whose motto, learned from a powerful, ruthless father, was 'seize every chance, turn everything to your advantage' would not turn away from this opportunity until he'd made the most of it.

Suddenly the figure on the bed before him changed, becoming not her but himself, long ago, shattered with the pain of broken ribs, half blinded by his own blood, but even more by his own tears, longing every moment to see her approach and comfort him, finally realising that she would never do so.

That was when his heart had died. He'd been glad of it ever since. Life was easier without feelings. The women who could be bought were no trouble. They knew their place, did their duty, counted their reward and departed smiling. In time he might choose a wife by the same set of rules. Friends too tended to be business acquaintances. There were plenty of both men and women, there whenever he wanted them. His life was full.

His life was empty. His heart was empty. Safer that way.

He kept quite still for several long minutes, hardly daring to breathe, before closing the door and retreating, careful that she should never know he'd been there.

She awoke to the knowledge that everything had changed. As she'd told Freya, she seemed to have been several people in the last few hours, without knowing which one was really her. But now she knew.

Cassie.

Somewhere in the depths of sleep the decision had been made. She was Cassie, but a different Cassie, angry, defiant, possessed by only one thought.

Make him pay.

He'd treated her with contempt, concealing his true identity because that had been his idea of fun. He hadn't meant any harm, but his silly joke had resulted in years of pain and suffering for her. Perhaps also for him, but she was in no mood to sympathise.

Freya knocked and entered. 'Just came to say goodbye,' she said. 'Marcel is waiting for you to have breakfast with him.'

She dressed hurriedly, twisted her hair into its usual bun and followed Freya out into the main room. Marcel was standing by the window with another man of about seventy, who turned and regarded her with interest.

'Good morning, Mrs Henshaw,' Marcel said politely. 'I'm glad to see you looking well again. This is my father, Amos Falcon.'

'Glad to meet you,' the old man said, shaking her hand while giving her the searching look she guessed was automatic with him. 'Marcel always chooses the best, so I expect great things of you.'

'Father—' Marcel said quickly.

'He's told me that your expertise is unrivalled,' Amos went on. 'So is your local knowledge, which he'll need.'

Since Cassie had refused the job this might have been expected to annoy her, but things were different now. In the last few hours she'd moved to a level so different that it was like being a new person. So she merely smiled and shook Amos Falcon's hand, replying smoothly, 'I hope he finds that I live up to his expectations.'

A slight frisson in the air told her that she'd taken Marcel by surprise. Whatever he'd expected from her, it wasn't this.

'If you'd care to go and sit at the table,' he said, 'I'll be with you in a minute.'

A maid served her at the table in the large window bay. She drank her coffee absent-mindedly, her attention on Marcel, who was bidding farewell to his father and Freya.

Now she had a better view of him than the night before. The lanky boy had turned into a fine man, not only handsome but with an air of confidence, almost haughtiness, that was to be expected from a member of the great Falcon dynasty.

But then haughtiness fell away and he smiled at Freya, bidding her goodbye and taking her into a friendly hug. Cassie noticed that, despite her avowed disdain for him, Freya embraced him cheerfully, while Amos stood back and regarded them with the air of a man calculating the odds.

So it was true what Freya had said. If Amos couldn't marry her to his eldest son, then Marcel was next in line. Doubtless she would bring a substantial dowry for which he could find good use.

Then it was over, they were gone and he was turning back into the room, joining her at the table.

'I owe you my thanks,' he said, 'for not making a fool of me before my father. If you'd told him of your intention to refuse the job I offered I would have looked absurd. I'm grateful to you for your restraint.'

'I doubt it's in my power to make you look absurd,' she said lightly. 'I'm sure you're well armoured against anything I could dream up.'

'Now you're making fun of me. Very well, perhaps I've earned it.'

'You must admit you left yourself rather exposed by allowing your father to think I'd already agreed. Still, I dare say that's a useful method of—shall we say—proceeding without hindrance?'

'It's worked in the past,' he conceded. 'But you're right, it can leave me vulnerable if someone decides to be difficult.' He saw her lips twitching. 'Have I said something funny?'

'How would you define "difficult"? No, on second thoughts don't say. I think I can guess. Someone who dares to hold onto their own opinion instead of meekly obeying you.' She struck an attitude. 'I wonder how I knew that.'

'Possibly because you're much the same?' he suggested.

'Certainly not. I'm far more subtle. But I don't suppose you need to bother with subtlety.'

'Not often,' he agreed, 'although I flatter myself I can manage it when the occasion demands.'

'Well, there's no demand for it now. Plain speaking will suit us both better, so I'll say straight out that I've decided it would suit me to work for you, on certain conditions.'

'The conditions being?'

'Double the salary I'm earning now, as we discussed.'

'And how much is that?'

She gave him the figure. It was a high one, but he seemed untroubled.

'It's a deal. Shake.'

She took the hand he held out to her, bracing herself for the feel of his flesh against hers. Even so, it took all her control not to react to the warmth of his skin. So much had changed, but not this. After ten years it was still the hand that had touched her reverently, then skilfully and with fierce joy. The sensation was so intense that she almost cried out.

From him there was no reaction.

'I'm glad we're agreed on that,' he said calmly. 'Now you can go and give in your notice. Be back here as soon as possible. Before you leave, we'd better exchange information. Email, cellphones.'

She gave him her cellphone number, but he said, 'And the other one.'

'What other one?'

'You've given me the number you give to everyone. Now I want the one you give to only a privileged few.'

'And what about your "privileged" number?'

He wrote it down and handed it to her. 'Now yours.'

She shook her head. 'I don't have one.'

'Mrs Henshaw—'

'It's the truth. I only need one number.'

Now, she realised, he could guess at the emptiness of her life, with no need for a 'privileged' number because there was nobody to give it to. But all he said was, 'You might have told me that before I gave you mine.'

'Then you wouldn't have given it to me. But if you object, here—take it back.'

She held out the paper but he shook his head.

'No point. You could have memorised it by now. Very clever, Mrs Henshaw. I can see I shall have to be careful.'

'If you're having doubts you can always refuse to employ me.'

His eyes met hers and she drew a sharp breath, for there was a gleam in their depths that she hadn't seen before—not for many years. It teased and enticed, challenged, lured her on to danger.

'I'm not going to accept that offer,' he said softly.

She nodded, but before she could speak he added significantly, 'And you know I'm not.'

It could have been no more than courtesy but there was a new note in his voice, an odd note, that made her tense. She was at a crossroads. If she admitted that she did actually know what he meant, the road ahead was a wilderness of confusion.

Ignore the challenge, said the warning voice in her head. Escape while you can.

'How could I know that?' she murmured. 'I don't know you.'

'I think we both know—all that we need to know. The decision has been taken.'

She wanted to cry out. He seemed to be saying that he really had recognised her, that the two of them still lived in a world that excluded the rest of the universe and only they understood the language they spoke.

But no! She wouldn't let herself believe it. She *must not* believe it, lest she go crazy.

Crazier than she'd been for the last ten years? Or was she already beyond hope? She drew a deep breath.

But then, while she was still spinning, he returned to earth with devastating suddenness.

'Now that we've settled that, tell me how you got here last night,' he said.

His voice sounded normal again. They were back to practical matters.

'In a taxi,' she said.

'I'm glad. It's better if you don't drive for a while after what happened.'

'My head's fine. It was only a tiny bump. But I'll take a taxi to the office.'

'Good. I'll call you later. Now I must go. I have an appointment with the bank. We'll meet tomorrow.'

He was gone.

At the office Mr Smith greeted her news with pleasure. When she'd cleared her desk he took her for a final lunch. Over the wine he became expansive.

'It can be a good job as long as you know to be careful. Men like him resemble lions hovering for the kill. Just be sure you're not the prey. Remember that however well he seems to treat you now, all he cares about is making the best use of you. When your usefulness is over you'll be out on your ear. So get what you can out of him before he dumps you.'

'Perhaps he won't,' she said, trying to speak lightly.

'He always does. People serve their purpose, then they're out in the cold. He's known for it.'

'Perhaps there's a reason,' she said quietly. 'Maybe someone deserted him.'

'Don't make me laugh! Dump him? Nobody would dare.'

'Not now perhaps, but in the past, maybe when he was vulnerable—'

Mr Smith's response was a guffaw. 'Him? Vulnerable?

Never. Amos Falcon's son was born fully formed and the image of his father. Hard. Armoured. Unfeeling. Oh, it's not how he comes across at first. He's good with the French fantasy lover stuff. Or so I've heard from some lady friends who were taken in when they should have known better. But don't believe it. It's all on the outside. Inside—nothing!'

'Thanks for the lunch,' she said hurriedly. 'I must be going.'

'Yes, you belong to him now, don't you?'

'My *time* belongs to him,' she corrected. 'Only my time.'

She fled, desperate to get away from the picture he showed her of Marcel—a man damaged beyond hope. Hearing him condemned so glibly made her want to scream.

You don't know him, don't know what he suffered. I knew him when he was generous and loving, with a heart that overflowed, to me at least. He was young and defenceless then, whatever you think.

Only a few hours ago her anger had been directed at Marcel, but now she knew a surge of protective fury that made her want to stand between him and the world. What did any of them understand when nobody knew him as she did?

She checked that her cellphone was switched on and waited for his call. It didn't come. She tried not to feel disappointed, guessing that the bank would occupy him for a long time. And she had something else in mind, for which she would need time to herself.

When she reached home she locked the front door behind her. For the next few hours nothing and nobody must disturb her.

Switching on her computer, she went online and settled down to an evening of research.

She forced herself to be patient, first studying Amos Falcon, which was easy because there were a dozen sites devoted to him. An online encyclopaedia described his life and career—the rise from poverty, the enormous gains in power and money. There was less detail about his private life beyond the fact that he'd had three wives and five sons.

As well as Darius and Marcel there was Jackson Falcon, a minor celebrity in nature broadcasting. Finding his picture, she realised that she'd seen him in several television programmes. Even better known was Travis Falcon, a television actor in America, star of a series just beginning to be shown in England. The last son was Leonid, born and raised in Russia and still living there. About him the encyclopaedia had little information, not even a picture.

There were various business sites analysing Amos's importance in the financial world, and a few ill-natured ones written in a spirit of 'set the record straight'. He was too successful to be popular, and his enemies vented their feelings while being careful to stay just the right side of libel.

The information about Marcel told her little that she hadn't already learned from Freya, but there was much about La Couronne, his hotel in Paris. From here she went to the hotel's own site, then several sites that gave customers' opinions. Mrs Henshaw studied these closely, making detailed notes.

Then Cassie took over, calling up photographs of Marcel that went back several years. Few of them were close-ups. Most had been taken at a distance, as though he was a reluctant subject who could only be caught by chance.

But then she came across a picture that made her grow tense. The date showed that it had been taken nine years ago, yet the change in him was already there. Shocked, she realised that the sternness in his face, the heaviness in his attitude, had settled over him within a year of their separation. This was what misery had done to him.

She reached out and touched the screen as though trying to reach him, turn time back and restore him to the vibrant, loving boy he'd once been. But that could never happen. She snatched her hand back, reminding herself how much of the tragedy was his own fault for concealing the truth. She must cling to that thought or go mad.

She came offline. But, as if driven by some will of their own, her fingers lingered over the keys, bringing up another picture, kept in a secret file. There they were, Cassie and Marcel, locked in each other's embrace. She had many such shots, taken on a delayed release camera borrowed from a photographer friend.

'I want lots of pictures,' she'd told Marcel, 'then we'll always have them to remember this time when we were so happy.'

'I won't need help to remember you,' he'd told her fervently. 'You'll always live in my heart and my memory as you are now, my beautiful Cassie. When I'm old and grey you'll still be there with me, always—always—'

Gently he'd removed her clothes.

'This is my one chance to have a picture of you naked, because I couldn't bear to have any other photographer take them. Nobody else must ever see you like this—only me. Promise me.'

'I promise.'

'Swear it. Swear by Cupid and his bow.'

'I swear by Cupid, his bow and all his arrows.'

As she spoke she was undressing him until they were both naked, and he took her into his arms, turning her towards the clicking camera so that her magnificent breasts could be seen in all their glory.

'This is how I'll always see you,' he murmured. 'When we're old and grey, I'll show you these to remind you that in my heart this is what you really look like.'

'You'll have forgotten me by then,' she teased.

To her surprise, he'd made a sound of anger. 'Why do you say things like that? Don't you know that we must always be together because I will never let you go?'

'I don't want you to let me go.'

But he hardly seemed to hear her.

'Why can't you understand how serious I am? There is only you. There will only ever be you. I'll never let you go, Cassie. Even if there were miles between us I would still be there, holding onto you, refusing to let you forget me. You might try to escape but you won't be able to.'

What mysterious insight had made him utter those words, so strangely prophetic of what was to come? Miles and years had stretched between them, yet always he'd been there as he'd promised—or was it threatened?—always on the edge of her consciousness until the day he'd appeared again to reclaim her.

There it was again, the tormenting question. Had he recognised her, or had she only imagined that he'd called her Cassie?

And his remark that the decision had already been taken, had she not simply read too much into it? Was she hearing what she wanted to hear?

But there was more. Just before she'd left him that morning there had been another clue, if only she could remember what it was. She'd barely noticed at the time, but now she realised that his words had been significant. If only—

Frantically she wracked her memory. It was connected with the cellphone number—something he'd said—something—something—

'What?' she cried out. *'What was it?'*

She dropped her head, resting it on one hand while she slammed the other hand on the table again and again with increasing desperation.

* * *

A few miles away someone else was conjuring up pictures online. The one word, 'Cassie' brought her before him in a website that analysed the careers of models who were no longer around.

For two years she rode high and could have ridden higher still, but suddenly she gave up modelling and disappeared from sight. After that she was occasionally seen in luxurious surroundings, places where only rich men gather. And always she seemed weighed down with diamonds.

Why hadn't he seen it happening? Her choice of himself over wealthy admirers had made him love her a million times more, but it had always been too good to be true. It was a game she'd played, until she'd succumbed to the lure of serious money. While he'd thought he was her true love, he'd been no more than her plaything.

He should have known when she'd failed to visit him in the hospital. He'd lain there in pain and anguish, certain that she would be here at any moment. Every time the door opened he'd tensed with longing, which was always crushed.

He'd clung to the fragile hope that she didn't know what had happened to him. If only he could reach her, all would be well. But her cellphone was switched off. When he'd called her apartment the phone rang and rang, but was never answered.

He'd known then, known with such certainty that he'd torn up the letter she'd sent him without even opening it. Who needed to read her miserable excuses?

He'd seen her just once more, the day he'd left for Paris. There she'd been at the airport with her new lover, as he went into the departure lounge.

'You!' he'd spat. 'The last person I ever want to see.'

She'd held out her arms, crying frantically, 'Marcel, you don't understand—please—please—'

'I loved you,' he raged. 'I trusted you—now I can't bear the sight of you!'

'Marcel—'

'Get out of my sight! *Whore!*'

He'd turned and ran from her. He remembered that afterwards with self-disgust. It was he who had run, not her.

But there would be no running now.

The time had come.

CHAPTER FOUR

WHEN she rose next morning her mind was firm and decided. Today she would start working for Marcel, getting close to the man he'd become, watching to see where the path led. And, wherever it led, she was ready to explore.

Now she was glad that his younger ghost haunted her. Far from trying to banish that spectre, she would enlist him onside and make use of his insights to confront the present man.

She made coffee and toast and sat eating it by the window, looking down at the street, thinking of another time, another window where she'd watched for a grocery delivery. Cassie had been riding high, with two great modelling jobs behind her and more in the offing. The world was wonderful.

And then the most wonderful thing of all had happened.

The grocery van had drawn up and the delivery man stepped out. That was her first view of Marcel's tall, vigorous body. Being only one floor up, she could appreciate every detail. When he'd glanced up she'd seen not only his good looks but the cheeky devil lurking in his eyes. That had been what really won her heart.

It was the same with him. She knew that by the way he came to a sudden halt, as though something had seized him, smiling at her with pleasure and an air of discovery. The words, *That's it! This is the one!* had sung in the air between them.

A week later, lying in each other's arms, he'd said, 'I knew then that I was going to love you.'

'I knew I'd love you too,' she'd assured him joyfully.

'Really? Me, the grocer's delivery lad? With all the men you could have?'

'If I can have them I can also reject them,' she'd pointed out. 'I choose the man I want. *I* choose.' With mock sternness she'd added, 'Don't forget that.'

'No, ma'am. Whatever you say, ma'am.'

He'd given her a comical salute and they'd dissolved into laughter, snuggling down deeper into the bed, and then not laughing at all.

How handsome he'd been that first day, getting out of the van and approaching her. How young, untouched by life!

'Good morning!'

She jumped, startled by the voice that came from below. A car had stopped and a man was calling up to her, pulling her back to the present, where she didn't want to be.

'I'm sorry…who…?'

'I said good morning,' Marcel repeated.

'Oh—it's you!'

'Who were you expecting?'

'Nobody. I thought you'd call me.'

'May I come up?'

'Of course.' She tossed down the keys.

She hadn't dressed and was suddenly conscious of the thin nightie. By the time he arrived she'd pulled on a house coat. It was unflattering, but it zipped up to the neck and at least he wouldn't think she was trying to be seductive. Anything but that.

When she emerged from the bedroom he was already there.

'I'm sorry to arrive so early, but I'm eager to get a close inspection of my new property.'

'Meaning me?' she asked, her head on one side and a satirical smile on her lips.

'A shrewd businesswoman like you should appreciate the description. So I came to collect you, which was perhaps a little thoughtless of me. Finish your breakfast.'

She fetched a cup and poured him a coffee. 'Let's talk. I can eat and work at the same time.'

'I see I've hired the right person. The hotel needs development, the sooner the better.'

'You spoke of making it like La Couronne, and there are several avenues that it would be profitable to explore. The success of your Paris hotel may be because of all the—' She launched into a list gleaned from her investigation of the hotel's website, adding, 'You could probably do some of these things more easily without the problems that arose in—' Here she made use of knowledge found on a business site that spilled the beans about some interesting battles.

'That man who caused you all the trouble didn't really give up, did he?' she asked. 'I gather he's still complaining about—'

Marcel listened to her with raised eyebrows. She could tell that he was impressed. Good. That was how she wanted him. She was taking charge.

'People who come to the London hotel should sense the connection with Paris,' she added. 'It'll be useful when you're ready to expand further.'

'That's looking rather far ahead.'

'But it's what you need to do. Eventually your hotels will be all over Europe, with your trademark. This one could be The Crown Hotel, and the one you'll open in Italy can be La Corona. Spain as well. Then it'll be Die Krone in Germany, De Kroon in Holland. Czech and Slovak will probably have to wait a while—'

'You don't say!' he exclaimed with a grin of wry appreciation.

'But when their time comes it'll be Koruna.'

'You've got this all worked out. And I thought *I* was organised.'

'I like to be prepared. Aren't I supposed to be?'

'Yes, indeed.' He added wryly, 'But how often are people what they're supposed to be?'

'People, rarely. But places can be exactly as planned, if you tackle the problem properly'

'Quite right.' He raised his coffee cup in her direction. 'And with your help that's what will happen.'

She clinked her cup against his. 'Now I must dash and get ready.'

When she'd gone Marcel looked around the apartment, surprised to find it so small and plain. Her fortunes might have dived over the years but a woman in her present position surely didn't need to live among second-hand furniture and walls that looked as though they needed repapering.

From the bathroom he could hear the sound of the shower, which made it awkward that the phone should ring at that moment. Since there was no way he could interrupt her now, he lifted the receiver.

'Is Jane there?' came a man's voice.

'She's occupied right now. Can I say who called?'

'Tell her it's Dave, and I need to talk to her quickly.'

The line went dead.

He replaced the receiver, frowning.

She emerged a few minutes later, fully dressed and with her hair swept back.

'Dave wants you to call him,' Marcel told her. 'It sounded urgent.'

She had seized the receiver before he even finished speaking, leaving him wondering even more curiously about Dave and the hold he evidently had over her.

He tried not to eavesdrop, or so he told himself, but certain phrases couldn't be shut out.

'Dave, it's all right, I'll take care of it. I can't talk now. I'll call you back later.' She hung up.

Marcel didn't speak. He wondered if he was being fanciful in imagining that she had ended the conversation quickly because he was there.

His mind went back years, to their time together. When had she ever spoken to himself in that placating tone? Never.

So what did this man have to make her subservient? Vast wealth?

No, she didn't live like a women with a rich admirer.

Good looks? Other attractions? Could his personal 'skills' make her cry out for more?

'Perhaps it's time we were going,' he said heavily.

She turned to him and her expression was as efficiently cheerful as a mask.

'Tell me something first,' she said briskly. 'Are they expecting you at the Alton?'

'No, I think I'll see more if I take them by surprise.'

'You'll see more if you take a room incognito. But I expect they'd recognise you, so it probably wouldn't work.'

'I doubt if anyone would know me. Are you serious?'

'You said you wanted to take them by surprise. There's no better way than this.'

'I suppose not,' he said slowly. 'I wonder—'

'Leave it to me.' She went to the phone and dialled the Alton's number.

'Hello, do you have a room free today? You do? Excellent. What kind of price? All prices? Really. Run them past me, single rooms and suites.'

As they were given to her, she recited them aloud, watching Marcel's expression of wry understanding. The Alton wasn't doing fantastic business.

'I'll take the best available suite,' he said quietly.

'What name?'

'My real name. I won't have anyone saying I deceived them.'

'Mr Marcel Falcon,' she said into the phone. 'He'll be there today.' She hung up.

He gave her a glance of grim appreciation. 'You're a wicked woman, Mrs Henshaw—I'm glad to say.'

'It has its uses,' she observed lightly.

'So I'll return to the Gloriana to check out. You'd better come with me, then we'll go on to the Alton. I'll wait for you downstairs.'

Once down in the street he glanced up at her window but there was no sign of her. He knew exactly what she was doing—calling Dave now that they could talk privately.

Whoever Dave was!

In this he was wrong. Cassie didn't return Dave's call immediately because there was no need. She knew what he wanted. Instead she went online, gave some instructions, shut the computer down and sent him a text saying, *All taken care of.*

Then she pushed Dave aside. Only Marcel occupied her thoughts now.

Against all reason, she was certain that he recognised her, but only against his will. And he refused to admit it to her.

But he could never deny it to himself. Instinct told her that. Try as he might, Marcel was fighting with Marcel, and it would be a losing battle on both sides.

That told her all she needed to know.

'Right,' she said to Mrs Henshaw in the mirror. 'Let's see if we can give him a run for his money.' She smiled. 'And maybe—just maybe—he'll give me a run for mine. That could be—interesting.'

She could almost have sworn Mrs Henshaw nodded.

The Alton Hotel had a disconsolate air.

'It used to be the London home of a duke,' she observed as they drew up in the car park, 'which is why it was built on such grand lines, but he had to sell it off, and the developers who bought it couldn't afford to complete their plans.'

Checking in went without a hitch. Nobody recognised Marcel and they were able to proceed upstairs to a luxurious suite of four rooms, one of which was dominated by a huge double bed.

Cassie ignored it and went to look out of the window, saying eagerly, 'Just the view I was hoping for. Look at that building next door. It's the one you need to buy to expand this place.'

'Let me see.' He came to stand beside her. 'Yes, it's ideal. I can connect the two and this side will be—'

He talked for a few more minutes but she barely heard him. Her whole body seemed to be hypnotised by the sensation of standing close to him so that the air between them seemed to sing. His extra height loomed over her in a way she'd once loved, and when he casually laid a hand on her shoulder she had to fight not to jump.

'Why don't we go and take a look?' she said.

'I can see all I want from here. I'm going to tear it down, and that's it.'

'I can put you in touch with three excellent building contractors—'

'Can't we just hire the best?'

'With three you can play them off against each other,' she pointed out.

'Splendid. I see you believe in reading your employer's mind and following his instructions exactly.'

'What else am I here for?'

'Then here's another instruction for you. I'll have no grim and forbidding ladies working for me.'

'Are you firing me?' she asked lightly.

'No, I'm telling you to make yourself less severe.'

'Flaunt myself, you mean?' she demanded in a voice that managed to sound shocked. 'Mr Falcon, I hope I've misunderstood you.'

'Only because you're determined to,' he replied with a smile that nearly destroyed her composure. 'I'm going to need you with me a lot of the time—'

'And you think I'm so ugly I'll frighten the horses?' she managed to say lightly.

'You're not ugly. But for some reason you're determined to pretend you are. Now that *is* frightening.'

'Why would any woman want to pretend that?' she murmured.

'A good question. We might talk about it later. Ah, I hear someone at the door. It must be the waiter with my order.'

He moved away and she clutched the windowsill to stop herself swaying. She was trembling from the feel of his hand on her shoulder, and also from the sensation that he too had been trembling.

It took several hours to walk slowly through the building, making notes, trying to be inconspicuous. They ended up back in his suite, thankfully drinking coffee.

'I'll just check my mail,' he said, opening his laptop, which he'd already connected to the hotel's Internet.

He didn't take long, sending a few messages and making a gesture of dismissal.

'Time to think of having some dinner,' he said. 'There's a place upstairs—'

Her phone rang. Marcel watched her face as she answered, saw her expression drop and heard her sigh.

'Dave, I've done my best—'

Dave, he thought. A man with some kind of hold over her, perhaps a man who'd once inspired her love and for whom she still felt some sympathy. Or was he blackmailing her?

'All right, all right,' she was saying. 'I'll send some more. Bye for now.' She turned to Marcel. 'Can I use your computer?'

'Be my guest.'

She was online in a moment, accessing her bank account. Marcel had the impression that she'd forgotten his existence. Totally absorbed, she was trying to transfer a large amount out of her account, into another one. But only trying. The bank refused, saying it would take her over her limit.

'Oh, no!' she said frantically.

'Look, I don't want to pry, but if this man is extorting money from you, then you need help,' Marcel told her.

She looked up as if wondering why he was there.

'Extorting—?'

'Why are you giving him money? Especially money that you clearly can't afford.'

'Dave's married to my sister Laura. They have a lot of financial problems, and I try to help them out.'

'He's…your brother-in-law?' he echoed, astounded.

'Yes, why do you sound so disbelieving?'

He couldn't have told her. It would take time to come to terms with the thoughts whirling chaotically in his head. All he knew was that somewhere the sun had come out.

'He didn't sound like a brother-in-law,' he said lamely.

'I know. He sounds like a needy child because that's what he is,' she said grimly. 'Also they have a little girl who needs a lot of care, so Laura can't take a job. Now, if you'd just give me a moment—'

'Well, I won't. Move over.'

She was forced to yield and let him get to the computer, where he accessed his own bank account in Paris, ordering them to transfer a sum of money to her.

'You'll have to fill in the details of your account,' he said.

She did so, too bewildered to argue, and in a moment it was done.

'Now, you just give the money to Dave and it's finished,' Marcel said.

'Actually, I give it to Laura. That way the bills get paid. He'd just be off down the pub.'

The contempt in her voice was plain. With more relief than he cared to admit, Marcel realised that Dave didn't have the place in her life that he'd suspected.

Dreaded?

'Thank you,' she said as she completed the transaction. 'I don't know how to—'

'Let's be clear. I've come to your aid for entirely selfish reasons. I want your whole attention and I won't get it if you're worried about money.'

'But you gave me so much.'

'Three months' wages in advance. Now you'll have to work for me whether you want to or not.'

'I've already said I will.'

'Yes, but you might have changed your mind.' His lips twisted. 'It's my opinion that women are notoriously unreliable about sticking to their word. So I've taken you prisoner. I'm sorry if you object.'

'I don't. I'm grateful. Laura needs all the help she can get.'

'By help you mean cash. Is that why you live in that shabby little dump?'

'What would you expect? Should I be revelling in the lap of luxury?'

It took him a moment to reply and she had the satisfying feeling that she'd caught him off-guard.

'I wouldn't know, would I?' he asked at last.

'No,' she said quietly. 'How could you?'

'I think we both need a good stiff drink and a large meal,' he said. 'The best restaurant seems to be the one on the roof, and so let's head up there.'

The restaurant had two halves, one with a glass roof, one with no roof at all. As the weather was clement they settled here with a magnificent view over London. In the distance the setting sun blazed crimson as it drifted slowly down the sky.

'It's like watching a fire that you don't have to be afraid of,' she said in wonder.

'Is there such a thing as a fire you need not fear?' he asked.

He spoke lightly, even casually, but she thought she sensed tension beneath the tone.

Only because you're listening for it, said her inner voice sternly. *Be careful of getting paranoid.*

'What did you say?' Marcel asked.

'Nothing, I—'

'It sounded like, "Sometimes paranoid is best."'

'Nonsense.' She laughed edgily. 'I didn't say anything.'

'I thought you did. Ah, here's the waiter. Time for a celebratory supper.'

He ordered the best of everything, including champagne and caviar, seeking her opinion, deferring to her as if she were a queen.

Until your usefulness is ended, Smith reminded her in her mind.

Get lost! she told him.

'What's so amusing?' Marcel asked, looking at her curiously. 'You suddenly started to smile in a very mysterious way. Share the joke.'

'I can't.'

'Ah, a private joke. They're often the most interesting.'

'Only while they stay private.'

'I see. All right, I'll back off—for the moment.'

Suddenly she came to a resolution. Clenching her hands beneath the table where he couldn't see, she said, 'There's something I meant to ask you,' she said.

'Go on.'

'When I fell against the tree, I thought I heard you call me Cassie. Who is she?'

He didn't reply at once, only looked at her strangely, as though trying to make up his mind. With sudden devastating insight she saw herself through his eyes—the severe clothes, the flattened hair, the steel-rimmed spectacles. She could even hear his thoughts. *How could I ever have thought this was her?*

'Just a girl I once knew,' he said at last.

'And you confused me with her? Am I like her?'

'Not at all,' he said instantly. 'The way she looked, the way she dressed—she gave herself to the world, at least—'

'Yes?' she urged when he didn't go on.

'Nothing.'

'She gave herself to the world, meaning I don't?'

'I think you prefer to withdraw and hide deep inside yourself.'

She laughed. 'That's one way of putting it. You said I looked grim and forbidding, and recently someone said I looked like a prison wardress.'

'To your face?'

'No, he didn't realise that I could hear.'

'You sound remarkably cheerful about it. Most women would be hurt or offended.'

'I'm not most women.'

'Indeed you're not. I'm beginning to understand that.'

'In my job it's an advantage if people think I'm dreary. They ignore me and overlook me, which is useful. You learn a lot when people have forgotten you're there.'

'But you're not at work every hour. What about the rest of the time?'

She gave a carefully calculated shrug. 'What rest of the time? Life is work, making a profit, turning everything to your advantage. What else?'

'You say that but you don't live by it, otherwise you wouldn't let your family bleed you dry.'

She shrugged. 'Their needs just mean that I have to make twice as much profit, be twice as determined to manage life my way. Eventually I'll make so much money that I can afford to help them *and* become a financial tyrant.'

'It has to be a tyrant, does it?'

'They seem to be the kind that flourish best.'

'Some people think there are other things that matter.' He was watching her.

'Some people are losers,' she observed.

'They certainly are,' he said slowly. 'No doubt about that. But not us. That's true, isn't it?'

'That's definitely true.'

The champagne arrived. Marcel filled both glasses and raised his. 'I think we should toast ourselves. To us and what we're going to achieve.' They clinked.

'I'm looking forward to the moment when you see La Couronne.'

'Am I going to?'

'Yes, I think we should head there as soon as possible. My lawyer here can deal with the formalities. When you've seen what there is in Paris you'll be better placed to take charge in London.'

'I must warn you that my French is very poor.'

'Really? I thought such an efficient lady must be an expert.'

'I know a few words—very limited—'

Mon seul amour, je t'aime pour toujours—

Words of passionate adoration that she had learned from him, and repeated with all her heart. To please him, as a surprise, she'd started to learn the language properly, but their parting had come before she could tell him.

'Don't worry,' he said now. 'There are so many English tourists in Paris that I insist that all my employees speak the language.'

'How long will I need to be in Paris?'

'Several weeks at least. Is that a problem?'

'No, but I shall need to sort out my affairs here. Perhaps I can take tomorrow off to make my arrangements.'

'Very well. Do you have other relatives? I assume you have no children since your sister and her family take so much from you. But what about Mr Henshaw? Does he have no claims?'

'None,' she said shortly. She held out her glass. 'Can I have another champagne?'

When Marcel had filled her glass she rose and went to the edge of the roof, leaning on the wall and looking down at London, where the lights had come on, glimmering in the darkness.

Mr Henshaw had never existed, although there had been a husband, one who still haunted her nightmares. She tried never to think of him and mostly succeeded, with that inner control that had become her most notable characteristic. But now events had brought him back so that he seemed to be there, infusing the air about her with fear and horror.

And there was no escape.

CHAPTER FIVE

LIFE with Jake had been a nightmare. He'd set his heart on marrying her and pestered her morning, noon and night. She'd refused, clinging to the hope that Marcel would come looking for her. Even after the agony of their last meeting she thought it might happen. He would suffer, lying in the darkness for long, sleepless nights, and during those nights the memories would come back to him. He would relive the joy of their youthful love, and at last he would realise that such love could never end in the way that theirs had seemed to. Then he would search for her, rescue her, and they would be together again.

But it hadn't happened. Days had become weeks, weeks passed into months and the silence stretched ahead endlessly. At last she'd faced the truth. Marcel hated her. For him she no longer existed. There would be no reunion, no hope of future happiness.

In this state of despair all energy had seemed to leave her. She no longer had the vigour to fight, and when Jake had marched in one day, seized her hand and slid a magnificent engagement ring onto it, she simply stared and left it there.

After that he was shrewd enough to move fast, arranging the wedding for the soonest possible date and never letting her out of his sight. In only one matter did she find the strength to oppose him, declaring that she would not be married in church. It must be a civil ceremony only. She refused to insult any religious establishment with this mockery of a wedding. Jake didn't care. As long as he claimed her it didn't matter how.

The ring he gave her was a spectacular creation of diamonds and sapphires, clearly designed to be a trophy. It was Jake's proof that he owned her.

The three years of her marriage were strange and haunted. He swore a thousand times that he was madly in love with her, and she came to believe that, in his own way, he was. He was cruel and egotistical, grasping whatever he wanted and careless of whom he hurt. But, like many selfish brutes, he had a sentimental streak. Cassie had a hold on his heart that nobody else could claim, and he took this as proof of his own humanity.

It gave her a kind of power, and she discovered that power could be enjoyable, especially when it was all you had. Jake's eagerness to please her was ironic, but she could use it to make him give money to charity. She supported two particular charities, one for children, one for animals, and for them she extracted as much as she could from Jake.

Afterwards he expected to be repaid. 'Now you'll be nice to me, won't you?' he'd say, and she would yield to the night that followed, trying not to show her revulsion. What Jake called 'love-making' was so horribly different to what she had known with Marcel that it came from another universe, one where she had to endure being slobbered over and violated.

At first she tried to pretend that she was back in the arms of her true love, but the contrast was so cruel that she gave it up in sheer self-defence. Otherwise she would have genuinely gone mad.

It was almost a relief to become pregnant, and have an excuse to banish Jake from her bed. Slightly to her surprise he accepted her decision without argument. At the thought of producing the next generation his sentimental streak was asserting itself again, and he withdrew to protect her.

And now she could at least feel that life held out some hope for her. She would have a child to love, a purpose in life.

But after five months she miscarried. No doctor could tell her why. There had been no accident, no trauma. It had simply happened, leaving her staring into a blank future.

Hope came from an unexpected source. By chance she discovered that Jake had been playing around.

'It's not my fault,' he defended himself. 'It's months since we could…well, it'll be different now.'

'Yes, it's going to be different,' she agreed. 'I'm divorcing you.'

His howls of protest left her unmoved, and so did his threats.

'If you want to destroy me, Jake, go ahead. What do you think is left to destroy? Do your worst. I don't care.'

Perhaps it was the thought of how many of his disreputable secrets she'd learned that warned him to be cautious. But something made him cave in. Before he could change his mind she hurled back at him every expensive gift he'd ever given her, including the engagement ring. Then she moved out the same day.

He made one last attempt to persuade her to remain his wife. When that failed he tried to get her to accept a financial settlement.

She agreed to very little for the sake of her family, but took nothing for herself. 'If I live off your money you'll still think you control me,' she told him. 'And I want to forget that you ever existed.'

He paled. 'You're breaking my heart,' he choked.

And he meant it, she thought afterwards. Oddly enough, this unpleasant man had a heart to break, where she was concerned. But it left her untouched. She no longer feared him. All she felt was a heady sensation of power at having brought him down.

She rejected his name, calling herself Henshaw because it had been her mother's maiden name, and using the 'Mrs' because she thought it made her sound older and more serious.

Refusing to live off Jake's money satisfied her but left her penniless. There was no chance of returning to modelling, even if she'd wanted to. Most people would still have called her beautiful, but she felt her magic 'something' had vanished for ever. She'd taken any menial job she could get, using her free time to go to evening classes, studying business to the point of exhaustion. She'd emerged triumphant, going to work in a bank and climbing fast. She had never looked back.

Now she was near the top of the tree, trying to believe it had all been worth it.

But as she looked back at Marcel, sitting quietly, watching her, she was filled with such a rush of hostility that she could have struck him down and enjoyed doing it.

You could have saved me, she thought. *If I'd known who you really were I'd have appealed to your father, and everything could have been different. Oh, why weren't you honest with me? You could have saved me from Jake, from that terrible marriage, losing my child. You could have stopped me turning into a heartless robot, but when it happened I had nowhere to turn. Damn you!*

'What's the matter?' Marcel asked, rising and coming beside her. 'You look upset.'

'Not at all,' she said brightly. 'I was just enjoying the view and the fresh air.'

'Come away from the ledge.' He led her firmly back to the table and stood over her until she was seated.

'Go on telling me about your life,' he said. 'What happened to your husband? Did you walk out on him?'

Like I did with you, you mean? she thought ironically. *That's what you're thinking right now, although you won't come out and say so.*

'Yes, I left him,' she said. 'But only because he was sleeping with someone else.'

Let's see what you make of that! If you want revenge I've just given it to you. But is that what you want? If only I knew.

'I hope he made some financial provision for you,' Marcel said politely.

'I wouldn't let him. It would have given him a hold on me, and no man has that. Ever.'

'When you finish with a man you really finish with him,' he murmured.

'It's the only way.' She gave a sharp, defiant laugh. 'When I've finished with him, he no longer exists.'

'No looking back?'

'Looking back is scary,' she whispered. 'It fills you with hate and makes you want to do things that you know you shouldn't, so then the person you hate is yourself.'

She didn't look at him as she said it. She didn't dare. And his reply was so soft that another person might have missed it. But she was alive to everything about him, and she heard the quiet words with their ominous warning.

'That's very true.'

She glanced at him just in time to meet his eyes, but not in time to read their expression before he looked away. She waited, hoping that he would turn back to her and they might even find a way to talk. But his eyes were fixed on the distance and the silence between them was as deafening as a roar.

All around them the lights were sparkling, arranged in arches by the walls, with dainty lamps near the tables.

The atmosphere on the roof had changed, grown softer, sentimental. This was a place for romantic trysts, with lovers' eyes meeting over the rims of wine glasses. Here there should be smiles of heartfelt understanding, unspoken promises of love. It was a world apart and anyone who did not belong in that world had no right to be here.

I don't belong, she thought wearily. *I did once. Not any more.*

Nearby was a couple sitting close together. The man was middle-aged and heavy. The girl was about twenty, gorgeous and flaunting it. She might have been the young Cassie.

'I guess there's no point in me trying to talk to him to-night,' said a male voice nearby. 'Sorry,' he added hastily, as Marcel and Cassie turned to look at him. 'It's just that I'd planned to talk business with that fellow.'

Marcel grinned. 'No chance now.'

'We should never have agreed to meet here. Too many good-time girls as a distraction. I gather this place is known for it. Everywhere you look there's a lush female trying to seduce a man into parting from his money.' He seemed to become aware of Cassie and hastily added, 'Forgive me. Not you, of course!'

'Of course,' she said.

'I mean you're obviously a very…sensible…businesslike woman, and I didn't mean to insult you.'

She regarded him with ironic humour. 'You mean it's quite impossible that I could ever lead a man down dark and dangerous paths? Some women would be more insulted by that than the other.'

'Look I…put my foot in it. I apologise.'

He retreated in a flurry of embarrassment.

'Well, you certainly made him sorry,' Marcel declared.

She managed to laugh. 'I did, didn't I? His face!'

The man had gone to join the couple at the other table,

talking wildly and making gestures, clearly explaining something to them. He glanced up, saw Cassie looking at him and gave her an embarrassed grin.

'He's terrified of me,' she murmured to Marcel.

'And you don't mind?'

'Why should I mind? I don't want to lead him down "dark and dangerous paths". Hey, the girl's looking at me now. I wonder if she's taking warning.'

'That your gaze might turn her to stone?' Marcel hazarded hilariously.

'No, that a woman can start out like her and end like me. Not that she'd believe it.'

She had a dizzying sensation of going too far. Surely now Marcel must be remembering the dark and dangerous paths down which they'd travelled together, and reading the truth in her eyes. But the time was not right. If things had been different she could have told him everything now, but that was impossible until he could bring himself to admit that he knew who she was.

And that day might never come.

Suddenly she doubted that she had the strength for this. She wanted to cry aloud and flee him. She even moved to rise from her seat, but his hand detained her.

'Are you all right? You look troubled.'

His voice was gentle, his eyes warm and concerned. It was as though another man had taken him over, or perhaps lured him back to the past, and it was her undoing.

'Look, I must go. It's late and I'm tired—'

'Of course. I'll take you home.'

'No!' The word was almost violent. 'No, there's no need for that. I'll be all right.'

'I'll tell Hotel Reception to send a car to the front for you. Then you'll be free of me.'

'It's not that—' she began wildly.

'Yes, it is,' he said. 'It's like that for both of us.' His voice grew softer, more intense. 'We both need some time to get our heads together.' His eyes met hers. 'Don't we?'

She nodded dumbly.

He escorted her out of the hotel and to the waiting car, assisted her into a seat at the rear, then stood with the door still open, leaning in slightly, holding onto her hand.

'It's all right about going to Paris, isn't it?' he asked.

'Of course.'

'Then be ready to travel tomorrow.'

'Tomorrow? But you said I could have the day off to sort out—'

'I've changed my mind. There's no time. You'll have to do it long-distance when you get there. I'll collect you at nine tomorrow morning.' His hand tightened on hers. 'You will be there, won't you?'

'Of course.'

'You won't vanish?'

'No.'

Promise me. His voice was almost harsh in its intensity. 'I promise,' she said.

His eyes held hers and for a moment she thought he would refuse to let go of her hand. But then he released her suddenly, slammed the door and stepped back. Her last view of him was standing there, completely still, his eyes fixed on the retreating car like a man clinging on to a vanishing hope.

He watched her until she was out of sight, then took out his phone and dialled a number given to him by his father. It was a private security firm. In a hard voice he gave her address.

'These are your instructions. You park outside and watch. If she comes out with a suitcase and gets into a taxi you call me. Then follow her. And don't let her out of your sight for a moment.'

* * *

In her time with Jake, Cassie had grown used to his ways of flaunting his wealth and what he fondly believed to be his status. He would book the most expensive seats on planes, then arrive at the last minute with the maximum of fuss.

Marcel, in contrast, reached the airport early, got through the formalities with courtesy and was driven quietly to the private jet that was waiting for him.

'My father's,' he explained.

The plane was pure luxury. It could seat eight people in soft, comfortable seats, and had its own galley from which food and drink was served to the two of them by a steward who existed solely for their comfort.

As they began to move down the runway he said, 'The weather's fine so it should be a smooth flight. Nothing to worry about.'

So he remembered that she was afraid of flying, she thought. After one modelling job she'd returned home still shaken and distraught from a bumpy flight. How bright his eyes had been, how full of expectancy for the night of passion to come. And how quickly he'd forgotten all thoughts of his own pleasure to take her trembling body in his arms and soothe her tenderly. There had been no sex that night, and in the morning she had loved him more than ever for his generosity.

'Have you ever been to Paris?' he asked now.

'No, but I've always wanted to. I'm looking forward to exploring it.'

'You won't have time for that. You'll live in the hotel, and have a desk in my office. Everything will be provided to help with your work and you'll be "confined to barracks", forbidden to leave.'

For a moment she almost thought he meant it, but just in time she saw the gleam of wicked humour in his eyes.

'Yeah, right!' she said cynically.

'You don't believe me? Wait until you see the locks on the doors.'

'Nonsense!'

'That's no way to talk to your employer.'

'If you were any other employer I wouldn't, but we both know that I'm not just here to study the facts of La Couronne. I'm here to absorb the atmosphere, and that means the atmosphere of the city as well.'

'Very subtle,' he said appreciatively. 'So you'll arrange the job to suit yourself.'

'It's what I'm good at,' she said impishly. 'Being in control.'

He grinned. She smiled back, happy in this brief moment of warmth and ease between them. But then a scream burst from her as the plane jerked and plunged a few feet.

'Sorry,' came the pilot's voice. 'Air pocket. It's going to be a little turbulent.'

'Don't worry.' Marcel took both her hands in his. 'It'll be over soon. There's no danger.'

'I know it's not dangerous,' she said huskily. 'It's just… being shaken…'

'Just hold onto me.' His hands tightened.

She did so, closing her eyes and shaking her head. It was foolish to be scared but she couldn't help it. As the plane shuddered she whispered, 'No, no, no—'

'Look at me,' Marcel commanded. 'Open your eyes.'

She did so, and the world vanished. His gaze held hers as firmly as if he had her in chains. And they were the most dangerous chains of all because she had no wish to break them.

'It's all right,' he said. 'It's finishing now.'

He was right. The plane's juddering was fading, then ceasing altogether. But that wasn't why the sense of peace and safety was stealing over her. She held him tightly because while he was there nothing could go wrong.

'I'm sorry,' she said in a shaking voice. 'It's stupid to be scared—'

'We all have our nightmares. They don't have to make sense.'

She managed an edgy laugh. 'So much for being in control.'

'We'd all like to be in control,' he said quietly. 'And we all spend our lives discovering how wrong we are.'

'No,' she said defensively. 'I don't believe it has to be like that.'

'I only wish you were right.'

He looked down at their hands, still clasped, and gently released her. She had to suppress the impulse to hold on, refusing to let him go. But she must not give in. She was strong. She was in control. She'd just said so.

At the airport a limousine was waiting to convey them into the heart of Paris. She watched in delight as the landmarks glided past, and they came to a halt in the Champs Elysées in the glamorous heart of the city.

La Couronne towered above her, grandiose and beautiful. Stewards hurried forward to greet their employer and regard herself with curiosity. One of them seized Cassie's bags and invited her to follow him.

'I'll join you later,' Marcel said.

Her accommodation was high up, a luxurious suite where a maid was waiting for her. She'd been wondering what to expect, but the reality took her breath away.

'My name is Tina,' said the maid. 'I am here to serve you. I will start unpacking.'

'Thank you. I'll go and freshen up.'

She went into the bathroom and regarded herself critically in the mirror. Marcel had told her to soften her appearance, but so far she hadn't done so. On the journey he'd glanced at her appearance but made no comment. Now she loosened her hair, letting it fall about her face, not in waves as he'd once known it, but long and straight.

I'm not really Cassie any more, she thought. *I've been fooling myself.*

Sighing in frustration, she left the bathroom and immediately halted at the sight that met her eyes.

'Tina let me in,' Marcel said. 'I came to see how you were settling. If you're ready I'll show you around.'

'Fine, I'm almost finished. I'll just—' She raised a hand to her hair, but he stopped her.

'Leave it.'

'But it's all over the place. I can't go around looking as though I'd been pulled through a hedge backwards.'

'True, but it won't take much to make you a little neater. Just brush it back here—and here—'

As he spoke he was flicking his fingers against her blonde locks, sending them spinning back over her shoulders, then smoothing them away. She tried not to be conscious of his fingertips softly brushing her face, but some things could never be driven away. The touch of a lover's hand, the feel of his breath whispering against her face in agitated waves.

But he's no longer my lover. Remember that.

Firmly she pushed feelings aside. She couldn't afford them.

'Let's go,' she said. 'I really want to see the hotel.'

'I suppose you've read enough to know the background,' he said, showing her outside.

'I know it was once the home of the Marquis de Montpelier, a friend of royalty, who could have anything he wanted, including three wives, five mistresses and more children than he could count.'

'Until the Revolution began, and they all went to the guillotine,' Marcel supplied. 'If you look out of this window you can almost see the place where they died.'

There in the distance she could just make out the Place de la Concorde, where the guillotine had once stood.

'I wonder how often they looked at that view, never dreaming of what would happen to them in the end,' she murmured.

Now, she thought, their palace was the centre of a business empire, and the man who controlled it was safely armoured against all life could do to him.

'Some of the building still looks as it did then,' Marcel told her. 'I keep it that way for the historical interest. Plus I have a friend who claims to have second sight and swears she can see the ghosts of the Montpelier family, carrying their heads under their arms.'

'And you make the most of it,' she said, amused.

'Let's say the rooms on that corridor are always the first to be hired.'

'Do you live on that corridor?'

He grinned. 'No, I don't like to be disturbed by howling spectres.'

As they went over the building she recorded her impressions into a small microphone while Marcel listened, impressed.

'Now let's go to my apartment,' he said, 'unless you're tired.'

'No, let's keep working.'

She was eager to see where he lived and learn what it could tell her about his present personality. But when they arrived she was disappointed. Only the room he used as an office was accessible. The rest was kept hidden behind closed doors.

'I'll be back in a moment,' he said. 'Access anything you want on the computer.'

He went out into the corridor, and she began to familiarise herself with his computer, which was state-of-the-art. She had expected no less. There was a mountain of information for her to take in and she went quickly from one item to the next. A casual onlooker would think she couldn't possibly be absorbing information with such brief glances, but that would be a mistake. She had a photographic memory, which in the old days she'd hidden because it clashed with her sexy image. Marcel had been one of the few people to discover that beneath the ditzy surface was a mind like a machine.

That was it!

She gasped as she realised that she had the answer to the question that had teased her. When she and Marcel had exchanged phone details yesterday, she'd offered to return his and he'd said, 'You could have memorised it by now.'

She'd barely glanced at the scrap of paper, yet he'd known that would be enough for her because he knew something about her that no stranger could have known.

'A great brain', he'd called her, laughing as he clasped her in his arms.

'How do I dare to make love to a woman with such a great brain? A mighty brain! A genius! Some men might find that intimidating.'

'But not you, hmm?'

'No, because she has other virtues. Come here!'

Now, sitting in Marcel's office, she began to shake with the violence of the emotion possessing her. She'd guessed that he recognised her, but now she was sure. He had brought her here, to the heart of his own world. Couldn't she dare to hope that they might open their arms to each other and put right the wrongs of the past?

She'd thought she wanted vengeance, but that was being crowded out by other sensations beyond her control.

Now was the moment, and she would seize it with eager hands. If only he would return quickly.

She heard footsteps in the corridor. He was coming. In just a few moments everything would be transformed. The old attraction was beginning to rise up inside her, and surely it was the same with him. There might even be happiness again.

But the next instant the dream died, smashed to smithereens by something she knew she should have anticipated, but had carelessly overlooked.

Which meant there was no one to blame but herself.

CHAPTER SIX

FROM outside came an urgent tapping on the door and a woman's voice in a high-pitched scream of excitement.

'*Marcel, mon chéri—ouvrez le porte et me prendre dans tes bras. Oh, combien je suis heureux que mon véritable amour est de retour.*'

Her limited French was just up to translating this.

'Marcel, my darling—open the door and take me in your arms. Oh, how happy I am that my true love has returned.'

So that was that. Another stupid fantasy destroyed.

Don't be so naïve again!

Bringing herself under control, she opened the door and backed away just in time to avoid being lovingly throttled by a girl who was young, sexy, beautiful, vibrant with life.

And she'd called Marcel 'my true love'.

The newcomer began to babble again in French, then switched abruptly to English.

'I'm sorry—you must be Mrs Henshaw—and English, yes?'

'Yes.'

'Marcel has told us all about you.'

'Us?'

'My papa is Raul Lenoir, Marcel's lawyer. He has spoken much of Mrs Henshaw, his new assistant who will handle important business for him in London. I am so pleased to meet you.'

Cassie took the hand she held out, murmuring untruthfully, 'And I am pleased to meet you.'

'My name is Brigitte Lenoir. Where is Marcel? I have missed him so much.'

'He went out a moment ago, but he'll be back soon.'

'Oh I can't wait. I have so much to tell him.'

'I think that's him now.'

The door opened and Marcel appeared, his face brightening as he saw his visitor. They next moment they were in each other's arms. Brigitte covered his face with kisses and he laughed, returning the compliment again and again.

'Brigitte, *ma chérie, mon amante*—'

Cassie returned to the computer, trying not to hear the sounds coming from behind her.

'Brigitte, I want you to meet Mrs Henshaw,' Marcel said at last, freeing himself from her clasp.

'But we have already met, and I am so impressed,' Brigitte declared.

'So you should be,' Marcel said. 'She's a great brain and we're all afraid of her.'

'Papa will be most interested to meet her. You must both come to dinner with us tonight.'

Cassie flinched. 'I'm not sure—'

'Oh, but you must,' Brigitte assured her.

Both her mind and heart rebelled at the thought of spending an evening with these two, watching them all over each other.

'I have a lot of work to do—'

Brigitte began to mutter in French. Without understanding every word, Cassie gathered that she was telling Marcel that he must persuade her. Another woman was vital and Mrs Henshaw would be useful.

'She's just what we need. She can keep Henri talking without—you know—'

The meaning of 'you know' was all too clear. Whoever Henri was, her duty was to keep him talking without attracting him in a way that might be 'inconvenient'. In other words, a plain woman. Like Mrs Henshaw.

'I applaud your desire to work,' Marcel told her, 'but joining us for dinner tonight will be part of that work. We'll dine in the hotel's most splendid restaurant, and you can give me your opinion of it later. Now, I suggest you return to your suite and prepare for tonight.'

Leaving him free to succumb to Brigitte's charms, she thought. As she walked away down the corridor she could hear shrieks of laughter which abruptly faded into murmurs. She increased her speed.

In her rooms she found Tina just finishing, and complimented her on the job.

'It looks so comfortable in here. If only I could just put my feet up, but I've got to attend a formal dinner tonight, with the lawyer and somebody called Henri. Why? What's up?' Tina had smothered a laugh.

'Forgive me, *madame,* but if Henri Lenoir is there it will not be formal.'

'You know him?'

'He is the son of the lawyer and Mademoiselle Brigitte's brother. But apart from that—' Tina hesitated before going on, 'Every girl knows him. He is a very naughty man. The rumour says that his wife has thrown him out for the third time.'

'Because of—?'

'Because he's naughty with many ladies. They say he's returned to his father's home, and the family is watching over him to make sure that…well…'

'That he isn't naughty again. I see.'

'If he behaves she may take him back.'

And evidently Brigitte saw no danger of her brother mis-behaving with Mrs Henshaw. It was practically an insult.

When Tina had gone she threw herself onto the bed, reliving the scene she had just endured. Something had happened that hurt more than anything else so far.

A great brain!

That was what Marcel had called her to Brigitte, but using the words so differently from the way he had once spoken them to herself that now the tears welled up and she rolled over, burying her face in the pillow. Suddenly there was only despair, with nothing to hope for, and she yielded to the darkness, weeping until she was too drained to weep any more.

As she recovered she realised that Marcel hadn't given her details about when, where and how to present herself tonight. Quickly she called his cellphone, but it had been switched off. She tried his hotel phone but it stayed unanswered.

Whatever he was doing left him with no attention for anything else.

She stared up at the ceiling, aware that she had reached a crossroads. Since Marcel had reappeared in her life she'd been cautious to the point of dithering.

'Not any more,' she vowed. 'Time for a final decision, and I'm making it.'

When Brigitte had finally departed Marcel paced the floor restlessly.

Today he'd shocked himself by doing things he'd never intended, and not doing things he'd vowed were essential.

He'd brought Cassie here to redress the past, although the meaning of that was still vague in his mind. To let her see the riches she'd thrown away, show her the life she could have had instead of the bleak impoverished existence she had now— yes, definitely.

Revenge? Possibly.

But during the flight there had been an unexpected change. At the first sign that she might be vulnerable he'd known a passionate desire to protect her. It was what he'd felt long ago and she'd thrown it back in his face, yet it had leapt out of the darkness at him, like an animal waiting to pounce. And, weakling that he was, he'd yielded to it.

No more weakness. Bringing her here had been a risk, but he wouldn't back down now. One day soon he would confront her with all the memories she seemed determined to avoid. Then she would answer for what she had done to him.

But that must wait until he was ready.

In one sense at least Cassie and Mrs Henshaw were the same person. When a decision was taken there were no second thoughts, no weakening, only a determined follow-through to the end.

This particular decision took her downstairs on winged feet, heading for the fashion shop at the back of the hotel. After studying several glamorous gowns she rejected them all in favour of a pair of tight black satin trousers. Only a woman with her very slender figure could have worn such a garment, but that suited her just fine. To go with them she bought a black silk top with a plunging neckline and bare arms.

It was outrageous, and for a brief moment she hesitated. But then she recalled Brigitte's face that afternoon, not in the least troubled by the sight of her.

'So you're not afraid of Mrs Henshaw,' she addressed the vision. 'Let's see if Cassie can scare you.' She gave a brief laugh. 'Perhaps she ought to. She's beginning to scare me.'

At the beauty salon she described how she wanted to look, aware of the stares of the assistants, incredulous that this plain Jane could indulge such fantasies. But they smiled and got to work, and when they'd finished her curled hair was tumbling over her shoulders, partly—but only partly—hiding her daring décolletage.

Back in her room she inspected the satin trousers, wondering if she was being wise. She had a dress that would do. It was adequate rather than outstanding, but that might just be better than outrageous.

She tried on the dress, then removed it and donned the trousers, fighting temptation as she studied her magnificent appearance in the mirror.

'Oh, heck!' she sighed at last. 'I can't do it, can I? But one day I will do it. I must. I can't settle for being "adequate" for ever, but just for tonight maybe I should.'

There was a knock at the door.

'I'm coming,' she called without opening it. 'Just give me a moment.'

'No, now,' came Marcel's voice. 'I need to talk to you at once.'

She opened the door, pulling it back against her and retreating so that she was mostly concealed behind it. Even so, he could see the cascade of her glorious hair and it stopped him short.

She could have screamed with frustration. The stunned look on his face was the one she'd longed to see, but what maddening fate had made it happen just at this moment?

'Mrs...I don't...I wasn't expecting...' He was stammering, which would have filled her with delight at any other time.

'You said I should look less severe,' she told him loftily. 'Is this sufficiently "un-severe" for you?'

'I...that wasn't...yes...I suppose...'

The last time she'd seen him lost for words was nine years ago when her landlady had walked in when they were lying naked on the floor.

'I'm glad you approve,' she said now, still taking care to

conceal as much of herself as possible. 'Is the Lenoir family here yet?'

'Part of it. Madame Lenoir won't be coming, but there's—'

'Marcel, *ou êtes vous?*' Brigitte's voice came floating down the corridor.

'I'm here, *chérie.*'

She was speaking French in a low voice, clearly meaning not to be overheard. Even so, Cassie managed to make out enough to learn that the mysterious Henri was reluctant to attend the dinner, not wanting to be saddled with 'the English woman nobody else wanted'. He'd agreed only on condition that he could leave early. Marcel gave a sharp intake of breath, but could say no more because of sounds from further along the corridor. Two men were approaching, hailing them, receiving Marcel's greeting in return. Then they were in the room, full of polite bonhomie.

'We can't wait to meet the brilliant lady you've brought with you,' Monsieur Lenoir declared. 'Isn't that so, Henri?'

'I've been looking forward to this moment all day,' came a courteous if unconvincing voice. 'Where is she?'

'Here,' Cassie said, stepping out from behind the door.

With the first glance Cassie understood everything she'd heard about Henri. Good looking in a 'pretty boy' style, he had a self-indulgent manner and dark hair worn slightly too long for his age, which she guessed at about forty. Definitely a 'naughty man', fighting the years.

His behaviour confirmed it. He was wide-eyed at the vision that confronted him.

'Madame,' he murmured, 'I am more glad to meet you than I can say.' He advanced with his hands out. 'What an evening we are going to have!'

He would have thrown his arms around Cassie, but she stopped him by placing her hands in his. Nothing daunted, he kissed the back of each hand. Then he jerked her forward and in this way managed to embrace her. Turning her head against his shoulder, she had a searing vision of Marcel's face as he gained his first complete sight of her.

What she saw would stay with her for ever. For one blinding second he looked like a man struck over the heart—astonished, bewildered, aghast, shattered. But in the next instant it was all gone, and only a stone mask remained.

No matter. She'd seen all that she needed to see. He'd expected to find Mrs Henshaw, but Cassie's ghost had walked and nothing would ever be the same.

Now she was glad there hadn't been time to change into something more respectable. There was a time for restraint and a time for defiance. Mrs Henshaw would have been left floundering, but Cassie was the expert.

Monsieur Lenoir cleared his throat and came forward, sounding embarrassed. 'Madame Henshaw, allow me to introduce my son.'

'Well, I think he's already introduced himself,' Cassie said with a little giggle.

'But you haven't introduced *your*self,' Henri said.

Brigitte intervened. 'Mrs Henshaw is masterminding Marcel's purchase of the London hotel.'

'That's a bit of an exaggeration,' Cassie said hastily. 'I'm not exactly masterminding it.'

'But Marcel says that you are a great brain,' Brigitte reminded her.

'I'm no such thing,' she defended herself.

Henri gave an exaggerated sigh of relief. 'Thank goodness for that. Brainy women terrify me.'

'Then you've nothing to fear from me,' she cooed, giving him her best teasing smile.

'But you must be brainy or Marcel wouldn't have employed you,' Brigitte pointed out.

'That's true,' Cassie said as if suddenly realising. 'I must be brighter than I thought.'

Her eyes met Marcel's, seeing in them floundering confusion wrestling ineffectively with anger. She was beginning to enjoy herself.

'It's time were going,' Monsieur Lenoir declared, edging his son firmly out of the way and offering Cassie his arm. 'Madame Henshaw, may I have the pleasure of escorting you?'

'The pleasure is mine,' she replied.

But then Henri too stepped forward, offering his other arm so that she walked out of the door with a man on each side, leaving Marcel to follow with Brigitte.

They made a glamorous spectacle as they went along the corridor, the men in dinner jackets and bow ties, Brigitte in flowing evening gown, and Cassie in her luxurious black satin that left nothing to the imagination.

Perhaps that was why Marcel never so much as glanced at her as they went down in the elevator.

But as they stepped out and headed for the restaurant he raised his voice. 'Mrs Henshaw, there's a small matter of business we need to clear up before the evening starts. The rest of you go on and we'll join you.'

His hand on her arm was urgent, holding her back and drawing her around a corner, where there was nobody to see them.

'Just what do you think you're doing?' he muttered furiously.

'Being civil to the people who are important to you.'

'You know what I mean—the way you're dressed—'

'But you told me to.'

'I—?'

'Be less severe, you said. And only today you brushed my hair forward so that—'

'Never mind that,' he said hastily.

'I'm only doing what I thought you wanted. Oh, dear!' She gasped as if in shocked discovery. 'Didn't I go far enough? Should the neckline be lower?'

She took hold as though to pull it down but he seized her hands in his own. Instinctively her fingers tightened on his, drawing them against her skin, so that she felt him next to the swell of her breasts just before they vanished into the neckline.

He stood for a moment as though fighting to move but unable to find the strength. There was murder in his eyes.

'Damn you!' he said softly. *'Damn you, Cassie!'*

He wrenched his hands free and stormed off without waiting for her to reply. She clutched the wall, her chest rising and falling as conflicting emotions raced through her. The signals coming from him had been of violence and hostility but, far from fearing him, she was full of triumph.

He recognised her. He'd admitted it.

He'd blurted it out against his better judgement and they both knew it. Whatever the future held, thus far the battle was hers.

As she turned the corner she saw that he was still there, standing by the door through which they must go. He offered her his arm without meeting her eyes, and together they went on their way.

The others were waiting for them just inside the restaurant, agog with curiosity, but their polite smiles acted as masks and curiosity went unsatisfied. Monsieur Lenoir pulled out a chair, indicating for her to sit beside him, and Henri nimbly seized the place on her other side. For a moment she thought Marcel would say something, but Brigitte touched his cheek and he hastened to smile at her.

Cassie looked about her, fascinated. Chandeliers hung from the ceiling, golden ornaments hung from the walls. The glasses were of the finest crystal, just as the champagne being poured into them was also the finest.

She wasn't usually impressed by luxury, having seen much of it in earlier years, but there was an elegance about this place that appealed to her. She sipped the champagne appreciatively, then took a notebook from her bag and began to scribble.

'What are you doing?' Henri murmured in a tone that suggested conspiracy.

'Observing,' she said briskly. 'That's what I'm here for.'

'Surely not,' he murmured. 'You're here to have a wonderful time with a man who admires you more than any other woman in the world.'

'No, I'm here to do a job,' she said severely. 'Monsieur Falcon has employed me for my efficiency—'

'Ah, but efficiency at what?' His eyes, raking her shape left no doubt of his meaning.

'At business matters,' she informed him in her best 'prison-wardress' voice.

'But there's business and business,' he pointed out. 'It's not just facts and figures he wants from you, I'll bet.'

'Monsieur Lenoir!' she exclaimed.

'Henri, please. I already feel that we know each other well.'

'Henri, I'm shocked!'

'And I'll bet you don't shock easily. Do go on.'

'You cannot know me well if you think *that* of me.'

'Think what of you?' he asked with an innocence that would have fooled anyone not forewarned. 'I don't know what you mean.'

'I'm sure you do.'

'Well, perhaps. I can't imagine Marcel wasting you on business efficiency when you have so many other lavish talents. He's known as a man with an eye for the ladies.'

He inclined his head slightly to where Marcel was sitting. Cassie waited for him to glance across at her, disapproving of Henri's attention, but he didn't. He seemed engrossed by Brigitte, sitting beside him, his eyes fixed on her as though nothing else existed in the world. Suddenly he smiled into her eyes and Cassie had to check a gasp. Surely no man smiled at a woman like that unless he meant it with all his heart?

There was a welcome distraction in choosing the food, which was of the high standard she'd expected. While they ate Henri surprised her by talking sensibly. Her questions about Paris received knowledgeable answers and she was able to listen with such genuine interest that when Marcel spoke to her across the table she failed to hear him.

'I'm sorry…what…?' she stammered.

'I was merely recommending the wine,' he said. 'It's a rare vintage and a speciality of this hotel.'

'Of course, yes. Thank you.'

'Never mind him,' Henri said. 'Let me finish telling you—'

'You've had your turn,' Monsieur Lenoir objected. 'I may be an old man, but I'm not too old to appreciate a beautiful woman.' He gave a rich chuckle. Liking him, Cassie gave him her most gracious smile and they were soon deep in conversation. On the surface he was more civilised and restrained than his son, but his observations about Paris tended to linger on the shadowy romantic places. Clearly Henri wasn't her only admirer.

At last an orchestra struck up and dancers took to the floor. Monsieur Lenoir extended his hand and she followed him cheerfully.

He was a reasonably good dancer for his age and weight, but what he really wanted, as she soon discovered, was to flaunt his sexy young companion, enjoying envious gazes from other men. She laughed and indulged him, careful not to go too far, and they finally left the floor, laughing together in perfect accord.

Henri was waiting for them, looking theatrically forlorn.

'I'm all alone,' he mourned. 'You've got my father. Marcel and Brigitte look like they're set up for the night.'

'Yes, they do, don't they,' Cassie said, observing them from a distance, dancing with eyes only for each other.

'So when will it be my turn?' Henri wanted to know.

'Right now,' she said firmly. 'Do you mind my leaving you alone?' This was to Monsieur Lenoir.

'No, you two young things go and enjoy yourself. I'm puffed.'

Before she knew it she was spinning around the floor. Henri was a good dancer. So was she, she suddenly remembered. How long had it been since she'd had the chance to let go and really enjoy herself?

For a little while she gave herself up to the thrill of moving fast. Her mind seemed to be linked to Henri, so that when he waggled his hips she instinctively did the same, and heard cheers and applause from the rest of the floor. The world was spinning by in a series of visions. They came and went in her consciousness, but the one that was always there was Marcel, watching her with narrowed, furious eyes. No matter how often she turned, he always seemed to be directly in front of her. She blinked and he vanished. And yet he was still there, because he was always there.

As the dance ended there was a mini riot, with Henri indicating that he wanted to partner her again, and at least three other men prepared to challenge for the privilege. But they all backed off when they saw Marcel, with murder in his eyes, stretching out his hand to her.

'My dance, I think,' he said.

His voice was soft but dangerous, and tonight danger had an edge that she relished.

'I don't think so,' she said with a challenging glance at her other suitors. 'I think you have to wait your turn.'

It was a crazy thing to say but she couldn't have stopped

herself for anything in the world. Suddenly she felt herself yanked fiercely against him, his arm so tight about her that she was breathless.

'I wait for no man,' he said. Then, in a voice even softer and more menacing than before, he added, 'And no woman.'

'Then I guess I have no choice,' she said. 'Let's go.'

The music had slowed, enabling him to draw her onto the floor in a waltz, his body moving against hers. She tried not to feel the rising excitement. That was to be her weapon against him, not his against her. But the shocking truth was that he was equally armed and her defences were weak. Now her only hope of standing up to him was not to let him suspect her weakness.

She reckoned a suit of armour would have been useful: something made of steel to protect her from the awareness of his body so dangerously close to hers. Lacking it, she could only assume the nearest thing to a visor, a beaming, rigid smile that should have alarmed him.

'I don't think you should hold me so tightly,' she said.

'Don't try to fool me,' he murmured in soft rage. 'This is exactly what you meant to happen.'

'You do me an injustice. I was going to wear something more conventional but you arrived before I could change.'

'Oh, please, try to think of something better.'

'Why must you always judge me so harshly?'

'If you don't know the answer to that—*mon dieu,* you're enjoying this, aren't you?'

'That's not fair.'

'When is the truth fair? I know how your deceiving little mind works—'

'How can you be so sure you know about me—a woman you met only a few days ago?'

His face was livid and she thought for a moment he would

do something violent. But he only dropped his head so that his mouth was close to her ear. *'Ne me tourmente pas ou je vais vous faire désolé. Prenez garde pendant qu'il est encore temps....'*

She drew in her breath. He'd warned her against tormenting him, telling her to take heed while there was still time.

'Don't torment me,' he groaned again. 'I warn you—I warn you—'

'Why?' she challenged. 'Whatever will happen?'

'Wait and see.'

'Suppose I can't wait. Suppose I'm impatient. What will you do then?'

'Wait and see,' he repeated with slow, deliberate emphasis.

She smiled. 'I'll look forward to that.'

His hand had been drifting lower until it almost rested on the satin curve of her behind. Suddenly he snatched it back, as though in fear, though whether of her or himself perhaps, neither of them could have said.

'Witch!' he breathed.

She chuckled. 'Anything you say. After all, you're my employer. Your word is law. I exist only to obey.'

Now his eyes were those of a man driven beyond endurance, and she really thought he would explode. But it lasted only a moment, then his steely control was in place again.

'I'm glad you realise that,' he said. 'There are things I won't tolerate.'

'You must tell me what they are,' she challenged.

His gaze was fierce and desperate. What would he say? she wondered. Was this her moment?

But the music was drawing to a close. The moment was over.

'Later,' he growled.

'Later,' she agreed.

'But soon.'

'Yes. Soon.' Her eyes met his. 'Because we've waited long enough.'

CHAPTER SEVEN

POLITELY they walked each other off the floor, slowing suddenly as they came within sight of the table.

'Oh, no!' Marcel groaned.

Cassie didn't need to ask about the newcomer. A woman in her thirties, tense, angular and furious, sat next to Henri, hectoring him as only a wife would have done.

'You found another floozie fast enough. I've been watching you dance with her.' Her eyes fell on the blonde bombshell approaching the table on Marcel's arm, and an expression of contempt overtook her face. 'And here she is.' She rose and confronted Cassie.

'Got another one, have you? Finished with my Henri, think this one'll have more money? That's how your kind operate, isn't it? Find out what they're worth and move from one to the other.' She glared at Marcel. 'Don't fool yourself. When she meets a man with more cash you'll be history. Don't suppose you know what it's like to be dumped, do you? Well, you'll find out with her.'

The air was singing about Cassie's head. How would Marcel respond to these words that seemed to home in on his own experience with such deadly accuracy?

His reply amazed her.

'Good evening, Madame Lenoir. I am so glad you could join your husband.'

'Join him? I'm going to get rid of him for good. I saw him dancing with *her,* and what an exhibition that was! Now she can have him.'

'You are mistaken, *madame,*' Marcel said coolly. 'Mrs Henshaw danced with your husband only out of courtesy. She is with me tonight, and I would prefer it if you did not insult her.'

'Oh, would you? Well, I'd prefer it if—'

She got no further. Scenting danger, Henri started to draw her away, apologizing frantically. When they had gone there were sighs of relief. Monsieur Lenoir indicated for Cassie to sit beside him but she'd had as much as she could stand.

'Forgive me,' she said, 'but I'm rather tired. I just want to go to bed. I'll be at work first thing tomorrow morning. Goodnight.'

She was backing away hastily as she spoke, giving Marcel no chance to object. Not that he wanted to, she thought. He must be glad to be rid of her.

In her room she stripped off, showered and dressed for the night. Her pyjamas were 'Mrs Henshaw', plain linen, loose trousers, high buttons.

Stick to Mrs Henshaw in future, she thought. You could argue that Cassie hadn't been a success.

Or you could argue that she'd been so much of a success that it had put the cat among the pigeons.

She paced the floor, too agitated to sleep. Everything that had happened this evening had been unexpected. She'd coped with surprise after surprise, and the biggest surprise of all had been Marcel's defence of her.

But it hadn't been personal, she thought with a sigh. Only what conventional courtesy demanded. If only...

There came a sharp knock on her door.

'Who is it?' she called.

'Me.' It was Marcel. He tried the door, rattling it. 'Open the door.'

She did so. Instantly his hand appeared, preventing her closing it if she'd wanted to. But she didn't want to. This moment had been too long in coming, and now she was ready for it with all guns blazing.

He pushed in so fast that she had to back away. His eyes darted around the room.

'I'm alone,' she said ironically. 'Henri left tamely with his wife. He didn't come flying back to me, whatever you think.'

'You'll pardon me if I don't take your word for that.'

'No, I won't pardon you,' she said. 'I'm not a liar. There's nobody here but us.'

He ignored her. He was opening doors, looking into the bathroom, the wardrobe. Her temper rose sharply.

'Look at me,' she said, indicating her dull attire. 'Do you think any woman entertains a lover dressed in clothes like this?'

'That depends how long she means to wear them. When she knows he'll rip them off her as soon as possible—'

'Is that what Henri wanted?' she asked sarcastically. 'He didn't say.'

'He didn't need to. It's what he wanted and every man in the room wanted. That's the truth and we both know it.'

'Now, look—'

He turned on her in swift fury. 'Don't take me for a fool!'

'But you are a fool,' she raged. 'The biggest fool in creation. Hey, what do you think you're doing?'

'Locking the door so that we're not disturbed. Since the conversation is getting down to basics, I have things to say to you.'

'I think we both have things to say.'

He nodded. 'Yes, and they've waited too long, *Mrs Henshaw.*'

For a moment she didn't speak. Then she said quietly, 'Are you sure that's what you want to call me?'

'I don't want to call you anything. I'd rather not have to endure the sight of you. I thought you were safely out of my life, just a bitter, evil memory that I could kick aside. But now—' He checked himself and looked her up and down, breathing hard with the emotion that threatened to overwhelm him.

'It is you, isn't it?' he said at last.

It was the question he'd promised himself not to ask, because that would be a sign of yielding. But now he knew there had never been a choice.

'It is you,' he repeated.

'You've known that all along.'

'I thought so—sometimes I wasn't sure—it didn't seem possible that you could be—' He broke off, breathing harshly. 'I've tried not to believe it,' he said at last.

'So you didn't want it to be true?'

'Of course I didn't,' he said with soft violence. 'Why should I want to meet you again? I can still hardly comprehend— what evil design made you come after me?'

'Don't flatter yourself,' she cried angrily. 'I didn't seek you out. I went to see Marcel Falcon. Until I saw you I had no idea it was the man I'd known as Marcel Degrande. If I *had* known I'd never have gone to that meeting. When I recognised you I ran away as fast as I could.'

'But you turned back.'

'I didn't mean to. At first I ran into the garden, but to finally escape I had to come back through the hotel and I met you coming out. Don't you understand? *I* didn't want to see *you* again. There was just too much—'

Suddenly the words choked her, and she turned away with a helpless gesture.

'Yes,' he growled. 'Too much. We could never have met peacefully.' He took hold of her and twisted her around.

'Don't turn your back on me. You flaunted your charms to-night, and I endured it, but no more! Did it please you to taunt and jeer at me?'

'I wasn't—' She tried to free herself but he gripped her more tightly.

'Don't lie. You knew exactly what you were doing to me, wearing those—those—you know what I mean. What kind of twisted pleasure did it give you? Or don't I need to ask? You played your games, the way you've always done—'

'I never played games with you,' she said desperately.

'Oh, but you did. You just weren't so frank about it in those days. Sweet, loving little Cassie, wide-eyed and inno-cent, honestly in love. And I believed it. Until I discovered that you were heartless, incapable of honest love. That was a useful lesson. Once learned, never forgotten. That's the Cassie I knew. So tell me, who is Mrs Henshaw?'

'She's who I am now,' she cried. 'At least I thought so. I thought Cassie had died a long time ago.'

'But tonight she rose again, didn't she? Because some crea-tures never die. You showed me that nothing had changed, and stood back laughing at the result. I hope I didn't disap-point you.'

'Can that be true?' she challenged him. 'That nothing has changed?'

She heard his swift intake of breath, saw the wild look in his eyes and knew that she'd hit a nerve. He didn't reply. He couldn't. So she answered for him.

'Of course it isn't true, Marcel. It *can't* be true.'

'You said yourself that Cassie hadn't really died,' he re-minded her coldly.

'But she's not the same Cassie. She's seen things she never thought to see, things she didn't want to see, but can't forget. She's trapped in her own memories. What about you?'

His terrible expression was her answer. It was the look of a man struggling to get free, knowing he was doomed to fail.

'I can cope with memories,' he said. 'But from some things there's no escape.'

'If you're accusing me of pursuing you, I've already explained—'

'I'm not. Not the way you mean.'

She had pursued him in dreams and fantasies, visions and nightmares. He'd tried to drive her off, crying out that he hated and despised her—that if they met again he would take revenge. But her ghost laughed at his rage, jeered that she was stronger than he, and haunted him so relentlessly that when she'd actually risen before his eyes it was as though he'd summoned her by the force of his will.

He knew he shouldn't tell her this. It would give her too much power, and her power was already alarming. But he couldn't stop himself saying, 'You were always there. A million times I tried to make you go, but you wouldn't. Now you're really here, and I'm no longer a callow boy to let you trick me and run.'

'Why must you think the worst of me?' she cried.

'Haven't I reason? Didn't you desert me when I was almost at death's door?'

'No, I didn't desert you,' she cried. 'I did it for you—'

'Surely you can think of something better than that,' he sneered.

'It's true. I had no choice.'

'You're lying and it's not even a clever lie. Anyone could see through it.'

'Listen to me—' she screamed.

'No, you listen to me. I hate you, Cassie, or Mrs Henshaw, whoever you are today. I shall hate you as long as I live. There's only one thing about you that I don't hate, and it's this.'

He pulled her hard against him and looked down into her face. She felt his hands move away from her shoulders to take her head, holding it in the right position so that she couldn't resist. She knew what he was about to do, but nothing could prepare her for the feel of his lips on hers after so long.

'Marcel,' she gasped.

'You've been trying to drive me insane all evening, and now you've done it. Are you pleased? Is this what you wanted?'

It was exactly what she wanted and only now did she admit the truth to herself. All her anger and defiance had been heading for this moment, trying to drive him to take her into his arms. Her body, her senses and, if she were honest, her heart, had been set on this, and if he'd resisted her it would have been an insult for which she would never have forgiven him. A sigh broke from her, and her warm breath against his mouth inflamed him more. He deepened the kiss with his tongue, seeking her response, sensing it, driven wild by it.

Her arms seemed to move of their own accord, gliding up around his neck, holding, drawing his head fiercely against hers, sending him a message with her lips and tongue.

But suddenly he drew back as though forcing himself with a great effort.

'Tell me to stop,' he growled. 'Tell me. Let me hear you say it.'

'How can I?' she said huskily. 'You never took orders from me.'

'You never needed to give me orders. I did what you wanted without you having to say it.'

'You were always so sure you knew what I wanted,' she murmured, looking up with teasing eyes that were as provocative as she meant them to be.

'You never complained.'

'Perhaps I was afraid of you.'

'You?' he echoed in a voice that was almost savage. 'Afraid of *me?'*

'Perhaps I'm afraid of you now. I'm in your power, aren't I?'

'Then tell me to stop,' he repeated with grim emphasis.

For answer she gave him a smile that tested his self control to the limit. She felt the tremor go through him, and smiled again.

'Tell me to stop!' he said desperately.

'Do *you* think you should stop?' she whispered.

'Damn you! *Damn you!'*

His hands were moving feverishly, finding the buttons of her pyjamas, wrenching them open, tossing the puritanical jacket aside. He touched her breasts with his fingers, then his lips, groaning softly so that his warm breath whispered over her skin, sending a frisson of delight through her.

She was aware of him moving towards the bedroom, taking her with him, but then all sensations merged until she felt the bed beneath her. He raised his head to gaze down at her and she instinctively began to work on his buttons, ripping them open even faster than he had ripped hers.

It was dark in this room and all they could see of each other was their eyes, fierce and gleaming with mutual desire. And then the moment came. After so many years they were one again, moving in a perfect physical harmony that defied their antagonism. The old memories were still alive, how to please each other, inflame each other, challenge, defy, infuriate each other. And then how to lie quietly in each other's arms, feeling the roar die away, leaving only fulfilment behind.

She could barely make out his features, but she sensed his confusion. For once in his life, Marcel was lost for words. She gave him a reassuring smile.

'Would you really have stopped if I'd asked you?' she murmured.

A long silence.

'Let's just say…I'm glad you didn't ask me,' he said at last, slowly.

She waited for him to say more. Whatever the past, they had suddenly discovered a new road that could lead back to each other. Surely now he would have words of tenderness for her?

Full of hope, she reached out, brushing her fingertips against his face.

But he drew back sharply, stared at her for a moment, then rose from the bed like a man fleeing the devil.

'No,' he said softly, then violently, *'no!'*

'Marcel—'

'No!' he repeated, then gave a sudden bitter laugh. 'Oh, *mon dieu!*' He laughed again, but there was no humour in it, only a grating edge.

'Look at me. How easily I…well done, Cassie. You won the first battle. I'll win the others but it's the first one that counts, isn't it? Did you hear me on the dance floor tonight, saying I waited for no woman? That has to be the biggest and stupidest piece of self deception of all time. All those years ago I waited for you—waited and waited, certain that you would come in the end because my Cassie loved me. Waited… waited…' He broke off with a shudder.

So the past couldn't be dealt with so easily, she thought. She must tell him everything, help him to understand that she'd had no choice but to save him from harm. But surely it would be easier now?

'Marcel, listen to me. I must tell you—'

But he couldn't hear her. He'd leapt up and was pacing about, talking frantically, lost in another world. Or perhaps trapped in a cage.

'Once I wouldn't have believed it possible to despise anyone as I've despised you. In those days I loved you more than my life, more than—' He stopped and a violent tremor went through him. 'Never mind that,' he said harshly.

'I guess you don't want to remember that we loved each other.'

'I said never mind,' he shouted. 'And don't talk about "each other". There was no love on your side, or you could never have done what you did.'

'You don't know what I did,' she cried.

'I know that I lay for days in the hospital, longing to see you. I was delirious, dreaming of you, certain that the next time I opened my eyes you'd be there. But you never were.

'I called your mobile phone but it was always switched off. The phone in your apartment was never answered. Tell me, Cassie, didn't you ever wonder why I vanished so suddenly? You never wanted to ask a single question?'

She stared. 'But I knew what had happened, that you'd had an accident and were in hospital. I told you that in my letter.'

'What letter?'

'I wrote, telling you everything, begging you to understand that it wasn't my fault. I put it through your door—I was sure you'd find it when you came home. Oh heavens! Do you mean—?'

'I never read any letter from you,' he said, and she was too distracted to notice how carefully he chose his words.

'Then you never knew that I was forced to leave you—I had no choice.'

He made a sound of impatience. 'Don't tell me things that a child couldn't believe. Of course there was a choice.'

'Not if I wanted you to live,' she cried. 'He said he'd kill you.'

'He? Who?'

'Jake Simpson.'

'Who the hell—?'

'I'd never heard of him either. He was a crook who knew how to keep his head down. People did what he wanted because they were scared of him. I wasn't scared at first. When he said he wanted me I told him to clear off. You were away at the time. I was going to tell you when you got home, but you had the accident. Only it wasn't an accident. Jake arranged it to warn me. He showed me a picture of you in hospital and said you'd die if I didn't drop you and turn to him. I couldn't even tell you what had happened because if I tried to visit you he'd know, and you'd have another "accident".

'I went with him because I had to. I didn't dare approach you, but I couldn't endure thinking of you believing that I'd played you false. In the end I wrote a letter and slipped it through your letter box. Obviously you never got it. Perhaps you'd already left by then. Oh, if only you could have read it. We'd still have been apart, but you'd have known that I didn't betray you, that I was forced to do what I did, and perhaps you wouldn't have hated me.'

She looked at him, standing quite still in the shadows.

'Or maybe you'd have hated me anyway. All these years—'

'Stop,' he said harshly. 'Don't say any more.'

'No, well, I guess there's no more to say. If I could turn back the clock I'd put that letter into your hands and make you read it and then perhaps I wouldn't have been such a monster in your heart—'

'I said stop!' he shouted.

She came to a sudden resolution. Reaching up from where she was sitting on the bed, she took his hand and urged him down until he was sitting beside her.

'You don't know whether to believe me or not, do you? Everything about us is different—except for one thing. Very well. If that's the only way I can make you listen to me, then that's the way I'll take.'

'Meaning?'

'You've implied that I'm a bad woman who'll use her physical charms to get her way with you. Well, maybe you're right. After all, I know now that I can do it, don't I?'

'What are you saying?'

'That I'll do what I have to. Maybe you know me better than I know myself. Perhaps I really am that unscrupulous. Maybe I'll enjoy it. Maybe we both will.'

As she spoke she was touching his face. She knew she was taking a huge risk, but there was no other way. At all costs she would soften him, drive the hostility from his eyes.

To her relief she could feel him softening, feel the hostile tension drain from him, replaced by a different kind of tension.

'Hold me,' she whispered.

He did so, reaching for her, drawing her down to stretch out on the bed, or letting her draw him down. Neither of them really knew.

Their first encounter had been entirely sexual. This one was on a different plane. No words were spoken, but none were needed. In each other's arms they seemed to find again the things that had been missing the first time—sweetness, warmth, the joy of the heart.

Afterwards they held each other with gentle hands.

'We'll get there,' she promised. 'We'll find a way, my darling, I promise we will.'

He didn't reply, and she suddenly became aware that his breathing was deep and steady. She turned her head, the better to see his face, and gave a tender smile as she saw him sunk in sleep.

It had always been this way, she remembered. He would love her with all the power and vigour of a great man, then fall asleep like a child.

'That's right, you sleep,' she murmured. 'Sleep and I'll take care of everything.'

Slowly her smile changed. Now it was one of triumph.

In the twilight world that came just before awakening she relived a dream. So many times she'd fallen asleep in his arms, knowing that he would still be there in the morning. Sometimes she'd opened her eyes to find him looking down at her adoringly. At other times he would be sunk in sleep, but always reaching for her, even if only with his fingertips. It was as though he could only relax with the assurance of her presence.

And me, she thought hazily, *knowing he would be there meant that life was good.*

She opened her eyes.

She was alone.

He was gone.

She sat up, looking around frantically, certain that there was some mistake. The room was empty. Hurrying out of bed, she searched all the rooms but there was no sign of him. Marcel had stolen away while she slept.

But he'd vowed to keep her a prisoner. The outer door would be locked.

It wasn't. It yielded at once and she found herself looking out into an empty corridor. Something about the silence was frightening.

She slammed the door and leaned back against it, refusing to believe that this could have happened. Last night they'd found each other again, not totally but enough for hope. They should have spent today talking, repairing the past. Instead he'd walked out.

But he might have fled through caution, she thought. Don't judge him until you've spoken to him.

She dressed carefully. Cassie or Mrs Henshaw today?

Finally she settled on a mixture, restrained clothing as befitted her job, but with her hair flowing freely. He would understand. A quick breakfast and she was ready to face whatever the challenge was.

The door to Marcel's apartment was opened by a middle-aged woman with a friendly face.

'*Bonjour.* I am Vera, Marcel's secretary. He has left me instructions to be of service to you.'

'Left you—? Isn't he here?'

'He had to leave suddenly. For what reason he did not say. I'm a little surprised because he has so much to do, and he didn't even tell me where he was going.'

So that was that. He was snubbing her, escaping to some place where she couldn't follow. Perhaps she should simply take the hint and leave, but that seemed too much like giving in without a fight. How he would triumph if he returned to find her gone. Grimly she settled down to work.

CHAPTER EIGHT

LAURA Degrande had settled contentedly in a small house in the suburbs of Paris. It wasn't a wealthy district, but she always said life was better without wealth. Her marriage to Amos Falcon had not been happy, and the only good thing to come from it was her son, Marcel. He would have kept her in luxury, but she refused, accepting an allowance that was comfortable, but no more, despite his indignant protests. It was the only blot on their otherwise affectionate relationship.

Her face lit up when he appeared at her door.

'My darling, how lovely to see you. I was thrilled to get your call this morning. What is it that's so urgent?'

Hugging her, Marcel said, 'I need to look through some old stuff that you stored for me.'

'Have you lost something?'

'You might say that. Are the bags where I left them?'

'Still in the attic.'

'See you later.'

He hurried up the stairs before she could answer, and shut himself away in the little room, where he began to pull open bags and boxes, tossing them aside when they didn't contain what he wanted. When Laura looked in he turned a haggard face towards her.

'There's something missing—a big grey envelope—I left it here—it's gone—'

'Oh, that. Yes, I found it but there was only rubbish inside, shreds of paper that you'd obviously torn up. I thought they should be thrown out.'

'What?' The sound that broke from him was a roar of anguish. His face was haggard, desperate. 'You threw it out?'

'No, calm down. I thought about it but then I remembered what you're like about not throwing things away. So I stored them safely—up here on this shelf. Yes, here's the envelope.'

He almost snatched it from her with a choking, 'Thank you!'

Laura left the room quickly, knowing that something desperately important had happened, and he needed to be alone to cope with it.

Marcel wrenched open the envelope and a load of small bits of paper cascaded onto the floor. Frantically he gathered them up, found a small table and began to piece them together. It was hard because his hands were shaking, and the paper had been torn into tiny shreds.

As he worked he could see himself again, on that night long ago, tearing, tearing, desperate with hate and misery.

He'd left the hospital as soon as he was strong enough, and gone straight to Cassie's home. The lights were out and he knew the worst as soon as he arrived, but he still banged on the door, crying her name, banging more desperately.

'You're wasting your time,' said a voice behind him. 'She's gone.'

Behind him stood a middle-aged man who Marcel knew vaguely. He was usually grumpy, but today he seemed pleased at the bad news he was imparting.

'Gone where?' Marcel demanded.

A shrug. 'How do I know? She packed up and left days ago. I saw her get into a posh car. Bloke who owned it must be a millionaire, so I reckon that's finished you. She saw sense at last.'

Seeing Marcel's face, he retreated hastily.

At first he refused to believe it, banging on the door again and screaming her name, until at last even he had to accept the truth. She'd gone without a backward glance.

He didn't remember the journey home, except that he sat drinking in the back of the taxi until he tumbled out onto the pavement and staggered into the building.

On the mat he found an envelope, with his name in Cassie's handwriting. The sight had been enough to make him explode with drunken rage and misery, tearing it, tearing, tearing, tearing—until only shreds were left.

He'd left England next morning. At the airport he'd had a brief glimpse of Cassie, dressed up to the nines, in the company of a man who clearly had money coming out of his ears. That sight answered all his questions. He'd screamed abuse, and fled.

In Paris he'd taken refuge in his mother's home, collapsing and letting her care for him. When he unpacked it was actually a surprise to discover that he'd brought Cassie's letter, although in shreds. He had no memory of putting it into his bag.

Now was the time to destroy it finally, but he hesitated. Better to keep it, and read it one day, years ahead. When he was an old man, ruling a financial empire, with an expensive wife and a gang of children, then he would read the whore's miserable excuses.

And laugh.

How he would laugh! He'd laugh as violently as he was weeping now.

When at last he could control his sobs he took the bits of paper to his room, stuffed them into an envelope and put it in a drawer by his bed. There it had stayed until he'd moved out. Then he'd hidden it away in the little attic, asking his mother to be sure never to touch his things.

As the years passed he'd sometimes thought of the day that would come when he could read her pathetic words and jeer at her memory. Now that day was here.

He worked feverishly, fixing the pieces together. But gradually his tension increased. Something was wrong. No, it was impossible. Be patient! It would come right.

But at last he could no longer delude himself. With every tiny wisp of paper scrutinised to no avail, with every last chance gone, he slammed his fist into the wall again and again.

When there was no word, and her calls went unanswered, Cassie came to a final reluctant decision. As she packed she chided herself for imagining that things could ever have been different. Her flesh was still warm from their encounters the night before, but she should never have fooled herself.

He was punishing her by abandoning her in the way he felt she'd abandoned him. The generous person he'd once been would never have taken such cruel, carefully thought out vengeance, but now he was a different man, one she didn't know.

She called the airport and booked herself onto the evening flight to London. There! It was done.

'You are leaving?' asked Vera, who'd been listening.

'Yes, I have to. Would you please give this to Marcel?' She handed over a sealed envelope. Inside was a small piece of paper, on which she'd written: *It's better this way. I'm sure you agree. Cassie.'*

'Can't you wait just a little?' Vera begged.

'No, I've stayed too long already.'

Take-off was not for three hours but she felt an urgent need to get away at once. She took a taxi to the airport and sat, trying not to brood. She should never have come to this place, never dreamed that the terrible wrongs of the past could be

put right. How triumphant he would feel, knowing his snub
had driven her away! How glad he would be to be rid of her!

At last it was time to check in. She rose and joined the
queue. She had almost reached the front when a yell rent the
air.

'Cassie!'

Everyone looked up to see the man standing at the top
of a flight of stairs, but he saw none of them. His eyes were
fixed only on her as he hurled himself down at breakneck
speed and ran to her so fast that he had to seize her in order
to steady himself.

'What do you think you're doing?' he demanded frantically.

'I'm going home.'

'You're staying here.'

'Let go of me.'

'No!' He was holding her in an unbreakable grip. 'You
can either agree to come back with me, or we can fight it out
right here and now. Which?'

'You're impossible!'

'It took you ten years to discover that? I thought you were
clever. Yes or no?'

'All right—yes.'

'Good. Is this yours?' He lifted her suitcase with one hand
while still holding her wrist with the other. Plainly he was
taking no chances.

In this awkward fashion they made it out of the building
to where the car from La Couronne was waiting for them.
While the chauffeur loaded the suitcase Marcel guided her
into the back and drew the glass partition across, isolating
them. As the car sped through the Paris traffic he kept hold
of her hand.

'There's no need to grip me so tightly,' she said. 'I'm hardly
going to jump out here.'

'I'm taking no chances. You could vanish at any time. You've done it twice, you won't do it to me again. You can count on that.'

'I went because you made it so obvious that you wanted to be rid of me.'

'Are you mad?' he demanded.

'I'm not the one who vanished into thin air. When a woman awakes to find the man gone in the morning that's a pretty clear message.'

'Tell me about vanishing into thin air,' he growled. 'You're the expert.'

'I left a note with Vera—'

'I didn't mean today.' The words came out as a cry of pain, and she cursed herself for stupidity.

'No, I guess not. I'm sorry. So when you left this morning, that was your way of paying me back?'

'I went because I had to, but…things happened. I never meant to stay away so long. When I got back and Vera told me you'd left for England I couldn't believe it. I tried to call you but you'd turned your phone off—*like last time.*'

She drew a sharp breath. Something in his voice, his eyes, revealed all his suffering as no mere words could have done.

'But why did you have to dash off?' she asked.

'To read the letter you wrote me ten years ago.'

'But you said you never got it.'

'No, I said I never read it. I was so blazing mad I tore it up without reading it.'

'Then how could you read it now?'

'Because I kept it,' he said savagely. 'Fool that I am, I kept it.'

She could hardly believe her ears. 'And you never—in all these years—?'

'No, I never read it. But neither did I throw it away. Today I went to my mother's home where it's been stored, meaning to fit it together. But it isn't all there. Some of the pieces are lost. I came straight back to find you, and you were gone. Vera heard you booking the flight so I had to act fast.'

'You only just got there in time,' she murmured.

'Well, actually—I have a friend who works in airport security. I called him. You wouldn't have been allowed to get on that plane.'

'*What?* You actually dared—?'

'I couldn't risk you getting away. It's too important.'

'And suppose I want to get away?'

He looked at her in silence. Words could never have said so clearly that what she wanted played no part in this. This was a man driven by demons that were too strong for him, and perhaps also for her.

'So you want me to explain the missing pieces?' she guessed.

'If you can remember them.'

'Oh, yes,' she murmured. 'I can remember everything.'

They had reached La Couronne. Marcel hurried her inside, his hand still on her arm. Several people tried to attract his attention, but he never saw them. Only one thing mattered now.

As soon as they were inside his apartment he locked the door. She almost told him there was no need, but then kept silent. Marcel was in the grip of an obsession and she, of all people, couldn't say it was irrational. She knew a burst of pity for him, standing on the edge of a dangerous pit. If he fell into its fearsome depths, wouldn't she be at least partly to blame?

He held out the letter, where she could see tiny scraps stuck onto a base sheet, but with gaping holes.

'Do you recognise this?' he demanded.

'Yes, of course.'

He thrust it into her hands and turned away. 'Read it to me.'

It felt weird to see the words over which she'd struggled so hard and wept so many tears. She began to read aloud.

"'My darling, beloved Marcel, you will wonder why I didn't come to you when you were in pain and trouble, but I didn't dare. What happened wasn't an accident. It was done on purpose by a man who wants to claim me for himself. I refused him, and—'" She stopped. 'There's a gap here.'

'What are the missing words?' he asked.

She closed her eyes, travelling back to the past. *"'He hurt you, to show me what would happen if I didn't give in,'"* she said slowly. She opened her eyes.

'Then the letter goes on, *"I couldn't risk coming to you in the hospital because he would have known and he might kill you. I'm delivering this through your door, because it's the only way I can think of that he won't find out. I hope and pray that it will be safe. I couldn't bear it if you believed I'd just walked away, or stopped loving you."* Then there's another gap.'

'Do you know what's missing?' When she didn't answer he turned and repeated harshly, 'Do you?'

'Yes. I said—*"'I will never stop loving you, until the very end of my days, but this is the last time I can ever say so.'"* The signature is still there if you want to read it.

'I don't need to read it,' he said quietly, and recited, *'Your very own Cassie, yours forever, however long "forever" may last.'* I don't suppose you remember writing that.'

'Yes, I remember writing every word, even the ones that aren't here any more.'

"'I will never stop loving you until the very end of my days,'" he repeated. 'You're sure you wrote that?'

'Yes, I'm quite sure. But even if you doubt me, the rest of the letter is there. I told you what had happened and why I had to leave you. If only you'd read it then, you'd have known that I still loved you—oh, Marcel—all these years!'

'Don't,' he begged, shuddering. 'If I think of that I'll go mad.'

'I'm surprised we haven't both gone mad long before this. And it was all so unnecessary.'

'Yes, if I'd read this then—'

'No, I mean more than that. There's another reason the last ten years could have been avoided.' She broke off, heaving.

'What do you mean?' he demanded.

She raised fierce eyes to his face.

'I mean that you played your part in what happened to us. It could all have been so different if only you'd been honest with me. Why didn't you tell me who you were, who your father was? We need never have been driven apart.'

He stared. 'What difference—?'

Her temper was rising fast. 'If I'd known you were the son of Amos Falcon I'd have gone to him for help. He's a powerful man. When he heard what Jake had done he would have dealt with him, had him arrested, sent to jail. We'd have been safe.

'Everything since then could have been different. You'd have been spared all that suffering and disillusion. I'd have been spared that terrible time with Jake. So much misery because you had to play a silly game.'

He tore his hair. 'I was just…I didn't want you to know I came from a rich family.'

'Because you thought I'd be too interested in your money. Charming!'

'No, because you thought I was poor and you chose me over your rich admirers. That meant the world to me—'

'Yes, but there was a high price, and you weren't the only one who paid it. You spoke of hating me, but I could hate *you* for what you did to my life with your juvenile games. When I found out the truth recently I…I just couldn't…so much misery, and so needless—*aaaargh!*'

The last word was a scream that seemed to tear itself from her body without her meaning it. It was followed by another, and another, and now she couldn't stop screaming.

'Cassie!' he tried, reaching for her. *'Cassie!'*

'Get away from me,' she screamed. 'Don't touch me. *I hate you.*'

He wouldn't let her fight him off, drawing her closer until her face was against his shoulder, murmuring in her ear, 'That's right, hate me. I deserve it. Hate me, hate me.'

'Yes,' she wept.

'I'm a damned fool and you suffered for it. Call me every name you can think of. Hit me if you like.' He drew back so that she could see his face. 'It's no more than I deserve. Go on, I won't stop you.'

She couldn't speak, just shook her head while the tears ran down her cheeks. Then she was back in his arms, held against him, feeling him pick her up, kick open a door and lay her down on a soft bed.

But this was no love-making. Lying beside her, he held her gently, murmuring soothing words, stroking her hair. Her efforts to stop weeping were in vain, and he seemed to understand this because he murmured, 'Go on, cry it out. Don't try to hold back.'

'All those wasted years,' she choked.

'Years when we could have been together,' he agreed, 'loving each other, making each other happy, having children. All gone because I was a conceited oaf.'

'No, you weren't,' she managed to say. 'You were just young—'

'Young and stupid,' he supplied. 'Not thinking of anyone but myself, imagining I could play games without people being hurt—'

'Don't be so hard on yourself,' she said huskily.

'Why not? It's true. I did it. My silly pretence meant you

couldn't seek my father's help and, even after that, if I'd only read your letter I—*imbécile, stupide!*'

'Marcel,' she wept, 'Marcel—'

Distress choked her again, but now it was the same with him. She could feel his body heaving, his arms around her as hers were around him.

'I did it,' he sobbed. 'I did it. It's all my fault.'

'No…no…' She tightened her embrace, tenderly stroking his head as a mother might have done with a child.

'Ten years,' he gasped. 'Ten years! Where did they go? How can we get them back?'

'We can't,' she said. 'What's done can never be undone.'

'I don't believe that!'

'Marcel, you can't turn the clock back; it isn't possible. We can only go on from here.'

He didn't reply in words, but she felt his arms tighten, as though he feared that she might slip away again.

Go on where? said the voice in her head. *And what do you mean by 'we'? Who are you? Who is he now?*

She silenced the voice. She had no answer to those troublesome questions. Everything she'd suffered, the lessons learned in the last ten years, all the confusion and despair, were uniting to cry with a thousand voices that from this moment nothing would be simple, nothing easy, and it might all end in more heartbreak.

It was a relief to realise that he was relaxing into sleep in her arms, as though in her he found the only true comfort. She stroked him some more, murmuring soft words in his ear. 'Sleep, my darling. We'll find a way. I only wish I knew…I wish I knew…'

But then sleep came to her rescue too, and the words faded into nothing.

It was dark when she awoke and the illuminated clock by the bed told her they had dozed for barely an hour. Careful not to awaken Marcel, she eased away and sat on the side of the bed, dropping her head into her hands, feeling drained.

The concerns that had worried her before were even stronger now. Their tumultuous discoveries could bring great happiness, or great despair. They had found each other again, and perhaps the troubles of the past could be made right. But it was too soon to be sure, and she had a strange sensation of watching everything from a distance.

She walked over to the window, looking out on the dazzling view. Paris was a blaze of light against the darkness.

'Are you all right?' came his voice from behind her.

'Yes, I'm fine,' she said quickly.

He came up behind her and she felt his hands on her shoulders. 'Are you sure? You seem very troubled.'

How had he divined that merely from her back view? she wondered. How and where had he gained such insight?

'What are you thinking?' he asked softly.

'I don't know. My thoughts come and go so quickly I can't keep up with them.'

'Me too,' he agreed. 'We must have many long talks.'

'But not now,' she said. 'I feel as though I'm choking. I need to go out into the fresh air.'

'Fine, let's go for a walk.'

'No, I have to be alone.'

'Cassie—'

'It's all right, I won't vanish again. I'll return, I promise.'

'It's dark,' he persisted. 'Do you know how late it is?'

'I have to do this,' she said in a tense voice. 'Please, Marcel, don't try to stop me.'

He was silent and she sensed his struggle. But at last he sighed and stood back to let her pass.

Without even going to her own apartment, she hurried directly down to the entrance. The hotel was close to the River Seine, and by following the signs she was able to find the way to the water. Here she could stand looking down at the little ripples, glittering through the darkness, and listen to the sounds of the city. Late as it was, Paris was still alive. Far in the distance she could see the Eiffel Tower reaching up into the heavens.

She turned around slowly and that was when she saw the man, fifty yards away along the embankment, standing quite still, watching her. At first she thought he was a stalker, but then she recognised him. Marcel.

When she began to walk towards him he backed away. When she turned and moved off he followed.

'Marcel,' she called. 'What do you think you're doing?'

At last he drew close enough for her to see a slightly sheepish look on his face.

'I was just concerned for your safety,' he responded. 'I'll keep my distance, and leave you in peace. But I'll always be there if you need me.'

Her annoyance died and she managed a shaky laugh. 'My guardian angel, huh?'

'That has to be the first time anyone's mistaken me for an angel,' he said wryly.

'Why do I find that so easy to believe? All right, you can stay.'

Recently she had forgotten how much charm he had when he was set on getting his own way. Suddenly she was remembering.

He completed the effect by taking two small wine bottles from his pockets and handing her one. 'Let's sit down,' he said.

She did so and drank the wine thankfully.

'It's a lot to take in all at once, isn't it?' he said.

'Yes, I guess so.'

'These last few years must have been terrible for you. The

man who had me run down—was that the man I saw you with at the airport?'

'Yes, that was Jake. I'd spent the previous few days at his house, "entertaining him" as he put it.'

'You don't need to say any more,' Marcel said in a strained voice.

'No, I guess not.

'We were travelling to America that day. After he'd seen you he kept on and on at me, demanding to know if I'd been in touch with you. I swore I hadn't, and in the end he believed me because he said if you'd known the truth you wouldn't have called me "Whore".

'I didn't know what to believe. I thought perhaps you'd read my letter and were pretending, or maybe you hadn't been home yet and would get it later. But I told Jake that he must be right about that.' She gave a wry smile. 'It was always wise to tell Jake he was right. He'd already destroyed my cellphone so that nobody could get in touch with me.'

'So you were his prisoner?' he said, aghast. 'All that time you were suffering and I did nothing to help you.'

'How could you? I must admit that I did hope for a while, but in the end I realised you'd accepted our parting and that was the end. So I married him.'

'You married him?'

'Why not? I felt my life was over. I just went with the tide. When I found he'd been fooling around with other women it gave me the weapon I needed to divorce him. Suddenly I wasn't afraid of him any more. I accepted some money from him because I had people who needed it, but I didn't keep any for myself. I didn't want anything from him, even his name. I used Henshaw because it was my mother's maiden name.'

'What's happened to him since? Does he trouble you?'

'He's in jail at the moment, for several years, hopefully. I told you how I took business courses after that, and started on the life I live now.' She raised her wine bottle to the moon. 'Independence every time. Cheers!'

'Independence or isolation?' he asked.

She shrugged. 'Does it matter? Either way, it's better to rely on yourself.'

He sighed. 'I guess so.'

He was glad she couldn't see his face, lest his thoughts showed. He was remembering one night, a lifetime ago, when she'd endured a bad day at work and thrown herself into his arms.

'What would I do without you?' she'd sighed. 'That rotten photographer—goodness, but he's nasty! Never mind. I can put up with anything as long as I know I have you—'

'And you'll always have me,' he'd assured her.

Three weeks later, the disaster had separated them.

'Better rely on yourself,' he repeated, 'rather than on a fool who thought it was funny to conceal his real background, and plunged you both into tragedy.'

'Hey, I wasn't getting at you. Nobody knows what's just around the corner.' She laughed. 'After all, we never saw this coming, did we?'

'And you'd have run a mile if you'd known. I remember you saying so.' He waited for her answer. It didn't come. 'How long ago since your divorce?' he asked.

'About five years. Since then I've been Mrs Henshaw, bestriding the financial world. It suits me. Remember you used to joke about my having a great brain?'

'It wasn't entirely a joke. I think I was a bit jealous of the way you could read something once and remember it like it was set in stone.'

'There now, I told you I was made to be a businesswoman.'

'But that's not your only talent. Why didn't you go back to modelling? You're still beautiful.'

'Not really.'

'I say you are,' he said fiercely.

'I won't argue about it. But it takes more than beauty and I've lost something special. I know that. I knew it then. I'd look in the mirror and see that a light had gone out inside me. Besides,' she hurried on before he could protest, 'I wanted to try something new. It was my choice. Life moves on, we don't stay in the same place.

'Cassie was one person. Mrs Henshaw is another. I became quite pleased with her. She takes people by surprise. Some of them are even scared of her.'

'And you like people being scared of you?'

'Not all the time, but it has its uses. She's a bright lady is Mrs Henshaw. Lots of common sense.'

'Now you're scaring *me*.'

'Good.'

'So I've got to get used to Mrs Henshaw hanging around, when the one I want is Cassie?'

'I'm not sure that's a wise choice. Mrs Henshaw has to get that hotel set up. You need her expertise, her "great brain". Cassie wouldn't be up to the job.'

She managed to say it in a teasing tone, and he managed a smile in reply. But they both knew that she was conveying a subtle warning.

Go slowly. Don't rush it. A false step could mean disaster.

'I think we should go back now,' she said.

She rose and offered him her hand. He hesitated only a moment before nodding and taking it. In this way, with him following her lead, they strolled back to the hotel.

CHAPTER NINE

SHE slept alone that night. Marcel kissed her at the door, touched her face with his fingertips and hurried away. She smiled at his retreating figure, glad that he had the sensitivity not to try to overwhelm her with passion at this moment.

After everything that had happened, all the unexpected revelations, the business of deciding her appearance next morning was a minefield. In the end she selected clothes that were respectable rather than forbidding, and wore her hair drawn back, but not scraped tightly, so that it framed her face softly before vanishing over her shoulders.

When she entered the office he was deep in a phone call, his manner agitated. He waved for her to come in, then turned away. He was talking French but she managed to make out that he was about to go away. The idea didn't seem to please him, for he slammed down the phone and snapped, '*Imbécile! Idiot!*'

'Somebody let you down?' she asked.

'Yes, he's made a mess of a deal I trusted to him, and now I have to go and rescue it. It'll take a few days. Come here!' He hugged her fiercely. 'I don't want to leave you. You should come with me and—'

'No,' she said firmly. 'I'd be a distraction and you've got to keep your mind on business.'

'I'd planned such a day for us. I was going to take you over Paris—'

'Paris will still be here when you get back.' She added significantly, 'And so will I.'

His brow darkened. 'Your word of honour?'

'I told you, I have no reason to leave now.'

Reluctantly he departed, giving her one last anxious look from the door. She saw him go with regret, yet also with a faint twinge of relief. His possessiveness was like a reproach to her. She couldn't blame him for it, but she sensed that it could be a problem, one to which he was blind.

Knowing herself better than Marcel could, she sensed that Mrs Henshaw was more than just an outward change. Her businesslike appearance really did represent a certain reality inside. For the moment Cassie and Mrs Henshaw must live side by side, each one taking the spotlight according to need. But which one of them would finally emerge as her true self? Even she could not be certain about that.

She'd hinted as much to Marcel the previous evening, but she knew he didn't really understand. Or perhaps didn't want to understand. That was the thought that made her a little uneasy.

For the next few days she was Mrs Henshaw, deep in business and thoroughly enjoying herself. Vera introduced her to the chief members of the staff, who had clearly been instructed to cooperate with her. She went through the books and knew she was impressing them with her knowledge of finance.

Then there were the builders who had renovated and extended La Couronne, and who spoke to her at Marcel's command. The more she listened, the more she understood what he'd been trying to do, how well he'd succeeded, and what he wanted in London. Ideas began to flower inside her. She would have much to tell him when he returned on Thursday.

He called her several times a day on the hotel's landline. Wryly she realised that in this way he could check that she was there. Just once he called her cellphone, and that was when she was out shopping. He managed to sound cheerful but she sensed the underlying tension, especially when he said, 'Don't be long getting back to the hotel. There's a lot to do.'

'I'm on my way back now,' she assured him.

Vera greeted her in a flurry of nerves. 'He was very upset when he called and found you not here,' she said.

'Don't worry; he tried my cellphone and I answered at once.' She added reassuringly, 'So when he calls, you can tell him that I'm not slacking on the job.'

Not wanting to embarrass the secretary, whom she liked, she got straight back to work. A few minutes later Vera's phone rang and she shut the door to answer it discreetly.

Poor Marcel, Cassie thought. *I suppose I can't blame him for expecting me to vanish in a puff of smoke. He'll understand, in time.*

By now everyone knew who she was, and the power she possessed, and they would scurry to give her only the best. On Wednesday evening the cook and head waiter joined her at the table for a few minutes, urging her to try new dishes.

They were both attractive men, middle-aged but with appreciative eyes, and they enjoyed talking to her about Paris, which they insisted on calling 'the city of love'.

'You work too hard, *madame,*' the cook told her. 'You should be out there exploring this magical place, becoming imbued with its spirit. Then you would know what to do for the hotel in London.'

'I'm afraid London lacks Paris's air of romance,' she mourned, and they solemnly agreed with her.

Once, long ago, Marcel had whispered in the night, 'I will take you to Paris and show you my city. We will walk the streets together, and you will breathe in the atmosphere of love that is to be found nowhere else.'

'You sound like a guidebook,' she'd complained.

'Actually, I got it out of a guidebook,' he'd admitted sheepishly.

She began to laugh, and he'd joined her. They had clung together, rocking back and forth in bed until the laughter ended in passionate silence, the way everything seemed to end in those days.

He never did take me to Paris, she thought now, sadly. And it would have been so wonderful.

Suddenly he seemed to be there in front of her, laughing joyfully as he'd done in his carefree youth, before cares had fallen on him in a cruel deluge.

'Ah, Monsieur Falcon,' the waiter called. 'How nice to see you back.'

She blinked in disbelief. It wasn't a fantasy. He really was there, standing before her, as though he'd risen from her dreams.

'Good evening,' he said cheerfully. 'I needn't ask if you've missed me. Clearly you haven't.'

'I've been so well looked after that I've barely noticed you were gone,' she teased.

His employees greeted him respectfully before rising from the table and leaving them alone.

'Come with me,' he said, drawing her to her feet.

'But the chef has spent hours preparing—'

'I said come *on.*'

He was laughing but also totally serious, she realised, as she felt herself drawn across the floor and out of the restaurant.

'Where are we going?' she asked breathlessly.

'Wait and see. *Taxi!*'

When they were settled in the back seat she said, 'You weren't supposed to come back until tomorrow.'

'Sorry to disappoint you. Shall I go away again?'

'No, I think I can just about put up with you. Hey, what are you doing?'

'What do you think? Come here.'

'Mmmmmmm!'

Suddenly the boy she'd loved long ago was in her arms again, banishing the severe man he'd become. Eventually that might prove unrealistic, but right now she was too delighted to care about anything else.

Especially being realistic.

'Where are we going?' she asked when she could breathe again.

'Sightseeing. Look.'

Gazing out, she could see that they were driving along the River Seine, with the Eiffel Tower growing closer and closer, until at last they turned over a bridge, heading across the water, straight to the Tower. There they took the elevator up higher and higher, to a restaurant more than four hundred feet above the ground, where he led her to a table by the window.

From here it seemed as if all Paris was laid out for her delight, glittering lights against the darkness, stretching into infinity. She regarded it in awed silence.

'I think it's the most beautiful thing I've ever seen,' she whispered.

'We dreamed of coming here. Do you remember?'

'Oh, yes, I remember.'

She didn't speak for a while, but gazed out, transfixed by the beauty.

'I've always wanted to come to Paris. I kept hoping that the next modelling job would take me there, but I was always unlucky.'

'So now I can show it to you, as I promised.'

'And every girl in Paris will envy me the attention of Marcel Falcon, famous for his harem.'

'Nonsense!'

'It's not.' She chuckled. 'After we met that first night I researched you online, and discovered a lot of interesting things.'

'Don't believe everything you read,' he said wryly.

'Oh, but I'd like to believe it. It was so fascinating. I looked in a web encyclopedia and the entry under "Personal Life" went on for ever. I couldn't keep up. Josie and Leyla, Myra, Ginette and—now, who was the other one? Just let me think.'

'All right,' he growled, 'you've had your fun.'

'After what I read, I don't think you should lecture me about having fun. Tell me about that woman who—'

His scowl stopped her in her tracks. 'Have you finished?' he grunted.

'I've barely started.'

'What would you think of me if I'd had no social life?'

'That you were honest, virtuous, shining white—and the biggest bore in the world. Of course you've had women, lots of them. So you should.'

'Now you sound like my father.'

'I take it that's not a compliment. I only saw him for a moment that night in London, but I thought you seemed tense in his company. Do you dislike him?'

'Sometimes. Sometimes I admire him.'

'Not love him?'

'I don't think he's bothered whether anyone loves him or not. If he was he wouldn't alienate them as he does. All he really cares about is making people do what he wants.' Seeing her wry smile, he ground his teeth, 'OK, fine! Say it.'

'You have been known to want your own way,' she teased.

'And to go about getting it in a way that's—shall we say, cunning and determined?'

'If you mean cheating and bullying, why not say so?'

'I didn't want to insult you. Or would it be a compliment?'

'My father would certainly take it as a compliment. A chip off the old block, that's what he'd call me.'

'Were you at odds with him when you were living in London, that time?'

'I resented him, the person he was, the way he lived, the way he treated people. He seemed to think he could do exactly as he liked, and everyone would just have to put up with it. When I was a child I thought he and my mother were married. They seemed like a normal couple. He wasn't at home very much but I thought that was just because of his work. Then suddenly it all changed. It seemed he'd had a wife in England all the time. At last she'd found out about his other family and divorced him, taking Darius and Jackson.'

Cassie had heard some of this before, from Freya, but Marcel's own view of his colourful childhood had a new significance.

'So then my mother married him and we went to live in England. After a couple of years his first wife died and Darius and Jackson came to live with us.'

'That must have made for a tense situation.'

'It could have been, but Darius and I got on better than you might expect. We were both naturally rebellious and we used to team up against Amos, be co-conspirators, give each other alibis when necessary. I really missed the fun of being wicked together when it was all over.

'Of course the marriage didn't last. He got up to his old tricks and she was expected to put up with it because he was Amos Falcon, a man with enough money to do as he liked.'

'That would be enough to put you off money for life,' she mused.

'That's what I felt, disgust with him and everything he stood for. We found out about his other sons, Travis in America, and Leonid in Russia. I often saw my mother crying, and there were times when I did hate him. I might be his son but I wanted to be as different from him as possible.

'Mama and I came back to Paris and tried to forget him. But he wouldn't let us. He kept turning up on the doorstep. Once his property, always his property. Especially me. I was his son so I was bound to be like him. It was no use telling him that I didn't feel at all like him and didn't want to.'

He made a wry face. 'I guess he knew me better than I knew myself. I fooled around in London, pretending I wasn't connected with him, not using his name, but when the crash came I fled back to my mother in Paris. At first I told myself the future was open, all paths were open to me. I didn't have to take the one that led to Amos.

'But in the end I faced reality. There was only one road, and he stood at the end, waiting for me to admit the truth. I called him in Monte Carlo, where he was living for tax reasons. After that I took lessons in being Amos Falcon.' He assumed a flourishing air. 'I passed them with flying colours.'

'Or you think you did,' she said gently.

'What does that mean?'

'It means I don't think you're as like him as you believe.'

'Maybe. I'm not sure any more. I was certain in those days because I thought he and his way of life was all I had left in the world. Nothing mattered but money, so I went after it because it could fill all the gaping holes.'

'And did it?' she asked.

He shook his head. 'Nothing could. But I wouldn't face it. I told myself it was all your fault. Every bad thing that happened, every cruel disappointment was your fault. That was the only way I—' His hand tightened on his glass.

'Steady, you'll break it,' she said.

'If you only knew—'

'But I do. I had a bad time too, but I don't think I suffered as much as you did. I missed you and grieved for you, but I never had the pain of thinking you'd betrayed me.'

'Didn't you? After what I called you when I saw you at the airport? Didn't I betray you when I tore up that letter?'

'Marcel, stop it,' she said firmly. Taking his hands in hers, she went on, 'You mustn't obsess about that.'

'How can I help it? I could have made it right and I made a mess of everything. I could have spared us ten years of suffering. Why don't you blame me? Why don't you hate me?'

'Would that make you feel better?' she asked softly. 'Shall I beat you up and then say, "Fine, now we're even"?'

'It's what you ought to do.'

'Yes, but I never did do what I ought to do. You said so a hundred times. I never hated you, and if anything good comes out of this it will be that you won't hate me any more.'

'If anything good—? Can you doubt it?'

'I hope for a thousand good things, but we don't know what they are yet.'

'But surely we—?'

'We have to be patient. We're strangers to each other now.'

'You'll never be a stranger to me.'

'That's lovely, but it isn't true. It can't be. We know the people we used to be, but not the people we are now. We have to discover each other again before—'

'Before we can love each other? Don't you want us to?'

Before the intensity of his eyes she looked away. 'I don't know,' she admitted. 'It frightens me. I guess I'm just easily scared these days.' She clasped his hands again. 'I need a friend.'

'Friend,' he echoed, as though trying to believe what he'd heard.

'Someone who understands things that nobody else in the

world understands. Please, Marcel, be my friend. Be that first, and then maybe—if we're patient—and lucky—'

'You know what you're telling me, don't you? You can't love me and you don't want me to love you.'

'No!' she said fiercely. 'It isn't that. But I'm scared. Aren't you?'

'I wasn't before. I am now. I thought the other night—'

'The other night we found each other again, but only in one way. And—' she gave a reminiscent smile '—it was so lovely.'

'But not enough,' he said.

'Would it be enough for you, always? Won't there come a time when you're lying in my arms wondering if you can really trust me?'

He didn't answer, and she followed his thoughts. She'd hit a nerve, leaving him shocked and appalled at himself. He'd had as much as he could stand, she decided, and she must bring this to an end.

'I want to look at the view again,' she said, rising and going to the window. 'I've never seen such beauty.'

He made a suitable reply, and they left the dangerous subject behind. For the rest of the evening they kept carefully to indifferent subjects, presenting the appearance of a conventional couple, with no sign of the turbulence whirling inside them.

She knew that she must face the fact that there was a sad but crucial difference between them. With the truth finally revealed he'd become open to her, as though he was hers again. It was she who was holding back.

The feeling of detachment was painful. She longed to throw open her arms in welcome, vowing that everything was good again and all suffering would be forgotten. But the lessons of the past few years couldn't simply be unlearned. Most piercing of all was the fear of hurting him again.

Returning to the hotel, he saw her to her door but, to her relief, didn't try to come in. He'd read the signal she'd sent him and accepted it, however reluctantly. He would give her time, but his eyes told of his turmoil.

'I'll see you tomorrow, then,' he said. 'There are some figures we must go through. Goodnight.'

'Goodnight,' she whispered.

He touched her cheek, then departed quickly.

He had to be away several times in the next couple of weeks. When he returned they would dine together and talk, just as she'd hoped. On those evenings he kept his distance both physically and emotionally, making her wonder if he was following her lead or if he'd really decided against her. That thought filled her with irrational dismay.

You're mad, she told herself. *You don't know what you want.*

Which was true.

One afternoon, working together in his apartment, they had a bickering disagreement which threatened to turn into a quarrel. Afterwards she could never remember exactly what it had been about. Or if it had been about anything except the fact that a final separation might be looming.

'I should never have taken this job,' she sighed. 'Let's end it now. I'll go back to England and we need never see or think of each other again.'

'Do you imagine I'll allow that?'

'I don't think you could stop me leaving.'

'I could stop you any time I want to. You won't leave me, Cassie. I won't stand for it.'

'Don't,' she said harshly. 'That's the sort of thing Jake used to say. I can't bear it when you talk like him.'

He stared. 'Do I talk like him very often?'

'Sometimes. He regarded me as bought and paid for, and he made it plain.'

'And you think that's how I see you?'

'No, I—'

'Can't you understand that I still dread the thought of waking up to find you not there? I try to tell myself to be sensible but in that great echoing vacuum there's no sense, only horror. Every time you leave the room there's a voice in my head that says you won't come back. You fill my dreams but you also fill my nightmares.'

'Then perhaps you should let me go, and never think of me again.'

'And know that you'll never think of *me* again? That's the biggest nightmare of all. Sometimes I wish I had the strength to let you go, because then I might find peace. Not happiness, but peace. But I can't do it.'

She nodded. 'I know,' she said huskily. 'Me too.'

Now, she thought hopefully, they could talk and rediscover each other in yet another way. The road lay open before them.

But he seemed reluctant to take it, turning back to the computer screen.

Never mind, she thought. The chance would come again.

Next day Marcel announced that they needed to spend a few days in London.

'My purchase of the hotel isn't finalised yet and I'm getting impatient, so let's see if we can put some rockets under people. Vera, we'll need train tickets.'

'Train tickets?' his secretary echoed.

'That's what I said,' he called over his shoulder as he left the room.

'First time I've ever known him not take a plane,' Vera mused. 'I wonder why.'

Cassie thought she knew why and her heart was warmed by his concern for her, although when she tried to thank him he loftily brushed the matter aside as 'Pure convenience.'

'Of course,' she said, and kissed him.

This was the side of him she had loved, and for which she could feel the love creeping back. That might be dangerous while she was still unsure who this new man was, and how much of his old self still existed. But right now she was happy to take the risk.

Rather than leave it to Vera, she volunteered to book their hotel rooms.

'At the Crown Hotel,' she announced.

'Not The Crown yet,' Marcel pointed out. 'Until I sign the final papers it's still The Alton.'

'To them it's The Alton, to us it's The Crown,' she declared triumphantly. 'Everything's going to go right, and nothing will go wrong.'

'Yes,' he said with a smile that touched her heart. 'Nothing will go wrong. We won't let it.'

But he frowned when he saw the bookings she'd made.

'Separate rooms? Surely we could be together?'

'You're going to be the big boss. We need to preserve your dignity,' she said.

'If that means Mrs Henshaw in steel spectacles, forget it. I don't like that woman.'

'Then why did you hire her?'

'Because she didn't fool me. I want the real woman, the one she hides inside.'

'Unfortunately,' she murmured, 'it's Mrs Henshaw who's good with figures.'

He seemed struck by this. 'Ah, yes! Problem!'

Then someone came into the room and it could be passed off as a joke. But it lingered in her mind as a warning that troubles might lie ahead.

When they arrived in London Mrs Henshaw was at her most efficient, ironing out last minute problems, talking with bank managers and accountants. Marcel dominated the meetings, but whenever she spoke he listened intently, even admiringly. But afterwards he observed, to nobody in particular, 'I shall be glad when this is all over.'

There was an infuriating delay in the finance, owing to the bank demanding extra guarantees.

'Is this going to make it impossible?' she asked, seeing him gloomy.

'No, I can manage it, one way or another. I just don't want to have to ask my father's help. His fingers are in too many pies already.' He gave a slight shudder. 'Now come on, let's have some dinner.'

'Yes, let's see if I can cheer you up.'

'*You* can't,' he said, eyeing her 'Mrs Henshaw' appearance. 'But *she* could.'

'Mmm, I'll see if she's free tonight.'

'She'd better be.'

She wore her hair long, tumbling over her shoulders, and when they met for dinner in the restaurant he nodded approval.

'Will I pass?' she teased.

'You will, but we can't go on like this. It's like living with Jekyll and Hyde.'

'Really? So am I Dr Jekyll, middle-aged, scientific, brainy and kind? Or am I Mr Hyde, young and cruel?'

He sipped his wine for a moment before saying, 'Joking apart, it's more subtle than that. With Jekyll and Hyde you could always tell from the appearance. But with you I can't always tell. Whichever one you look like, the other one is always likely to pop out for a few moments, then dash back.'

'Yes, we exist side by side,' she agreed. 'Which may be confusing.'

'*May* be?'

'But why worry if ditzy Cassie sometimes has a great brain? There was a time when you knew that.'

'I know, I know. In those days—the great brain was just a part of you. I never dreamed it would take over your whole life in the form of Mrs Henshaw!'

'I know. But Mrs Henshaw was always there, lurking.'

'Yes, lurking, but now she's pounced. She's a bit alarming.'

'Maybe she wouldn't be if you knew her better,' she said, smiling.

This was the tone of the rest of the evening, light, easy, full of merriment and goodwill. She was happy, although still disturbed by a feeling that was half hope, half caution.

On the one hand there was the thoughtfulness that had made Marcel take the train for her sake. On the other hand was his reluctance to accept Mrs Henshaw as part of who she was. But that would sort itself out soon, she reassured herself.

In the meantime she was feeling exhausted. She'd worked through most of last night and all today, determined to stay on top of her duties. Now she would have given much to be able to sleep.

Hoping to liven herself up a little she took an extra glass of wine, and knew fairly soon that she'd made a mistake. If anything, she was woozier than before.

'I think I'll have an early night,' she said, and he rose at once, giving her his arm.

He followed her into her room and turned her towards him, looking down at her face with a questioning look. 'Are you all right?'

'Yes, just tired.'

'I'll say goodnight then.' He lifted her chin and laid his lips gently against hers.

Her head swam. The last time they had kissed there had been an edge of hostility, even violence, on her side as well as his. But now his touch was gentle, reminding her of happier times, and she responded with pleasure, although its edge was blunted by drowsiness.

'Cassie,' he murmured, 'Cassie…don't shut me out… please…'

'I don't…mean to…'

'Kiss me—I've waited for this so long and now…kiss me…'

She could feel the softness of the bed beneath her, his fingers opening her dress. Deep inside she sensed her own response, but waves of sleep washed over her brain.

Now, she thought, he would take what he pleased, knowing she was beyond resistance. She hadn't wanted it this way. Their next love-making should have been a union of hearts as well as bodies—not like this.

'Cassie—Cassie—*Cassie?*'

She opened her eyes, whispering, 'Marcel.'

His face was full of sudden suspicion. 'Are you entirely sober?'

'I…don't think so. I shouldn't have…oh. dear.'

His face tensed. He drew back and looked down at where her breasts were partially exposed, showing all the lushness that he'd always enjoyed. For a brief moment he let his fingertips linger on the swell, relishing the silky skin. His head drooped and she waited for the feel of his lips. But then he stiffened as though a bolt of lightning had gone through him. Next moment he'd practically hurled himself off the bed.

'Marcel—' she whispered.

He was breathing hard. 'Goodnight.'

He yanked at the duvet and threw it over her so that he could no longer see the glorious temptation, and moved towards the door.

'You're going?' she asked vaguely.

'Of course I'm going,' he answered. 'You really think I'm

going to—when you don't really know what you're doing? A fine opinion you have of me. Goodnight.'

'Marcel—'

The door slammed. There followed the noise of his footsteps running down the corridor, but she never heard them. She was already asleep.

CHAPTER TEN

NEXT morning he greeted her briskly. 'Just one more day and then we can be gone. There's some papers over there that need—' He couldn't meet her eyes.

It was almost funny, she thought. Last night he'd behaved like a perfect gentleman, refusing to take advantage of her vulnerability. It was practically worth a medal for chivalry. And he was secretly ashamed of it.

Which was a pity, because she couldn't tell him how proud she was of his generosity.

That evening they were invited to a business dinner, where networking would be a high priority.

'And I promise not to touch anything stronger than orange juice,' she said.

'And then—?'

'And then I'll be fully awake and alert, and I'll know exactly what I'm doing.'

She gave him a quick kiss and vanished, leaving him staring at her door in frustration, admiration and bemusement.

In her preparations, Cassie and Mrs Henshaw came together, the dress with a mysterious combination of severity and temptation, the hair drawn lightly back, but not scraped. She was a huge success. It was Marcel who had a lacklustre evening, unable to take his eyes off her and letting business opportunities slip by.

Later, as they approached his suite, she pulled her hair free, shaking it so that it flowed over her shoulders and forward down her breasts.

'You should be careful,' he murmured. 'A conceited man might interpret that as a hint.'

'Better a conceited man than a slow-witted one,' she said, slipping her arms around his neck. 'Just when will you get the message?'

'Right now,' he said, clasping her with one hand and pushing the door open with the other.

Twice since their meeting they had shared passion. The first time had been in anger, the second time the feeling had been gentler, but still tense.

But now they rediscovered many things they had both thought lost for ever. His touch brought her only delight, the look in his eyes raised her to the heights. He loved her slowly, prolonging every moment so that she could feel his tenderness.

And something else, perhaps. Love? Did she dare to hope?

When he finally abandoned control and yielded to her completely she held him close, hoping and praying for the miracle.

At last he whispered, 'Is everything all right?'

'Yes,' she said slowly. 'Very much all right.'

In the next few hours they loved, slept, and loved again. Now she was filled with deep joy, sensing the approaching moment when all would be made well.

Next day they returned to Paris and plunged back into work, both content to do so, knowing that better times were coming.

Soon, she promised herself, she would say the words that would make everything different between them. But first she would enjoy the pleasure that only he could give her. There would be plenty of time for talk.

He didn't even ask if he could come to her room. Now he knew he didn't need to ask. Nestled down in bed, they found themselves and each other again and again, before sleeping in utter contentment.

She awoke to find him watching her, and made a decision.

'Marcel—'

'Yes, Cassie?'

She took a deep breath. All hesitation gone. What better time could there ever be?

But before she could speak his cellphone shrilled.

He swore and grappled for it in his clothes. Cassie closed her eyes and groaned.

'Yes?' he answered. Then his face changed and he grew alert. 'Freya! What's the matter? You sound upset—all right, calm down. How can I help? What?—What's got into the old man now?—I don't believe it, even of him.'

At last he hung up and flung her a despairing glance.

'My father's up to his tricks again. He's on his way here. I think he's beginning to realise that he's not going to marry her off to Darius so he's turning his fire on me.'

Groaning, she covered her eyes with her hands. Of all the times for this to happen! Now she couldn't say what she'd meant to. For the moment the spell was broken.

'I need your help,' Marcel continued. 'So does Freya. If there's one thing she doesn't want it's to be stuck with me.'

Cassie forced herself to concentrate. 'Well, Freya was very kind to me, so I'll do all I can to save her from that terrible fate. Just tell me what to do.'

'When we take them to dinner we must act like a couple, just until he gets the message.'

'When are they going to arrive here?'

'Soon. Let's hurry.'

He was out of bed, throwing on his clothes. She sighed

and followed suit. The time would come, she promised herself. But she must be patient for a while.

Amos and Freya arrived two hours later. When Marcel had shown them to their rooms Amos said, 'I thought you'd still be in London working on that new place. But I dare say the admirable Mrs Henshaw is taking care of everything.'

'Admirable certainly,' Marcel agreed. 'In fact I've brought her here to study La Couronne so that she'll have a more precise idea of my wishes. She's looking forward to meeting you again when we all have dinner tonight.'

Amos made a displeased face. 'No need to invite her to dinner. I'm not in the mood for business.'

'But I'm in the mood to meet Mrs Henshaw again,' Freya said quickly. 'I liked her so much when we met in England.'

'She's eager to see you too,' Marcel assured her. 'Why don't you go up to the office and talk to her?'

The meeting between the two women was friendly and eager. Cassie had pleasant memories of Freya's kindly attention when she'd banged her head, but she'd been too confused to notice much about her. Now she saw an attractive young woman in her late twenties, slim and vigorous, with light brown hair that was almost auburn, green eyes and a cheeky smile. She ordered tea for them both and they settled down comfortably.

'I'm so glad you took the job with Marcel,' Freya said. 'He was so afraid that you wouldn't.'

'He thought I'd refuse it?'

'I don't know, but he seemed very worried about it. He must have heard a lot about your business skills.'

'Yes, I guess it must have been that,' Cassie murmured.

'He says you're having dinner with us. I'm so glad.'

Her fervent tone prompted Cassie to say cautiously, 'I gather Mr Falcon is trying to throw the two of you together.'

'Sort of. I don't think he's quite given up hope of Darius, but—'

'But he's keeping all his options open,' Cassie supplied. 'Just what you'd expect an entrepreneur to do.'

'Yes. Do you know what they're talking about now, why Amos originally came here? Bringing me was just an after-thought. He's helping Marcel raise extra funds for the London hotel. Somebody owes him money and there's a loophole in the contract by which Amos can get repaid earlier. So he's twisting the poor fellow's arm.'

'Not a nice man,' Cassie agreed.

'He's always thought Darius was that way inclined too. And Marcel is next in the money-making stakes. Honestly, who'd want to marry a man like that?'

'Nobody in their right mind,' Cassie agreed.

The phone rang. It was Marcel, wanting Vera, but the sec-retary had just left.

'I need some papers. Can you bring them to me? You'll find them—'

'No problem,' she said when he'd explained. 'I'll be right down with them.'

Approaching Amos's room, she could hear raised voices. One of them was Amos, but the loudest belonged to a young man who seemed almost hysterical.

'But it isn't fair. Can't you see that?'

'It's in the contract.' That was Amos.

'But you said it was just a fallback, and you'd never make use of it—'

'I said I probably wouldn't make use of it. It wasn't a guar-antee.'

'You made it sound like one—as long as I kept up the re-payments—'

'Which have sometimes been late.'

'They're up-to-date at this moment. Surely that's what counts?'

'*I* say what counts.' Amos's voice was as harsh as sandpaper, and Cassie stepped back from the door in revulsion.

The next moment she was glad of it for the door was yanked open by a man who came flying out. He turned to scream back, 'Be damned to you! I hope you rot in hell!'

Then he dashed off, forcing her to flatten herself against the wall. She stayed there, breathing out, trying to calm down. But before she was ready to enter the room she heard Marcel's voice.

'There was no need to go quite so far.'

'Don't give me that. I know just how far to go. I didn't get where I am by weakening. Nor should you.'

'I don't. I can be tough when I have to, but it's a new age. Subtlety can be better.'

'Only one thing matters,' came Amos's rasping voice. 'Does he have the cash or doesn't he?'

'According to him he doesn't. It might not be wise to press him too far.'

'Give me patience! Will nothing cure you of the habit of believing what people say?'

'It can actually be useful sometimes.'

'Not this time. Leave that man for me to deal with.'

Cassie backed away, wishing she could run far away from this horrible conversation that exhibited all the worst of Amos Falcon. She was glad that Marcel had had the decency to argue against him, although she wished he'd done so more strongly.

He'd advised his father to soften his stance, not out of kindness, but because subtlety offered a better chance of a profit. It was only a different road to the same money-filled destination.

Suddenly she was glad that she hadn't opened her heart to him that morning.

Amos Falcon was exactly as Cassie remembered him from their brief earlier meeting—in his seventies, heavily built with a harsh face and piercing eyes. He smiled a lot and his words were often cordial, but his eyes were cold.

He greeted her politely at dinner that evening and indicated a chair next to himself. Since the table was oblong, this effectively separated them from Marcel and Freya, sitting on the other side.

As so often these days, her appearance was a subtle combination of the two women who seemed to inhabit her. Amos regarded her with admiration.

'I'm going to enjoy talking to you this evening. Marcel, you entertain Freya. I want to get to know Mrs Henshaw.'

He proceeded to give Cassie all his attention, asking about her career, her abilities, the recent trip to England.

'Don't know why problems are cropping up now,' he growled. 'Those damned banks!'

'Well, I suppose they—' Cassie began.

She continued in this way for a while, talking generally without giving away any information about Marcel's dealings. Amos listened, nodding sometimes, and in this way the meal passed.

Over coffee things changed. Marcel joined in and the talk became all business. Amos mentioned the man who'd been there earlier, refusing to hand over money.

'He'll see sense,' he said. 'I'll make sure of that. He thinks he can defy me and get away with it. The best way—'

The two women met each other's eyes.

'You two don't need us for this kind of talk,' Freya said. 'Shall we—?'

'Yes, let's,' Cassie said, rising and following her. 'Goodnight, gentlemen.'

They said goodnight and returned at once to their discussion.

'They hardly noticed us go,' Freya said as they went up in the elevator, and Cassie nodded.

Upstairs in Cassie's rooms, Freya threw herself into an armchair with a sigh of relief. 'Oh, thank heavens!' she said. 'I'd had as much as I could stand.' She gave a laugh. 'Of course you probably find it interesting. Sorry, I forgot about that.'

'No, I was just as glad to get away,' Cassie said. 'I don't like it when it gets brutal.'

'Me too. I much prefer a good TV show and a handsome man. Hey, look at him!'

She'd flicked on the set, and suddenly the screen was filled with a staggeringly handsome young man.

'Know who that is?' she asked.

'Yes, it's Marcel's half-brother, Travis,' Cassie said. 'They started showing *The Man From Heaven* a few weeks ago, and I've been watching it because of Marcel. Who was his mother? Another of Amos's wives?'

'No, she was an American girl he met while he was over there on business.'

'So if he can't marry you to Darius or Marcel, Travis is the next in line?' Cassie asked, amused.

'Either him or Leonid, who lives in Russia, and who nobody seems to meet. Or Jackson, the naturalist. I'd have to be crazy to marry any of them, but especially Travis. His wife would never have a moment's peace he's so handsome. Mind you, it would be much the same with Marcel, who's also very handsome.'

'Is he?' Cassie asked indifferently.

'Well, some women think so. Is that tea? Thank you, I could do with it. Sometimes I think Amos insists on champagne all the time as a kind of status symbol, just to underline how far he's come from his days of poverty, when actually I'm dying for a cuppa.'

They sipped their tea in deep contentment.

'Why do you put up with it?' Cassie asked. 'Can't you escape him?'

'Yes, soon, hopefully. I'd like to go back to working as a nurse. The high life doesn't really suit me. I suppose I shouldn't complain. He's decent to my mother, and good to me. He wants me in the family.'

'I suppose that's nice of him.'

'Ye-es,' Freya said, unconvinced. 'It's only because he's never had a daughter and he sees a chance of "completing the set". A sharp businessman covers every angle.'

'That's true.'

'A few months ago Amos had a scare with his heart. He's too stubborn to admit that it might be serious so my mother asked me to come and stay with them for a while. This way he always has a nurse on hand, but he can pretend I'm just visiting.

'All his sons came to see him, just in case it was the last time. From things he said, I know he wanted to take a good look at them and decide which one was really his true heir. Whichever one he decides on will get an extra share of his fortune. And whichever one marries me will get an extra dose of money too, as a reward for "doing what Daddy wants".'

'Oh, heavens!' Cassie exclaimed in horror. 'How do you put up with it?'

'Because basically I'm free. I can walk out and get a job elsewhere any time I want. He got me on this trip by staging a dizzy spell at the last moment, so I came with him to keep my mother happy. But that's it! From now on I'm going to reclaim my life.'

A sense of mischief made Cassie say, 'Amos is a man very used to getting his own way. You might yet end up as his daughter-in-law.'

'I suppose anything's possible, however unlikely. But it won't be Darius because I think he's going to make it work with Harriet, the young woman he brought to the wedding in London. And it won't be Marcel. He wouldn't suit me at all.'

'You sound very sure,' Cassie said, not looking at her. 'Why is that?'

'He just sees things in black and white all the time. Where brains are concerned he's as sharp as they come. But emotionally I think he imagines things are more straightforward than they ever really are. Maybe that's because he doesn't seem to have much emotional life.'

'Doesn't he? Let me pour you some more tea.'

'I don't think so. Women galore but no real involvement. And if that's what satisfies him, he's not for me. And he won't marry for Amos's money because he doesn't need it. Sometimes I think he's just that little bit too much like Amos.'

'Or maybe he just likes to believe that things can work out simply and straightforwardly,' Cassie mused.

'True. Actually, I think a lot of men are like that—just not geared up to see how complicated life can be.'

'Yes,' Cassie said quietly. 'That's it.'

'Oh well, let them get on with it.'

Freya gave a theatrical shudder and glanced back at the screen where the drama series was still showing. Travis's face was still there.

'Why is this show called *The Man From Heaven?*' she queried.

'I think he's supposed to be at least partly an angel,' Cassie said.

'No guy as good-looking as that was ever an angel. But hey, don't you dare tell Amos I said that. I'd get no peace afterwards.'

Cassie chuckled and they continued the evening in perfect accord. She was beginning to feel that Freya was exactly the kind of person she would like to have as a close friend.

But she couldn't guess the astonishing way in which that would one day become true.

It was a couple of weeks later that she opened Marcel's door, stopped on the threshold, then prepared to back off, saying, 'I'm sorry, I didn't know you had someone here.'

'Come in, Mrs Henshaw,' Marcel called cheerfully. 'This is my brother, Darius.'

She'd recognised him from her research of the Falcon family, and knew part of his history. Eldest son of Amos Falcon and a skilled entrepreneur in his own right. Like many others, he'd been hit by the credit crunch and was now the owner of Herringdean, an island that a debtor had dumped on him by way of repayment.

'Darius has just invited me to his wedding,' Marcel explained now. 'He's finally persuaded Harriet to put up with him.'

'It wasn't easy.' Darius grinned. 'She's part of the lifeboat crew on Herringdean and she saved me from drowning in the first few days. Now I never feel safe if she's not around.' He thumped Marcel's shoulder. 'You've got to come. The other lads are all going to be there.'

'Yes, you have brothers all over the world,' Cassie said. 'I remember Freya telling me.'

'That's right, Jackson's going to get a few days off from interviewing animals. I had to twist his arm for that because he finds ferrets more interesting than people. Leonid's going to drop whatever he's doing in Russia and come on over, and the man from heaven has promised to put in an appearance.'

'Ah, yes, I've been watching that on television,' she said, smiling.

'So Travis will be there for the wedding, and so will Marcel. Come on Marcel, say you will.'

'Oh, no. I'm avoiding Amos at the moment. Now he can't marry you to Freya I'm in danger.'

'Dad probably won't be there. He's that mad at me for marrying Harriet that he's snubbing our wedding.'

'Yes and, knowing him, he'll drop in at the last minute,' Marcel observed.

'Coward,' Darius said amiably.

'No, I'll be there, but I want some protection. Mrs Henshaw must come with me and if Dad starts any funny business she'll deal with it.'

'That's the spirit,' Darius said. 'Mrs Henshaw, are you up to the job?'

'I think so,' she said cheerfully. 'If Mr Falcon tries to speak to Marcel I just tell him he must make an appointment through me first.'

'Hey, she's good.' Darius grinned. 'I'll leave you in safe hands. The wedding is next week. I know it's short notice but I can't risk Harriet changing her mind. Besides, she's got this dog—lovely fellow called Phantom. He did a lot to bring us together but he's very old and we want to marry while he's alive to see it.'

'It's not like you to be sentimental,' Marcel said.

'It's not like me to do a lot of things I'm doing these days. But Harriet…well… I don't know how to describe her…she's "the one"…no, that's not it. Well, yes, it is, but it's much more…at least…'

'You're stammering,' Marcel observed.

Darius gave an awkward laugh. 'I guess I am. It's the effect she has on me. She kept her distance for a while because she thought I only wanted to marry her for the sake of the children. I had to…persuade her otherwise.'

'Now you're blushing,' Marcel accused him. 'You, the man I've always admired because he could make everyone scramble to please him, you're scrambling to please Harriet.'

'Yes, I am,' Darius said with a touch of belligerence. 'I've finally got my priorities right, and she's what matters. I know you think I'm making a fool of myself, but I don't care what anyone else thinks. When you find the one, grab her, or you'll regret it all your life.'

'But that's assuming that you find the one in the first place,' Mrs Henshaw pointed out with a friendly smile.

'True. Marcel will probably never find her. Too busy playing the field. Never could commit himself. Probably never will now. Right, I must be off. Here's the details.' He gave her a sheet of paper. 'Get him there on time, see that he behaves.'

'That won't be easy,' she joked. 'But I'll do my best.'

When Darius had gone Marcel said, 'We need to go to London for a few more days to sort out some final details. Then we'll go on to Herringdean in time for the wedding.' He added significantly, 'I'm looking forward to that.'

In the atmosphere of a wedding anything might happen. Answers could be found, love might flower. His eyes told her that he was thinking the same thing.

He began to reach for her, but suddenly her cellphone rang. She answered it, then tensed, growing so still and silent that Marcel was alarmed.

'Don't hang up,' said a man's voice at the other end. 'You know who this is.'

Without replying, she ended the call.

'What's the matter?' Marcel asked, concerned. 'Why are you looking like that? Who was it?'

'Jake,' she said. 'I don't know how he got my number. He must be out of prison. How dare he contact me again!'

'Don't worry; I'll keep you safe,' he promised. 'I won't let him get to you again.'

She longed to believe him, but Jake could always get to her because he never really left her. That was the cruel truth that poisoned her life. Even now he must have been keeping tabs on her to have discovered her new phone number.

It rang again. She answered, saying sharply, 'I'm shutting this down—'

'I'm dying,' Jake said.

'What?'

'I've only got a few days left. I want to see you, Cassie— one last time.'

'No!'

'I'm not in prison any more. They let me out to die in hospital. You know the place—'

He gave her the name, while she clenched her free hand, whispering, 'No…no…no…'

'Please—I beg you—'

'No. Understand me, Jake, I don't care if you are dying. I don't want to see you again, ever.'

'Dying?' Marcel echoed.

'He wants me to go and see him.'

'Then tell him you'll go.'

'What?'

'I'll take you. You won't be alone.'

'Are you mad?'

'No, I want you to find closure, and this may be the only way you can do it. See him, Cassie. Tie up the ends. Then tell him from both of us to go to hell.'

She stared at him, mesmerised by something fierce and desperate in his voice. This mattered to Marcel. It was there in the tension of his body and the sharp edge of his voice.

'Tell him,' he said. 'Say you'll do it. Say it!'

'Marcel—'

'Say it!'

'Jake,' she said slowly, 'I'm on my way.'

CHAPTER ELEVEN

THIS time they took the plane to London. On the flight Marcel held her hand in his. She gave him a brief wan smile, but mostly she stared out of the window.

To see Jake again. To be forced back into his company. This was the stuff of nightmares, yet the road was taking her inexorably there and she had no chance of escape.

At last she turned to Marcel, trying to read his expression.

'Why are you doing this?' she murmured. 'It's not just for me, is it?'

'No,' he conceded. 'I need to see him myself. Can you understand that?'

'Yes, I suppose I can understand, but I'm afraid, Marcel.'

'Don't be. I'm here.'

The thought, *Not afraid of him—afraid of you*, winged its way through her mind and vanished into the distance. She didn't really know what she meant by it, and there was no way she could have told him, even if she had known.

She realised that Marcel was pursuing some goal of his own, and she was only part of it. He was like a man who'd travelled on an epic journey and who saw the end in sight.

'I heard you ask how he got your number,' he said. 'Do you think he's been keeping tabs on you?'

'He must have been. Even in prison he's had people on the outside taking his orders. When we were together he had a horrible obsession with me. All he saw was that I was his property. We'd go out to dinner and he'd flaunt me—that's the only word for it. And I'd have to smile and look proud, knowing that as soon as we got home he'd grab me and—'

'Don't!' Marcel said with soft violence. 'Don't.'

He threw himself back in his seat, his eyes closed.

'I'm sorry,' he said at last. 'I can't bear to hear it, but you had to live through it. You must despise me. I don't blame you.'

'We're past that,' she said gently. 'Neither of us knows what it was really like for the other. Let's take it carefully.'

He nodded and they held each other for a few moments.

'Talk to me,' he said at last. 'Tell me anything you like. I want to be part of your life, even that stage of it.'

She sighed. 'There was one moment when I hoped life might not be completely wretched. I was pregnant.'

'You've had a child?' he asked, startled.

'No, I miscarried. That was when Jake went sleeping around. I didn't mind. The less I saw of him, the better. And it gave me a way of divorcing him. He fought me but I had one big weapon.'

'Yes, you must have known a lot of his dark secrets by then.'

'I did, but that wasn't it. The real weapon was the fact that I didn't care about anything. He defeated people by scaring them, and when he knew I couldn't be scared he was left floundering.

'The last thing he said to me was, "You think you've got away from me, but you haven't really." And he was right. Once I'd escaped him all the feelings he'd killed began to come back, and I started caring again. He was always there in my nightmares, and I haven't been able to banish him.'

'But things are different now,' Marcel said firmly. 'We'll defeat him together.' Seeing the confused look in her eyes, he put his hands on either side of her face. 'We will. I promise you.'

'Will we?' she mused. 'Perhaps.'

'You don't believe me, do you? *Do you?*'

'I want to,' she said desperately. 'You don't know how much I want to believe that all the problems could be swept away so simply, but oh, my darling, it's more complicated than that, more worrying, more frightening.'

'But we're together now. How can we be frightened, either of us, while we have each other? We're going to defeat Jake, I promise you.'

She longed to believe him. She didn't have the words to tell him how confused and bewildering was the universe in which they lived now. He'd always seen things in simple black and white, she remembered. And sometimes he'd been right. If only he could be right now. But she was full of apprehension.

They were beginning the descent, and there was no chance to say more.

They had booked a hotel near Heathrow Airport, and after checking in they went straight to the hospital where Jake was living out his last few days.

They found him in a private ward. A guard was sitting by the bed, but he moved discreetly away.

Marcel had kept a firm, comforting grip on her hand, but then he released her and backed into the shadows.

She barely recognised Jake. Once a big, beefy man, he was now skeletally thin.

'Cassie?' he croaked. 'Is that you? I can't see you properly.'

'Yes, it's me.'

'Come closer.'

Reluctantly she leaned down and he reached up a hand to touch her cheek. With an effort she stopped herself from flinching and sat on the bed. He managed a ghastly travesty of a smile, croaking, 'You're still beautiful, still my Cassie.'

'I was never your Cassie,' she said at once.

'You were my wife.'

'Not in my heart. Never.'

'But you're here,' he gasped. 'I knew you'd come.'

'No,' she said quietly. 'Don't fool yourself, Jake. I'm sorry for you, but there's nothing between us. There never was.'

'Oh, you always played hard to get. That's what I loved about you. Yes, we belonged together. I always knew it.'

'And you deluded yourself,' she said, filled with disgust. 'You hurt the man I loved and I stayed with you to protect him. That's the only reason.'

'Him? Don't make me laugh. He was nobody. By now he's probably scraping a living sweeping the streets.'

This was Marcel's moment and he took it, moving out of the shadows to stand beside Cassie.

'You were wrong about that,' he said, 'as you have been wrong about everything.'

'Who the hell are you?' Jake demanded.

'You don't know me? No, I suppose you wouldn't. You got someone else to do your dirty work. They left me lying in a pool of blood in the street. But here I am and now I've seen all I needed to.'

Then Jake did something that astounded them both. He began to laugh.

'Fine talk,' he gasped. 'You think you've won, don't you? If you'd *won* back *then* you would have won. She was young and glorious, better than she'll ever be again in her life. Those were her best years, and they were mine, d'you hear? Mine. I had things you'll never know.'

'No, he had things *you* never knew,' Cassie said. 'He had my love, given freely. That's something you never had.'

Jake barely heard her. His hate-filled eyes were on Marcel.

'You didn't win,' he spat, 'and one day you'll realise that. Cassie died years ago. All you've got now is the shell. You think you have a future? What kind of future? No children. She can't have any.'

'Not with you, maybe,' Marcel said softly.

Jake turned to Cassie and he was suddenly shaken with a coughing fit. His hands gripped her arms with the last of his strength. She hated him but a feeling of pity made her clasp him back.

'You came to me,' he choked. 'You came…you couldn't stay away…'

'I came because he asked me to,' she said with a fierce glance at Marcel. 'Nothing else would have brought me here.'

'You're lying…I'm your husband…Cassie…my Cassie… mine…'

Gasps tore him, growing faster, noisier, until at last he fell back against the pillows.

'You were always mine,' he murmured as his eyes closed.

'No,' she breathed. 'Never, *never!*'

He could no longer hear her. His eyes, half open, stared unseeingly into a hidden distance. His rigid hands, clasping her arms, held her prisoner.

'No,' she wept. 'Please, no.'

In a flash Marcel was there, wrenching Jake's hands away, setting her free.

'Let's go,' he said.

In the taxi he held her shuddering body.

'Everything's all right,' he said. 'It's over now.'

But it wasn't over. And suddenly she doubted that everything would ever be all right.

Back in the hotel he came to her room and immediately called Room Service to order supper. While they waited he went to his own room, returning with his night clothes. When the food arrived he prepared to serve her.

'I'm not really hungry,' she sighed.

'I know, but you have to eat anyway. Don't argue.'

His tone was gentle but firm, and she let him take over. She felt drained and defeated. Where was the sense of triumph that should have filled her? Nothing. Only the troubling sense that Jake had mysteriously won again.

He helped her to undress, then he put her to bed and got in beside her, taking her into his arms, holding her as though in this way he could keep her safe. She snuggled against him, reaching out for that safety.

She fell into a contented sleep and awoke to find him touching her intimately. She responded, giving and seeking love, letting him take her into the dream.

'It's all right,' Marcel murmured. 'He's gone. Now it's just us.'

'Yes,' she said, trying to believe that this was really so.

But there was still a dark and worrying cloud hanging over her. She didn't look at it too closely. She didn't want to understand it.

But some kind of understanding was forced on her when she awoke in the early hours with a headache. Moving quietly not to wake Marcel, she slipped out of bed, and went to her bag, seeking a pill. Not finding what she wanted, she reached her fingers into a small pocket inside that normally she never used. What she found there almost made her heart stop.

Drawing the tiny object out into the light, she surveyed it with horror. It was the ring Jake had given her long ago, and which she'd flung back at him during the divorce.

She remembered how she'd sat by his bed that afternoon, leaning over him, the bag lying on the coverlet. He must have slipped the ring inside when his hand moved towards her. It had fallen into the pocket without her noticing.

With a horrified, sick feeling she realised that it was what he'd always meant to do. By returning it he'd reasserted his claim on her from beyond the grave.

'Cassie?' Marcel appeared, rubbing sleep from his eyes. 'Are you all right?'

'Yes, fine,' she said, closing the bag. 'I'm just coming back to bed.'

Briefly she thought of confiding in him and letting him deal with the matter. But she rejected the thought. Her head was invaded by confusion, and she wouldn't have known what to say.

In bed he took her back into his arms, comforting her with his warmth and strength. Seeking more, she ran her hands over him, taking reassurance from the feel of him. Suddenly she stopped.

'What is it?' he whispered.

She switched on the light and leaned back to survey his chest with the livid scar that ran across it. Slowly, almost fearfully, she touched it.

'That's what he did,' she murmured. 'Oh, God!' She laid her face against it.

'It's all right,' he said gently. 'It was bad at the time but they made me right again. I'm fine now. Don't grieve. It's over.'

'It's not over,' she wept. 'It'll never be over. You might have died.'

'I didn't die.'

But in another sense he had died, and so had she. The wounds had healed but the scars would be there for ever, and they both knew it. Through the barrier of time, from prison, from beyond the grave, Jake had put the shackles back on her.

Darius's wedding was drawing near. Back in Paris, Cassie booked them both into The Conway Hotel on Herringdean

Island. Freya called to say she would be there, but not Amos, which was a relief to them both.

'And my mother's coming,' Marcel said.

Since Laura Degrande also lived in Paris she would join them the night before their departure and travel with them. Cassie was curious to meet her, but also a little apprehensive, wondering what Marcel would have told her. Laura greeted her civilly but was not forthcoming. Sometimes Cassie would look up to find Marcel's mother watching her. Then Laura would smile, but not speak.

Between herself and Marcel, recent events were never mentioned. She shut him, and all to do with him, away in a compartment of her mind, which she bolted, barred, and threw away the key.

Marcel too never spoke of that time. He might have been waiting for a signal from her, which never came. With the wedding coming up they both assumed a cheerful demeanour. Nor was it entirely a pretence. She discovered that a locked compartment could work well, even if only intermittently.

Since it wasn't possible to take the train to Herringdean they travelled by helicopter and Cassie forgot her fear in the dazzling pleasure of skimming low over the Channel and seeing the island come into view.

'How beautiful,' she murmured.

'Yes, you really have to envy Darius,' Marcel agreed.

'Living in a place like this? I agree.'

'I meant more than that,' he murmured.

She turned her head and found him looking at her with a mysterious smile, but the helicopter was descending and there was no time to talk.

Darius was waiting as they landed, with a cheerful young woman by his side. Cassie took to Harriet at once.

Darius seemed on good terms with Laura, whom he hugged. After the introductions he said, 'I'll drive you to the hotel. When you've settled in, you come on to my place. We're having a big party.'

'Who else is here?' Marcel called.

'Jackson's arrived, and Travis. Travis is staying with me so that he can hide. He daren't go out in the street without girls shrieking, *"That's him!"* Jackson ribs him something terrible. They've started showing his series on Herringdean now, so there's no escape.'

'But not Amos,' Laura said. 'You assured me—'

'No, not Amos. Promise.'

They got through the hotel formalities as fast as possible, and were taken straight to Giant's Beacon, where Darius lived, which turned out to be a magnificent building overlooking the sea. They arrived to find Jackson and Travis standing outside, watching for them.

She recognised Travis at once as the actor she'd seen on screen. He greeted her with charm and practised friendliness, and she immediately understood why Freya was wary of him. Too charming. Too handsome.

She also recognised Jackson as a naturalist she'd seen on-screen. Not handsome in the Travis style, but good-looking in a 'kid brother' fashion. She liked him.

The house was decked out with flowers in the halls and one huge room filled with tables. Because this had to be saved for the wedding reception the next day, the family gathered outside that night and partied under lights hanging from the trees.

The Falcon family might be riven with divisions, but tonight they were forgotten and only the warmth could be felt. Cassie thought that Harry, as everyone called her, was exactly as a bride should be, full of happiness at her love but, more than that, the deep contentment of someone who knew, beyond all possible doubt, that she had come to the right place.

'When did you know for sure?' she asked when they were alone for a moment.

'It was him,' Harry said, pointing to a large dog who lay curled up on the sofa.

'Is that Phantom?' Cassie asked. 'Darius said he'd done a lot to bring you together, and you wanted him at the wedding.'

'That's right. We thought he was going to die one day, and I was called out on the lifeboat. I hated leaving him to die without me, but Darius stayed with him, talking to him, letting him know he was loved and wanted. And he didn't die. I still have my darling Phantom, and it's all because of Darius. I'd been wondering about him for a while, but that was the turning point, when it all became clear.'

Cassie nodded. 'If you were lucky enough to have a turning point everything would be easy,' she mused.

'Of course most people aren't that lucky,' Harry agreed. 'They have to just hope they've got it right. But I knew then that I mustn't let this wonderful man get away. When you find a man who understands you so perfectly you've got to hold onto him.'

'Yes,' Cassie murmured. 'If he understood you, and you understood him—everything would be simple.'

She reached down and stroked Phantom's head, wishing that she too could have a Phantom instead of the unruly ghosts who seemed bent on confusing her.

There was an excited murmur in the hall.

'That'll be Leonid,' Harry said. 'Darius went to collect him. He's the mystery man of the family, and I'm dying to meet him.'

From the first moment Leonid lived up to the tag 'mystery man'. He had black hair, dark blue eyes and an ultra-lean face.

'Haunted,' Cassie murmured. 'Or am I being too melodramatic?'

'I don't think so,' Harry murmured back.

Freya joined in. 'Where has he come from and where is he going?' she said. 'The rest of the world will never know.'

'Oh, that's really being a bit fanciful,' Harry protested.

'No,' said Freya. 'It isn't.'

The other two women exchanged glances that said, *Maybe he's the one she'll marry. This is going to be interesting.*

Watching Leonid make the rounds, Cassie had the impression that he knew none of his family well. She wondered how often he left Russia. He greeted her courteously, speaking in a deep voice with a distinctive accent. He was an attractive man, she thought, but very reserved, which some women might find intriguing.

Cassie suddenly realised that Laura was looking at her, then towards the trees with a question in her face. She nodded and rose, moving quietly away from the lights and under the trees, where she waited for Marcel's mother, who joined her a moment later.

'I have wanted to meet you for some time,' she said.

'Yes, I suppose Marcel has told you all about me. You must hate me.'

'I did once,' Laura agreed, 'many years ago. He came flying home from London, ran to me and shut himself away in his room. I used to stand outside the door and hear him sobbing. When he told me how his beautiful girlfriend had betrayed him when he was ill, then I hated you.

'I hated you even more as the years passed and I saw my generous, gentle son retreat into himself and turn into a terrible copy of his father. But a few weeks ago he came back home and found the letter. I saw his distress when he discovered pieces missing. It mattered so much to him. I wonder if you can understand how much it meant.

'When he was back in Paris he called me to say he'd spoken to you and all was now well. You had never betrayed him, and he could have known that if he hadn't torn up the letter. I've never heard him so happy. I thought soon he would tell me that you were reunited, but there has been nothing. And I came to ask you—to beg you—please don't break his heart again.'

'I don't want to, but—'

'But you're not sure you love him?'

'How can I be when I don't know who he is? We've both changed in ten years. I love—part of him, but the other part worries me. You said he'd become like his father. I need to know how much before I can make a decision.

'He's compared it to Jekyll and Hyde, and he's right. There are two people living inside each of us, and we all four have to learn to love each other. Otherwise there will only be more heartbreak and misery.'

'It will happen,' Laura said earnestly. 'It must. Look.' She reached into her bag and pulled out a little black box which she opened, revealing a ring with the biggest diamond Cassie had ever seen.

'Amos gave it to me when I first knew him. I've kept it all these years for Marcel, so that he can give it to the girl he loves.'

'It's beautiful,' Cassie said, gazing at the ring.

'Would you like to try it on?'

'No,' she said quickly. 'You're very kind but no thank you.'

Laura sighed and put the ring away. 'I shall hope for better things soon.'

As they strolled back together Jackson came out to call, 'Come on in! You'll never guess who's on the box *again!*'

'Travis?' Cassie laughed.

'Honestly, I swear he thinks he really comes from heaven. There's no getting away from him.'

In fact the episode was nearly over and they arrived just in time to hear Travis announce heroically, 'That's what we must all remember. Seize the moment whenever it comes. Don't let the chance slip away, or we may regret it for ever.'

Everyone in the room laughed and cheered, Travis looked sheepish and held out his glass for another drink.

Cassie cheered with the others, glancing across at Marcel to see if he shared the amusement, but he seemed sunk in thought, as though something had taken him by surprise.

But then he looked up and smiled. Someone appeared at Cassie's side, offering wine, and the party engulfed her again.

It was only later that she remembered Travis's dramatic pronouncement, because of its devastating consequences.

Next morning the family gathered on the beach for the wedding to take place. When Harry appeared she was accompanied by Darius's children, his daughter Frankie and son Mark. With them came Phantom, whom Mark led to the front and settled him where he had a good view.

Cassie watched, entranced, not only by the beauty of the ceremony and the surroundings, but by the love that blazed from the bride and groom.

She remembered Harry's words about the turning point, the moment when the road ahead became clear. Would she and Marcel ever reach that point? Or was it too much to hope for?

She stole a glance at him and found him looking at her intently. She smiled, receiving his smile in return. And something else? Had she imagined it or had he nodded? And if so, what had he meant?

Then he looked away, and she was left with her thoughts.

For a long time after that she wondered about that moment, and how differently everything might have turned out.

The reception was much as expected—speeches, laughter, happiness. Then they spilled out into the garden again and someone put on some music so that there could be dancing.

'Are you glad we came?' Marcel asked as they twirled under the trees.

'I wouldn't have missed it for the world. Everything was perfect.'

'Yes, they seized the chance when it came. Travis was right. That's what we should always do. Now, watch this!'

Plunging a hand into his pocket, he drew out the diamond ring Cassie had last seen in Laura's hand. Before she knew what he meant to do, he took her hand and slid it onto her finger.

'Marcel—'

'Seize the moment,' he said. 'This is our moment and I'm seizing it. *Listen, everybody!*'

They all stopped and looked at him eagerly.

'I've got wonderful news,' he cried. He held up Cassie's hand so that they could all see the glittering diamond.

'She's said yes, and the wedding will be as soon as possible.'

Cheers and applause. The family crowded around them, smiling, patting them on the back, embracing Cassie, asking to see the ring.

She showed it mechanically. Inwardly she was in turmoil, her mind whirling with a thousand desperate thoughts, of which the chief one was, *No!*

CHAPTER TWELVE

THE crowd waved and cheered. Harry flung her arms around Cassie, crying, 'You next. I'm so glad.'

Cassie maintained a determined smile, practically fixed on with rivets to hide her real thoughts.

She loved this man, so why wasn't she over the moon at his declaration of love?

Because there had been no such declaration, only a pronouncement without asking her opinion first. And this was the side of him that roused her hostility.

It would take a heart of stone to resist the way Marcel was gazing at her now, but she forced her heart to be stone.

'Aren't you going to ask me to dance?' she said and he swept her onto the floor.

Here there was a kind of safety. Nobody could hear them or study their whirling forms too closely.

'Well,' he said, smiling in a way that would have dazzled her with delight at any other time, 'we finally got that settled.'

'Did we?' she retorted. 'You didn't even wait for my reply.'

'I didn't need to,' he said, still smiling. 'I won't take no for an answer.'

Give in, cried a voice deep inside her. *You love him. Isn't that enough?*

But it wasn't enough to quell the indignation rising in her.

'But I won't have to, will I?' he persisted. 'You know this is what we both want.'

'If you're so sure of that, why won't you wait for me to answer?'

He sighed, humouring her. 'All right, we'll do it your way. Cassie my love, will you marry me?'

She looked into his eyes and shook her head. 'No, Marcel, I won't.'

'Oh, I see, you're going to make me beg.'

'No, don't beg. It would only make it worse when you have to accept my refusal.'

'Darling—'

'I mean it. Let's get out of here.'

The way back to the village lay along a road overlooking the sea. Halfway there, he stopped the car.

'Better if we talk here,' he said.

'Yes.' She left the car and went to stand looking out over the waves. 'I can't marry you, Marcel.'

'I know we've needed time to sort things out, but I thought we'd managed that by now.'

'But you didn't ask me. You just assumed I agreed with you and claimed me in front of everyone, almost as though the decision didn't concern me. That's the side of you I dislike so much, the side that makes you check up on me when I'm out, making phone calls to see if I'm there.'

'I never give up something that belongs to me. If it's mine, it's mine. You belong to me, and I won't give you up.'

'You talk as though I was an inanimate object, nothing but a possession.'

'You are a possession, but not inanimate. You belong to me because you once gave yourself to me of your own free will.'

'And then took myself back.'

'But not of your own free will. You yourself told me that, so it doesn't invalidate your original gift.'

'But you can't—we can't—'

'Maybe you can't, but I can. And I'm going to. All those years ago we made a verbal contract and I'm holding you to it.'

She regarded him with disbelief. She didn't know this man. He called himself Marcel, but there was a glint in his eyes that took her by surprise. It might almost have been humour, and the curve of his lips suggested a hint of teasing that went back to the other Marcel, years ago.

'A contract is a contract,' he said. 'You told me a thousand times that you belonged to me and nobody else. Nothing that's happened since invalidates that, so the deal still stands.'

'And that's what I am to you—a business arrangement.'

'Of course. But you'll find that I conduct business at very close quarters.' As he spoke he drew her close.

It was sweet to be in his arms again, but the voice of reason rose up and screamed, reminding her of all the sensible resolutions she'd made.

'No,' she said, pushing him away. 'Can't you understand? *No!*'

He stepped back. 'Then you don't love me?'

She sighed. 'Cassie loves you, but Mrs Henshaw can't stay with a man who behaves like this.'

'Isn't it time we forgot that Jekyll and Hyde nonsense?'

'But it's how things are, except that I'm content to be both people. But you aren't content. You only want one of us and you can't accept that we come as a package. But so do you. You're just as much two people as I am. One of you is the Marcel I loved. The other one acts more like Amos, or even J—'

'Don't!' he shouted. 'Don't dare to compare me to Jake Simpson.'

'Why not? He used to give me orders, and drive me up a blind alley so that there was no choice but to do as he wanted.'

Silence. Only the wind and the murmur of the waves.

'You'd better take this,' she said, handing him the ring. 'It might have fitted me years ago, but not now.'

By common consent, not a word was spoken as they returned to the hotel. Laura was already there.

'I didn't expect you two back so soon,' she teased.

'I'm tired,' Cassie said quickly. 'I'm going straight to bed.'

Laura's eager questioning look was more than she could endure. There was no way she could talk about what was happening, so she went quickly to her room and locked the door. Tonight she needed to be alone, perhaps to think, or perhaps to yield herself up to the confusion and dismay that was now all she could feel. She longed to go to sleep but could only stare up at the ceiling, longing for the night to be over.

Next day they all returned to Paris. Marcel drove Laura back to her home.

'Did you tell her?' Cassie asked when he returned.

'No. I wasn't sure what to say.'

'Tell her everything when I've left. I think I should go to London tomorrow.'

'And that's it?' he asked, aghast.

'When you see the end of the road there's nothing to do but head for it.'

'But is that really the end of the road? Cassie—'

'Don't,' she begged. 'I can't make you happy, Marcel, any more than you could make me happy. We're each of us too different from what the other wants.'

'Is that really true?' he whispered. 'I can't make you happy?'

Dumbly she shook her head.

It was as though someone had struck him a blow. He sagged, his head drooped and he turned away in defeat. Cassie reached out her hand, driven by the impulse to comfort him. But then she drew back. She had to stick to her resolve for both their sakes.

She spent the rest of the day alone in her room, tying up ends, leaving him notes. The night was sleepless. Every moment she expected him to come to her.

But he did not. He had accepted her decision.

Nor did he come next morning, and she wondered if he was going to let her go without another word. But there were surely words to be spoken at the last. She went along to his apartment and found Vera just leaving.

'He's given me the day off,' she said. 'Bye!'

She sped along the corridor and Cassie slipped inside. There was no sign of Marcel. She closed her eyes, full of confusion. Her mind and heart were full of so many feelings and impressions, and they all seemed to contradict each other.

She looked into the bedroom which, by now, she knew, with its extra large double bed that was so comfortable for the indulgence of pleasure followed by sleep. But he wasn't there. Next stood another door which she'd only half noticed before. She tried the handle and felt it give.

Probably a cupboard, she thought, easing it open, meaning just to take a quick glance. But what she found made her push the door wide and stand on the threshold, confused and trying desperately to understand.

It was a bedroom, although prison cell might have described it better. Pushed up against the wall was a bed so narrow that it sent a dismal message. No lovers could ever share that restricted space. The man who slept here slept alone. There was no wardrobe. A small bedside chest of drawers was the only other furniture.

But surely, she thought, Marcel slept in the huge bed in the other room? But this one looked as if it had been recently slept in, and only clumsily made. It couldn't be anyone but him, which meant—surely not?

She sensed the truth by instinct. The outer room was the bedroom 'for show', the place where he took good-time girls who would expect to find him sleeping in lush surroundings, no expense spared. To keep up his reputation, he provided the background they expected, wined and dined them, made the speeches they would expect of a playboy and seduced them

But then he retreated to this bleak little place, because this was where he felt he belonged. Here he could be his true self. At least, that was how he felt.

The warm, life-loving, open-hearted boy she had loved had become the man who only felt truly comfortable in retreat. That thought distressed her more than any other.

And he'd loved the same about her, she thought, remembering how he'd said only recently, 'She gave herself to the world.'

They had both changed, both been damaged. She had thought she understood the extent of the injury to him, but now she was being forced to recognise how badly he'd been hurt.

'So now you know,' said a voice behind her.

Turning, she saw Marcel in the doorway, watching her. She searched his face for anger but found only weariness and resignation.

'Why didn't you tell me?' she whispered, gesturing to the bleak surroundings.

'Why do you think? Do you imagine I wanted you to know what a hopeless, miserable specimen I'd become? Look at it!'

'It…doesn't look very comfortable,' she said, searching for the right words.

'It doesn't need to be comfortable. It serves its purpose.'

She couldn't bear any more. She put her arms about him in an embrace of comfort. She thought he would cling to her, but at first he didn't. Instead his hands reached up hesitantly, barely touching her, then down again, as though he wasn't quite sure.

But at last he seemed to summon up his courage, wrapping his arms about her, drawing her against him and dropping his head so that his face was hidden against her neck. Cassie stroked his hair softly and they stood like that for a long time.

'I usually keep this door locked,' he said. 'Nobody else has any idea. Nobody ever will.'

'Nobody?' she asked.

'Nobody at all. This is me, deep inside, where nobody else ever gets to look. Not since…well…'

She stroked his face. 'Oh, my dear, dear Marcel—how long have you had this?'

'Since I bought the hotel, five years ago. Out there is the "official bedroom", and in here is the real one.'

'You never brought me in here.'

'I was waiting for the right moment—' He looked at her.

'It's now,' she said, drawing him down.

In the narrow bed there was only one way to make love, and that was to cling together, arms holding each other close, faces touching gently. When he claimed her she felt herself become one with him as never before. When he'd finished she offered herself to him again, and felt him accept her gift gratefully. In return he gave her gifts of power and tenderness that made her heart rejoice as never before in her life.

As the storm died away and she felt peace return she knew a passionate gratitude that this had happened while there was still time.

She looked up at him, eyes shining with love, waiting for him to utter the words that would start their life together.

'Goodbye,' he said.

* * *

Later that day he took her to the airport.

'There's the line for Check In,' he said. 'You're in good time. I'll go now.'

She turned tortured eyes towards him.

'Don't worry,' he said. 'I won't trouble you any more. I'm glad we had this morning. It means we can part on good terms, and that's important after the way we parted last time.'

He was silent, searching her face for something he needed to find there.

'At least we met again and found out…well, things we needed to find out. We'll always have that.'

'Marcel—'

'I told you it's all right. You're free of me now. No one stalking you, checking up on you, trying to back you into a corner. You were right about that. Goodbye, my darling. Be happy.'

'And you,' she said.

'Happy? Without you? Surely you understand that the only happiness I can have now is knowing that I set you free. Heaven forbid that you should regard me as you regarded him, a bully who forced you to do what he wanted. It's the way I was going, wasn't it? I wouldn't face it, but it was true. Thank goodness you showed me in time.'

'Why did it have to be this way?' she whispered.

'I don't know, but I do know that if we'd stayed together you'd have come to hate me, and I'll endure anything but that. Goodbye, my dearest. Find a man who deserves you, and be happy with him.'

'You can wish that?' she asked, amazed.

'I can wish anything for you that's good.'

'And you—oh, heavens, we both harmed each other so much. If only—'

'I know. But I won't risk harming you any more.' He leaned down and kissed her cheek. 'Goodbye.'

She watched as he walked away. Last time they had been in this airport he'd cried out her name in desperate determination to stop her leaving. But now he kept walking, not once looking back.

She stood there for a long, long time before moving off very slowly.

She was numb for the journey. Only when she was at home, behind a locked door, staring into the darkness, did she finally face what had happened.

Marcel had opened his arms and set her free because it was the only way he could show himself better than her fears. By doing this he'd proved the strength of his love for her.

It was the moment she'd been secretly waiting for, what Harry had called 'the turning point, when it all became clear.'

The clarity was blinding. Marcel had done what she hadn't believed possible, behaving with a generosity that paradoxically freed her to love him completely. Now she knew beyond all doubt that he was the one. The only one.

And she had lost him. It was over. Final.

Perhaps it was the best thing for him too, she thought, trying to comfort herself. If they had stayed together she might have made him wretched. He deserved better than that. He deserved better than *her*.

And with the thought came a sense of pride and even happiness that she'd thought never to know again. Marcel had loved her enough to ignore his own needs, his own pain. His generosity raised him head and shoulders above all other men. To be loved by him was an honour.

She might never see or hear from him again, but as long as she lived she would know that she'd won the heart of the finest, bravest, strongest, most honourable man in the world. That thought would sustain her throughout the long, sad years ahead.

* * *

Back in London, she realised that it was time to be practical. She was out of a job. There was more in her bank account than she had realised, owing to a sudden infusion of funds from Paris on the day she'd left. Marcel had put in three months' wages as a farewell gift.

She texted him, *Thank you.* And received in return, *Good luck!*

Nothing else. Not a word.

But the money wouldn't last for ever, as she realised when she visited her family, and her brother-in-law exclaimed, 'Do you mean you're out of a job?'

'Don't worry,' she said, handing him a cheque. 'I'll get another.'

But what? That was the question. The business world beckoned, but it no longer satisfied her. She needed more to fill the emptiness inside.

A few evenings later she went for a walk along the Thames, sometimes stopping to lean on the wall and watch the blazing sunset over the river. As she gazed she suddenly heard the sound of a familiar click, and turned to see a man aiming a camera at her.

'Don't move,' he called. 'I haven't finished.'

'You've got a cheek,' she began, then stopped. 'Hey, aren't you—Toby?'

Toby had been the eager young assistant of the photographer who had helped to make Cassie's name ten years ago. Since then he'd become successful on his own account.

'How lovely to see you after all this time!' she said, embracing him warmly. 'Let's go and have a coffee.'

'Not just yet,' he said. 'I'm not passing up my chance of a photo session with the great Cassie.'

'She's not the great Cassie any more. Let's get back to the studio.'

The pictures astonished her so much that she yielded readily to his suggestion of a 'proper shoot'. It was simple fun until he said, 'I've had a brilliant idea. The return of Cassie, more beautiful than ever.'

'You're mad,' she said, laughing.

'Sure I'm mad. That's what's most fun. Now, here's what we'll do…'

Her return was a sensation. Voluptuous Cassie belonged to the past. This was another age, Toby told her. Lean and boyish was 'in'. Now she was in demand again.

One evening a few weeks later, there was a knock at her door and she opened to find—

'Freya!'

When they were both settled over tea and cakes, Freya said, 'I hear you're making a modelling comeback.'

'Not really. Just a few shoots. I simply wanted to be sure I could do it.'

'Cassie still lives, huh?'

'Yes, she does. That was a nice surprise, and Mrs Henshaw thinks the money's nice, so we'll see. What about you?'

'I've come back to London to get a nursing job. Amos was just getting too much for me. You'll never guess what his latest wheeze is.'

'Jackson? Leonid? Travis?'

'Still Marcel. Honestly, that man doesn't understand the word "no". He's only put a load of money into my bank account, without even asking me. He knows Marcel needs money and he thought that would sway him.'

'Why is he still in need of money? I thought that was all sorted.'

'So did Amos. He was going to squeeze it out of that man—remember him?'

'I remember,' Cassie said quietly.

'But Marcel made him back off.'

'Marcel did?' Cassie asked quickly.

'Yes, I gather there were some very tough discussions and Marcel prevailed. So then they needed money from somewhere else, and he's raised it by selling shares in La Couronne.'

'But that place is his pride and joy!'

'Yes, but his mind was made up. He raised the cash and he's bought the London hotel but he's not out of the woods yet. So Amos thought making me rich would make Marcel go down on one knee.'

'And you don't think it will?' Cassie asked, pouring tea with great concentration.

'I've warned him if he does I'll thump him. Besides, he's still pining for you.'

A pause while her heart lurched, then a shaky laugh. 'That's nonsense.'

'No, it's not. I called in on him in Paris on my way here and we had a talk. He told me how your engagement ended. Not that there was really an engagement, was there? What an idiot he was to do it that way! I told him what I thought of him. But you two are right for each other and I won't see it come to nothing just because he's made a stupid mistake.'

Cassie shook her head helplessly. 'It's too late for that.'

'You mean you don't love him any more?'

'Of course I love him. I always will, but—'

'Do you want to talk?' Freya asked.

'Yes, I need to. When I first returned to London I was sad at losing Marcel, but I could bear it because I was so proud of him for leaving me. He did it to protect me. I'm still proud of him but—'

'But there's a lot of life still to get through,' Freya said shrewdly.

'I want him back, but I can't try to tempt him back. That's not the way.'

'Right, because if he could be tempted you wouldn't still be proud of him,' Freya said.

'Right. You're so clever. I really wish you were my sister.'

'If we play our cards right, I soon will be. Tempting is out. Compulsion is in. You've got to grab him by the scruff of the neck and not give him any choice. Now, listen carefully. This is what we're going to do…'

A few weeks later Vera glanced up as her employer hurried in. His face was tense and troubled, as always these days. But she thought that might be about to change.

'You have a visitor,' she said. 'Someone has just bought some shares in this place and says they need to see you urgently.' She nodded in the direction of her office door. 'In there.'

Frowning, he went in and stopped on the threshold.

'Hello,' said Cassie.

He drew a long breath, fighting for the control that he would need at this moment more than any other. 'What… Vera said…shareholder…'

'That's right. I've bought shares in La Couronne and I thought I should tell you soon.'

'But…it must have cost you a fortune. How did you—?'

'Raise the cash? From Freya. She's made me a big loan, which I shall pay off from the money I'll make from the hotel.'

'But surely she can't have loaned you enough to—'

'No, I have another source of income. That time we visited Jake, he sneakily returned my ring to me, the one he gave me just before we married. I found it in my bag afterwards, and now I've sold it, and I've invested the money in you.

'It's only for a short while. I don't want to keep anything of his permanently. His ring sold for nearly half a million. As soon as I can afford it I'll give an equal amount to charity. By then, Jake will have served his purpose.'

'Bringing you back to me,' he murmured.

'Exactly. Jake separated us, and now Jake has helped us find each other again.'

'He'd hate that,' Marcel said with relish.

'Yes, that's the thought I enjoy most. My other source of income is this.'

She opened a magazine, displaying Cassie, centrefold. She was stretched out, in a tiny bikini, looking directly into the camera with eyes that were almost as seductive as her barely clothed body.

'Take a good look,' she purred.

'I don't need to. I have my own copy. I'm amazed. I thought Mrs Henshaw had taken over.'

'So do the people I deal with, until they learn their mistake. It's Cassie who poses but Mrs Henshaw who draws up Cassie's contracts. They're the best of friends now.'

'I'm glad to know that,' he said carefully. 'It could make life…a lot easier.'

'It certainly does. Cassie's going to have to flaunt herself for quite a while yet, to help pay off Mrs Henshaw's debts, so the two of them decided to live together in harmony. Take one, you get the other.' She slipped her arms about his neck. 'I hope that's all right with you.'

It was hard to speak, but he managed to say, 'You once told me to get out of your life, and stay out.'

'That was then, this is now.'

He was suddenly tense. 'Cassie, my love, don't do this unless you mean it with all your heart. I couldn't endure to lose you again. I must be sure—to know that you're sure. I was torn from you once, and the last time I left you because it was the right thing to do. I thought it would help me keep your love, even if we could only love from a distance.'

'Yes, I understood that. I thought you were wonderful, even though losing you again broke my heart.'

'But—you said it yourself. That was then, this is now.' He met her eyes and spoke softly. 'Another parting would kill me.'

'There will be no other parting,' she vowed. 'I'm as sure as you want me to be, but sure in a way you don't know about yet. Things have changed. It's probably your influence. I'm not afraid of your controlling side because I've got one too. You brought it out in me and now it's out it's out for good.

'You need to know this. I'm in charge. From now on we're going to do things my way.' She laid her lips softly against his. 'Understand?'

'Understand.'

She could feel temptation trembling through him, making him draw back after a moment.

'You know that we'll fight,' he said.

'Of course we will. We'll have terrible fights, call each other all sorts of names, dig up our memories and use them to hurt each other. Sometimes we'll even hate each other. But we'll do it equally.'

'Oh, really? Well, let me tell you, conquering Cassie is a pleasure, but conquering Mrs Henshaw—that's something I'm really looking forward to.'

She smiled, nodding towards the door of the little bedroom.

'Better get started then. I don't know what you're waiting for.'

He lifted her high and headed for the door.

'Who's waiting?' he said.

* * * * *

LET'S TALK
Romance

For exclusive extracts, competitions
and special offers, find us online:

f facebook.com/millsandboon

🐦 @MillsandBoon

📷 @MillsandBoonUK

Get in touch on 01413 063232

MILLS & BOON

THE HEART OF ROMANCE

A ROMANCE FOR EVERY KIND OF READER

MODERN

Prepare to be swept off your feet by sophisticated, sexy and seductive heroes, in some of the world's most glamourous and romantic locations, where power and passion collide.
8 stories per month.

HISTORICAL

Escape with historical heroes from time gone by. Whether your passion is for wicked Regency Rakes, muscled Vikings or rugged Highlanders, awaken the romance of the past.
6 stories per month.

MEDICAL

Set your pulse racing with dedicated, delectable doctors in the high-pressure world of medicine, where emotions run high and passion, comfort and love are the best medicine.
6 stories per month.

True Love

Celebrate true love with tender stories of heartfelt romance, from the rush of falling in love to the joy a new baby can bring, and a focus on the emotional heart of a relationship.
8 stories per month.

Desire

Indulge in secrets and scandal, intense drama and plenty of sizzlin hot action with powerful and passionate heroes who have it all: wealth, status, good looks...everything but the right woman.
6 stories per month.

HEROES

Experience all the excitement of a gripping thriller, with an intense romance at its heart. Resourceful, true-to-life women and strong, fearless men face danger and desire - a killer combination!
8 stories per month.

DARE

Sensual love stories featuring smart, sassy heroines you'd want as a best friend, and compelling intense heroes who are worthy of them
4 stories per month.

To see which titles are coming soon, please visit

millsandboon.co.uk/nextmonth

JOIN US ON SOCIAL MEDIA!

Stay up to date with our latest releases, author news and gossip, special offers and discounts, and all the behind-the-scenes action from Mills & Boon...

 millsandboon

 millsandboonuk

 millsandboon

It might just be true love...